# Family Holiday

# Family Holiday

(In A Strange Land)

## Raymond Dodds

Copyright © 2015 by Raymond Dodds.
Map copyright © Raymond Dodds 2015

| Library of Congress Control Number: | 2015914821 |
|---|---|
| ISBN: Hardcover | 978-1-5144-6340-6 |
| Softcover | 978-1-5144-6339-0 |
| eBook | 978-1-5144-6338-3 |

All rights reserved. No part of this book may be reproduced or transmitted in any form or by any means, electronic or mechanical, including photocopying, recording, or by any information storage and retrieval system, without permission in writing from the copyright owner.

This is a work of fiction. Names, characters, places and incidents either are the product of the author's imagination or are used fictitiously, and any resemblance to any actual persons, living or dead, events, or locales is entirely coincidental.

Any people depicted in stock imagery provided by Thinkstock are models, and such images are being used for illustrative purposes only.
Certain stock imagery © Thinkstock.

Print information available on the last page.

Rev. date: 09/07/2015

To order additional copies of this book, contact:
Xlibris
800-056-3182
www.Xlibrispublishing.co.uk
Orders@Xlibrispublishing.co.uk

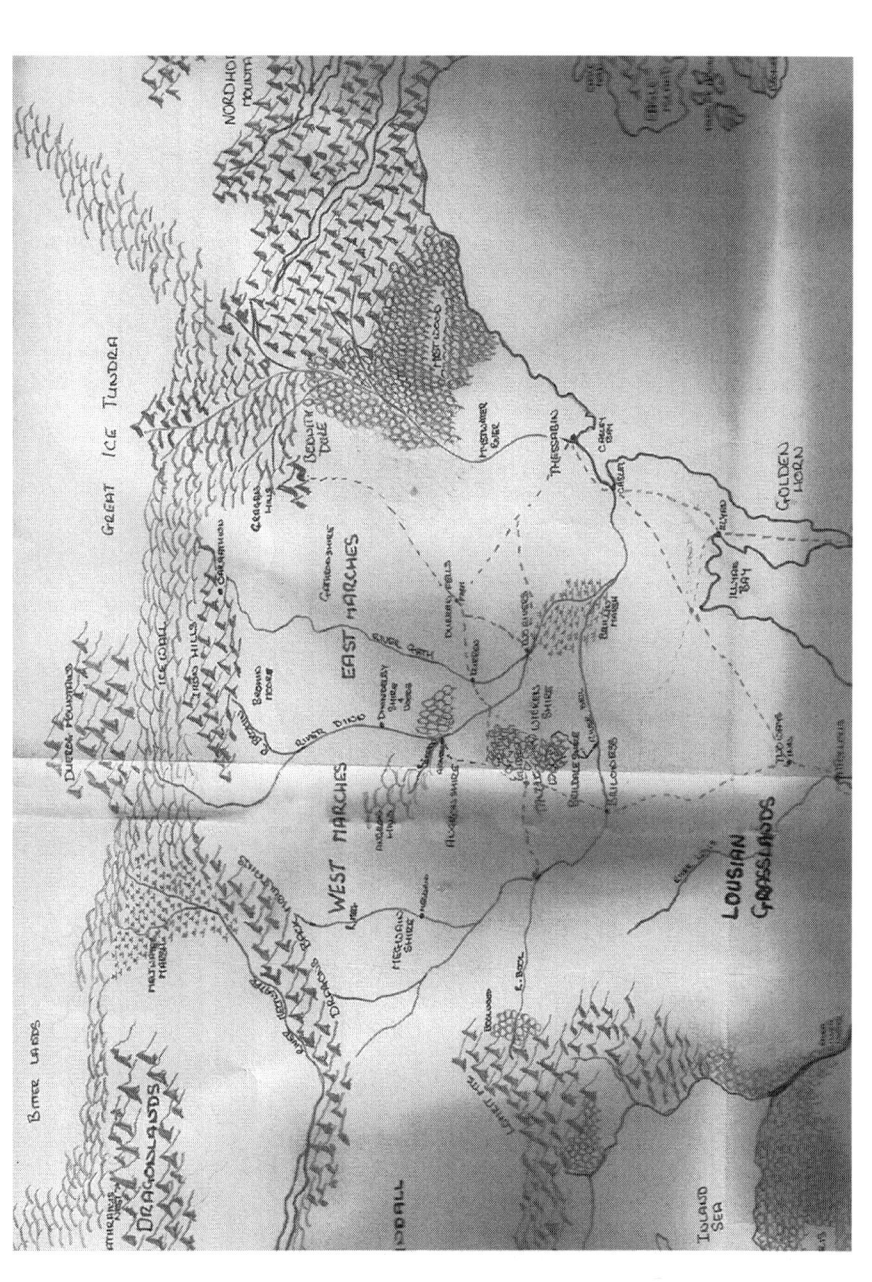

# Contents

Chapter 1   The Show ......................................................................... 1
Chapter 2   Diversion ...................................................................... 15
Chapter 3   Draygon's Farm ........................................................... 30
Chapter 4   GuidePost ..................................................................... 47
Chapter 5   New Friends ................................................................. 83
Chapter 6   Thieves in the Night ................................................. 107
Chapter 7   A New Day ................................................................. 129
Chapter 8   Tangle Wood .............................................................. 148
Chapter 9   Brownie Council ....................................................... 166
Chapter 10  Grassland and Grog ................................................. 191
Chapter 11  Factor Drayloc .......................................................... 197
Chapter 12  The Day after the Night Before ............................. 225
Chapter 13  Riders in the Wild .................................................... 240
Chapter 14  Two Rivers and the Party ....................................... 259
Chapter 15  Meetings and Waiting for Meetings ..................... 272
Chapter 16  Moorbe ...................................................................... 289
Chapter 17  Wolfric's Company .................................................. 313
Chapter 18  Into the Wilds .......................................................... 336
Chapter 19  Cooper Kettles and Rotting Fruits ........................ 353

Chapter 20  The Hunt.................................................................361

Chapter 21  The Magic of Books and Books of Magic ..................375

Chapter 22  Walls, Wiglaf, and the Watch ......................................401

Chapter 23  Work for Willing Hands ..............................................420

Chapter 24  A Glimer of Hope .......................................................429

Chapter 25  The Battle of Two Rivers.............................................446

Chapter 26 ......................................................................................476

# Chapter 1

## The Show

The loudspeakers surrounding the showground crackled into life, and in a dry tone, the announcer's voice again warned everyone, 'All visitors are reminded to stay behind white rope of the main arena for their own safety.' The announcer cleared his throat, making the speakers screech, before adding, 'We have a lost child so, could the parents Sue Pennifree please make your way to the event manager's tent, that's the green tent next to the beer tent on the north of the grounds, to collect your child.'

Then, and in a much more dramatic tone, accompanied with the blaring of many trumpets, or at least a recording of blaring trumpets, the announcer proclaimed: 'And now, ladies and gentlemen, boys and girls, to begin our tribute to warriors through the ages. Make way for the Fifth Cohort.'

In the grandstand overlooking the field, Jay Deeks shifted eagerly in his seat, the program of the day's attractions clutched in his hand. 'This is the Romans, Dad,' he proclaimed excitedly as he shoved the program under his backside and sitting on it, all the while straining to get a better view of the re-enactors.

Off to the right a lone trumpet sounded, drawing the attention of everyone to the gates of the castle. For a moment there was nothing to be seen, but there was one lone and very loud voice barking orders: in Latin no less.

First there was just the one voice, no doubt calling the men to attention. Then came the sound of men in armour snapping to attention, of metal clanking on metal. The trumpet sounded again, further orders were shouted out, and the Fifth Cohort marched proudly out of the castle gates.

Their armour was shining brightly in the sun and their heads were held high. There may well have been only twenty-five of them – two were on holiday and another had gotten a puncture on the way and was late – but they had the pride of a thousand. Then, as they marched, the applause of the crowd seemed to swell that pride more. They marched down to the field, shields held to their left sides and with two javelins on their right shoulders, except for their commander, who carried a heavy walking stick instead and the standard bearer who carried the golden eagle. Once in the centre of the field they began their drill. The announcer explained how every Roman solider had to drill everyday he was in camp for the term of his twenty-five year enlistment.

'They drilled like this,' the announcement said, 'until they were inch perfect, and until every man of the cohort knew exactly what he had to do, at what order, and to what trumpet call of whistle blow.'

Jay was wrapped in concentration. He sat forward on his seat, his eyes straining to catch every last detail of the cohort's drill.

After the cohort had marched for several minutes they paused, coming to attention once more a few paces in front of the grandstand. 'Let's hear it for the Fifth Cohort,' the speakers blared out and the crowd responded with a big round of applause.

At the right of the group of Romans, a Centurion, after waiting till the applause had died down, blew a long note on his whistle. He shouted another order in Latin, and quickly the cohort wheeled to the left. Ahead of them several targets had been set up. More orders were shouted. The cohort halted, closed their ranks, and stood ready.

'Now we can see the fire power of the legions,' the announcer's voice crackled.

The Centurion's whistle blew and twenty-four light javelins were lurched towards the targets. As the first javelins struck home, the cohort was moving forward at a slow walking pace, the second, heavier, javelins at the ready. Another whistle sounded, and another volley of javelins sailed towards the targets. Even before they struck home the men of the cohort had drawn their swords, and banging sword on shield, they continued their menacing advancing. They wheeled again, facing the crowd, and advanced once more. But this time they did a 'combat advance'. Their shields locked together and held high to protect their faces, only the tips of their swords showing as they came on. Instead of walking, as they had before, the men of the cohort did a kind of shuffle, their left foot forwards, taking a half pace and pushing with their shields as they stabbed out with their short swords. Then, protecting themselves with their shields again, they brought up the right foot, planting it ready to push forwards again. 'Push, stab, recover, step', the announcer said, 'push, stab, recover, step, push, stab, recover, step, until the first man is too tired to push any more, then ...' the announcement paused for the centurion to blow his whistle. With that the first man suddenly turned, his shield held to cover his back as he quickly filtered between the ranks following him. 'Now there is a new man at the front and the cohort begins again. Push, stab, recover, step.'

Several times the men of cohort performed their manoeuvres, all the time coming closer and closer to the crowd. Jay was by then near off his seat. He was leaning further and further forward as the cohort came ever closer. And, like so many there, in his mind he was no doubt wondering what it would have been like to have to face a real Roman Cohort in a real battle. All that bright armour, all those brilliant red shields, and those fearsome stabbing swords.

It was all totally gripping, at least it was to a fifteen-year-old boy like Jay. His father, sitting next to him, was also watching the cohort, and every bit as enthralled as Jay. Jay's mother and sister however were not so enthralled.

Liz, Jay's mother, was watching, though not that closely, and from the way she was looking about her, with not a great deal of interest either. Kate, his sister, was even less interested. Rather than watch the men of the cohort she was absorbed in her game boy, playing some game or other while the Romans went about their last few drill manoeuvres.

This had been planned as a family holiday. Ed and Liz had always wanted to spend some time touring England and now, with Kate sixteen and Jay fifteen, it had appeared to be the perfect time. It was the sort of holiday that they had always promised themselves, and promised the children. Each of them, each member of the family, had their own reasons for wanting to spend their holiday in England. Liz wanted to see Yorkshire because that was where her mother came from. Ed wanted to see England because, as an engineer and as an amateur historian, he wanted to see the birthplace of the industrial revolution. Kate had said she wanted to see London, maybe even the Queen, but what she had went to see first and foremost were the designer's shops. But for Jay there was only one reason for a holiday in England and that was the history. And from the very moment they had arrived, Jay had managed to produce a whole long list of things to see and that meant castles, military museums, and more castles.

The Deeks had done all the usual touristy things. They had been to see the Tower of London. They had watched the changing of the guard outside of Buckingham Place, though they never did get to see the Queen who, as luck would have it, was on a state visit to America. They paid a visit to Covent Gardens and, at Kate's and Liz's insistence, the ballet: something that Ed and Jay had to put up with if they were going to be allowed to spend all the next day at the Greenwich. There was, after all, an enormous amount of interesting exhibits to be seen at Greenwich, the Naval Museum, the Observatory and so on. So, one night at the ballet was a small price to pay.

After a week in London the Deeks had begun their trip north, taking in many of the castle, cathedrals, and country houses on the way. Later they had gone to see the sights of Yorkshire, the Minster and walled city. Though Ed and Jay found the National Railway Museum far more interesting than churches and textile factories, or indeed the factory outlet shops where Liz had managed to buy a whole load of new sheets, tableclothes, and just about anything else she thought might fit in her suitcase.

In truth Kate didn't really seem interested in anything she saw. The ballet had been good, but that had been the only thing that had held her attention for any amount of time. Liz had loved the country houses. Her mother had told her about them but she could never have imagined that they were as grand or as beautifully furnished as they turned out to be.

They had seen a lot, but there were loads more still to see. Even with the three weeks that the Deeks had taken for their vacation Ed and Liz were coming to terms with the fact that they really didn't have the time to see everything on their lists. Ed, for instance, had wanted to see the SS Great Britain and HMS Warrior, but he accepted that they would have to wait for another day, for another trip. Liz had her list also. Places like the Glass Museum and the Wedgwood pottery, but it could only be imagined how much more she would have bought for the house if they had of managed to fit them in. Ed had been sure that you could buy the very same things back home in Seattle, even if it wasn't 'the same' as Liz had maintained. Jay wanted to see more castles, the Royal Armoury, or anything else to do with war, while Kate just made the rest of the family feel uncomfortable with her attitude. For her the malls were boring, the country houses were old, and boring, and the castles were just old . . . old and very boring.

Kate's attitude was best summed up at the Alnwick show as wholeheartedly disinterested. While Jay and his father were watching the show intently, and even Liz was a little interested in the cohort's drills, Kate was transfixed with her game boy.

As the men of the cohort demonstrated the tortoise, the announcer was introducing the ancient Britains. The main character was a warrior on his chariot. He was dressed in blue-and-white stripped pants but above the waist he was naked. His body was painted blue and his hair, coated in ash and mud, was stuck up in fearsome spikes. As the chariot raced round the tortoise, the warrior shouted abuse and taunted the Romans as he brandished his trophy at them: a bloody, severed head.

Ed hadn't known that the ancient Britains had taken heads as trophies. Jay was, as ever, enthralled, and watching every twist and turn that the warrior and chariot made. Even Liz was interested. But, as Kate looked up to see the warrior ride past the grandstand, with the bloody head held aloft, she summed up her views on the trip thus far when she groaned, 'Gross, like, really gross,' before going back to her game boy.

Perhaps it was a bit much to expect Kate to be interested in the show. In fact it seemed to have been a bit much just to expect her to be interested in the trip at all. Kate was more interested in the mall and hanging with her friends. If she'd had been given the choice between a trip to England and summer camp Kate would have chosen summer camp, which was why her parents didn't give her the choice. The only time Kate had been remotely interested was while shopping in London. Had the holiday ended then Kate would have been delighted. The fact that it didn't had done nothing other than to give Kate a serious case of teenage angst.

'Ed,' Liz said, tapping her husband on the shoulder. When he looked round she nodded towards Kate, 'I'll take her round the fair.'

'OK,' Ed said, then quickly added, 'you want us to come too?'

'No no,' Liz said. She nodded at Jay. 'Anyhow, you would need the whole cohort to drag somebody away.'

Ed could only smile, give his wife a goodbye kiss, and then go back to watching the show: they did have a heap more to see after all. Once the Romans and ancient Britains were finished there were the Saxons. They would then be followed by the Vikings, a display of the

Border Reivers, the Sealed Knot Society, English Civil War, and finally a Napoleonic re-enactment group.

Kate and Liz left the grandstand and made their way over to the re-enactors fair. They spent time walking round the various displays, the small camps set up by the different warrior bands, the Saxon village, the Napoleonic 'camp followers' camp, complete with brothel and tented tavern. There were tables set up where visitors could buy various things, food, jams, bread and cakes, swords and uniforms, and also demonstrations of how some of the things for sale were made.

Only once did Kate show any interest, and that was a small Viking jewellery stand. There were five people there, all clad in authentic-looking Viking garb and each one taking part in the various stages of making the jewellery. One man was casting tiny bronze and silver brooches from the liquid metals he was heating in a hand-built kiln. Another man was sitting at a table, carefully working the recently cast pieces and cleaning them up before fixing coloured stones into them. A woman was sitting beside him, soldering the clasps onto the rear of the broaches, and beside her, another man was polishing the finished jewellery ready for sale. The fifth person was clearly the salesman. At first he went round, explaining what each of the steps were in the jewellery making process then, after his guided tour was over, he shifted into sales mode.

'I love that ring,' Kate informed her mother, pointing at a silver ring amidst the display.

Liz glanced at the ring Kate was pointing at. 'A bit garish, isn't it?'

'No, it's lovely,' Kate insisted.

'Your sister is right,' the salesman said, smiling broadly at Liz. 'It is a lovely ring. It's a copy, a very accurate copy of a power ring worn by a Viking shield maiden that was found in a burial just up the coast from here.'

Liz smiled. 'Nice try,' she grinned. 'Kate is my daughter not my sister and you need to work on your sales pitch.'

The man laughed loudly. 'Fair cop. But you have to give me points for trying.' He looked at Liz more seriously and asked, 'You're American, aren't you?'

'Yes,' Liz replied, 'from Seattle Washington, but my mother was born in Yorkshire.'

'Nice part of the country,' said the salesman. 'So how are you enjoying your tour?'

'It's lovely,' Liz said, but then she would hardly say anything else. 'At least we have had some lovely weather.' She laughed to herself, adding, 'People warned me before we came over that it always rains in England, but it's been beautiful for the past two weeks. I just hope it holds for the rest of our time here.'

'I hope so too,' the salesman said as he took the ring Kate had pointed to from the display. 'Want to try it on?'

'Sure,' Kate said reaching for the ring only to stop herself just before taking it, 'Can I, Mom?'

'Well OK, you can try it,' Liz replied.

'We didn't make that one at the shows,' the salesman explained. 'We have a small workshop where we make the finer pieces. They are too fiddly to make here in the open. Plus that ring has a much higher silver content than the stuff we do at the shows.'

Kate slipped the ring on her finger, admiring it, and how it looked on her hand then asked, 'What were you saying about it being a power ring?'

'The Vikings used to believe that rings could be given or hold magical powers,' he explained. 'The original that the ring was copied off was found at a burial up the coast. It was on the finger of a female warrior. Unusual but not unheard of; I mean female warriors. Anyway, it was so beautiful that we took a cast of it and have been making copies. What do you think of it?'

'It's really nice,' Kate said holding her hand for her mother to see. 'What do you think, Mom, can we get it?'

'Kate,' Liz groaned, 'it is sixty pounds.'

'I know, Mom, but it is a power ring,' Kate smiled.

'Power ring?' Liz said, raising her eyebrows.

'I know,' the salesman sniggered. 'But it's not what you are thinking. To tell you the truth in the real world I'm a very boring archaeologist.' He held out his hand to Liz. 'Doctor Geoff Bellman at your service, and over there, playing with fire as he often does, is Doctor Ian Summerville. It was we two that ran the dig on the Spindlestone Lady; that's where the ring came from or rather where the original ring came from.'

'Doctor Liz Deeks, MD,' Liz replied as she shook hands. 'And this is my daughter Kate.'

'Hi,' Kate said waving her hand. 'What about the ring, Mom?'

He turned around suddenly and began hunting through a box behind him. 'I have some photos of the dig here if you would like to see them.' Moments later he came back to face Liz with a large portfolio of photos in his hands. 'This is her,' he began, pointing at the photo of a skeleton. 'She was quite tall, over six feet and had long blonde hair, much like your daughter's hair, but a lot longer.' He flipped through a few more photos till he found one of the skeleton's hands. 'Here, you can see the ring on her hand.' He had another look at the photo himself and thoughtfully added, 'Surprisingly well preserved. Lucky really as silver doesn't always last very well.'

Liz looked at the photo closely. 'What is she holding?' She held the photo closer in an attempt to discern exactly what was in the woman's hands. But, whether because of the dirt and rust on the item, or because of the angle of the photo, it was hard to see what it was.

'It's a sword,' Geoff replied. 'Well, a sword hilt to be precise. And a very fine sword at that. We made a copy of it.'

'Who made a copy?' Ian, the other man who, until them, had been busy at the kiln's fire. 'I would shake hands but as you can see . . .' He held out his hands to show the dirt and soot on them from his work.

'The sword is Ian's pride and joy,' Geoff said as he lifted a copy of the sword from the display. He laid it before Liz and Kate saying, 'Did you ever see a sword like it?' The pommel was gold, with a large red gemstone set at the very top. The handle was sharkskin and bound with gold wire that had been twisted into a fine chain. The guard was thick and wide, almost seven inches across, and made of silver. In the guard were more gemstones, rubies, and sapphires, and it was inlaid with gold that formed the outline of a great dragon.

'That is beautiful,' Liz exclaimed breathlessly.

'And,' Geoff said proudly, 'in the original all the gems are real and have been valued at nearly two million pounds. Unfortunately the blade hasn't survived. The soil was simply too acidic. All that was left was an oxide impression in the grave.' He flipped to another photo. 'That wasn't all we found at the dig. Take a look at her funeral treasures: gold, silver, and more gems than you can poke a stick at. We figure she must have been some sort of princess; she was of noble birth at the very least.'

'Perhaps she was a Queen or something?' Kate offered.

Geoff shook his head. 'No, she was definitely a warrior. In fact she had several wounds that must have come from battle.'

'Is that what killed her?' Liz asked, her medical curiosity aroused.

'No no,' Geoff said. 'She had a number of wounds but they had all healed. In fact they had been healed so well that we are having to rethink Viking medicine. But as to how she died, we think that she died of nothing more than old age. She was after all about sixty-five or seventy years old. And back then that was really old.'

'Fascinating,' Liz thought for a few minutes as she studied the photos. She flipped through the portfolio, her professional curiosity drawing her further and further in. Then she came to a set of enlargements of the jeweller and asked, 'What are those markings on the ring?'

Geoff, the salesman, cleared his throat. 'Well there are two figures as you can see. One is Odin, King of the gods and war, and the other we think is a Valkyrie. As you can see, they are reaching out to, or supporting, depending on your viewpoint, what is an endless knot.

We think that is a sign that they are touching the wearer's soul. One to give strength in battle and, if the wearer dies in battle like every true Viking should, the other as a sort of marker so that the Valkyrie may find them and take them up to Valhalla.' He held his hand out to Kate saying, 'May I?' Kate removed the ring and handed it back. 'If you take a close look inside you can just see some markings. But those however were pretty well worn on the original and we can't be sure what they said.' He handed the ring back to Kate and turned his attention back to Liz asking, 'What do you think?'

'I think sixty pounds is a lot for a "magic" ring,' Liz stated flatly. 'In spite of where it came from.'

'Not a magic ring, a power ring,' Geoff corrected her.

'There's a difference?'

'Quite a lot, yes,' Geoff smiled. 'A magic ring implies that it can grant the wearer some sort of special abilities. A power ring only grants the wearer the ability to place their own power into the ring. For example, a good swordsman, if he wears the ring while training, will be a better swordsman in battle. At least that is what the sagas say about them. It all comes down to what the Vikings believed. If they thought that rings like this made them better warriors, then perhaps they did. A sort of talisman or good luck charm if you like. Or maybe the people they were fighting against had heard the sagas and were put in fear of someone wearing such a ring. Who really knows?'

'Mom?'

'I'll tell you what,' Geoff said, 'fifty pounds and the ring is yours.'

'Forty.'

'Forty-five. And I will throw in the power of a warrior for free.'

'Done,' Liz said.

'I think I have been.'

They left the Viking stall and began looking round the remainder of the rest of the displays. After a while they stopped to partake of a Saxon lunch of black bread, cheese, and fruit. Liz also had small ale, while Kate was allowed a not so Saxon coke. At the end of the stalls they found the archery range.

Liz was the first to have a go, recalling her days at college when she had taken up archery as a hobby. She would be the first to admit that she was never anywhere near good enough to make it onto the college team, but she had enjoyed it. Kate, who had never picked up a bow before, was understandably nervous to begin with. But, whether she was just enjoying the experience, or the close attention of a rather rugged-looking instructor, Kate was soon into it. And after a little bit of instruction, she was getting really good at it. Once she had been shown how to use her right eye to keep the arrow on line and how to judge the range with her knuckles, Kate was soon hitting the gold with every arrow, admittedly only from twenty-five metres, but she was hitting the gold.

At long last the military show was over in the main field and the family reunited by the archery butts. On their way Ed and Jay had also taken a tour of the re-enactors stands, and whereas Kate had found her ring, Jay had found a whole heap of leaflets and flyers, and yet another book on ancient weapons and warfare.

'Where's Kate?' Ed asked.

Liz nodded towards the butts. 'Still doing her Robin Hood impression.' She turned her attention back to Jay. 'More books?'

'Yes but, Mom . . .'

Liz held up her hand, laughing. 'Don't tell me. You haven't got that one and it's really good.'

'It's really really good,' Jay corrected her.

'I bet it is,' Liz sniggered. 'And your father just happened to have the right money.'

'It's just one book,' Ed shrugged.

Liz grinned. 'Just one more to go with the . . . how many is it now, Jay?'

Before Jay answered his father changed the subject. 'Listen,' he said, 'if we're going to get up to Scotland tonight then we had better get going.'

'And we have to stop at Bamburgh,' Jay pointed out.

'Another castle,' Kate groaned, having rejoined the family.

'Well it is on the way, and we could stop there to have something for dinner,' Ed interjected, in an almost apologetic fashion. 'By the way, Kate, that is a nice ring.'

'It's a Viking power ring, Dad,' Kate said enthusiastically. 'Mom bought it for me.'

'Really,' Ed said, smiling a little. He glanced over at Liz, playfully mocking her words. 'Another ring, Kate, ho many is that now?'

Bamburgh was a short drive up the A1 from Alnwick; however, with all the trouble getting out of the jammed car park at the fair, and all the road works taking place, by the time the Deeks reached the castle it was near to closing time. It was a disappointment for them all but they did at least find a cosy little restaurant where they could eat. Time however was marching on, and after finishing their dinner, they all began to think it was past time for driving up to Edinburgh.

The rental car was equipped with a Sat Nav – Ed had insisted upon it. After all, being in a strange country, going to places he had never been to before, and often along roads he had no idea about, the family would have spent more time lost than found without a Sat Nav.

With the family all seated and belted up, and with the sun setting at last on that summer's evening, Ed set the Sat Nav for their hotel in Edinburgh.

There were five ways into, or out of, Bamburgh. There was the coast road, coming up from Seahouses, which then continued on north hugging the coast all the way to Holy Island and beyond. There was the main road from the A1 which, while just a little bit longer, was much easier than the road from Lucker. But the road that the Sat Nav took them on was a back road that went between the coast and the A1. According to the little box of electronics it was the shortest route, but once they started driving along those narrow lanes it was hard to believe.

The road, if one could indeed call it that, was a twisting winding lane that was bordered on both sides by high earth banks topped with thick hedges. From time to time it was possible, just possible, to catch sight of farmland beyond the hedges. Occasionally the road cut through a wood, then turned this way and that, dropped down a hill or climbed up yet another. Strictly speaking, there was little need for the Sat Nav, for there was nowhere to turn off the narrow road. All Ed had to do was drive and make sure that he didn't run into any of the banks.

In the rear seats Jay was falling asleep. He had spent sometime reading his new book but, as weariness from a long day, and a heavy meal, overcame him, he drifted off. Kate was also drowsy, her head resting against a folded sweater that was pressed against the window. Even Liz was beginning to succumb to sleep. Only Ed was left awake, and only because he had to drive them all safely north.

There was little wonder that the family was feeling sleepy; it was getting late, very late. They had been told that during the summer the sun set very late at night. But none of them had realised just how late that sunset could be. They had left the restaurant after ten o'clock, yet the sky was still light. But soon, and quiet suddenly, the sun was gone and Ed was driving in near pitch-dark.

# Chapter 2

## Diversion

Ed may well have been warned about the light nights, but nobody had warned him about the endless road works on the A1. And despite all those old movies that always depicted England to be damp and foggy, nothing could have prepared Ed for the pea soup he found himself driving through.

It had begun shortly after he had managed to get back on to the A1. At first Ed had made good time. The road had been clear, and there was a full moon. But then came the road works, and not just one set of road works, but an entire series of them.

He had to stop and wait in the northbound carriageway while a convoy system was in force. That had cost Ed ten, perhaps fifteen minutes, before he was been able to move on again. Then came the diversion just short of Berwick. Something to do with the bridge perhaps, Ed didn't know, he couldn't tell, as he never got near enough to see what was happening. All he knew, all anybody knew, was that one minute he was driving towards Berwick, then the next he was being sent off along one more of those closed-in country roads. That was when Ed got really lost.

Initially the Sat Nav kept repeating its instructions to do a U turn. But what was the point in a U turn when the U turn would only take you back to the diversion. So Ed pressed on, just like all the other drivers, not that there were that many at that time of the night. Then the fog really set in, a thick, clinging fog that filled every low-laying point of the road.

The night had begun to get colder. The day had been a beautiful sunny day without a cloud in the sky, but suddenly, and out of seemingly nowhere, the clouds rolled in and the temperature dropped like a stone. In scarcely more than an hour it had gone from the day's high of thirty-two to a night of less than four degrees. That had caused the fog. It started forming on the streams and rivers, a thin mist at first but, as the temperature fell, the mist thickened and built into clinging banks of white vapour. Yet this was no passing haze; rather it was a solid miasma that allowed only a few meagre feet of visibility.

Ed slowed the car, subsequently slowing it again until he was driving at little more than walking pace. There were no road signs anymore; even the diversion signs had seemingly disappeared. He might not want to admit it, but Ed was well past lost. Even the Sat Nav seemed lost. No longer was it telling Ed to do a U turn; now it just sat there silently flashing, recalculating. The road, if that was what the country track passed for, had narrowed till there was no room to turn the car around. There were high banks and hedges either side of the road and that impenetrable fog everywhere. There was nothing for it other than to push on, no matter how slow he was travelling, Ed had no other choice than to keep driving until he found some place to turn around.

Pothole by bone-jarring pothole Ed inched the car forward. The tarmac had vanished suddenly, miles back. There were conceivably passing places along the road, or driveways into the bordering fields, but they were impossible to see in all the fog. Nor could any lights be seen through the fog. Ed might have been driving past a house at that very moment, but there would have been no way to tell, not unless he got out of the car and walked right up to the door. The simple fact was that he could not see a thing.

'Where are we?' Liz asked sleepily.

'The hell if I know,' Ed replied in a hoarse whisper.

Liz looked about her then back at her husband, her face etched with concern. 'Can you see in all this fog?'

'Not very well,' Ed answered, 'just enough to see where the road is.' They hit another pothole and the car jarred to the left.

'This is a road?' Liz asked.

'Supposed to be.'

'What time is it by the way?'

Ed looked down at the dashboard clock. 'Half past one.'

'You're joking, right?' but then seeing Ed shaking his head Liz asked, 'Did you think to ring the hotel and let them know we will be late.'

Ed shook his head again.

'Thought not,' Liz said. She picked her bag up from the foot well and fished inside for her phone. Finding it, and the paper with the hotel details, Liz switched her phone on. 'Great,' she groaned.

'What?'

'You'll not believe this.'

'Let me have a go,' Ed smirked. 'No signal.'

'Nobody likes a wise ass,' Liz scoffed.

'Who's a wise ass?' Kate asked.

Liz looked round. 'I thought you were asleep.'

'And watch that language, young lady,' Ed added.

'I was asleep,' Kate said as she gazed out of the window. 'What the hell is it with this fog?'

'Did I not just tell you,' Ed snapped. He turned round in his seat and would have said more had the car not jerked violently to the left.

The road had been filled with potholes but this was different. This time the suspension didn't just drop and then rebound with a bump. This time the whole car seemed to drop abruptly, lurching over to the left before slanting and slewing over onto the hedge row. A loud bang rang out, as the car bottomed out, a fraction of a second later, another, as the airbags inflated. The engine began to race for a few moments, followed by the most painful noise of metal grinding on metal.

'Goddam it,' Ed barked. He snatched at the keys and switched the engine off then, quickly turning round, he checked that his family was unhurt. 'Everyone OK?'

'I'm OK,' Liz said, beating down the airbag in front of her. 'A little ringing in my ears but that's all.'

'Kate?' Ed asked.

'Fine,' she replied. 'But have a look at this.'

Liz and Ed turned to see Jay still sound asleep. Kate was shaking him. 'I swear this kid would sleep through World War Three. Hey, hey, wake up, dummy.'

Jay stirred. He yawned and stretched before taking a good look around him. 'Are we there yet?'

Ed climbed back into the car. 'And you said we wouldn't need a torch,' he said tossing it on the dash as he sat down. 'The good news, nobody got hurt. The bad news, this car isn't going anywhere. The sump is cracked wide open and one of the half shafts is sheared. It also looks like the front left suspension is wedged up and the shock's gone.'

'So what do we do now?' Liz asked.

'Well we could sit here and hope that somebody comes along before we freeze,' Ed said, 'or we could walk. There's bound to be somewhere.'

'Did we pass anywhere?' Kate asked.

'Not that I saw, back that ways,' Ed said, 'but that just means that we know there is nowhere behind us; therefore going on is the best chance of finding some help.'

'Or getting total lost,' Liz retorted sharply. 'And anyway, why didn't you turn back when you saw you were lost? Surely you must have realised this road was going nowhere?'

'And where exactly was I supposed to turn round?'

Liz didn't answer, rather she said, 'That's just like you though, isn't it?'

'Mom,' Kate, cut in sharply.

'Look,' Ed said, 'we are in England not the States, there has got to be somewhere close by. It's not like back home where you might be walking for miles and miles before you see anyone.'

'That's right, Dad,' Kate smiled. 'Here we just have to walk for miles, not miles and miles. It's so much better.'

'Well, come on then,' Liz said at last. 'If we have to walk we have to walk.'

'And we better wrap up warm,' Ed added.

'But we only have summer clothes, Dad,' Kate said.

'Then you had better put lots of them on,' Liz said. 'It's cold outside and even if we stay it's going to get cold here. So come on people, let's get wrapped up and ready to go.'

Soon they were ready. Each dressed in three to four T-shirts, whatever jackets they could find, and jeans. There were two rucksacks in the car, just small affairs that they used to carry water and something to eat while they were walking. These were now pressed into service to carry everything they might need till they found somewhere to get in from the cold. They all carried their socks and shoes in their hands, for, as Ed found out while checking the car, the first part of their trek was through a shallow ford. The water was not deep, no more than eight or nine inches, but it was freezing cold and would, had they worn their shoes, left them with cold wet feet for their walk.

Their greatest problem was however the fog. Even after they had crossed the ford and replaced their footwear for the walk, they could walk for miles along the lane but never see anything either side of them because of the fog. Not only that, but the very act of walking a few paces ahead of the group made them quickly lose sight of the others. Therefore they had to stick close together, almost within touching distance of each other, and they had to remain alert as to where the others were at all times. It made for very slow going. And as the long dark night dragged on, the cold, damp air sapping their wills, tempers within the family soon began to show.

Ed was leading the family, shining the torch so that he could both see the road ahead, even if just a few feet ahead, and so that he could be seen by the others. Behind him, close enough that he could have held onto his father's belt was Jay. Kate was third, a short way behind Jay and just able to see the torchlight, and almost walking beside her was Liz.

'Ed, will you slow it down a bit?' Liz called out. 'We can't see where you are back here.'

Ed stopped and turned round, shining the torch back along the road for them to see. 'OK I've stopped. Just kept walking towards the light.'

'We can't see the light. Just keep talking, Ed,' Liz called back.

'Ooooooo,' Jay sniggered at his own ghostly voice, 'don't go into the light, don't go into the light.'

Suddenly Liz and Kate loomed out of the fog and Kate stood over Jay. 'That's not funny,'

Jay chuckled, 'What's the matter, Kate? You scared!'

Kate jumped at Jay's sudden shout. 'Mom, Dad, Jay is being a pain again.'

'Jay, leave your sister alone,' Ed said, his tone somewhat irritated, and not just because of Jay fooling around but also because of the need to find somewhere to get out of the cold.

'Jay, leave your sister alone,' Liz said quietly as she stormed towards Ed. 'You two go strolling off ahead, leaving us without knowing where you are, or without any light and all you can say is "Jay, leave your sister alone".'

'Look,' Ed began, but Liz quickly cut him off.

'Look nothing,' she turned swiftly to face Jay and in an abrupt tone said, 'Jay, apologise to your sister.'

Jay sighed heavily and looked down, saying, 'Sorry, Kate.'

'That's better,' Liz said.

'Sorry that you're such a scaredy-cat.'

'Jay,' Liz snapped.

'Sorry.'

'And so you should be,' Kate said haughtily.

'Well then,' Ed began, 'now that that is all sorted, shall we get on?' He began to wind the handle on the torch, recharging it as the light was dimming.

'Yes it's sorted,' Liz replied. 'And thank you for all your input, Ed.'

Still winding Ed asked, 'Now what did I do?'

'Apart from crash the car, get us out on a freezing night, and totally lost to boot, no, Ed, you didn't do a thing. But then you never do, do you?'

'Look,' Ed said, trying to sound a little more conciliatory, 'we have gone about three miles, perhaps a little more, and we just began to go uphill. Maybe we will be able to see over the top of all this fog from high ground.'

'Oh well pardon me,' Liz hissed, 'but then we don't all have the benefit of your Marine training. Sorry, I meant to say "Marine Reserves" training.'

'Big deal, I wasn't regular,' Ed retorted. 'But I still know when I'm going uphill.'

'You do surprise me,' Liz scoffed. 'You went downhill without noticing.'

'Stop it,' Kate barked. 'Just stop it. Can't you two give it a rest just once?'

'Kate, honey,' Liz said as she stepped towards her daughter.

Kate pushed her mother away. 'No, Mom. Do you think Jay and me haven't heard you two, night after night. I thought that was why we came on this goddamned holiday to this goddamned country. Wasn't that what your counsellor told you to do?'

'What counsellor?' Liz asked.

'Come on, Mom,' Kate groaned loudly. 'Do you think Jay and me are stupid? Do you think we haven't heard you two talking when you get back late on Wednesday nights? Voices travel in the heating ducts, you know.' She turned round to her brother for support saying, 'Jay, tell them.'

'It's true, Mom, Dad, we've heard just about everything.'

'Look, honey,' Liz said softly only to be cut short by Kate once more.

'Look nothing, Mom. We know what has been going on. We know about Dad's job.'

'Kate, please . . .' Ed said softly, attempting to appease his daughter.

Kate heaved a heavy sigh. 'Look, Dad, I'm sorry. But since you lost your job you and Mom have been fighting all the time.'

'Listen, sweetheart,' Liz began, in a tone designed to be both comforting and reassuring. 'It's true that your dad and me have been having some problems, but we are trying to work them out.'

'Yeah, it sounds like it,' Jay scoffed.

'Sorry?' Liz said brusquely.

'Look, Mom,' Kate began, her voice raised. 'We know all about Dad getting laid off. Even though you two tried to keep a secret. And we know that he has been having a hard time finding another job. There is a recession on after all. But he is trying so why don't you just cut him some slack?'

'So I'm the bad guy?' Liz said.

'Nobody is the bad guy,' Ed cut in, 'and this is neither the time nor place to be talking about this.'

'It's never the time to talk according to you, Ed,' Liz shot back at him.

'See, Mom,' Kate snapped, 'you're hopeless.' With that she grabbed the torch from her father's hand and, quickly winding it a few more turns, turned away and began to walk hastily up the road. Jay followed close behind her and, before the torchlight had totally vanished from sight, Ed and Liz followed on at the rear.

For some time no one spoke. Kate and Jay led the way, walking side by side but hardly even looking at each other, while Ed and Liz tagged along at the back. Occasionally Ed and Liz would steal a glance at each other, but they did not speak; they did not know what they should say to one another. The fact was that Kate had been right; they had been having some problems in their marriage and for some time; Ed's plant closing down and him being laid off had only magnified the problems. They had tried to keep it from the kids, hoping that he could find another job before things got too bad. But the credit crunch, or recession, or whatever was the latest catchphrase for the crap that the world economy was in, was making finding work near impossible. Ed was a highly educated and highly trained engineer, and that was apparently working against him. Several times he had gone for interviews only to be told that he was over qualified for the position or that he was too specialised in his field. Either way it came down to the same thing: he didn't get the job. Liz thankfully didn't have that problem. She was a doctor and there wasn't any likelihood of a cut back in sick people. But it meant that she was, or at least for over the last year, the breadwinner. And it was perhaps that reversal of roles that was putting an ever increasing pressure on their marriage.

The night drew out in an endless silence. They had been walking for hours; at least in that taut hush that gripped the family it seemed like hours. From time to time Kate would spot, rapidly wind the torch handle, then begin walking again. Even Jay, normally the most talkative of the four, had nothing to say, or if he did he was keeping his thoughts to himself. But there was little, if anything, to say. The night was just as black as it had been. The fog was just as thick and impenetrable. And the cold was gradually seeping through their clothes, chilling each and every one of them.

'You were right,' Liz finally broke the silence with a whisper.

'About what?' Ed asked, his voice hushed, just as Liz's had been.

'About going uphill,' Liz thought for a moment and added. 'Well, I think we've been going uphill but it's so hard to tell.'

'I know what you mean,' Ed smiled weakly. 'I've been trying to figure out how far we've gone but in all this fog it's hard to tell. We're making slow progress, I know that much. But if it is uphill or down I'm not sure any more.' He breathed a heavy sigh. 'I just wish we could see something. But there is nothing. There's no moon, no stars, nothing to get a bearing off.'

'I know,' Liz whispered. She looked at Ed, her face etched with concern. 'Ed, I don't like this. I mean this fog, it's . . . well . . . it's not natural.'

Ed placed his arm around her shoulders, attempting to reassure her as they walked. He drew her closer to him saying, 'Don't start thinking things like that, honey, that's just fatigue talking.'

'No!' Liz insisted. 'It's not fatigue. There is something different about this fog, something wrong.' She thought for a second, looking about her the whole time as she tried to make sense of the impenetrable mist that surrounded them. 'Take a good look, Ed. Have you ever seen fog like this before? Anything that moves just a few feet away is lost from view. And even sounds seem to be deadened, muffled somehow, it's so thick. It almost as if the sound was under water; it gets distorted and with no sense of direction.'

She would have said more but Kate had stopped suddenly and Ed and Liz walked right into her.

Kate was standing motionless. She held the torch in her hands, one hand holding the torch the other the winding handle. But she was not winding; rather she stood, frozen in time, and staring off into the fog ahead of her. Jay was beside her, and he too was silently staring ahead of them, hopelessly struggling to see something within the thick vapour.

'What is it?' Ed asked in a whisper.

Kate flinched slightly, shocked out of her concentration by her father's voice. She said nothing but turned quickly to face her father and pressed her finger to her lips motioning him to be quiet. Then Ed and Liz, following the example of their children, stood silently listening and straining to see whatever they might see in the fog.

Jay held up his hand, one finger extended to indicate that something had caught his attention. He turned his head slowly left to right, trying to pinpoint whatever it was. Time stood motionless; seconds and minutes lost all meaning. They strained their senses to hear or see whatever it was that Jay had noticed. There was nothing, not even the sound of breathing, for they had all stopped breathing for fear of missing whatever it was that Jay had spotted.

All eyes began to slowly turn towards Jay as they each wondered what he had heard or saw. No one spoke; they just stared at Jay and waited for him to react again.

Gradually Jay's finger curled back into his hand. He slowly lowered his arm and began to edge silently forward. Like a hunter creeping closer to his prey, Jay inched his way along the road. Kate followed half a pace behind Jay, careful to be as silent as her younger brother. Ed and Liz followed just behind, and just as silently. Then Jay halted once again. This time he paused for a second, then turned to Kate saying, 'There, can you hear it?'

They all listened.

How Jay had heard it was anyone's guess, and just what Jay had heard was also as much of a mystery. But there was a sound, very faint and indistinct, but a sound all the same.

It was distant; at least it seemed to be distant. And it came and went as if carried away on the wind. But there was no wind, not even the slightest hint of a breeze. Yet the sound, whatever it was, never seemed to be constant. Sometimes it was like a bubbling noise, at other times like a chinking, a tapping almost, And still at other times it was like the sound of coins jingling together in a pocket. None of them had any idea what it was, yet there was an unspoken agreement between them that they had to get closer and find out what was making the sound.

Ed took the lead as they began to slowly edge towards where they thought the sound was coming from. By then the torch was out of charge and they had been plunged into an inky blackness. They were walking blind, and yet no one wanted to wind up the torch for fear of missing the sound that lay ahead of them.

They had no idea what the sound was. It may have been some animal, and the sound of the torch being charged might scare it away. Then again it might be someone on the road, or worse it might be the sound of another car approaching them, and winding up the torch right then might mean them not hearing the car clearly until it was too late. So, and at a snail's pace in total darkness, they crept anxiously forward.

Ed reached back and took Kate's hand. If he could not see her then at least he could hold her hand to be sure where she was. In turn Kate took Jay's hand and finally he took his mother's. Then they set off again, a blind chain snaking their way forward so very, very slowly.

How long they went on like that they had no way of knowing. Each step forward brought them closer to the sound, and yet it never seemed to be any louder or clearer. Like chasing after a mosquito in a dark room, sometimes the sound was there and sometimes not.

But then, all of a sudden, Ed's foot was not on a road. He stepped forward, placing his foot down firmly, only to hear the sound of wood creaking as his weight was place onto the foot. He stopped, stepping back in surprise, and then put his foot down again. Again there came the creaking sound and he inched his foot forward in an attempt to find out what he was stepping on. There were more timbers under foot. They were stout but old. He stepped onto them, testing their strength with his weight. The timber held, creaking softly with complaint at the load, but they held easily. Ed stepped forward more confidently, still holding hands with Kate, and drawing the rest of the family behind him.

Unexpectedly the sound they had been following became clear. Like someone lifting a muffling blanket off a stereo speaker, the sound became much louder. It was the noise of water: more accurately the sound of a small, shallow river. The chinking and clinking they had heard was the sound of small stones being jostled about by the flowing water. And the bubbling and gurgling was the sound of the water lapping round the post of the small bridge that they were then crossing.

Ed stepped onto the far bank and it was as if he had stepped out from behind a curtain. The fog had vanished and he was standing in bright moonlight. Above him was a night sky filled with stars brighter than he had ever seen before. As each of the family stepped from the bridge they all gasped at the abrupt change. But, when they turned to look back at the fog, it had gone.

The bridge was little more than thirty feet from bank to bank, and in the bright moonlight they could clearly see the other side of the stream, but still, the fog that had haunted their steps for so long had completely and utterly disappeared. Behind them was the small bridge; beyond that was the road they had just walked, though now they could see it was little more than a dirt track. Either side of the road there were trees, a thick crowded wood and not the earthen banks and hedges that they had imagined. Ahead of them lay the same dirt track. It stretched out before them like two broad, parallel paths, little more than deep ruts cut into the landscape by the passage of many wheels.

The night was near cloudless, and the moon was full. There was no wind, just a stillness disturbed only by the sound of the bubbling stream.

Suddenly, and seemingly without reason, Ed sprinted back over the bridge the way they had just come. Just as suddenly he stopped when he had reached the other bank. For a moment he was still. He looked about him, straining his eyes to see something in the dark. Then, after perhaps no more than two minutes, he turned and walked back to where the rest of his family was waiting for him, yet all the while glancing back over his shoulder at the wood.

'What was that about?' Liz asked quietly.

'I'm not sure,' Ed replied looking back again at the distant bank. 'For a second I thought I saw something move back there. But then, when I got to the other side there was nothing, just . . .'

'Just what?'

Ed thought for a while then said, 'It's weird, but for a second I could have sworn I heard someone, well, it sounded like somebody laughing, you know, in the distance.'

Liz bent closer to Ed so as not to be overheard. 'I told you there was something unnatural about the fog.'

Ed didn't reply, other than to frown at Liz. He quickly adjusted his clothes, hitching the small rucksack upon his shoulders then he smiled at Kate and Jay. 'Come on then, people. I don't know about you all but I am cold, wet, and hungry. What say we press on and find somewhere for the night?'

No one argued with Ed's suggestion; rather, had he not made it then anyone of the other three would have suggested the very same thing. They were all cold, wet and hungry, and though no one said it, they were all a little nervous about hanging round by the bridge.

They walked on, following the two deep ruts of the track. They did not need the torch now; the moonlight was bright, and where the ruts cut into the earth, the chalky under soil showed up white in the moonlight. It was an easy path to follow and they made good time. Whereas before they had been grouping aimlessly in the fog, now they were walking at a good pace and able to see several hundred yards ahead of them.

'We shouldn't have any problems seeing a house or farm in this,' Ed stated confidently.

'Assuming there is a farm around here,' Liz corrected him.

'Well, yes,' Ed conceded. 'But there is a road, of sorts, and where there is a road there is some sort of farm, village, something at least.'

'So long as that something has a fire,' Jay put in.

'And a bathroom,' Kate added.

Ed stopped and looked at Kate. 'I'm sorry,' he said. 'What with everything else I clean forgot.' He quickly looked about before turning back to his family saying, 'If anyone needs a bathroom break there are some bushes over there. Not that anybody is about to see you.'

'I'm not going in the bushes, Dad,' Kate protested. 'It's too gross.'

'You might have to,' Jay giggled.

'Mom?' Kate groaned.

'Mom,' Jay mocked. He set off, running towards the bushes shouting, 'Last one in is a smelly pants.'

'Mom, Dad,' moaned Kate.

Liz just sighed, 'There's nothing for it, sweetheart.' And with that she took Kate's hand and walked off towards another group of bushes.

Directly they were back on the road and feeling a tiny bit more comfortable. They walked for roughly an hour before Ed called a short halt. He was looking at something up ahead, endeavouring to untangle the shadows fashioned by the moonlight.

'See something?' asked Liz.

'May be,' Ed said, staring off into the distance. 'Just along there a bit on the right. Can you see it?'

Liz gave him a long, sideways look before saying, 'All I can see is night. You sure you're not imagining things?'

'Humm,' Ed replied before turning his attention back to the road ahead. 'I'm not sure but it looks like there is some sort of house just up there. A mile or so I would guess. But it's hard to be sure.'

'Well, come on then, Kit Carson,' said Liz sarcastically. 'Whatever it is, I just want to get in out of this cold.'

And so they carried on.

# Chapter 3

## Draygon's Farm

They reached the building in the last light of a setting moon. The shadows that had distorted the building, and its surrounding, were deepening and the whole world seemed plunged into an inky darkness. Even the stars were dimming, snuffed out one by one by the approaching dawn. In that pre-dawn gloom they turned off the road at last and stood before the building.

Set back from the road by a distance of a hundred feet there was a wall. It was a little over eight feet high, a dry wall of rough stones. Facing the road, and facing the family, was a gate of old but very stout timbers topped with spikes. Looking more closely Ed could see that the wall also had wooden spikes set in its top. Though in truth both wall and gate looked somewhat neglected, stout, to be sure, but neglected.

Ed pushed at the gate; there was no handle by which to open it, nor was there any knocker with which to call the attention of those within, so he pushed at the gate. The old timbers creaked, but did not yield. Ed pushed again, harder this time, much harder. Again the gates groaned and the hinges squeaked a little at Ed's assault, but they did not give.

'No joy there,' Ed said, heaving a sigh.

'Do ya think?' Liz asked, her tone mocking Ed's efforts.

Ed ignored her comment and began looking around him, searching the ground until he saw what he was after. Walking off to the side a short way Ed picked up a rock the size of a large coconut. Coming back to the gate, and using both hands to hold the rock, he beat the rock against the solid timbers several times.

*Bang, bang, bang.* 'Hello,' Ed shouted. *Bang, bang, bang.* 'Anybody there? Hello.'

Somewhere inside a dog barked and growled after being woken from its slumber.

'At least we know there's a dog inside,' Liz mused.

*Bang, bang, bang.* 'Hello,' Ed shouted louder.

The dog barked again, snarling angrily at the noisy intrusion. Other noises could also be heard coming from within the walled house. A man's voice telling the dog to be still, which the dog ignored until he shouted at the dog to 'get down'. Then, at length came the sounds of bolts being drawn and a door opening. There was also the sound of hushed voices chattering. One voice, a woman's voice, was saying something indistinct. Then came the man's voice again, louder than the woman, and saying, 'I'll know that when I ask. Now get inside, wife and stand you ready.'

Shortly the sound of footsteps was heard approaching the gate. But, rather than open the gate, the man's head suddenly appeared looking over the wall. 'Who goes?' the man demanded crossly.

Initially Ed was startled by the man's sharp tone. Also, in the dark, it was difficult to make out exactly where the man was. Yes he was above them, calling down to them from atop the wall, but it was nearly impossible to make out which was the man's head and which was just another big stone. 'Hello, sir,' Ed said, as his eye scanned the area where the voice had emanated. 'We are sorry to disturb you, but we had an accident back along the road there.' Ed waved his arm in the general direction. 'I am Ed Deeks, and this is my wife Liz and my children Kate and Jay. If you could be so kind, we are cold; we've been walking most of the night and we need to call for some help. Do you think you might let us in and maybe use your phone?'

'Accident you say?'

'Yes.'

'Wife and children you say?'

'Yes.'

'Wait there.'

'Thank you,' Ed shouted at the disappearing head. He turned to Liz and shrugged, adding in a hushed voice, 'A bit odd, don't you think?'

'Trust me, Ed,' she whispered back, 'you really don't want to know what I think right now.'

From the far side of the gate there came the muted sounds of an argument. Once more the woman's voice could be heard, but again it was too quiet for her words to be understood. The man's voice, however, was a little louder and clearer. From the one side of the conversation that could be heard it appeared as if the man was telling the woman everything that had just been said at the wall. Then he told her the whole thing again, and finally he told her to get back inside; several times in fact he told her to get back inside.

Eventually there came the sound of a heavy bolt being drawn, closely followed by the sound of wood hammering on wood. With each blow the gate gave a tiny shudder until finally the hammering stopped and the gate was pulled open.

A man stepped into the gap of the open gates; he held up a small lantern saying, 'Show yourselves then.'

'Hello, Ed Deeks, thank you for opening up,' Ed held out his hand, offering it to the man, but the man did not take it; the reason soon became apparent.

'They call me Braygon,' the man said.

He was short, no more than five feet six tall, but stocky and broad-shouldered. His hair was long, hanging down past his strong shoulders and set with two plaits, one either side of his head to draw his hair back from his face. He had a small beard that was thick and unkempt and also appeared to have a portion of his last meal hiding in it. The lantern he held was small and gave only a little light but it was still possible to see that the man was dressed in some sort of long shirt-cum-smock over a type of woollen pants that didn't quite reach his ankles. On his feet were clogs, wooden-soled and with leather upper that appeared to be handmade, but not very skilfully. In the dim lamplight it was also possible to see that he carried a short-handled bill hook in his other hand.

'Mr Braygon, this is my wife Liz. And back there is Kate and Jay,'

'Hi, hello,' the family said together, following Ed's introductions.

'Accident you said,' Braygon said, his voice gruff and perhaps a little inpatient. 'Anyone hurt?'

'No, thankfully,' Liz said, 'just our car.'

'Your what?'

'Our car,' Liz replied. 'I know it must be an inconvenience, Mr Braygon, but could we please come in from the cold and use your phone?'

'My what?'

Braygon looked from Ed to Liz and back again, eyeing them both suspiciously. He seemed to be weighing up whether or not to allow them in but then the woman's voice started up again, and it apparently made his mind up for him.

'Braygon, Braygon, you big lard tub,' the woman called out from somewhere within the yard. 'Let them in out of the chill; they have little ones, so let them in.'

'Be still, woman,' Braygon shouted back over his shoulder without ever once taking his eyes off the family at his gate. He shrugged and sighed, saying, 'You had better come in then.' With that he drew the gate back further and allowed the family in.

Within the gate there was a muddy courtyard. To the left, set in the corner of the wall that surrounded the courtyard, was a small fenced-off area that had a chicken coop within. Next to that, taking up most of the remainder of the left hand wall, was an open-fronted shelter. Under the shelter there stood a sorry-looking, shaggy-haired horse. It faced the wall, its rear end presented to the courtyard, as it aimlessly chewed some hay. Occasionally, when it wasn't pulling another mouthful of hay from the bundle hanging from the wall, the horse would look back to see what was happening in the yard, but only because what was happening in the yard was fractionally more interesting than the wall it was tethered to.

Next to the horse's shelter were several bales of hay and finally, neatly stacked, log and other cut firewood. On the right hand side of the yard, and able to be smelt before it was seen, was a pigsty. Beside that, and further along the wall, was a low building with a door and several small windows. Five men were congregated just outside its door, one of them holding back a vicious-looking dog that had been making so much noise before. The men said nothing, but stood there watching the family intently as they walked through the yard.

Ed gave the group a small wave. 'Hi there,' he said in a low voice, 'sorry to disturb you.'

The men did not reply.

Liz, likewise, gave the men a wave then turned to Ed saying, in a hushed tone, 'Aren't those men . . .'

'Yes,' Ed said quickly, cutting Liz off. He took her arm, gently drawing her away from the men and placing himself between her and them as he whispered, 'They're all carrying weapons.'

Lastly, at the rear of the yard, and facing the gate, was a two storey house. It, like the walls and the remainder of the buildings, was stone-built. And again like the walls, in need of some repair. The roof appeared to be thatch, but the edges were uneven and hanging untidily over the eves. There were several small windows on the upper floor, all of which were shuttered against the night. However the strangest feature was that there was no door at ground level. The entrance door to the house was also on the upper floor and could only be accessed by a ladder.

'Come along now,' the woman said cheerfully as she mounted the ladder. 'This way, my loves, and we'll get you out of the cold.' She carried on climbing, talking all the time as she climbed. 'We got a nice fire within. Soon have the chill out of your bones. Come along then, it's an easy climb.' With that she disappeared through the door.

Jay went first, closely followed by his sister, his mother and finally his father. Once up the ladder they found themselves in an open room that filled the whole of the upper floor of the house. There were no interior walls, only coarse-looking blankets strung across the room to divide off various bits. To the right of the door was an open fire set against the wall, a fire that served both to heat the room and as the cooking stove. A small chimney carried the smoke up and out of the building. The floor was bare wood and the walls were neither plastered nor covered in any other fashion. The only light in the room came from several lanterns hanging from hooks in the bare stone walls and from the small fire in the hearth.

In the middle of the room was a long, rough wooden table with two benches, one set either side and both equally as rough as the table. On the table were six wooden bowls, each with a spoon. In the centre of the table was a large black iron pot filled with what appeared to be some form of steaming porridge.

'We were just ready to break our fast,' the woman said merrily.

She was a short woman, little more than five feet tall, and a little rotund, though perhaps her limited height made her look rounder than she really was. Her face was round, her cheeks rosy, and her bright eyes were edged with deep laugh lines. Like Braygon she was dressed in a shirt-cum-smock, a long woollen skirt and clogs.

She turned to face the family as they came through the door and, waving her hand to motion them inside added, 'Come on now, sit you down, sit you down.' With that she turned away and gathered up more wooden bowls and spoons. She set them on the table before quickly scurrying off to one of the blankets hanging across the one room.

'Come now, children, time to break fast, soon be dawn, and, come see, we have guests.' She clapped her hands, 'Come, come.'

Small voices could be heard from behind the blankets at the far end of the room. It was soon followed by the sounds of rustling and then the blanket was slowly drawn aside.

Four children emerged nervously from what must have been the sleeping area of the one room. As they came out the woman, who had maintained a cheery smile throughout, introduced them. 'This is our oldest Boargon,' the woman said as the boy came to the table. Like his father, Braygon, he was stocky and had broad shoulders. He also had long hair and braids, though he did not yet have a beard. Next out was a girl. 'This is Poppy,' said her mother as a pretty blonde girl came to the table. 'And there is little Rosemary.' Rosemary was barely as tall as the table top and had the sweetest round face with rosy red cheeks just like her mother. She was also impossibly shy, using her bigger sister to hide behind until she was close enough to quickly jump behind her mother's skirt. As her mother went about the task of doling out the porridge into the bowls, Rosemary clung onto the skirt, only peeking out occasionally and even then only very briefly. It was her own little game of hide-and-seek. Lastly, from behind the blanket, came another boy. He was carrying a baby. 'Last as usual,' the woman said to the boy. Then she turned to Ed and Liz saying, 'This is our second son Hargon, and in his arms is our latest girl.'

'She's lovely,' Liz said with a smile as she bent closer to the baby. 'What's her name?'

The woman chuckled. 'Oh deary dear, she is not a year old yet.'

Liz looked up from the baby, a puzzled expression on her face. 'I'm sorry. A year old?'

'But of course,' the woman smiled. 'When baby is a year old we have the naming.' She thought for a minute then asked Liz, 'You are strangers here, yes? I mean, not to be impolite, but your clothes are strange and you talk funny.'

'We're from Seattle,' Liz said.

The woman shrugged her shoulders, looking blankly first at her husband and then back at Liz.

'You know,' Liz said, glancing at Ed for support. 'Seattle, Washington. In the States.'

Again the woman just stared at Liz with the same blank expression on her round face, finally asking hesitantly, 'So is that far from here?'

'Yes,' Liz said at length. 'It's a seven-hour flight.'

'Oh,' said the woman as she finished dishing out the porridge, 'that is a long way then.' Suddenly, remembering something from earlier, she turned to her husband. 'Braygon, you big lump, you never introduced me.' Her words may have been sharp but there was a lilt in her tone and a playful glint in her bright eyes.

'Since when did you stop talking long enough for me to introduce you, woman?'

'Well, I am not talking now, am I?'

'Yes, you are woman, you're still talking now telling me you're not talking now,' Braygon said flippantly. 'If you just shut up a minute then I'll introduce you.'

'Shut up telling me to shut up. You shut up and introduce me.'

'How do I shut up and introduce you, woman?'

'Braygon,' the woman smiled, 'be a dear and introduce me, then shut up and eat.'

Braygon sighed heavily and rolled his eyes upwards. 'Ed, was it?' he asked at length. 'I have the honour to introduce my wife-man Salsify,' then, covering his mouth with his hand, added with a wry smile and lowered voice, 'It means the "Raging One", as you can tell.'

Ed returned the introductions, and once everybody knew who everybody was, they all took their places at the table, places that they were directed to by Salsify.

'You sit there dear, next to Braygon husband,' Salsify said to Liz, pointing at one side of the table. 'And you sit next to me, dear,' she told Ed. 'Kate, was it?'

'Yes.'

'What a sweet name that is. You sit next to Boargon.' And so it went on till all had been assigned a place.

Before each of them was a bowl of porridge and a spoon. In the middle of the table Salsify placed a large earthenware jar filled with honey. Next to that was a similar jug with milk.

'Let us not be shy,' Salsify said with a merry smile. 'Eat up while it's hot.'

Boargon made a dive for the honey, but was beaten to it by his father. Meanwhile Poppy had grabbed the jug of milk and, after pouring some on her porridge, passed it down the table to Jay and away from her brother at whom she stuck out her tongue.

If truth be told breakfast was something of a scramble, with everyone in Salsify's family trying to be the first to obtain both honey and milk for their porridge. It left Ed, Liz, Kate, and Jay looking at each other in bemusement. But then Salsify did something that none of them was expecting. She put milk and honey on her porridge then, before taking her seat, she took the baby in her arms, unfastened the front of her smock, and began to feed the baby from her breast.

Had Ed been able to see his own face at that moment he would have known what Liz was grinning at: when a total stranger had bared her breast, sat down next to him, on a rather cramped bench, and begun to feed a baby while, with her free hand, wolf her porridge down. But Ed couldn't see his own face: he could however see both Kate's and Jay's faces, and they both looked horrified. Jay in particular appeared to have been struck rigid. His fist clutched a porridge-laden spoon several inches from his yawning mouth and his eyes were glued to Salsify's naked breast.

And yet, while Ed's family might have been staring at Salsify, her family were eyeing his with intense curiosity. The reason for that curiosity was simple: it was the way Ed, Liz, Kate, and Jay were dressed.

When they had been forced to abandon the car, Ed and his family had grabbed whatever clothes they could without unpacking all of their suitcases. As a result they were wearing a couple of T-shirts each, jeans, hooded sweatshirts and wind-proof jackets. All of which could not have been in greater contrast to Braygon and Salsify's family that were all clothed in heavy woollen pants or skirts and grubby smocks. The girls, just like their mother, also wore knitted shawls.

'So Braygon,' Ed began, trying to divert everyone's attention from Salsify breastfeeding. 'What exactly do you do here?'

Braygon looked a little confused. 'We farm,' he said with a mouth full of porridge.

'Well yes,' Ed stammered. 'But what I meant was, is this like a historic farm or something?'

'Historic?' Braygon puzzled, adding after a long pause. 'If by that you mean that the farm belonged to my father before me and his father before him and so on back, then yes, you could say it is a historic farm.'

Ed ate more porridge before saying, 'Well, no Braygon, not exactly. What I was meaning was is this like a farm for like tourists?'

'No. No tourists,' Braygon said shaking his head. 'We got cows, chickens, pigs and some sheep, but no tourists.'

Liz coughed, almost choking on her porridge.

Ed glanced at her in surprise before saying to Braygon, 'Surely you know what tourists are?'

But Braygon just shook his head again and stared back at Ed with a confused expression planted firmly on his round, red-cheeked face.

'Tourists,' Ed repeated, 'visitors that come to see how the farm is run.'

'No,' Braygon said. 'No visitors, just yourselves.' He looked across the table at Salsify for support.

'That's right, no visitors or them, what did you call 'em?' Salsify asked.

'Tourists,' Ed offered.

'Aye them, tourists. No none of them,' stated Braygon matter-of-factly.

'But Mr Braygon,' Liz said in a slow gentle tone. 'We are tourists. That is to say that we are on tour. You know, touring, going around and seeing things. Tourists, you see.'

Braygon thought deeply for a moment then asked, 'So is that what you do then? Just go round places and see them.'

'Well yes,' Liz smiled.

Again Braygon thought deeply. 'Doesn't sound like much of a trade that.' He pondered aloud, 'How do you get paid?'

'What?' Liz exclaimed. 'We don't get paid. We have to pay to tour. It's our vacation not our job.'

'Your va-what?' Braygon asked.

'Va-ca-tion,' Liz said for emphasis. 'Our holiday, time off, break away from work.'

'That's nice, dearie,' Salsify smiled. 'But how do you live? Do you have a farm somewhere?'

'No, no farm,' Ed said. 'Liz here is a doctor, Jay and Kate are still at school, though she will be going to college soon, and I am an engineer.' But his words fell upon Braygon and Salsify like soap bubbles: as soon as they landed they burst and had no meaning.

Salsify, after a long pause, spoke first, turning her attention to Liz. 'So what do you then? I mean, a doctor, what's that then?'

Liz gawked at Salsify in disbelief. 'A doctor? You mean you don't know what a doctor is?'

Salsify just smiled an innocent, dim-witted smile.

'I work with sick people,' Liz stressed. 'In a hospital.'

For a long moment there was silence in the room, like a stone falling into a deep well, and then came the sudden splash of realisation. 'Oh a healer, she means a healer,' Salsify said loudly. 'You do mean a healer, don't you, dearie?'

'Well, yes I suppose so,' Liz agreed, somewhat reluctantly.

'See Braygon, she's a healer,' Salsify said, seemingly quite pleased with herself for working it out. Braygon merely grunted some unintelligible reply. Then Salsify turned her attention to Ed, asking, 'And you dear, what did you say you did?'

'An engineer,' Ed replied. 'Well I was till the credit crunch I got laid off.'

'Engineer? Was that right, dearie?'

'Yes.'

'And what does they do, dearie?'

'An engineer, we design and build things; at least I used to.'

'Build things, what things?' Braygon asked.

'Well, anything really,' Ed explained. 'I used to design machine tools, but engineers work in all fields.'

Braygon appeared to be totally perplexed when he heard that. 'So you work in a field, and that is where you build whatever it is you build, right?'

'Err no, not quite,' Ed groaned. 'My field is machine tools.'

'So then you have a field of tools?' Braygon said.

Now it was Ed's turn to stare in disbelief. 'No, when I say "field" I mean that is the area I work in.'

'I see now,' Braygon smiled. 'You have an area of fields with tools in them. Do you have any animals in your fields or is it just tools?'

'No, no animals,' Ed said wearily. 'Just tools.'

'But, and I am sorry to go back a bit,' Salsify interjected, 'but didn't you say that you don't work in your fields now?'

'That's right,' Ed sighed. 'What with the credit crunch and the recession my plant closed and I was laid off.'

'Could you not grow another plant?' Braygon asked.

'It's not that type of plant,' Ed said, a bit puzzled. 'By plant I mean the place where I work, where I worked. A plant is a factory, you know what a factory is?'

'I know what a factory is,' Salsify stated proudly.

'You do?' Ed smiled.

'Well, of course,' Salsify replied. 'Old Drayloc, that fat tub of dripping up at Guidepost, he's the local factor, and where he lives that would be the factory, right?'

'Err no, not quite,' Ed said giving Liz a disappointed glance. He turned back to Salsify, trying to explain but with a growing realisation that his explanation was going clear over her head. 'A factory is a place where things are made. Materials come in one end, things like steel or wood or whatever, and finished goods go out the other end.'

Braygon nodded but didn't appear convinced.

'So what is a, how did you call it, a rescission?' Salsify asked.

'A recession. That is when there is little or no money about,' Ed explained. 'No money means people don't buy things, which mean people that make things can't sell them, then they lose their jobs and they have no money to buy things and so on.'

'Aye now that I understand,' Braygon said loudly. 'Few years back we could get a good price for our sheep, now we can't get more than a few copper coins. Cost more to feed them than you make off them.'

'That's right,' Ed smiled, 'that's a recession.' Then he stopped smiling. 'Yes, that is a recession.'

Ed's words seemingly struck a note that everyone understood and all fell silent for a long moment as they thought about them. Finally Salsify broke the silence.

'So dear,' she said, addressing Liz, 'What were you doing travelling in these parts, and at night too?'

'Well,' Liz began hesitantly, 'like we said before, we are on vacation. My mother came from Yorkshire originally so we wanted to see where she came from. You know, having a look at the old country, so to speak.'

'The old country,' Salsify smiled. 'That's nice, dearie.'

'My folks came from Germany,' Ed offered, though it was obvious that it meant nothing to either Braygon or Salsify.

'Well,' Braygon said slowly, helping himself to more of the porridge from the pot. 'I don't know these places you talk of, but then I have never been outside of Angron. Never had the time, or the need.'

'Never been outside of this farm you mean,' Salsify mocked. 'Leastways not unless you were taking the sheep to market.'

'And who else is going to take the sheep to market? They don't get there by themselves, you know,' Braygon protested without much conviction.

'Still,' Salsify said thoughtfully, 'it might be nice to see some place else. Some place like . . .' She turned to Liz asking, 'Where was it you said you came from, dear?'

'Seattle,' Liz replied.

'Seattle, and what's that like?'

Liz gave a little smile as she began. 'Oh it's really quite beautiful. There is the harbour and the old town. The Pacific Ocean is right on our doorstep and then there are the Cascade Mountains. It's lovely.'

'That sounds nice,' Salsify said. 'Doesn't that sound nice, Braygon?'

Braygon snorted, 'Ocean? Mountains? And who is going to look after the animals?'

'Ah true,' Salsify finally agreed.

'If I may,' Ed said at length. 'Just to get things clear in my own mind.' He faced Braygon and asked, 'You are telling me that you have never been on vacation, never taken a holiday. In fact you have never left this area.'

Braygon merely shrugged and answered, 'Never had the time.'

'And you have never had other tourists here?'

'No,' Braygon said flatly.

'Mind you,' Salsify began, pausing for a moment as she changed the baby round to feed on her other breast. 'There has been some strangers of late, not round here but up by the ford at Bywater. Leastways that's what Molly, the miller's wife-man, tells me.'

'Molly talks too much,' Braygon snapped.

'Mayhap she does,' Salsify replied, looking at her husband keenly. 'But her cousin has a farm near Bywater and he tells of strange folk coming and going in dead of night. He says they are meeting up with some of them new folk that have moved in south of Guidepost, and they be a most unsavoury sort to be sure. Lording it over folk that have lived here for years.'

'Be still, woman,' Braygon said sharply, giving a tiny, almost imperceptible nod towards Ed and his family. 'We mean no offence, sir,' he said to Ed directly. 'We are just farming folk and know nought about the outside world. Live and let, as we say, live and let.'

An awkward silence hung over the table for a while, until finally Ed broke it.

'Well we know nothing about what goes on here. As we said, we are from the States, and well, we're lost. It was just that we thought you might be like some type of re-enactors,' Ed explained. 'We were at Alnwick yesterday and they had a whole horde of them. We sort of assumed that you might have been part of that.'

Braygon and Salsify just looked at each other and then began to chuckle.

'Actors,' Salsify laughed heartily. 'No dear, there are no actors here. Not unless you mean my Braygon there acting the goat after he's been at the cider.'

Braygon smiled broadly at that. 'Tell truth, wife-man, I'm not the only one with the cider.' And they both laughed.

'So how then did you come to this road?' Braygon asked Ed at length.

'We got turned off the main road by the road works,' Ed replied with a shrug. 'Then we got sent down some side roads and that was when the fog came in. After that we just got plain lost.'

'We got lost?' Liz asked.

'Sorry,' Ed corrected himself. 'I got lost, these three were asleep.' He cleared his throat. 'The next thing I know I am driving through the thickest fog I have ever seen without the faintest idea where we are.'

'Fog?' Braygon said sharply.

'Sure as hell was; the worst I've ever seen.'

Braygon eyed Ed suspiciously. 'Was that east of here in Tangle Wood?'

Ed gave Liz a quizzical glance before answering, 'To tell the truth, I really have no idea. In all that fog I don't know if we were heading east, west or round in circles.' He thought for a minute then added, 'I know we had to cross a ford; that was just after we had the accident. Then we walked for a good while, but how far we walked I wouldn't like to say. What with the fog being that thick it was impossible to see where we were, and we were travelling very slow. Next we came to a wooden bridge over another river. Right after that the fog just up and vanished. Then the weirdest thing.'

'Yes?' Braygon said, willing Ed to continue.

'Well after we crossed the bridge, it was like . . .' Ed suddenly appeared embarrassed about what he was going to say. 'Well, it sounded like somebody was laughing in the trees behind us. I know it sound stupid, and maybe it was just the wind or something, but for a second I truly believed that I had heard it.'

'We bless you, sir,' Salsify said placing her hand upon Ed's hand. She looked across the table at the others and smiled reassuringly. 'Sounds to me like you came through Tangle Wood, and what with the wood folk up to their mischief, you should all count you blessings that you came out alive. Not many do, you know.'

'Aye,' Braygon agreed. 'Think yourselves lucky it was just your cart and horse you lost.' He looked to his family saying, 'Children, what have we told you?'

As one the children replied with a little rhyme.

*When sun is fading, and moon on the rise.*
*When heavy cloud fills the skies.*
*From Tangle Wood, so full of lies.*
*Stay you clear and homeward fly.*

'That's right, children,' Salsify smiled. 'And mark it well all of you.'

'Well,' Liz said, having difficulty suppressing her mirth, 'children's rhymes aside. We still require some help, like a phone, so we can get the car recovered. And maybe a good hotel so that we can get showered and some sleep.'

'You can sleep here if you like,' Salsify said brightly, 'and the beds will still be warm so, so much the better.'

'No,' Liz said sharply, then noticing that her tone seemed to have offended Salsify, she said more conciliatorily, 'We could not possibly impose on you any further. You have been more than generous, and this porridge is particularly good. But the truth is that we really should be getting on. Isn't that right, Ed?'

'For sure,' Ed agreed. 'If you could just point us in the direction of a phone, or a garage, breakdown recovery, anything like that, it would be most appreciated.'

Braygon finished his second bowl of porridge and gave a loud burp. 'Delightful as ever, Salsify.' He looked at Ed, cleaning the porridge from his beard with the back of sleeve and saying, 'Well sir, I don't rightly know what it is that you are after, all that talk of phones and things, but there be a smithy in Guidepost, man by the name of Maullen. Can't miss him, big man, about your height, and as wide as my gate. He can fix most things but, if you left your cart in Tangle Wood, then there's little luck that it will still be there. The wood folk would have their sport with it and no mistake.'

'Great,' Ed moaned. 'There goes the excess.'

'Never mind the excess,' Liz said. 'We left most of our stuff in it. I told you we should have bought the better cover.'

'Makes no never mind,' Braygon sighed. 'The wood folk will have the cover too.'

Both Liz and Ed stared at Braygon, asking him in unison, 'What?'

Braygon did not answer, but he did burp again, very loud and very long, a burp of which he was immensely proud.

# Chapter 4

## GuidePost

The directions to Guidepost were simple enough to follow.

Beginning at Braygon's farm, take the track back to the road and then turn right. From there follow the road for a few miles until you reach a crossroad. At the crossroad turn left. It would be hard to miss the turn as a big old oak marked the crossroad and the road to Guidepost was lined by a row of poplars that goes on for a mile or so. All Ed and his family had to do was follow that road and Guidepost was directly before them.

Braygon had been happy to give them directions while, at the same time, apologising for not having anyone he could spare to show them the way. Salsify was likewise sorry, but her apologies were more heartfelt and profuse.

'Stay on the road and you should be there by midday,' Salsify told Ed with a smile, more comforting than cheerful. She handed Liz a bundle, a small package wrapped in a grubby canvas cloth. 'Just a little something for the road, dears,' she said, giving Liz a kiss on the cheek before adding in a whisper, 'Be watchful on the road and make for the smithies as soon as you get there. Maullen is good man, but not all at Guidepost can be trusted.'

With those words and handshakes the two families parted.

It was shortly after dawn but already the sun was climbing high in the sky and the day was set to be bright and hot. In fact, it was just the type of day for a pleasant country walk, and would have been, had the circumstances been different.

Ed and Liz walked side by side, the children walked a little way ahead of them. For a good while no one spoke but they did, every few yards or so, turn and wave goodbye. Salsify was standing by the gate, holding her baby in her arms and watching them as they followed the road that Braygon had directed them to follow. Each time the family turned, Salsify would give a little wave, or hold up the baby's arm and wave that. And so they went on, until finally they lost sight of the farm.

The men that had been in Braygon's yard when the Deeks had arrived were in the fields. Some were tending to the animals; others were fixing a plough harness to the horse in readiness to begin their ploughing for the day. As the family walked past, both the men and Deeks waved to each other, and yet, while there was genuine warmth from the Deeks there appeared to be only indifference returned from the workmen. The fact was that while Braygon and Salsify may have been welcoming and friendly, the men, who Ed and Liz assumed worked for Braygon, had been watching them suspiciously the whole time. It had left both Ed and Liz feeling a little uncomfortable and now, as they walked away from the farm, they could not help feeling uncomfortable all over again. Both got the feeling that they were being watched, and watched for some malevolent purpose. Even when they were some distance from the farm, they still felt like they were being watched.

'I wonder why we did that,' Liz said at last.

'Did what?' Ed asked.

'Kept waving but not talking till the farm was out of sight,' Liz began with a nervous giggle. 'Do you think they might have overheard us?'

'You're right,' Ed laughed. 'Very friendly folk but, my heavens, the only thing missing was the Banjo music.'

'And those accents,' Liz scoffed, then, doing her best impression of Salsify, she said, 'Stay on the road, dears; there be some strange folk hereabouts.'

Ed likewise tried to copy Braygon's accent. 'There be strange folk at the farm.' Ed chuckled. 'What the hell was that all about, them acting dumb like that, "We don't got no tourists, sir."'

'Nor no telephones, whatever they be,' Liz added.

They both laughed, wondering exactly what sort of people they had just spent their breakfast with.

'I will tell you one thing though,' Liz said, 'and I am not joking around here. But somebody should really have a word with Child Services or whatever they call them in this country.'

'Liz honey,' Ed sighed. 'We are supposed to be on holiday. Please don't go getting involved.'

'Getting involved, Ed?' Liz groaned. 'Did you have a close look at the children back there? They all looked malnourished, there was no running water in that place, no heating, and they appear to be suffering from vitamin D and C deficiency.'

'Look, is it really any of our business?' Ed asked.

'If not us, who then?' Liz retorted. 'And another thing, did you get a good look at Rosemary's head? I am sure I saw something crawling around there. We had better check each other, come to think about it, just in case we have picked up a few hitch-hikers.'

'Are you for real?'

'Absolutely.'

They both walked for a while, keeping their thoughts to themselves. Finally Liz broke the silence.

'You know, Ed I never thought I would see poverty like that, least not unless it was a third world country.'

'Well, if I am being honest,' Ed began hesitantly. 'I think I was a little surprised.'

'How so?'

'Well, remember about six years ago I went off with the reserves for two weeks in South Carolina?' Ed waited until Liz nodded. 'Well we saw some places, real backwoods miles from anywhere, places that were dirt poor. But I didn't think we would see anything like that here.'

'And what about the people there? How did they look?' Liz asked.

'Come to think about it. Just like the kids back there. You know, thin, lacking any colour in their faces, sallow, sunken eyes with dark patches round them.'

'Exactly,' Liz said. 'Now do you think we should talk to somebody about those kids?'

'Weeeell,' Ed sighed. 'May be we should. But I just feel awkward reporting them, especially as they were so friendly and helpful.'

'Maybe so, but the fact is that those children need attention. A proper diet at the very least.'

'Maybe so,' Ed agreed, adding softly, almost to himself. 'Maybe so.' He glanced about him as they walked saying, as if he was simply thinking out loud. 'But before we get to that I just wish I knew where the hell we were.'

They were walking on a road that was nothing more than a track, just like the road they had walked the night before. It was a dirt track really, a dirt track deeply rutted by cartwheels and potholed where wind and weather had eroded away the soft chalky soil. Either side of the road there were fields, small fields with thick Hawthorn hedges as boundaries. And each of the fields was apparently subdivided into narrow strips roughly forty feet wide and about 200 feet long, which seemed awfully small. Then again, perhaps the fields just looked small because they came from the States.

They had walked for nearly two hours when the crossroad eventually came into sight. The road had taken an almost straight course from Braygon's farm. And the country round about was gently rolling with a few low hills. To their right, to the north, was a low valley, a slow gurgling river at its base meandering leisurely upon its way to who knew where. They paused a while, standing on a moderate rise in the road, where the road crested one of the few folds in the land thereabouts, looking down at the crossroad.

To the north, and about half a mile away, was a ford over the river. Beside the ford was another house within a walled enclosure, just like Braygon's farm. The large oak tree, that Salsify had told them to look for was just to the south side of the crossroad and, a little further on from that, two lines of poplars, one either side of the road, led away off to the south. To the west the land was again mostly flat. It was only to the far north that the land appeared to change. There, it rose up gradually into tree-covered hills in the far distance. The hills arced round the whole of the northern horizon, surrounding the low plains like the serrated edge of some vast grassy bowl. What there wasn't, however, was any sign of the town of Guidepost: that was obviously further away than Salsify had told them it was.

In the fields around the house by the river they could see both men and women toiling with the land, some ploughing, others planting while still other tended animals. All of them were dressed the same as Braygon and his family had been. They all wore one of those discoloured smocks, either brown or a greenish coloured pants and of course, clogs. At first the people in the fields paid no attention to the Deeks as they approached, but then, as the family got closer, heads began to turn; the farmers began to point as they gathered in the fields to talk among themselves.

Getting closer, Ed raised a hand in the air, 'Hi there,' he called out.

But the people in the fields answered with a muttered, but distinctly indifferent, 'Hello.' Some waved, in a very perfunctory fashion. The sort of wave that said 'Yes we know you are there, but do us all a favour and be on your way.'

'Well,' Ed sighed, 'what the hell do you make of that?'

Liz shrugged. 'I guess what Salsify said was right. Not all the folks here are to be trusted, not even trusted to be a little bit friendly.'

'May be,' Ed groaned. 'Let's just hope that they are bit more sociable at Guidepost.'

'Yeah we can hope, I suppose,' Liz said.

They walked on for another hour, following the road up from the crossroad, walking between the rows of poplars. Then, after the trees, the road began to climb gently, steadily, but gently for a mile or more until it came to a small wood atop a hill. From there they could see all along the river valley to the north, and to the south they had their first glimpse of the small town of Guidepost. Between the two were several more walled farms. Some were small, like Braygon's and the one by the ford, while others were large, having a tall tower rather than a farm house within the walls. One, set back from the road to the east of Guidepost, was very large. It looked as if three farm houses and one tower had been built within the walls. And from the way the buildings had been placed, it looked more like a small castle than a farm. The fields around it were different also in that they were larger, had higher walls, and what appeared to be smaller towers set at the far corners of the fields. In some ways its appearance could best be described as a prison. But looking closer it was clear that the walls and towers were to keep people out, and not to keep anyone in.

'You ever seen anything like that?' Liz asked.

'Never.'

'Not even when you came over with the reserves?'

'Not even then,' Ed said. 'And I will tell you something else; it's what we haven't seen that worries me.'

Liz turned to him, 'What's that?'

'Well,' Ed began, 'take a look around you, I mean take a really good hard look and tell me what you notice.'

Liz did as he asked, sweeping her eyes around at the green fields, the tall woods, and wide open spaces around them. 'It's beautiful country,' she said at length. 'Beautiful and unspoilt. And we got a fantastic view from up here.' She turned to Ed smiling. 'You know darling, this is the type of place most people would give their right arm live. I mean, did you ever smell air so clean and crisp?'

'Exactly,' Ed said. 'So where's the power lines or phone lines, where's the blacktop roads, where's the tractors in the fields or even their tier marks, and where are the cars? It is nearly midday and we haven't seen a single car.'

'Well I don't know,' Liz shrugged. 'May be we just ended up in some national park or something. You know they do have them here sweetheart. Maybe that's it.'

'Come on, honey,' Ed groaned. 'Even the best national park has some sign of the modern world, something, anything, even if it's only a "DO NOT FEED THE ANIMALS" sign. There's not even a contrail of a plane in the sky. Nothing is ever this pristine and unspoilt.'

'Honestly,' Liz huffed. 'You always have to look for the downside, don't you?'

Ed rolled his eyes skywards. 'I'm not trying to see the downside. I'm just saying that there is something wrong; well, at least something is not right.'

'For the sake of Mike and little green apples,' Kate shouted. 'Will you two give it a rest. I swear, it's like you could find an argument in an empty room.'

Both Ed and Liz had all but forgotten about their children walking slightly ahead of them. They had been in their own small world and once again that world had proven to be a world where tension ruled and an argument was never further than a word away. It wasn't that Ed and Liz didn't love each other but, times were hard, very hard, and their love was being tested at every turn. Perhaps it was Ed losing his job, and Liz having to work extra shifts in order to pay the bills, that had placed such a strain on their relationship. Then again, perhaps it was any number of other factors. Whatever the reason, and there seemed to be many of them, both silently accepted that this holiday was perhaps their last chance to save their marriage. If they could not find a way past their current difficulties, and increasingly it looked as if they might not, then a separation on their return to the States seemed inevitable.

Once more they set off on their slow walk towards Guidepost. It was, after all, right where Salsify had said it would be: a lot further away than she had indicated but in the right direction.

They had reached the end of the small wood on the hill when Liz asked. 'Shall we stop for a short while and have something to eat?'

'Good idea, Mum,' Jay smiled. 'I'm starving.'

'Like that's something new,' Kate scoffed.

Before Ed could answer his attention was abruptly drawn away. On the road, from the north, came the pounding of horse's hoofs. Ed spun round, just in time to see four riders bearing down on them at full gallop. All were dressed in black, their pants, shirts, and jackets were all black; even the long cloaks about their shoulders were black. The riders pressed their mounts, pushing them on harder and faster as they charged up the hill.

Quickly Ed grabbed Liz and pulled her from the road. At the same time he shouted to Kate and Jay, telling them to look out. For the riders seemed bent on charging them down and riding over them. In seconds the four riders thundered past without so much as a glance in the direction of the family. Their horses were breathing hard from the exertion and their sides were white with sweat, yet still the riders pressed them, beating their flanks with whips in a demand for yet greater speed as they left the family far behind.

'Do you believe that?' Liz gasped.

'Sons of . . .'

'Ed,' Liz cut him off sharply, adding more thoughtfully. 'But yes, you're right.'

'Kate, Jay,' Ed shouted, 'you two OK there.'

'We're fine, yeah,' Kate shouted back.

'Speak for yourself,' Jay cried out sorely. He had been so startled by the sudden appearance of the horsemen that he had hurtled himself, without looking, out of their way and right into a thick gorse bush. The thick mate of claw-like thorns had snagged his clothes and scratched his flesh from head to toe as he dived in. Now, as he attempted to extricate himself, he was being scratched all anew.

The rest of the family ran forward to help Jay, holding aside the thorny braches of the gorse as a dishevelled son and brother crawled out. It was a view that, after the suddenness of the charging horses, made them all laugh: all that is with the exception of poor Jay who was still being scratched repeatedly. Each time another thorn cut him he protested loudly, and each time he protested the rest of the family, despite their best efforts, laughed all the more: particularly as Jay had gone in head first and he was forced to extricate himself rear end first. Finally, and amidst much remonstration from Jay, he was out.

'I don't see what you all have to laugh at,' Jay moaned.

'That, little brother, is because you can't see yourself,' Kate sniggered. She brushed his hair back from his face with her hand and, in doing so, picked up a liberal dusting of bright yellow on her fingers. 'You seen all this, Jay?' she giggled.

Gorse is blessed not only with thick, sharp thorns to keep would-be herbivores away, but also with an enormity of bright yellow flowers, all of which are packed with a huge amount of bright yellow pollen. Most of that pollen was now covering Jay.

'Aha man,' Jay groaned when he saw himself. He made to wipe the pollen off, but each time he rubbed his jacket sleeve or trouser leg, the pollen merely got rubbed in and left a yellow stain behind. He tried to blow it off, but the pollen was sticky and simply refused to budge. Jay rubbed his hair, but that only left him looking like he had recently visited a hairdresser and come away with the worst highlights ever. Finally, angry and frustrated, not to mention just a little bit sore and stinging from all the small scratches he had received, Jay took off his sweatshirt and shook it violently in an effort to dislodge the clinking yellow dust. It worked, in fact it worked only too well, and a cloud of the yellow dust was propelled into the air, so much so that the dust instantly engulfed the rest of the family who just happened to be standing downwind of Jay the pollen giver.

'Jay,' Kate shouted as she tried to duck out of the way of the fine yellow storm. 'Like, come on, man.'

But it was too late. Kate had managed to turn away but that only meant that she now had a slightly yellow back and yellow hair. Not too great a problem as the pollen seemed to almost blend in with Kate's blonde tresses. Ed was standing closer to Jay as he wafted the dust into the air and consequently had no time to turn away. He therefore got a blast of pollen full in the face, leaving him looking as if he'd had a sudden attack of jaundice.

Now they were all covered in pollen, all that is with the exception of Liz. She stepped forwards to help Jay when the yellow dust had settled. From somewhere, most likely from her shoulder bag, where she always seemed to have just the right thing for the right moment, Liz offered Jay some wet wipes and a small tube of antiseptic. She set about cleaning Jay up and, more importantly, cleaning the many scratches on his face and hands.

While Liz was doing that Ed and Kate set about cleaning each other up as best they could. Finally Ed looked at Liz and asked, 'OK sweetheart, how come you didn't get that dust all over you? Kate and I got covered.'

Liz looked herself over; she was still as clean and as fresh as she had been when she had stepped out of the hotel more than twenty-four hours before. 'Just lucky, I guess,' Liz shrugged. 'That, and when I saw what Jay was going to do, I ducked behind my big ex-marine husband.'

'Nice to know I still have some uses,' Ed groaned good-naturedly.

'Of course you do, honey,' Liz smiled. She walked to Ed and raised her head ready to kiss him then, on second thoughts, she stepped back, got another wet-wipe out and quickly cleaned Ed's lips. Then, she leant in quickly, so as not to get any of the pollen on her clothes, and kissed him.

They had their lunch in the shade of a large tree at the edge of the wood. Salsify had been more than generous in what she had included in her 'little something for the road': there was freshly baked herb bread, a creamy soft cheese, honey water, and some small sweet cakes. They sat there for some time, enjoying the food and enjoying the view. While it was an ideal day and an ideal location for a family picnic – just the type of place to sit for a long while and watch the world go by – time however was pressing, and they still had to get to Guidepost and get something organised about the car.

'Shall we go then,' Liz said at length, clearing away the remains of the package Salsify had given them. Then, once more, they set off towards Guidepost.

Whatever they had expected to find at Guidepost it certainly wasn't what they did find. Braygon and Salsify had led them to understand that Guidepost was the main town in the area. And to be fair, it was the biggest place around. It was much bigger than the farms they had passed; it was even bigger than the farm that looked like a prison. But it was not what any of them would have called a 'main town'.

Guidepost sat on a crossroad in a shallow but wide valley. All around it was green, lush pasture with a few cattle grazing happily under the watchful eyes of their herder. To the west of the town, the broad river that they had been seeing all day took a leisurely course through the pastures, making its way south. To the east there were wheat fields, the grain looking ripe as it swayed gently in the summer breeze. There was a wall around the town. And where the road entered the town, there were stout wooden gates, drawn open to allow people in and out as they went about their daily business. Next to the gates, looking more like a tollbooth, was a small gatehouse. Just outside the door of the gatehouse, two men sat on crudely made stools next to an equally crudely made table. They both wore thick, padded jackets that were heavily stained with dirt and much worse besides. The jackets were also far too thick for a sunny day and that made both of them sweat profusely, adding yet more deposits onto their already filthy garments. Over the top of the jackets they wore black tabards which had some form of crest on the front. Whatever the purpose of the men, there was something about them that instantly put everyone on their guard. For they were, to say the least, a very unsavoury-looking pair: all bad teeth and worse body odour. Both men were dirty, almost as dirty as the clothes that they wore. Their faces were unshaved, their hair unkempt, and every wrinkle was highlighted by a dark grimy line of muck that bore testament to their distinct lack of personal hygiene. Their hands, with which they ate, were so ingrained with grunge that any self-respecting sewerage worker would have been ashamed to show them in public.

They were eating their lunch of bread, cheese, and some type of cured meat, meat that was in truth more fat than flesh. This they washed down with what appeared to be a rather flat brew of beer. The men gave the impression of total disinterest as the Deeks family passed them by. They were enjoying the sun and, when the mood took them, ripping off hunks of bread, which was sometimes dipped into the beer and sometimes not before being thrust into their wide gaping mouths, quickly followed by a slack handful of meat or cheese and yet another gulp of beer. After each sequence they would wipe their mouths on the sleeves of their thick, padded jackets, sleeves that showed the greasy evidence of countless repartitions of their eating habits.

'Morning,' Ed said, as they entered the town gates. Neither man replied, but they did pause and look at Ed for a moment, before thrusting more food into already overfull mouths.

'We're looking for somebody called Maullen,' Ed said, realising the two men were more interested in lunch than pleasantries. 'We have been told he is the smithy.'

One of the men, a round-faced, overweight fellow with slightly greying hair and greenish teeth, gulped back more beer, burped noisily and wiped his mouth. 'Up at the square,' he said, spitting out tiny fragment of uneaten food as he spoke, which he attempted to catch before it could fly too far. He gestured in the general direction with his flagon of beer, an action that caused the stale smelling brew to splash out of the flagon and onto the sleeve of his companion. Rather than complain the second man simply looked down at his sleeve, then back at the first man. 'Tar,' he grinned. Then he lifted the sleeve to his mouth and sucked the beer from the filthy clothes.

'Come on,' Liz said, ushering the family away from the men at the gatehouse.

But hardly had they gone more than a few paces when a rough voice from the gatehouse called out, 'If Maullen doesn't do it for you come and see me Goldie.'

'Like that's going to happen,' Kate snapped back.

'Yeah,' said the fat-faced man, flashing his green teeth in a leering smile. 'I'll be waiting right here for you, beautiful.'

'Hey now wait a minute,' Ed shouted at the man.

But the man simply looked at Ed, grinned a mocking smile, drew a sword out from under the table and slapped it down next to his beer. The implication was only too clear, and Ed, despite his anger, took the sensible decision to keep his family moving.

'Did you see that?' Liz asked after they had put some distance between themselves and the two men. 'I mean, what sort of place is this where someone can go round carrying a blade like that. Where are the police?'

'I told you,' Ed said pensively. 'There is something really wrong with this place.'

'You might be right,' Liz said.

'You think?' Ed replied, raising an eyebrow.

They walked on but much more warily now.

Around them was not so much a town as a collection of hovels with each one looking very much like the filthy fleapit next to it. They were built from coarse grey stone, bonded together with mud. Some had tiny windows in the walls, but without glass; rather they had rough wooden shutters blocking up the holes against the weather.

Even the doors appeared to have been taken from some dilapidated old garden shed and simply thrust into the frames, and if they fit, that was a bonus. There were gardens, of sorts, to the fronts of the houses and low wooden fences. But the gardens were overgrown and littered with weeds, and the fences were mostly broken, falling down or kicked over. The only way to distinguish between an occupied house and an abandoned one was by how much the weeds before the houses had been trampled to form a path.

The roofs of the houses were made from turf, most of which was as overgrown as the gardens. And almost every house had moss coming down from the roofs and creepers growing up from the weeds; it was as if nature was slowly clawing back what was once its own.

There were some people around, a few of them at least, and they looked as cheerless as their little town. All appeared to be dressed in the same scruffy smocks and pants, just about everyone else they had seen up till then. But, almost everyone they saw in Guidepost quickly ducked out of sight as soon as they saw Ed and his family. One or two did stick around long enough to have a good look at the family but, as soon as Ed, or any of the others made eye contact, the local would scurry off indoors.

Guidepost gave one impression above all else: an impression of overwhelming decay. It was not just the broken-down state of the houses, nor the destitute condition of the people, but the very atmosphere spoke of putrefaction. It was everywhere, and it was wholly daunting. Every house looked to be falling deeper and deeper into disrepair, even those that were occupied. The very air smelt of decay, that stale, musty smell of mildew and neglect.

Things did not improve as they got closer to the centre of Guidepost. The houses were perhaps a tiny bit larger, but no better looked after. If anything there seemed to be less people living in those houses. Most had been boarded up; though without exception those boards had been smashed or torn off and the houses ransacked for any valuables that may have been left behind. Above all there was the smell. It was the smell of open sewers, of a cesspool, and it was everywhere.

For all that it was Ed, Liz, Kate, and Jay that were the odd ones. And they were being watched, of that they were all sure. And not just watched by the two men at the gate. It was more than just a feeling that they got as they walked through Guidepost. In the silence that surrounded them it was possible to hear the distinctive sound of a rusty door hinge creaking. If, as they did from time to time, they turned round to search where the noise came from, it was only to see a door being hastily closed. No one acknowledged them, spoke to them, or greeted them as they walked into town. Rather they had been met with distinct disregard.

In the centre of town there was little if anything to differentiate it from the rest Guidepost. There was however a market, of a kind, in the open area. It was not so much a market square but more exactly a muddy patch of land with a well and water trough in the middle. Here there were several stalls, people selling their wears or whatever produce they had. There were a couple of stalls selling vegetables, though neither one of them had much on display. A few potatoes here, some carrots there, ten, perhaps twelve apples and the odd, slightly bruised pear was all that was on offer. To one side there was a cart, loaded with logs. Beside it a strong-looking man with an axe and saw was cutting the log down into more manageable lengths before selling them to the locals. An old woman sat next to the axe man. She was snapping long twigs and tying them into bundles to be sold as kindling. Then, after the man finished chopping another log, she would get herself up, gather up the wood chips, and put them in to a small basket ready to be sold on also. Down from the vegetable stalls another stall was selling meat. Half a sheep, a skinny-looking specimen moreover, was laid out on the bare wooden boards of the stall. The butcher, if that indeed was what he was, would basically hack off lumps of meat for sale to anyone that was interested. Other cuts were hanging from a wooden cross beam that was above the stall. But there was nothing covering the meat, no refrigeration; there was a black swarm of flies around the stall that simply ignored the butcher as he half-heartedly attempted to swat them away.

At one side of the square was a large stone building with a much larger wooden building attached to it. That one combined structure filled almost the whole west side of the square. Smoke rose from the chimney in the stone portion of the building, and intermittently, the sound of hammering could be heard emanating from the open doors. That stone-and-wood structure had to be the smithies they had been looking for.

On the east side of the square was another large building with a shingle hung above the door. The shingle was old and grubby but the picture and the words that were painted on the shingle could still be seen. The picture was of a man smiling and several sheep round his legs. 'The Jolly Shepard' the sign said, yet one quick glance round the town showed there was very little to be jolly about.

Apart from the smithies, the tavern, and the stalls, there was nothing else of note.

'Is this it?' Kate asked. 'Is this like, all of it?'

'What were you expecting? A mall maybe,' Ed replied.

Kate shot him a withering glance before saying, 'I dunno, but maybe like a few shops.'

Liz took another look round the square before saying, 'You notice something? There are no shops, no post office, no tea room, nothing. Ed, can you tell me one place we have been to on this vacation that doesn't have a post office or tea room?'

'Now who sounds like they are looking for the downside in all this natural beauty?' Ed mocked in a muted tone. 'I tried to tell you before. There is something really wrong here. And I do mean really wrong.'

Liz stared at him for a moment. 'Is this really the time for "I told you so"?'

'I'm not saying that,' Ed told her. 'But look, you three stay together and I will go and see if I can find this Maullen fella. The truth is, the sooner we are out of here, the better I'll like it.' With that Ed set off across the square towards the large building that they had assumed was the smithies.

Entering the building, Ed saw a boy of around ten or eleven sweating heavily as he worked the leaver attached to bellows. It was taking a huge effort to work the bellows, all the boy could muster, but the result was a brilliant fire in the hearth. Next to the boy, and sweating even more, if it were possible, was a large bull of a man. He was dressed in nothing more than pants, clogs, and a thick leather apron. In one hand he held a set of long steel tongs, in which he held a glowing horseshoe. In his other hand he held a large hammer, with which to beat and shape the shoe upon the anvil that was before him. His shoulders were broad and his arms pure muscle. His eyes were fixed upon his work and his face, which was round and friendly, was set in a mask of concentration.

Ed watched for a while without speaking, watched as the man beat on the steel shoe with his hammer until the red glow had left the steel and it had died to a bluish colour. Only then did the man place the shoe back in the fire. He racked about in the hot coals for a few seconds, drew it out, and made ready to beat it into shape again.

'Excuse me,' Ed said, taking his chance to get the man's attention before he began hammering loudly on the shoe. 'I am looking for a Mr Maullen.'

'Aye that's me,' the man said, noticing Ed for the first time. Then he suddenly straightened himself to his full, and quite considerable height, gave a tiny bow of the head saying, 'I mean that's me, sir.'

'Ah good,' Ed began, somewhat thrown by the big man's reaction. 'I was told that you might be able to help. We had an accident last night, broke the axle on the car and had to walk miles to get here. Do you do break-down recovery? Or can you phone and get somebody to come out?'

'I'm sorry, sir,' Maullen said slowly. 'And no disrespect, you understand, but you talk funny. You are not from round here are you, sir?'

'No, we're from America, Seattle to be exact,' Ed smiled.

'Ah I see, sir,' Maullen said politely, though obviously puzzled.

He was the same height as Ed, six feet three inches, but much broader in the shoulders and with a much greater chest and arms. Had Maullen been a bit younger, and had he grown up in the States, he would have made a first class tight end just as Ed had been at college, though with all the power in those arms he could have made a hell of a linebacker too.

'If I might ask, sir,' Maullen said as he put his tools aside. 'But who said as I could help you, sir. Theys that do me a favour is I dos them is one as it were.'

Ed looked at Maullen for a moment, trying to make sense out of what he had just heard. 'A couple that helped us out this morning,' Ed said at last. 'Fella by the name of Braygon and his wife, Salsify.'

Something in what Ed had said made Maullen smile warmly. 'Braygon,' he said loudly, the mirth obvious in his tone. 'How is the old boy, sir? Still at the cider, is he? I shoe that old nag of his, you know, sir? And how is that fruitful wife-man of his, sir? She's my wife-man's brother cousin, so I suppose that makes her some manner of family. Nice woman is Salsify, not a bad bone in her, sir.' Maullen stood for a while looking up and past Ed, as if he was recalling some fond, but half forgot memory. Then, shaking himself out of his momentary trance, his expression changed and he was back to business. 'So sir, this cart of your, I could possibly fix it but have to see it first. I gota finish up here, horse needs two shoes you see, sir, then I can have us a look.' For a second the smile fell away from his face and he looked intently at Ed asking, 'How you going to pay, sir?'

'That all depends,' Ed said. 'I don't know how much it's going to cost but I've got a hundred pounds in cash with me.'

'A hundred pounds, sir?' Maullen asked curiously. 'A hundred pounds of what?'

'Pardon?' Ed asked in return. 'A hundred pounds, you know, a hundred pounds, pounds, sterling.'

Maullen stood, slowly shaking his head; clearly he didn't know.

'Look,' Ed said, 'if a hundred pounds isn't enough then I have my American Express; it's gold so there should be no problem.'

Maullen's face lit up at that. 'Gold, sir,' he beamed. 'That'll do nicely.'

'Now we're getting somewhere,' Ed smiled. He reached into his pocket and brought out his wallet. Opening it, he took out the card and offered it to Maullen. But Maullen didn't take it; rather he looked from the card to Ed and back at the card again.

'What's that?' Maullen demanded.

'My gold card,' Ed said. 'Look here, it says American Express, accepted all round the world.'

Maullen still did not take the card. He stood back, drawing himself up to his full height as he glared at Ed. The smile had vanished from his lips, and the friendly light in his eyes had been replaced with one tinged with anger.

'Would you make sport of me, sir?' Maullen challenged Ed.

'Make sport? No of course not,' Ed insisted, not knowing what he had done or said to upset the big man. 'The card is as good as cash anywhere. I really don't see what the problem is.'

'The problem, sir. The problem is that it's not a gold crown, it's not a silver shilling, and it's not even a copper bit. What it is is, well I don't rights know what it is but it's not cash.'

'Well, all right,' Ed said. He placed the card back into his wallet and took out the five twenty pound notes he had obtained from the cash machine the morning before. 'Here, look, 100 pounds, sterling, your money not American dollars.'

Maullen looked down at the crisp new bank notes for a moment then, picking up the very large hammer he had placed aside just minutes before, said, 'I think sir had best leave now. Honest folk have got work to do and no time for tomfoolery.'

Ed placed the notes back into his wallet, momentarily lost for something to say. But what could he say? His money was no good, his credit card was no good; what else did he have to offer? 'Look Maullen,' he said, more out of desperation than hope, 'Salsify told us you were a good man and one that could be trusted.'

'Please sir,' Maullen cut Ed off. 'Salsify is family, sort of, but you're not.'

Ed made one last appeal. 'Look, if you could just help us out, we can surely come to some arrangement. We just have to go and get the car; it's just past Braygon's farm in the woods.'

'Tangle Wood?' Maullen demanded.

'Yeah that's it,' Ed said.

'Then I cannot help you, in fact nobody can,' Maullen stated flatly. 'There is not enough gold in the land to get me, or anybody else to go into that wood. If that is where you lost your cart then it's lost for good and all. And if you were in the wood then thank whatever you hold sacred that you came out alive. The woodland folk don't suffer fools, nor do I. Now, with respect, be gone with you, there's a good sir.'

'Well OK then,' Ed said firmly. 'If you are not willing to help then be so good as to point us towards someone that is willing.'

'Don't you understand, sir?' Maullen groaned. 'There is no one willing to help, not there, not ever.'

'There has to be someone?'

'No sir, no one,' Maullen insisted. 'Tangle Wood is a big place, a dark place and very very old. It's full of dark magic, and not just the Woodland Folk. There are other things there, things older than time itself. Take my advice sir, stay away from Tangle Wood. And that is an end of it.' With that Maullen went back to work, hammering the steel shoe harder and far louder than was strictly necessary.

There was nothing that Ed could do, so pushing his wallet back into his pocket, he headed back towards the square. On the way out, and for no real reason Ed took one last look back at the smithy. Perhaps trying to think of something persuasive to say, something that might possibly change Maullen's mind, but there was nothing. In a dejected state Ed turned away again.

Something stopped Ed, something half noticed that he had not even been aware of until he made to walk away. There, in the wooden building next to smithies, through the open door, Ed saw four dark horses. Their sides were white with sweat and their tack was all black. A woman was rubbing them down, washing the sweat from their flanks with water and a stiff brush. Ed was about to ask who the horses belonged to when he was interrupted by Jay who came charging over to him in a highly excited state.

'Dad, Dad you gota come and see this,' Jay shouted as he ran across the square.

'See what?' Ed asked.

'Come and see the Dwarves; they're great.'

'Now Jay,' Ed began, a little annoyed at the disagreeable terminology his son had used. 'We don't call them Dwarves; it's not polite.'

'But, Dad,' Jay insisted. 'They're real Dwarves; I mean real, genuine Dwarves.'

Jay grabbed his father's hand and was dragging him towards a small crowd that had gathered at the other side of the square. Liz and Kate where standing near the crowd, both of them looking at him with bewildered expressions on their faces.

Ed walked towards the commotion and Liz gave him a most unusual smile. 'Brother, when you get lost you really get lost,' she laughed.

'It wasn't me that got us lost,' Ed protested. 'It was the damn road works and then . . .'

Ed's words stopped in his throat; his mouth kept moving but no sound came out. Jay had called to someone among the crowd and waved for them to come forwards, which they did. But nothing could have prepared Ed for what he saw next.

From out of the small crowd that was gathering around a cart strode a dwarf. He gave Jay a friendly wave as a broad smile played upon his bearded face. 'Yes, young master,' he called to Jay, 'coming right along.'

The dwarf was all of five feet tall and nearly as wide. His hair was long and black, as was his beard, and both were carefully plaited and tipped with silver rings and beads. He wore a knee-length, black leather jerkin over a dark brown jacket and pants. His boots were of thick leather and shod with steel tips and heels. Around his waist was a stout belt, of dark brown leather, and hanging from the belt was a small dagger.

The dwarf came forward, smiling broadly as he held out his hand. 'Hello stranger well met,' he said in a loud booming, though very friendly voice. The dwarf turned to Jay, saying, 'You were right, young fellow, your father is tall.' Then, turning back to Ed, 'Greetings Longshanks. They call me Grooflin, and over there, that is my sister Grizlan.'

Ed was stunned, and more than stunned, he was somewhere between dumbfounded and befuddled. His hand went out to shake with the dwarf's, more as an automated response than as a genuine greeting. 'It's not possible,' he muttered. 'It's simply not possible.'

Grooflin shook hands but as he did so a frown crept over his smile. He glanced back over his shoulder then back to Ed. 'No, it is possible, Grizlan really is my sister.' And it was true; the resemblance was unmistakeable, right down to the silver rings and beads in her long black beard. In fact the only obvious difference between the two was that Grizlan wore an embroidered white cotton dress under her leather jerkin and over her trousers and iron shod boots.

'I didn't mean that,' Ed said. He would have said more except that he was interrupted by the sounds of a growing disturbance around the cart.

Grooflin had heard the commotion too and quickly headed back to his sister.

The small crowd that had gathered around the cart was beginning to slowly disperse. They had been replaced by a fattish man, with a round, ruddy face and flabby jowls. There was something else that distinguished this man from the remainder of the villagers, apart from his much great girth, and that was his clothes. Whereas all the villagers seemed to be dressed in rags, or at the very least rough and dirty clothing, the fat man was dressed in a fine woollen jacket and clean white shirt. Over his shoulders was a thick woollen cloak that fastened at his throat with a large silver clasp and chain. Standing a short distance behind him but clearly close enough to intimidate, were four cloaked men dressed head to toe in black.

'That's must be the four that nearly rode over us on the road,' Ed said to Liz as they both watched the argument around the cart unfold.

The four men, who they had only just glimpsed on the road, were unmistakeable. They were standing there, and given that they were dressed so distinctively in all black, including tight-fitting helmets that left only their callous eyes exposed, they made very imposing figures.

'It's five shillings so pay the tax or get out of town, *now*,' The ruddy-faced fat man stated. 'Besides, we don't want no filthy, thieffing Dwarves round here anyhow.'

'Yeah, yeah,' the four men agreed laughing and jeering.

'Who you calling filthy, and who you calling thieffing?' Grizlan shouted at the fat man. 'Just cause you got a fancy coat and some gobs at your back you think you can rob honest folk?'

Something in what she had said seemed to have unsettled the four figures behind the fat man. One of them stepped forward, flipping his black cloak over his left shoulder to show the handle of his sword. Doing so he also showed something else: on his chest, on the tabard he wore, was a crest, a fist, no, a gauntlet holding a lightning bolt. It was the same as the men at the gate had worn.

'My companions are of no consequence,' the fat man said sternly, holding up his hand, but it was hard to distinguish as to whom he was signalling: was it to the Dwarves, or to the four cloaked figures backing him up? 'The law is the law and law says it is five shillings. And if you filthy Dwarves don't pay up then my companions will help enforce the law. Got it, *dwarf*.'

'Law, what law?' Grizlan demanded.

'I'm the law, you ugly dwarf,' the fat man sneered, making the four men laugh again. 'I am the factor of this town, and this county, and I say what the law is. Now did that get through your thick *dwarf* skull?'

'That's enough,' Grooflin shouted. He made to run at the fat man but one of the four cloaked men stuck out a leg and tripped him as soon as he moved.

Grooflin fell face first into the mud. Suddenly encouraged by Grooflin's fall the other three jumped forward, lowering their shoulders and ramming the cart with such force as to knock Grizlan off her feet and back onto the seat. Just as quickly she jumped back up again, but then the three men at the cart began to rock it back and forth. Grizlan struggled to keep her balance as the three repeatedly rocked the cart with all their combined strength. She hung onto the back of the seat with one hand while, with her other, she had to pull back on the reins to stop the two small ponies that pulled the cart from being panicked by all the hullabaloo taking place behind them.

The one standing over Grooflin made a great show of slowly drawing out his sword. He held the sharp tip of the long curved blade over the dwarf's face. 'Ready to die, dwarf,' he sniggered.

'Hey, enough,' Ed shouted. Liz must have sensed he was going to do something for she had been holding on to his arm the whole time. Now Ed broke free and stepped forward, trying to stop the whole thing from getting totally out of hand. Besides, five against two was just unfair, not to mention that the two were people of limited stature.

'Shut your mouth, *man*,' the one holding the sword at Grooflin's throat sneered.

The other three forgot about the cart for a moment and started directly towards Ed.

'Someone's got a big mouth,' one of them scoffed.

'Better shut it then, 'aden't we?' hissed another as all three slowly made their way around the cart.

'Now look,' said Ed, holding his hand out. 'Let's just all calm down a minute. There's no need for anyone to get hurt.'

'Yous is gonna get hurt,' the nearest one hissed at Ed. 'Gonna get hurt dead.' He flipped his cloak over his shoulder and drew out a dagger. The blade was a good ten inches long, double-edged and slightly curved. The cloaked figure advanced upon Ed, waving the blade from side to side as he advanced. 'Yous gonna learn to keep your mouth shut, *man*. Cause I'm gonna cut me a nice big hole in your guts.'

'Look, I don't want any trouble,' Ed said backing away slightly as the knife-wielding figure advanced.

'Well, you got trouble now.'

Unnoticed by anyone, until he shouted, one of the three cloaked men had made not towards Ed but towards Liz and her children. Abruptly he shouted out, partly in triumph and partly in surprise, 'Here, look here, this one has gold.' He grabbed Liz's left hand, almost lifting her off the ground as he roughly thrust her hand up in the air for the others to see. Then, as Liz attempted to snatch her arm back, the cloaked man used his free hand to grab hold of Liz's throat. 'Gimme the gold or I takes the finger,' he hissed.

'Get off my mum,' Jay shouted, running at the much taller figure and repeatedly punching at the man's chest.

However the cloaked man did not let go. Maintaining a solid grip on Liz's throat he swung her round; his right hand released her wrist, but only so that he could knock Jay aside before reaching under his cloak and pulling out his knife, a knife that he then taunted Jay with.

Ed stopped backing away; he had to do something, and do it fast.

'That's it,' he shouted at the one approaching him, making the cloaked figure freeze momentarily. 'Put the knives away, get out of here, and that will be the end of it.'

All four cloaked men looked at each other and laughed. The one nearest Ed waved the blade in front of Ed. 'I don'ts want to put my knife away; nots until I cuts you, cuts you good,' he jeered.

What happened next was not planned by Ed; it just happened.

The cloaked figure lunged at Ed, and in an instant, his instincts took over.

Ed quickly sidestepped the thrust, catching the knife hand in with his right; at the same moment his left hand chopped down hard onto the cloaked man's elbow, bending it painfully as he twisted the wrist. The man's momentum carried him forwards, and as Ed bent the arm backwards, the knife came up swiftly and plunged deep into the man's throat. It was a move right out of the US Marine Corp training handbook, a move practised many times in both boot camp and unarmed combat training. Consciously, Ed had forgotten the move, forgotten most of the things he had been taught in combat school, but subconsciously, somewhere deep within his memory, the move was stamped upon his instincts.

Silence fell over the square as all eyes were fixed on Ed and the cloaked man. They stood together, close enough together that Ed could smell the foul odour of the man's last breath. They stood together for a second or two then, very slowly, the cloaked figure slipped to the muddy ground with blood spraying out of the gaping wound in his neck.

The figure standing over Grooflin cried out. It was a strange, unearthly cry. A cry of rage, of anguish, and wrath all rolled into one chilling screech. He forgot all about Grooflin at his feet and charged headlong at Ed. But the cry had alerted Ed and he was facing the oncoming figure as it ran towards him. The cloaked man raised his sword as he ran then; closing the distance quickly, he swung at Ed with all the force he could muster.

The blade flashed down and across Ed's body. Ed jumped back just in time, pulling his hips and stomach back as far as he could and narrowly avoiding the blade that slashed at him. It was just enough, although the blade tip still managed to snag the front of Ed's sweatshirt tearing it wide open.

Quickly Ed regained his footing and faced the man again. The man, thrown temporarily off balance by the force of his own swing, now swung the sword again, this time backhandedly and aiming higher, aiming at Ed's neck.

Ed ducked under the swing, dropping into a low crouch and letting the blade pass harmlessly over his head. He felt the draft of air coming off the blade as it passed, then, at that moment, with the swordsman stance wide open, Ed made his move. Like an American football lineman Ed shot up, up and forward, driving his body at his assailant with all the power his leg could supply. Ed's hands came up, catching the man under his chin. In an instant the man's head was thrust backwards, his body was lifted and pushed, over balancing him and knocking him into reverse.

The cloaked man stumbled, back-peddled for an instant but, as Ed drove relentlessly forward, the man tripped and fell back. Ed was on him; he lifted the helmeted head with both of his hands, only to slam it down against the ground as hard as he could. He lifted it again only to swiftly let go and roll out of the way as yet another of the cloaked attacker charged towards him.

This was the fourth man, the man that had been standing half way between Ed and Liz and who Ed had temporarily lost sight of but who was now making his very unpleasant presence felt. The man charged at Ed, his sword raised high above his head. He hacked downwards, like a man chopping firewood, fully intent on decapitating Ed. But Ed's fast reactions surprised the man. Ed rolled away as the sword whistled down past where his neck had been, missing him completely, but not missing the man Ed had been crouched over. The sword sliced straight through the exposed throat of the man lying on the ground, neatly parting his head from his body.

'Oops,' came a voice from within the black helmet.

For a second the fourth man was so stunned by what he had just done that he froze. It was all the opening that Ed needed. As he rolled away, he flipped his body and landed on his feet facing this new enemy. With the man frozen Ed lunged forward, crashing into the man and knocking the sword from his hand. The man landed on his back in the mud and Ed went for him again. The man twisted away in an attempt to regain his footing. Ed had to be quick. He slipped behind the cloaked man before he could get up. Then, seizing the man's chin in one hand, and the crown of his helmet with the other, Ed gave the man's head an almighty jerk. The neck snapped with a sickening crunch. His body went as limp as a jellyfish. And even before Ed dropped the man's face into the mud, he was dead.

Ed stood up, facing the man that had threatened to cut off Liz's ring finger. This one didn't rush in; this one was a little wiser, if only because of seeing his companions die, but he was too shrewd to let anger rule him. He walked towards Ed, slowly and deliberately, making a great show of drawing out both his knife and sword.

The sword was easily three feet long, slightly curved and with edges that were chipped and notched from many combats. The black figure came on, levelling the blades at Ed. Like a wolf stalking its prey, the man closed in on Ed. His cruel eyes were fixed on Ed. He leant forward, his knees bent slightly, and his footsteps were slow, well balanced, and methodical. He did not come straight on; rather he sidestepped, his feet searching out the firmest ground from which to launch his final assault.

Ed too began to sidestep, moving away from the three bodies so that, when the attack came, he would not be tripping over the corpses that now littered the ground. Slowly, Ed and the cloaked man began to circle each other, Ed waiting for the attack which would surely come and the cloaked man waiting until he saw the clear opening he wanted and to be sure of the kill he was after. Around they went, oblivious of everyone in the square watching them. Each man was tense, ready to do what they knew they had to do: kill or be killed.

Ed looked around him; to his right he saw the discarded sword of the man whose neck he had snapped. It was a few feet away but perhaps just close enough that he might be able to rush and snatch it up ready to use it to defend himself. But even then Ed was unsure what he would do with a sword. The only time he had ever had a sword in his hand was during his short officer cadet training at West Point and then only to learn how to salute without cutting his own nose off.

But the black-cloaked figure had also seen the sword and Ed glancing at it. He stepped to his left quickly, coming between Ed and the sword and letting a small mocking laugh escape from within his helmet as he did so.

There came a hiss and a thud, a dull thumping sound that only just managed to break the silence filling the square. Everyone had been holding their breaths, even the birds seemed to have stopped singing, as Ed and the man circled each other like two prize fighters in an ill-matched bout. Then had come that swift hissing sound closely followed by that solid thud and a collective gasp from the small crowd.

For a brief second the cloaked man froze, just as Ed was frozen, trying to figure out what the noise was and where it had come from. The man slowly stood upright, his arms dropping to his sides. Both sword and dagger fell from his hands, clinking noisily together as they landed in the mud. His hands reached behind his back, raking frantically at something under his shoulder blades. Blood spit from his mouth, dripping from under his helmet as he arched his body backwards and his breath came as a hiss of pain. Just as suddenly as the thud, the man fell face first into the mud, a short, thick, feathered shaft sticking out of his spine. For a moment Ed didn't know what had happened, then he saw Grizlan standing on the cart with a crossbow in her hands and he understood.

'Way to go, Dad,' Jay shouted excitedly as he rushed forwards, only to be stopped by Liz.

But Ed did not answer him; he did not react at all. The adrenalin was passing and shock was beginning to set in. Ed was numb, left speechless by what had just occurred.

Liz came to his side, hugging him as only a loving wife could, and checking him out as only a concerned doctor would. 'Are you hurt, have you been cut anywhere?'

'No I'm fine,' Ed mumbled.

'Come on, we have to get you cleaned up,' Liz told him. 'You're filthy and I need to make sure you're OK.' She took his hand and began to pull him towards the water trough by the well.

'Ah Longshanks,' Grooflin cried out merrily. 'What a fight. Never did I see such moves.' The dwarf came striding towards Ed, a grin a mile wide on his bearded face. 'Three you got, three, and you without so much as a blade. What a song this will make; three with nought but your bare hands. All right, strictly speaking you did get a little help from a badly aimed swing, but we won't tell.'

'I got one too,' Grizlan cut in, her smile every inch as wide as her brother's. 'What about a song about me?'

'Songs?' Ed gasped. 'Songs?' he repeated, louder than before. 'Are you mad? I just killed three men. And you, Grizlan, you just killed a man as well; this is not the time for songs.'

'Men?' Grooflin said very slowly, and more than a little confused. 'They are not men, they're gobs. Well that's what we call them. We Dwarves, I mean. You humans call them half-goblins; least that's what I heard yous say.'

Ed stared at the two Dwarves for a long moment. 'What are you talking about? Goblins? Half-Goblins? There is no such thing.'

'Really?' Grooflin asked. 'Then come here, Longshanks.' He grabbed hold of Ed's hand and pulled him over to where the nearest of the four cloaked figures lay. It had been the first to attack and the first to die. Grooflin bent down and took hold of the close-fitting helmet on the figure's head. 'No such things aye; here.' And with that he pulled the helmet off to expose the face beneath.

The skin was leathery and tinged with a strange greyish-green colour. The eyes were somewhat slanted, almost oriental in shape but more narrowed and all together callous. The eyeballs however were over large and bulging. The nose was flattened, upturned to the point where it was more like a pig's snout. And the mouth, the mouth, even in death, was a mocking sneer, its thin lips drawn back over teeth that had been filed to sharp points. In general shape and proportion, the creature's face was human, but in every detail it was far from human.

'What the hell is that?' Ed moaned.

'I told you, Longshanks,' Grooflin grinned. 'It's a gob, a goblin, and a good one; it's dead.' Then Grooflin's mood changed; the smile dropped from his lips and his head came up sharply as he scrutinized the crowd in the square. 'Where did the fat one go?' he asked abruptly.

'The fat one?' Kate said. 'Do you mean the guy in the fancy cloak that was with these four?'

'Yes,' snapped Grooflin. 'Where did he go, quickly now.'

Kate pointed back across the square towards the north gate. 'He went that way. Started running off right after Grizlan fired the crossbow. Well, when I say running, I mean sort of waddled really. He's like soooo fat, he couldn't . . .'

'Enough,' Grooflin broke in. 'Grizlan Sister, get the cart,' he ordered then, turning to Ed and his family, he quickly said, 'Where are their horses? Do you know where they put their horses?'

'How do you know they had horses?' Liz asked.

'Because,' Grooflin began as he stood up, 'these gobs never walk anywhere if they can help it. Now, find their horses and be quick about it; you can ride I take it?'

'Well yes,' Liz replied truthfully, but more than a little curious. It was true, they could all ride. The Deeks might have been from Seattle, but they did not live in the centre; rather they lived on the outskirts of the city and around them were several riding schools and numerous farms. Each and everyone of the family were accomplished riders.

'Good, let's get going then, quick as,' Grooflin insisted. He bent down over the first goblin, unfastening the belt around the creature's waist. After removing the belt from the body he picked up the knife, cleaned off the blood on the black cloak, and slipped it back into the scabbard. Then he removed the purse that was hanging from the belt and, calling to Ed, 'Here, Longshanks,' he tossed the purse. Ed caught it, and it made a very heavy jingling sound as it landed in his hands. 'To the victors,' Grooflin laughed. 'Now be quick, horses, come on.'

'Are you robbing them?' Liz asked.

'No,' Grooflin smiled as he set about removing the belt from the second fallen gob. 'Not robbing them, just easing their burden so as to hasten their passage into whatever afterlife these things believe in.'

The purses from the other two Ed had killed Grooflin set to one side in the cart, the fourth he handed to his sister saying, 'A good day's trading sweet sister, a purse of coin for one bolt.' Grizlan laughed at that and tucked the heavy purse under her seat. Grooflin then tossed the belts and swords into the cart and covered then with a canvas, but not before he had fished out a vicious-looking axe that he had hidden there. Then, climbing up on the cart next to his sister, he anxiously looked around for Ed.

Ed had gone to the stable only to be met by Maullen who had witnessed the whole fight. As Ed approached Maullen stared harshly at him, but as he got closer the harsh look fell from the smithy's face only to be replaced by one of surprise and wonder.

Maullen bowed low; he placed a hand across his middle, bowing to Ed and saying, 'Sorry if I spoke out of turn, good sir.' Then, straightening himself up, he added, 'Anything I can do for a king's man, sir, I will do; you only have to command it, sir.'

Ed was puzzled but was both in too great a hurry and too drained by the fight to even try and figure out what Maullen was talking about.

He stopped before the smithy saying, 'Those four had horses, are they ready to ride?'

'Yes sir,' Maullen said quickly, and with that he spun round and ran into the stable. Moments later Maullen was back leading the four dark horses out, two in each of his large, strong hands.

Ed took the reins from the smithy and walked back to his family, towing the horses behind him. As he walked the people in the square began to stare at Ed anew. There were looks of wonderment, of astonishment, of happiness and joy touched with disbelief. Some of the people stepped forwards, only to hold back as if unwilling to let themselves believe they were seeing what they were seeing. But, as Ed got the rest of his family mounted, the old woman who had been bundling up the kindling overcame her fear and stepped close to Ed. She placed her painfully thin hand upon Ed's sleeve saying, 'Tell me, sir, has the King come back? Are you one of his knights? Please, sir, are these unhappy days coming to an end? Please sir, tell us, sir.'

Other people in the square began to close in around Ed and his family, and they all began to ask the same questions of Ed. At first it was a soft whisper, but it grew louder and louder as they got ever closer to Ed. 'Has the king come back?' they asked. 'Are you his knight? Are there more coming? How many knights are there, sir? When will they come, sir?' On and on it went. The small crowd closing in around him as they repeatedly demanded of him, 'Stay with us good sir, please stay, defend us. Save us . . .' For the first time that day, for the first time in a very long time, Ed was fearful.

Ed spurred his horse forward after an insistent cry from Grooflin and before the crowd got too close. He never answered any of the questions that they asked; he couldn't; they were asking about things he could not possibly know.

However, what the dwarf knew, what Grooflin realised as soon as Kate told him that the fat factor had run off to the north, was that the north gate would have been barred and bolted as soon as the fat man got there. Once that gate was bolted it was anyone's guess which way they'd go then; it was a fifty-fifty chance that they might go to the east or west gate and bolt that next. So, with no time to lose, the south gate was the best option, the only option. It was to this gate that they rode as fast as horse and the pony cart could travel.

Just in time they reached the gate. From their left could be heard frantic cries: 'Alarm, alarm, close the gate.' But the two men at the south gate were drunker than the two they had passed at the north gate. Too late the guards came out of their stupor, too sluggishly did they react to the cries. By the time they had got to their feet Ed, his family, and the cart carrying Grooflin and Grizlan had already passed.

Quickly they put some miles between themselves and Guidepost, though all the while looking back over their shoulders for signs of pursuit. Seeing none, and at a distance where they could no longer be seen from the town, Grooflin called a halt. The horses, which had already been ridden hard by the gobs earlier that morning, were nearly blown. Even the sturdy ponies that pulled the cart were winded and breathing heavily.

Once they had all stopped, dismounted and gathered themselves together, Grooflin quickly asked if everyone was all right: each in turn said they were. Then, as the dwarf looked them over he began to laugh. He placed his hand upon his hips, his head tilted back and he fair roared with merriment.

'Well, well, Longshanks,' Grooflin roared. 'Fancy that, you a knight.'

'I know,' Ed said, more than a little embarrassed. 'Wonder why they said that?'

Grooflin stopped laughing for a moment; he gazed at Ed then, slapping his legs hard as he bent over laughing even louder than before. 'You play it well good, Sir Knight,' Grooflin howled. 'Look at

Longshanks's face, not a flicker. Remind me never to play a chance game with this one; he'd have the shirt off my back and the britches off my ass in a trice.' Again Grooflin laughed and so did Grizlan. But Ed was left looking confused.

'Grooflin please,' Ed said, a little annoyed. 'But what the hell are you talking about. I am no knight; I'm an engineer. Well, in fact, right now I am just a tourist, and a very lost and confused one at that.' Ed waited until Grooflin and Grizlan stopped their laughing, and they only did so when they realised that nobody else was laughing along with them. 'Listen, my small friends; I don't know what on earth is happening round here. Yesterday I was on vacation and today, today I have been involved in a fight that left four . . . well four I don't know what, dead. All I do know is that I want to go to the nearest police station explain it all to them and hope that I don't end up getting locked away for life. It was self-defence after all.'

Grooflin stared at Ed for a moment then a smile began to break out across his face, he laughed again. 'He really is good. You missed your calling, Sir Knight, you should have been an actor.'

'But I am not a knight,' Ed shouted impatiently. He stepped forward and took Grooflin by the shoulders. 'Stop laughing will you? This isn't funny. Look, understand one thing, I am not a knight, got it?'

'Why then?' Grooflin asked pulling open the torn sweatshirt Ed was wearing. 'Why then do you wear the herald of the King?'

'What?' Ed demanded.

'The herald you wear,' Grooflin said, pointing at Ed's chest. 'A silver eagle on a sea of blue. It is the standard of the King of Angron and only he, his family, his thane, and his knights may wear it upon pain of death.'

Ed looked down at himself: the sword tip that had so nearly cut him in half had ripped his sweatshirt wide open and exposed the T-shirt he had on underneath. There, right where Grooflin was pointing, and what the people of the town must have also seen, was a head of an eagle, painted in sliver on a blue background. Now it was his turn to laugh.

'That's not the herald of a King,' Ed chuckled; he whipped the sweatshirt off over his head. 'Look, it's my football team. See, Seattle Seahawks.'

# Chapter 5

## New Friends

When Grooflin finally overcame his mirth they set off once more. For a short while they kept to a southerly course then, at a signal for Grooflin, they turned off the road and began to trek cross-country. The dwarf had explained that there was another settlement further down the road; however, as that was a gob shanty town and they might wonder how the family came by the horses, it was therefore best to give the area as wide a berth as possible.

They all walked, the family leading their tired mounts while Grooflin led the ponies. Ed and Grooflin walked at the head of the small caravan talking quietly as they went. Grooflin had been curious about football; he had never heard of such a game and wanted to know more. For his part, as Liz would happily inform anyone, there was nothing more that Ed liked talking about than football. And perhaps it was just as well that Ed had something to talk about, for Liz had been watching him, and she must have guessed just how tired he was and how the adrenalin rush of the fight had left him shaken.

Ed was walking but he often failed to lift his feet high enough and tripped or stumbled repeatedly. Each time they took a short break Ed would sit down heavily; he would take a small drink of water but, after each short halt, Ed was finding it harder and harder to get back onto his feet and set off again.

For all Liz may have been a doctor, there was nothing that she could actually do for Ed. But she was thankful for Grooflin, for the dwarf apparently knew just what to do. He kept Ed talking, kept his mind off earlier events, kept him moving and, most importantly, kept putting more and more distance between them and any possible pursuit. Grooflin also appeared to have a clear idea where he was going; though the route he was taking gave the impression of being very circuitous.

A number of times Grooflin would make sudden and seemingly needless changes of directions. First he led the party to the east but, as the ground there began to rise, Grooflin turned north, keeping to the low ground. Then, when they came to a small stream, Grooflin followed its banks, even though that meant walking in somewhat marshy ground, while it would have been much quicker to cross the hills in a straight line. For all this, for all the twists and turns that Grooflin took, no one questioned his leadership.

For her part, Grizlan walked beside Liz and Kate. She may well have been a dwarf, may well have been a small bearded woman, but she was a woman and seemed only too happy to have other women to talk to. Grizlan wanted to know all about Liz's home in Seattle, wanted to know all about what a doctor was and did and, strangest of all, wanted to know what this thing called school, that Kate went to, was all about.

Eventually they came to a low valley with a shallow stream at its base. Up ahead, no more than half a mile, there was a tiny copse. Around the copse, from the edge of the stream and half way up the side of the valley, was a gorse thicket.

'Nearly there,' Grooflin announced as they approached the thicket. He gave a whistle, placing two fingers into his mouth and letting out a sharp blast.

A moment later the whistle was answered from somewhere within the thicket.

A short way up from the stream the gorse began to move, first shaking and swaying, then lifting up and being moved aside to reveal an entrance. Two Dwarves stood at the entrance, crossbows held at the ready and vicious-looking war axes tucked into their belts. They were dressed like Grooflin, dark earthy-coloured jackets and pants with a long, heavy leather jerkin over the top. Also, and just like Grooflin, they had long beards and hairs, all of which was braided and decorated with silver fastenings. The two Dwarves at the entrance looked at Grooflin then at Ed and his family, deep curiosity etched on their faces.

'Greeting brothers, well met,' Grooflin said cheerfully at he reached the entrance. He clasped hands with the other two Dwarves, grasping their forearms and shaking them. 'This, brothers, is an indebted friend, Ed the Longshanks,' Grooflin explained.

Ed stepped forward and offered his hand to the first of the two Dwarves. 'Hi,' he said. 'It just Ed, Grooflin has added the Longshanks bit because I am so tall, to him at least, and I suppose to you also.'

They stared up at Ed for a second then, when he had finished his somewhat embarrassed explanation of his name, they smiled a polite smile and shook his hand.

'Well met . . . Longshanks,' the first said. 'Call me Hamfast.'

'Well met, friend. Gammet is my name,' the second said.

Then, once they were inside the small encampment and saw the other eight Dwarves around the small fire, the whole 'greetings, well met' routine began all over again, followed by a whole series of introductions. Grooflin took the family round the camp, pointing at each dwarf in turn saying, 'This is Harlin and Maklin, over there, the fattish one is Polmet. Beside him is Shamlin and the short one is his younger brother Dannit. That ugly one sharpening his axe is Cromlin. And there, sitting by the fire is Balelin.' Each introduction was followed by a greeting from the named dwarf, a lot of 'well met, Ed', and 'well met, Liz', and not forgetting Kate and Jay.

The introductions came at the family so thick and so fast that it was difficult for them to remember who was who or, more accurately, which dwarf was which except Polmet; well he was easy to remember on account of his girth. Grooflin had said, 'the fattish one' when what he should have said was 'the one the size of a blimp.' For Polmet was huge round the middle and looked more like an over-inflated basketball with legs than anything else. His hair was black and drawn back into a long, tight plait that stretched down to his enormous waist, with the exception of two smaller plaits at the front that framed his face. Silver bands encircled his hair, band large enough to be used as bracelets, and sliver and coloured beads were woven into the plaits. Cromlin, on the other hand, was a great deal thinner than Polmet, by dwarf standards at least. True he was very broad-shouldered, but then all Dwarves are broad-shouldered, but at least for the time being, his middle had not yet expanded in the way some of the other Dwarves had. His hair was also shorter than the other Dwarves, though every bit as elaborately decorated.

Dannit also had shorter hair and a short beard, but that was put down to his young age, for he was the youngest of the little band of Dwarves. His eyes were a very dark brown, but bright and clear. His cheeks were rosy and he possessed a ready smile, though he was soft spoken, and a bit shy, again compared to other Dwarves. He was a tiny bit shorter and thinner than all the other, yet from the firmness of his hand shake, he was every bit as strong. His hair was not as yet in plaits or braids, it still being too short for that; however he did have several sliver beads and rings woven into his hair and beard. Shamlin, Dannit's elder brother, was an altogether different matter. While he had the same dark, laughing eyes as his little brother, no doubt a family trait, he was as similar to his brother as a loaf of bread is similar to roast beef. Shamlin was loud and brash. His handshake was nearly enough to dislocate a shoulder and a simple hug from him would break a rib or two. He had the strength of a whole team of wild horses and just about the same level of self-restraint. And as loud and as brash as Shamlin was, so too were the decorations in his hair and beard. Shamlin's beard was divided into six tight plaits, his moustache into two further plaits, and all of them heavily waxed and festooned with small silver rings and beads.

At the encampment the family had a chance to rest. The horses were unsaddled, given some water and allowed to forage freely: there was little chance of them finding another way out of the surrounding gorse and wandering off. Ed, Liz, and the children were shown to a dry, shady spot where they all sat down, or at least three sat down while Ed seemed to simply flop onto the ground.

'You OK, honey?' Liz asked, obviously concerned for her husband.

'Sure,' Ed forced a weak smile. 'I'm just a bit tired.'

'When did you last sleep?' Liz enquired. 'You look beat.'

'Yesterday, no, the night before, wasn't it? It's over twenty-four hours, I know that. Anyway you're right, I am beat.'

'Why not try and get a bit of shut eye?' Liz suggested; she needn't have bothered, Ed had lain back and, within seconds of closing his eyes, was sound asleep.

One of the Dwarves within the encampment came over to the family, offering them steaming mugs of tea and bowls of a thin rabbit soup. This dwarf, who introduced themselves as Bromlan, explained that the tea and soup were the best they could manage on the road. Grooflin and Grizlan were to have traded for some fresh vegetables at Guidepost, but things hadn't worked out, as they all knew. As to the tea, Bromlan apologised, it was made from Nettles: it was all that they could find.

Liz thanked Bromlan for the tea, though that was before she had tasted it. Then, finding it hard to recall which face went with what name, she asked, 'I am so sorry, I got a terrible memory. What was your name again?'

'I am Bromlan, Polmet's wife.'

Liz stared at the broad-shouldered and heavily bearded dwarf for a few second, finding it hard to reconcile the evidence of her own eyes with what Bromlan was saying. 'I don't believe it,' she whispered, to herself at last.

Bromlan quickly looked over her shoulder at Polmet then, with a growing smile on her lip and a blush in her cheeks, she turned back to Liz saying, 'I know, I can hardly believe it myself sometimes. Polmet is such a fine figure of a dwarf he could have had any dwarf maiden he chose. Aren't I just the luckiest girl?'

'Y . . . y . . . yes,' Liz stammered. 'I am sure you are.'

So saying Bromlan flicked some imagined hairs from her face, then turned and positively skipped back to her cooking fire.

Bromlan's hair was divided into numerous long braids, some of them rolled up and pinned to the side of her head like Chelsea buns, while others were waxed or somehow teased to curve up and out away from her head. Bromlan was also quite broad in both shoulders and hips and every bit as strong as her male counterparts.

The nettle tea was bitter and stewed, making for a very dark brew that would take a lot of getting used to. The soup, on the other hand, was thin, very very thin and must have had a whole rabbit in it, which sadly had been shared between sixteen of them. There were however some bit of green, and something that looked like very thin, white carrots, though not tasting anything like a carrot. Exactly what those green and white bits were was anyone's guess, and if the truth be told, nobody really wanted to know. But, for all that, both the tea and the soup were hot, and if they did nothing else, they filled a hole in a grumbling belly, for which they could only be thankful.

Around by the fire, Grooflin and Grizlan were explaining what had happened at Guidepost. They were talking to what must have been the head of the small party. He was a grey-haired dwarf sitting on an uprooted tree trunk. He was also a rotund fellow, even more rotund than most of the other Dwarves with the exception of Polmet. His grey hair was positively festooned with silver decorations, as was his beard. Even the buckles on his jerkin and his belt were of ornate silver. Never once had this fellow got up from his seat on the tree trunk and, while the other went to collect their tea and soup, his was taken to him by Bromlan.

# Family Holiday

Liz watched as Grooflin explained what had happened. He spoke in a strange language, a language that she guessed could only be Dwarfish.

Dwarves, while perfectly able to communicate in the common tongue while among other folk, always reverted to their own, somewhat mysterious tongue while in their own groups. It was a language that apparently involved as many actions and gestures as words and syllables. Sort of like an advanced form of charades. And because of that, it was possible to follow the conversation.

Grooflin began by telling how they had went into Guidepost then, using his arms and blowing out his cheeks to show a fat man, he was saying something about the local factor. In fact Grooflin and the factor were about as round as each other, but apparently gross exaggerations were also part of Dwarfish. Then he told the part about the market tax that the factor had tried to impose, holding up all ten fingers, something that irritated the other Dwarves greatly. Grooflin, once he had calmed the party down, then went on to tell about four cloaked men, at least he got the four right. From there he pointed at Ed, then went back to the gathered Dwarves, and with a great flourish he showed just how much bigger the four men were. Ed would have told the Dwarves that the cloaked men were in truth slightly shorter than himself, but then why let the truth get in the way of a good tale. Then Grooflin came to the fight: it was a very animated and energetic description, and one that evidently entertained all the others. Grizlan also offered her support in the tale telling. She showed how the men had tried to tip her cart over and how Grooflin had been tripped and how she fell in the mud. That was something that embarrassed Grooflin but amused the others considerably.

The conversation went on with Grooflin re-enacting each and every action, right down to rolling himself over in the dirt much like Ed had done in the square in his effort to avoid the sword aimed at him. The part about the head coming clean off one of the gobs got a round of applause and many an approving nod.

Finally the tale was told, even if the telling took much longer than the fight itself. All the Dwarves appeared suitably impressed, and from time to time, they would glance over to Ed, nod their head and smile, then go back to watching and listening to Grooflin's tale. At the end they seemed more than pleased. They clapped and cheered, they patted Grooflin on the back, and they hugged Grizlan. But, and most importantly, they all seemed only too happy to have a man like Ed with them.

Ed had been asleep for perhaps an hour when Grooflin came and gently woke him up. He was offered a steaming cup of tea, which Ed thanked Grooflin for. Ed coughed and spluttered, nearly choking on the surprising brew. 'What on earth is that?' he asked Liz in a hushed tone after Grooflin had left them.

'Nettle tea,' Liz smiled. 'It takes some getting used to.'

'You got that right,' Ed grimaced before trying another sip.

Liz smiled, brushing a few leaves out of his hair as she asked, 'How you feeling?'

'Better,' Ed said. 'I really needed some sleep.' He took another reluctant sip of the tea then nodded towards the party of Dwarves. 'Did I miss anything?'

'You wouldn't believe it,' Liz smiled.

Before Ed could ask more they saw Grizlan walking over to them. 'Ed, Liz, if you are feeling up to it, we need to have a talk to you, all of you.'

'Please be seated,' the old dwarf sitting on the tree trunk said as the family approached. All of the other Dwarves had moved away, getting busy with odd jobs around the camp. 'Have you eaten? I'm sorry that it could not be more but we are, as you can see, a little ill-prepared to offer the hospitality we would normally offer.'

'You have been more than welcoming,' Ed said.

The old dwarf smiled and nodded his head, a sign of thanks and an accord between them. 'Come then, Ed Longshanks, Dwarf-friend, sit with me.'

Ed grinned broadly and sat down.

'Did I say something humorous?' the old dwarf asked.

'No,' Ed smiled. 'It's just that each time somebody says my name it seems to get longer and more elaborate.'

The old dwarf tilted his head to one side, smiled softly and nodded. 'We cannot always shape how others see us, or the names and titles they heap upon us.' He sat upright and faced Ed squarely. 'How then would you wish to be known?'

'Ed, just plain, simple Ed, if that is all right.'

The old dwarf nodded his agreement. 'Then we shall call you Ed, if that is what you wish. But we will always know you as dwarf-friend among ourselves.'

'That sound fair,' Ed nodded.

He sat down beside the old dwarf, Liz, on the old dwarf's signal, sat on the other side. Kate and Jay sat either side of the small fire facing them.

'They call me Balelin,' the old dwarf began. 'It falls to me to be the leader of this little band, an honour to be sure, but one that brings with it some responsibilities.'

'And my killing those . . . those things back at Guidepost has given you extra troubles to worry about,' Ed offered.

Balelin nodded. 'Exactly so,' he said softly. 'We are indebted to you, far more than you know, for Grizlan is very dear and important to us.' The old dwarf sighed then went on. 'That Grizlan is safe, we thank you, but whisper and rumour travel fast in Angron, especially among the gobs. I had hoped that we might pass without notice but, alas, that will not be possible after today.'

'So,' Ed said. 'I take your point and we will level as soon as possible. But where we go, I don't know.'

Balelin laughed quietly. 'Level, no, never. You are Dwarf-friend, and that means more than you understand. Dwarf-friend means till death, all of you. Do you understand? Till death.'

'What then?' Liz asked.

Balelin patted her knee gently saying, 'I am going to give you a word and this is very important, perhaps the most important word you will ever learn. Grif-balin.' He said slowly, looking deep into each of their faces, 'Now each of you must repeat that: Grif-balin.'

'Grif-balin,' They said in unison.

Balelin smiled and nodded his head.

'What exactly does that mean?' Liz asked.

Balelin sat back. 'It means many things, depending on how and when you say it. If a Dwarf or Dwarf-friend is in dire need, but only in the most dire need, then he may use it to another dwarf and that dwarf is obliged to help in any way they can. If, however, you are in battle, Grif-balin is a rallying call, a call to arms and any dwarf that hears that call will fight by your side, and if it shall go ill, they will die at your side also.'

'So not a word to be used lightly,' Ed said.

'No indeed not,' Balelin stated flatly. 'It is a powerful word, perhaps the most powerful word you may ever learn. It is only ever to be used when in the greatest of need.'

'And what if we hear it used by a dwarf?' Ed asked.

Balelin tilted his head as he thought. 'There is no possible way that other Dwarves, other Dwarves not gathered here that is, will know you as dwarf-friend. However, if you hear the call, then it is up to your conscience how you react. But you have already shown more than your readiness to help a dwarf in need.'

Ed nodded. 'I think we can all understand that, and thank you.'

'No,' insisted Balelin. 'It is we that thank you. Firstly, as I said Grizlan is very dear to us. But secondly because, as you may have seen, we Dwarves are not always made welcome here. To have a total stranger come to our aid is most uncommon.'

'It was only what any decent person would do,' Ed blushed.

'Then it would seem that there are very few decent people on this earth,' Balelin observed.

'Speaking of a few descent people,' Liz said. 'Why didn't anybody else so much as speak up?'

Balelin sighed heavily, 'Because those gobs have this land in a grip of fear.'

'Yeah,' Kate said quickly. 'What exactly are those things, and why is everyone, like, running off when they show up?'

'They are goblin-men,' Balelin said. 'Half men and half goblin, and wholly corrupt of sprit.'

'Yuck,' Kate gasped. 'What type of woman would sleep with something like that?'

'The type that have no choice in the matter,' Balelin muttered softly.

'You mean . . . you can't mean . . . do you mean . . .'

'Sadly yes,' Balelin said. 'Have you not noticed that there are no young women in these parts? When the gobs move into an area any young folks with half a wit about them move out. For soon after those thing arrive the young women begin to disappear.'

'Surely somebody must do something,' Liz said sharply. 'There are police around here somewhere, I take it?'

Balelin shook his head and gave Liz a puzzled look, 'What are police?'

'You know, police, the law, who enforces the law in these parts?'

'Why the factors, of course; leastways he is supposed to,' Balelin shrugged. 'But these gobs are not stupid. The first thing they do, if a factor objects or tries to stop them, is kill the factor. Then, after the factor, each town used to have Bondsmen. These were men in the service of the king and ready to take arms if the town was attacked. But, the King of Angron has been surprisingly absent of late, and without leadership, the Bondsmen have been reluctant to act.' Balelin took a deep breath then went on, 'It is a pattern that these fell creatures have followed several times. First kill the factor, then, with the Bondsmen unsure what to do, they are picked off one at a time. All the while young women of child-bearing age disappear. At that point the young, who can, pack up and leave. All that is left are the old, the weak and sick, those and the gobs and anyone corrupt enough to work for them.'

'For evil to succeed it is only necessary for good men to do nothing,' Ed said quietly, more to himself than anything.

Balelin nodded in agreement. 'That is very true, and very wise.'

'And sadly not mine,' Ed said. 'It was said by a man much wiser than me.'

'Then he was a truly wise man,' Balelin said. 'And you Ed Longshanks, you too are wise to remember that, and to live by it, honest also for not claiming it as your own. Two qualities that are becoming uncommon in these sad days.'

'One thing I would like to know,' Liz said. 'The king, people back at Guidepost mentioned the king, what happened to him?'

'That, I wish I knew, and what I am hoping to find out soon,' Balelin sighed heavily. 'There was a time, many, many years ago, when men and Dwarves stood side by side against great evil. And the Kings of Angron remembered it and made us welcome in this land as we made kings and men welcome in our halls. It was a time when we fought side by side, and when friendship flowered between us. We traded, silver and gold, food and fine clothes, and all manner of trinkets.' Balelin sighed heavily and was silent for a long while. His eyes were fixed on the small fire, but they did not see the flames; rather they saw the memories of the good times: the times when men and Dwarves were friends. 'But those times appear passed away now. Now we are only tolerated in this land; now there is only mistrust and fear between our peoples. As for the king? I, much like his own people, more so perhaps, I wish I knew where he was and why he allows these evil creatures to befoul his land.'

'Somebody must know,' Jay interrupted.

'Indeed,' Balelin smiled weakly, 'but not I. Rumour did tell that the king and his thanes went off on a quest. Some tale of a dragon and gold and such like but, and how true that may be, I cannot say. All I can say is that the king of this land is more noticeable by his inaction towards the growing malignancy of these half-goblins than by his actions to aid his own people.'

'You don't paint a happy picture,' Ed said, thinking out loud.

'Indeed, these are not happy times,' Balelin agreed. 'But perhaps we might see happier times.'

'We can hope,' Liz said.

A silence fell over the little group as each became absorbed in their own thoughts. Around them the other Dwarves had been busy. Unnoticed by the group the Dwarves had been breaking up the camp. Now, with the talking round the fire at an end, and the carts ready to move, Grizlan approached.

'Ed, Liz, if you would saddle your horses we are ready to move,' she said. She turned then to Kate and Jay, asking, 'Will you two ride or would you care to come in the wagons?'

'We'll ride,' Jay said quickly. 'Meaning no offence, mind you, and thank you for the offer, but we will ride.'

'Yes,' Kate echoed her brother. 'We'll ride if it's all the same to you.'

'As you wish,' Grizlan smiled. Then she turned to Balelin, saying, 'You shall come with me in the wagon, Grandfather.'

'Grandfather?' Ed said.

'Yes,' smiled Balelin. 'I told you, Grizlan is more precious to us than you know, and in ways that you do not yet understand, for she is family, and much more than family.'

They set off towards the east. For a while they followed a meandering course along the low valleys. As the ground flattened out, they headed directly east. No longer did they hug cover, no longer did they attempt to disguise their path; once in open ground, only speed mattered. The two carts bounced and rocked as they picked up a steady pace. Grizlan and Balelin were in the lead cart, Grooflin and Hamfast in the second. Either side of the carts, jogging along methodically, were four other Dwarves, with the horses carrying the family bringing up the rear.

At first none of the Deeks family noticed it; they were just a party of Dwarves making quick time to wherever they were going. But, looking more closely, it could be seen that all of the Dwarves were now heavily armed. The Dwarves on foot had formed a screen around the two carts. They were carrying lethal-looking war axes in their hands and shields upon their arms. In their belts they had more weapons, smaller axes, swords, and daggers, and some had placed helmets upon their heads. Even those in the carts were armed; both Grizlan and Grooflin drove their carts with crossbows resting on their knees. More crossbows and quivers of bolts had been placed around the carts ready, should they be needed.

The Dwarves hastened along at the trotting pace of the horses. Despite the burden of their weapons, despite their heavy boots that were more iron than leather, they moved at a steady pace. Never once did they slacken, slow, or falter. They pounded out the miles as if they were merely out for a Sunday stroll. Whether they were going uphill or down, the Dwarves' pace remained constant. All the while their heads were held high, alert and swivelling side to side as they scanned the land around them. It seemed as if they could run in that way for miles, and indeed that was just what they were doing. Never tiring, never stopping for a drink or to catch their breath, they simply ran and ran and ran.

Eventually a great mass of trees came into view. At first it was nothing more than a dark greenish, uneven line in the far distance. But, as the Dwarves progressed in that unwavering run of theirs, the tops of tall trees could soon be seen. A short time later, the shapes of the trees could be clearly distinguished. Presently, the first of the tree trunks at the edges of the wood became visible. And all too soon the party was in among the trees and heading deeper into the forest.

Still the pace did not slacken. They ran deeper and deeper into the woods, not following any road or track but rather making their own path as they went. At the edge of the wood the tree had been close together, leaving very little room for the carts. There had been many small bushes, which the Dwarves did their best to avoid, picking a twisting path that never once appeared to have slowed their progress.

Gradually the trees became taller and the distance between them became greater. They were approaching the deeper part of the forest, where the tree trunks were thick and strong. High above them was lush green canopy, giving them shade but also blocking out light so that very little brushwood could grow. The eight Dwarves on foot now spread out slightly, checking either side of the large trees as they went. Only now did their pace slow as they cautiously searched the area.

They came to a stream, a shallow, rapidly flowing ribbon of clear water. It was here that the Dwarves called a halt to their advance. At once the eight on foot spread out, searching deeper into the trees all around where they had stopped. Grooflin, Hamfast, and Grizlan all jumped to the ground when they stopped, their crossbows held at the ready.

Slowly Ed dismounted, holding onto the reins as he led his horse over to the three Dwarves standing round the carts. 'What's up?' he asked quietly.

'Hopefully nothing,' Grooflin said quietly, and then he smiled broadly and tapped the stock of his crossbow. 'But just in case.'

Balelin turned to look at Liz, a solemn expression set upon his old face. 'We are in Tangle Wood and the woodland folk claim dominion over every part of it, and everything within it.'

Liz looked around her, probing the wood with her eyes. 'It's just a wood,' she mused softly to herself.

Grizlan came beside her, stretching herself up so that she might whisper into Liz's ear. 'This is no ordinary wood,' she said softly. 'There is magic is this wood, sometimes playful, but more often mischievous, and other times cruel and malicious.'

'Is that why the locals stay away?' Ed whispered to Grizlan. 'Even that big smithy Maullen was afraid of this place.'

Grizlan nodded. 'That is why we have come this way,' she replied in hushed tones. 'This is the one way that the gobs will not come.' She turned to face Ed and Liz, and seeing the worry upon their faces, she smiled reassuringly. 'Fear nought, dwarf-friend. We will stay the night and be on the other side tomorrow.'

'Wouldn't it be better to just keep going?' Liz asked nervously.

'No,' Balelin said as he stepped down from the cart. 'This wood is too wide to cross in what is left of today. We have all need of rest, dwarf, man, and beast. And what better place to rest than where no one will follow you?' He shook himself dramatically, twisting his face as he looked about him. 'I hate the woods; there is no warmth in them; give me good solid stone every time.'

A camp was established once all the Dwarves had returned from their brief exploration of the wood. The ponies and horses were unharnessed and unsaddled and taken to the stream for a drink. They were, for a while, also allowed to graze on the long grass that grew on the banks.

Presently a small fire was started with the dead wood that littered the ground. A kettle of water was set over it, hanging from a small steel tripod. Pot and pans were unloaded from the carts, along with some grain and other supplies. Hamfast took charge of the cooking and soon had a plain, simple meal bubbling away in a black, cast-iron pot. From his pack, Hamfast produced a little wooden box of seasonings. He carefully selected some of the contents, holding it tenderly between his fingers before sprinkling it lovingly over whatever it was that he was cooking.

Grizlan dished out more of the nettle tea, apologising profusely to Liz once more for not having anything better.

Balelin was by the fire, sitting on a low box that had been taken from one of the carts to use as a makeshift stool. He wrapped himself in a thick fur and made himself as comfortable as possible. The old dwarf sipped his tea and edged closer to the fire as he warmed his old bones. 'Don't allow yourself to think we Dwarves always eat and drink such poor fare,' he smiled at Liz.

Liz shook herself. Her mind had been drifting when Balelin spoke to her then, hearing him, she snapped back to the present. 'Sorry,' she said quickly, 'I wasn't thinking that, I was . . . well, I was, just trying to figure things out.'

Balelin nodded thoughtfully, willing Liz to continue.

'Well, it is just that yesterday we were like any other family,' Liz said. 'And now . . .' she reached out and took Ed's hand, squeezing it tightly. 'And now we are, I don't know, the best way I can describe it is like, in a strange world where everything has been turned upside down.'

Balelin said nothing but instead he turned towards Ed and waited for him to speak.

Ed, seeing the old dwarf was then looking at him then, began by taking a long slow sip of tea before saying, 'I think Liz has put it in a nutshell: our world has been turned upside down. Yesterday was like any other day, to begin with at any rate. But then that fog and now . . . Balelin please don't be offended by what I am about to say but, well, in our world Dwarves simply don't exist, nor do goblins or who knows what else.'

'What, no Dwarves?' Grizlan asked surprised.

'No, well, only in stories,' Ed explained. 'Fairy story and the like.'

'Ah,' Grizlan smiled. 'So you do know something of fairies then.'

Kate and Jay giggled at that, but they stopped when their mother shot them a withering look.

'No,' Ed said, shaking his head. 'When I say fairy stories I don't mean that we have fairies.'

'Oh,' Grizlan began to giggle herself realising her mistake. 'I thought you meant stories told to you by fairies.'

'I'm afraid not,' Liz said. 'We don't have fairies; they are just stories, that's all. My grandmother, she was from Yorkshire, she was always telling us stories like that. But they were just stories, made-up things to tell the kids.'

Balelin looked keenly at Liz, 'Can you really be sure of that?' he asked.

'I believe you,' Jay blurted out, which made the old dwarf smile softly.

'You still believe in the Easter Bunny,' Kate hissed at her brother sardonically.

'Not true,' Jay protested.

Balelin's expression suddenly became very serious. 'What is the, "Easter Bunny", was it?'

Neither Jay nor Kate had time to answer as they were interrupted.

'Food's ready,' Hamfast said, and then he added apologetically, 'Such as it.'

They ate in near silence as the sun began to set, a melancholy meal of boiled barley and a few herbs. It was a fitting meal for such a night for, as the sun dipped lower in the sky and shadows lengthened, a depressing gloom spread over the forest and over the camp. The light faded, and as it did so, the Dwarves finished up their meal and began checking weapons.

While Hamfast washed up, and Balelin warmed himself by the fire, the other Dwarves examined their swords, axes, and daggers. Each blade was inspected, checked for sharpness, and then checked again to ensure it was close at hand, should it be required. They collected blankets and furs from the carts, wrapping them about themselves as they again took their places around the fire. But, as they sat back down, the Dwarves made sure that they were ready to defend the camp if needs be. No one had said anything, no orders had been given, yet each of the Dwarves instinctively knew what was necessary.

For their part both Liz and Ed were tired, too tire to be fully aware of what was actually going on around them. Ed had lain back on the blanket he had been given, and almost at once, he was sound asleep. Liz had laid a fur over him to keep him warm as the heat of the day was slowly replaced by the night's chill. Even Kate, who had grumbled so often about the tiniest discomfort in her life, was soon finding herself a warm place by the fire and wrapping herself in a blanket. Only Jay seemed unable to sleep; he was wrapped up in his blanket but, rather than finding somewhere to sleep, he moved closer to Balelin who remained sitting, deep in his own thoughts.

'Excuse me, sir,' Jay said softly, and a little bit nervously.

'Yes,' Balelin replied slowly, leaving whatever had occupied his mind till then.

'Can I ask you, sir, not having met any Dwarves before today but, if I may, sir, how old are you?' he gave a tiny, anxious smile as he asked his question and hoped that he had not given offence.

But it was Liz that spoke next. 'Jay,' she snapped quietly. 'Leave the man, sorry, the dwarf, alone and get to sleep.'

Balelin chuckled softly. 'Please, good lady, indulge an old dwarf and young boy. For dose not youth and old age delight in the company of the other?'

Liz sighed. 'All right,' she said. 'But don't let him make a nuisance of himself. And Jay, don't stay up too long.'

'All right, Mom,' Jay groaned.

Balelin smiled gently. 'He is no nuisance, good lady,' then to Jay he said, 'Sit by me little man so that we do not disturb the others.'

So Jay shifted himself, sitting closer to Balelin. He wrapped the blanket tight around his shoulders and looked up into the dwarf's seemingly ancient eyes. Eyes that were framed by a thick, heavy brow, and creased by many years. Balelin's forehead was furrowed by deep wrinkles. But the eyes themselves were bright and clear, giving ample evidence of a lively mind.

'Well, sir?' Jay said.

'Well what?' Balelin smiled, teasing Jay like any grandfather would tease a child.

'How old are you, sir?' Jay asked again.

Balelin sat back, brushing his beard thoughtfully and meaningfully, and obviously wasting time so as to tease Jay still further. 'Let me think now,' Balelin said slowly, 'I was three hundred and twenty-seven at the last counting.'

'Three hundred?' Jay gasped.

'And twenty-seven,' Balelin corrected him light-heartedly. 'Do not forget the twenty-seven.'

Jay smiled, nodding yes, he would remember. 'Boy you must have seen lots.'

'Boy?' Balelin said, staring quizzically at Jay.

'Sorry, sir. It's just an expression,' Jay explained. 'You know like "Oh boy", when something is good, or surprising, or, well, just about anytime and for a whole host of reasons.'

Balelin nodded. 'Well I have learnt something new, and at my age that is no shabby achievement.'

'So?' Jay asked.

'Ah yes, so,' Balelin said. 'Yes indeed I have seen many things, many, many things. I have seen kings of men come and, sadly, go; not all of them have been good kings, mark you. I have seen bad times and good, I have seen the fat years and the thin. I have seen Elves and giants; I even saw a dragon once.'

'Elves, giants, and dragons?' Jay gasped wide-eyed.

'Yes,' Balelin nodded. 'And what about you, little man? What do you do and what have you seen?'

'Me? Up till now I haven't seen anything,' Jay groaned. 'I'm still at school, and that takes up most of my time. Sure we have been on vacation before, you know the regular things.'

'The regular things' Balelin echoed.

'Yeah, like going to Yellowstone national park, looking at the mountains, and watching Old Faithful.'

'Old Faithful?'

'It's a geezer, you know,' Jay said, 'water filters down to molten rock deep in the earth then races back to the surface as steam where, *whoosh*, it blasts out and high into the sky.'

'But this is not usual or ordinary; this is wonderful,' Balelin said, his eyes wide with astonishment. 'Never have I seen such a remarkable thing. And mountains, are they great mountains? Do they stand high and proud, and do their roots reach deep into the earth?'

'I suppose they do,' Jay shrugged.

'Oh I should dearly like to see such mountains,' Balelin reflected. 'To walk in them, to feel them under my feet, to touch them, and delve into them.' He paused, looking keenly at Jay then he laughed softly. 'You do not understand what I am talking about do you, little one?'

'No, sir,' Jay said.

Balelin smiled and patted Jay's head. 'Then there is something that you must learn,' he said. 'You have looked at wonderful things, but you have not seen them.'

''Course I seen them,' Jay protested.

'No,' Balelin shook his head. 'You look with your eyes yes, but you see with your heart.' He patted his chest. 'It is in here. It is how it makes you feel, and if you do not feel, then you have not seen. Tell me, Jay, how do you feel when you watch the sun rise, or when you look at the last glow of a sunset? What do you feel when you look at the clouds gently kissing the peaks of snow-covered mountains. Or when you watch the water of a mighty fall as it spills from the side of some high precipice? But it is not just in the big things, it is in the small, even in the tiny. Have you seen the beauty in a tiny flower, or have you just looked at it?'

Jay thought for a long moment before saying, 'Well, I suppose I have just looked at them.'

'Then look closer, and hopefully, when you have learnt to look, to really look, you might begin to feel, and then you might see.' Balelin bent down and carefully selected a small stone from among the dirt at his feet. He held it up, turning it over and over as he studied it. 'Take any rock, Jay, look at it, see it. What type of stone is it? Where has it come from? What forces made it and worked upon it? Try it, Jay, pick up a stone and look at it; look deeply into it.'

Jay did as Balelin had bid. He picked up a stone, just as the old dwarf had done and, mimicking his actions, turned it over and over as he looked closely at it. Finally Jay looked up at the old dwarf in amazement. 'So,' he said slowly, 'tell me about the dragon then. Did you really see a dragon?'

Balelin looked up from his stone and then smiled. 'Very well then,' he said discarding the rock. 'Let me see now, it was a very long time ago and I was just a small dwarf at the time, no more than fifteen years.' Balelin looked up, recalling long-forgotten events, ordering them meticulously in his mind as he made ready to relay them to Jay. 'Yes, I was fifteen, a boy really, and much shorter than you are now. We lived in a small farm, not much of a farm, truth be told; we Dwarves farm but our hearts are not really in it. Our hearts are in the mountains, in the good solid rock or in shaping and crafting fine stone. Dwarves always make the best masons, much better than men because we feel the stone, feel the life within it. And Elves,' Balelin scoffed. 'Those pointy-eared fools only think about trees and woods and silly things like that. But you let me wander off the point, little man: our old farm. Well, I lived there with my father, mother, and twelve brothers.'

'You had twelve brothers?' Jay sat up sharply.

'Have,' Balelin corrected him. 'I have twelve brothers, and seven sisters; we Dwarves like large families, you know. But again you have let me wander off the point. As I was saying, we lived on the farm. It was not a very big farm, though it was close to the great Lomrit Mountains. Yet the times were hard for our farm, and for the whole valley. A dragon, Azwrath, a fearsome black dragon, and black dragons are the worst you know, well, she lived in the mountains also. Now black dragons are terrible creatures, full of rage and malice. Their hearts are as black as their thick, scaly hides, and they are driven by one thing and one thing only: greed. They are large, very large, perhaps the largest of all the dragons. And their breath is fire, a hideous blazing fume that can melt iron and consume the flesh from a dwarf's bones in seconds.

'At first it was just a sheep here, or a cow there, but then, when Azwrath got a taste for our animals and saw how easy they were to get, well then, she came every night. So the elders got together and they made up their minds that the best thing would be to get rid of that beast. No easy thing that, killing a dragon, especially one as all together wicked as Azwrath. Many times I saw her, her huge black wings spread wide, blotting out the moon as she swept down the valley. Some say that her very shadow was enough to still the hearts of weaker folk, and as she hunted, that shadow was spread over every corner of our valley.

'Her wings were vast, twenty times the stretch of my arms, and when she raised up on her hind legs, she stood the height of ten good Dwarves. She had claws, immense claws on her hind legs that could pick up and carry away a whole cow in each of them. Her fore claws were smaller but so sharp that she could tear apart her victim with a single swipe. I saw her do it once, killing a cow, ripping the poor thing apart like you or I might rip apart soft bread.

'She liked to come at night, when the animals were drowsy and even the Dwarves on watch were sleepy. Then she would come, silently sweeping over the mountains and down into the valley. She didn't bat her great black wings; rather she glided noiselessly like some huge, terrible bird. Down she would come, the wind whooshing around her as she came on faster and faster. Then, having selected her prey, she would sweep low over the ground and spew fire as she passed.

'She did not aim for the animals. No, no, Azwrath was too canny for that. No she wanted to scare the animals, make them run, getting their blood nice and hot and ready for her. She would lay long curtains of fire to panic the animals but also to hem them in and to thwart anyone that may try to help them. Soon she had what she wanted, a wall of flames surrounding her prey, and them petrified within the walls.

'Then she would fly down into the flaming trap she had made. She would breathe out a terrible fume, not fire, mark you, but a foul corruption of air and bile. She would breathe this at the trapped animals and they would scream and die. Then she would eat, gorging herself, safe within her walls of fire and with all the food she needed. When she had had her fill she would fly out, leaving us to put out the fires before they burnt all our crops and to bury those poor beasts that she had killed in her greed but not eaten.

'Now, Dwarves are brave; it is in our nature. In fact it is often said of Dwarves, and rightly so, that we never ask how many the enemy are, but rather where they are at. But a dragon, a black dragon to boot, that is a whole other thing. Still, something had to be done, and done soon. For winter was approaching, and if Azwrath was left unchecked, then there would be little food left to feed the valley. Someone had to go up into the mountains, find Azwrath's lair, and kill the great beast.

'Well, the elders argued, as elders often do, yet there was no one willing to take onto themselves this quest. No one that is until Harmlin One Eye, my cousin on my father's side stepped forward. Mind you, he wasn't Harmlin One Eye then, just simple Harmlin' the "One Eye' got added later or should that be taken away. Anyway, Harmlin knew what he was up against, had seen for himself how evil and cruel Azwrath was. But he, of all the Dwarves in the valley, was willing to set forth and slay that fell creature.'

'Grandfather,' Grizlan whispered, making the old dwarf pause. She nodded towards Jay saying softly, 'the boy is asleep.'

Balelin chuckled to himself. He placed a fur over Jay, whispering, 'Another time I will tell you the tale of Harmlin One Eye and his quest. Till then, little man, sleep, and may the night keep you safe.'

# Chapter 6

## Thieves in the Night

Kate had found herself a place near her mother and father. She placed her blanket upon a pile of hastily racked together leaves, lay down on it, and pulled the thick fur over herself. She was surprisingly warm and comfortable. Close by her father was deep into a sound sleep, her mother snuggled tight against him. Only Jay was fighting off sleep, fighting it off and talking to Balelin as they sat near the fire.

For a while Kate listened to Balelin and Jay talking. She listened until day finally surrendered to night then, when she could hold her eyes open no longer, Kate fell asleep.

It was pitch-dark when Kate next opened her eyes. Something, she didn't know what, had woken her. She did not sit up, in truth Kate barely moved, but she opened her eyes and took a cautious look about her.

The sky was as black as it had been when she had closed her eyes. The air was every bit as chilled as before, if not more so. But there was movement within the camp, and that was different.

Kate looked over at the fire. Several of the Dwarves that had bedded down there were now on their feet. They moved slowly, casually, as they placed more wood on the fire and went about doing whatever they were doing. Then Kate noticed something else: all of the Dwarves were now fully armed and carrying their shields. They attempted to look nonchalant, although in doing so their actions only look more deliberate. Kate watched them as they went unhurriedly round the camp, unhurried but with a definite intent. Those on their feet went round waking the rest of the party, and while doing so, they signalled everyone to be silent.

One of the Dwarves came to Kate – she could not tell who it was for they all looked much alike. With their long hair and beards, both male and female Dwarves were too similar to tell apart, more than ever in the deep shadowy light of the fire. The dwarf, seeing Kate had her eyes open, pressed a finger to his lips. Then, with only the slightest hand gesture, signalled that she should get up and follow him. She did so, but then the dwarf stepped closer to her. He placed his left arm around her so that his shield protected her back, and all the while the dwarf repeatedly scanned the woods.

Kate was ushered by the dwarf over to her mother who was crouching close by Balelin's side. Liz reached up, pulling Kate down beside her and wrapping a thick fur around her daughter's shoulders. Over by one of the carts her father was standing, Grooflin fastening round his waist one of the sword belts that they had taken from the four dead goblin-men in Guidepost.

Jay also made to collect a sword and shield, only for his mother to pull him back, 'I don't think so, young man,' she said firmly.

'But, Mum,' Jay protested, making all the Dwarves gathering round them smile.

Ed rejoined the group, taking his place in the circle that had formed up. In the centre of the circle Liz was hunkered down, her arms wrapped tightly around both Kate and Jay. Beside them Grizlan stood, her eyes surveying the wood.

With everyone in position the group fell silent. No one moved, scarcely daring to breathe: they merely stood and peered outwards into the dark. Kate looked out from the circle also, though it was very difficult with those broad-shouldered Dwarves drawn tight around her. She could see a little, either between their legs or through the tiny gaps between their shields.

Beyond the circle, beyond the small fire and the carts, at the very edge of vision in that blackest night, nothing moved. Kate turned her head left and right, but she could see nothing. She could however hear the faint sound of the wind whispering in the trees, the soft creaking of the branches and leaves as they gently tumbled over each other; whipped up on the breeze. For a long time they were the only sounds, the trees, the branches, and the leaves and with each soft sound the Dwarves would quickly turn their heads, hoping to see something, anything.

Time appeared to slow. Seconds stretched out into prolonged minutes and the minutes seemed endless. About them the very air buzzed, charged with some unnatural energy. It was stifling, becoming harder to breathe, and the once-chilled night was somehow suddenly humid, oppressive. The circle of Dwarves drew even tighter together.

But how could the wind whisper and whistle in the trees when there was no wind. The air was still, stagnant, with not the slightest rumour of wind. There was no breeze to make the branches sway or to cause leaves to tumble over one another. Yet nonetheless those noises were in the wood all around the party, and they were getting closer.

At last, peering out between the Dwarves, Kate saw something that made her body shake with fear. Among the trees, and seemingly surrounding them, there was a fog rising. It was a thick rolling fog, very white and very dense, and getting closer and closer to them with each passing second.

The fog closed in around them, creeping ever nearer with every long second. Inch by agonising inch it came on, surrounding them with an eerie white curtain. This was no ordinary fog, however; it had no wispy edges thinner than the rest. It was just a thick white mass closing ever tighter around the group, like some giant blanket being wrapped around them by unseen hands. On it came, swallowing up the trees one by one as it crept nearer. It was like the walls of a trap closing in upon its victim, surrounding the Dwarves and the family.

'When sun is fading, and moon on the rise,' Kate began to whisper to herself. 'When heavy cloud fills the skies. From Tangle Wood, so full of lies. Stay you clear and homeward fly.' And as she recounted the little poem that Braygon's children had recited, Kate began to tremble.

Liz pulled her daughter close, her arm about Kate's shoulder holding so tight that it was almost painful.

'Stop,' Grizlan cried, as the fog neared the camp. She held a hand in the air, like some traffic cop on point duty. 'Stop and come no closer, I command you.'

The fog stopped, and so did all the little noises within the woods. No more could they hear the non-existing wind whistling in the trees. No more was there the sound of branches creaking or of the leaves brushing over themselves. There was only silence, and the silence was thunderous.

Kate held her breath just as her mother, holding her too tightly, held her breath also. Each and every one of the Dwarves, drawn up in their protective circle, held their breaths also. And all peered out at the fog, waiting for who knew what.

New sounds came to their ears. Very low and distorted but unmistakeable: the sound of mocking laughter.

'*He he he,*' a small voice went. It was distant and high-pitched. '*He he he,* we come close ifs we wants.'

'*Comes verys verys close,*' other voices in the fog all around them answered.

'This is our's woods,' said the first voice.

'*Our's woods our's woods,*' the other voices chanted.

'Yous no welcomes. Yous trespasses.'

'*Trespasses yesss.*'

'Be still,' Grizlan called out, her voice firm and unshaken. 'We mean you no harm and ask only that you leave us to pass in peace.'

'You no passes,' said the voice in the fog. 'Yous no friends, yous no passes.'

*'He he, no passes no passes. Our's woods, no passes.'*

'Yous got carts. We wants, we takes.'

*'Takes carts yeses. We wants we takes. Our's woods, we takes we takes.'*

'There is nothing in the carts for you,' Grizlan called out. 'Now be gone.'

Again the wood, and the fog, was filled with the sound of mocking laughter. As suddenly as it began it stopped, only to be replaced by a noise like the buzzing of hundreds of mosquitoes. At first the buzzing seemed to just zip quickly over their heads, but then each rapid hissing sound was followed by a distinctive pinging.

Grizlan ducked down next to Kate. 'Stay low and stay covered,' she ordered Liz and her children. 'Those darts are poisoned.'

'Darts?' Kate gasped. She looked up and saw the Dwarves holding their shields up, covering their faces from the mass of tiny darts that whizzed through the air. They could not see the darts, nor could they see who was firing them, for they were hidden by the thick fog. All the Dwarves could do was hold their shields up and hope for the best.

'We's wants what yous got,' the voice in the fog taunted.

*'We's wants it. Yous give us it.'*

'We's wants its, yous give us its or we's kills yous; thens we's takes it.'

*'Give us its or we's kills.'*

'Give us its now.'

*'Give us its give us its give us its.'*

The voices in the fog began chanting again, and still those little darts whizzed and zipped all around them.

Swiftly Grizlan drew herself up to her full height. Her face was turned up towards the night sky and her arms reaching up over her head. 'Fire, water, earth, air, I am Grizlan, hear me,' she called out in a commanding voice. 'Water, fire, earth, air, I am Grizlan, I call to you. Earth, fire, water, air, I am Grizlan, I command you. I Grizlan, I command you. Air, I command you.'

The laughter in the fog came to an abrupt halt, even the whizzing and hissing of the darts stopped. The wood fell silent once more but, as Grizlan held her arms aloft, the very air seemed to hum and crackle with electricity.

Around them the fog began to fluoresce, illuminated by some ghostly internal glow. Even the leaves on the trees appeared to glow, tiny sparks of light dancing around their edges as they shivered upon their branches.

Grizlan called out again, 'Hear me, Air, I am Grizlan, I command you, air, I command you blow, wind, blow. *Blow.*' She swept her arms around, turning about again and again in some trance-induced dance.

Slowly, at first, but building all the time, a wind began to blow. At first it was barely strong enough to move the branches above the party's heads but, as Grizlan called to the air again and again, commanding it, the wind quickly picked up. The leaves on the ground were lifted into the air, tossed about by the ever increasing gust. Stronger and stronger the wind became, and faster and faster did it blow around the group. They were standing then in the centre of a storm, a storm that Grizlan had somehow called forth.

'Blow, wind,' Grizlan called out. 'Blow.' And at once the wind responded until it was as if the party was standing in the eye of a tornado. Grizlan spun around, her arms outstretched to the night sky. 'Blow, blow, I command you,' she cried as she spun faster and faster, and the wind blew stronger and stronger.

Around them the fog was blown away, ripped apart, and sucked up by the tornado that Grizlan commanded. It swirled around them, moving ever upward, lifting any loose object up with it. The laughter was then replaced by cries of fear and shouts of, '*No no stops, no.*' But Grizlan did not stop the wind. She stood, rooted to the spot, her arms spread wide and her fingers outstretched as she swept them around and around. Her face a mask of concentration as her eyes peered out at the mass of leaves, twigs, and many other things that tumbled in the windstorm she directed.

When Grizlan judged that the time was right, she called again, 'Air, be still.' And at once the wind died to nothing.

Kate watched in astonishment as the tornado vanished quicker than it had appeared. She watched as all the leaves suddenly froze in midair then, without the wind to hold them up, she watched as they tumbled back to the forest floor. And while the leaves may have drifted down, twigs, branches and small stones taken up by the storm fell swiftly, crashing noisily to the ground all around them. But something else fell to the ground also. They appeared to be small rag dolls, at least that is what they looked like in the dark of the forest night. For a split second after the wind died, they hung in the air then, and with many cries and shouts of, *'ouch, outch, eek,'* they too fell heavily to the ground.

Kate watched as the small doll-like creatures, dozens of them, went tumbling to the ground. Some cartwheeled, others crashed into the trees, bounced off then fell, while still others collided with each other and lay moaning and groaning where they dropped.

Quickly the Dwarves broke their circle, racing out and grabbing several of the small figures as they lay stunned on the ground. They scooped up the little things, turned, and raced back to reform the circle. As soon as they had, Grizlan raised her arms again calling out, 'Water, I am Grizlan, I command you rain.' And it began to rain; it began to rain heavily, but not on the group; an incredible powerful driving rain, just like the wind was all around them, but not on them.

In the woods it was dark, but there was just enough light to see those little figures picking themselves up. It looked like they were many small children getting to their feet and dusting themselves off then, as the rain began to beat down on them, they quickly turned and ran away, shrieking noisily as they went. That left only the four little figures that the Dwarves had caught.

Kate stared in disbelief at the four tiny little figures that were now prisoners. They looked like any human, two arms two legs, a head and body, and all in perfect proportion, but they stood no more than two feet tall. It looked like they were dressed in doll's clothing, roughly made clothing that were of a motley pattern of greens and browns. Over their clothes, and even woven into them, they had small twigs and leaves, with mud splashed and smeared all over. Even their tiny faces were painted these same earthy colours: a perfect camouflage for the woods in which they lived. But, whereas they had been brave and menacing before, when they had been hidden by their fog, now they just appeared a bit wretched.

'What are they?' Kate asked.

'Brownies,' Grizlan said looking down at the four little figures. 'Well, that is one name for them. Some people call them Poppets, others call them gnomes and . . .'

'We's nots no gnomes,' one of the little creatures snapped. 'And we's will fights anys that says we's is.' He stepped quickly towards Grizlan, putting his tiny fists up ready to take on the dwarf who towered over him.

'Game little fella, ain't he?' Ed laughed.

The little guy spun round to face Ed, rolling his tiny fists as he did. 'And yous, yous longs streak of nought,' the little Brownie shouted in a high-pitched voice. 'Come on thens,' he yelled swinging his right fist in an exaggerated hook that lifted him off his tiny feet. 'Ones at a times or alls togethers.'

Balelin reached over and grabbed hold of the back of the fearless little fellow's jacket. He lifted him up, turning him so that they faced each other. 'Calm down, little fella,' he said, 'no one wishes to fight you.'

The little guy kicked out and swung his fists at Balelin, but all his efforts were for nothing as he was too far away. 'Puts me's down, you miserable Dwarves, puts me's down and fights fair.'

'Nobody wants a fight,' Balelin said reassuringly.

'I's dos, Dwarves,' the frisky Brownie retorted, kicking and punching out at the dwarf holding him. 'Puts me's down and we'lls fights.'

Balelin gave a heavy sigh. He held the Brownie up for all to see then, then turning to face Kate, he said, 'See these little fellas; they're more mischievous than dangerous.'

'Put's me's down and I'lls show yous who's dangerous.'

Balelin laughed softly. 'Do you know what these little fellas do?' he asked Kate. She shook her head. 'Well,' Balelin said slowly, 'what they do is play their little games in the woods. You ever been walking in the woods and then suddenly found yourself lost?' Again Kate replied silently, this time nodding yes. 'Well, that's these fellows. They are the ones that hide your trail. When you walk past, they run out of their little hidey holes and put the leaves back, or they brush away your footprints. And then, when you try to find your way, they move branches or tree roots to trip you up. In fact they will do anything to get you lost, just so they can have their sport with you. And when you make camp and sleep for the night, they come out again and filch anything they can carry off.'

'Hey, Dad,' Jay interrupted, 'do you think that is what happened to my compass?'

'No,' Ed said laughingly.

Balelin didn't say anything; he simply stared at Ed, waiting for him to explain.

'We went camping two years ago, in the Cascades, and Jay lost a brand-new compass that I had just bought him. That was all; it was just a simple accident; the compass got mislaid.'

Balelin nodded slowly. 'If that is what you wish to believe,' he said knowingly.

As her father was talking Kate crept closer to the three little figures standing in the middle of the group. They had been captured by the Dwarves, but they were in no way conquered. If anything the three little Poppets, or Brownies, or whatever it was that they were called, were the epitome of defiance. They stood, back to back, three tiny beings amidst sixteen much taller and much more powerful beings, and they showed no fear or concern.

Kate looked closely at the three little Brownies. They appeared, at first glance, to be nothing more than miniature versions of a human being. But looking closer Kate could see that their heads were slightly larger than what a scaled-down version ought to have been. Their eyes were a deep, dark brown, just like the eyes of a deer, and much bigger in proportion to the size of their heads. Their eyes seemed to bulge a little also, more like the eyes of some nocturnal animal. Their ears were likewise comparatively large, finishing in a small point at the top. Other than that, they were in every way exactly like a fully grown human. They had five fingers on each hand and five toes on each of their bare, muddy feet.

'Be careful,' Grizlan cautioned Kate, as the young girl got closer.

'But they're so cute,' Kate exclaimed, looking up at the dwarf. She turned back to take a closer look at the three Brownies, just in time to see one of the Brownies jump at her.

Moving with a quickness that Kate could never have imagined, the Brownie hurtled itself at her. It caught her hair, flipped head over heels, twisting itself as it did, until Kate's hair was tightly knotted over her face. Then, with Kate's hair already in an awkward and painful knot, the Brownie leant backwards and, planting its feet on her face for leverage, yanked as hard as it could.

Kate let out a cry of surprise and pain which the other Brownies used as the signal to make their escape.

One of the three Brownies that had been standing in the middle of the Dwarves suddenly darted under the long leather jerkin of one of its guards. A second later the dwarf, between whose legs it had disappeared, suddenly let out a breathless huff, his eyes closed as a pained expression crossed his face. Then, as his knees clamped together and buckled, tears filled his eyes and the dwarf fell to the ground his hand covering his most delicate parts.

'Catch them,' Balelin shouted, just as the one he had been holding unexpectedly began to wriggle and twist violently. With the skill of both an escapologist and gymnast the Brownie somehow managed to drop out of its little jacket, catch hold of the edge and swing on it, flipping itself through the air to land on top of Balelin's arm. In a second it had wrapped its legs around the old dwarf's arm, riding it like a bronco, as it sank its needle-sharp teeth into the soft flesh between Balelin's thumb and fingers. '*Owwww,*' Balelin cried out.

Balelin began shaking his arm, trying to knock the Brownie off, but the little fella hung on. 'Do you give up?' the Brownie shouted before sinking its teeth into Balelin's hand again.

Balelin went to swat the Brownie, as one would swat a worrisome wasp. But, seeing the dwarf's hand coming at it, the Brownie let go, jumped and tumbled through the air, then landed on Balelin's other arm. It grabbed hold of Balelin's little finger, wrenched it back with all its strength, causing Balelin to cry out again. 'Surrender and we will not hurt you, dwarf.'

Grizlan went to grab the Brownie on her grandfather's hand just as Liz made to grab the Brownie pulling her daughter's hair out by the roots. Then the other Brownie threw itself at Grizlan's feet, tripping her and sending her sprawling into Liz who in turn crashed into Kate and all three ended up on the ground, a tangle of arms and legs. At that moment the Brownie that had been pulling Kate's hair disappeared, jumping off her face to who knew where. Then, as the three women tried to untangle themselves, each shouted in dismay to discover their hair all tied together.

In years to come, around many tiny little camp fires, baby Brownies would be told the tale of the Battle of Tangle Wood. Older Brownies would recount how four, very brave Brownies bested three times their number heavily armed and vicious Dwarves and as many humans. The Dwarves, however, would never speak of it, ever. For, once the Brownies had got loose, it was near impossible to catch them again.

Grooflin saw one of the Brownies standing next to the fire; he dived at it, arms outstretched, only to see the Brownie dart out of the way. Then, as he landed heavily, the Brownie kicked the burning embers of the fire at Grooflin, setting fire to his beard. Grooflin howled, frantically patting out his burning beard, only for the Brownie to jump onto his head and stomp on his helmet till it slipped down and covered his eyes.

The Brownie pulling at Balelin's finger abruptly stopped. It vaulted into the air, somersaulted, and then with both feet, drop kicked Balelin right on the end of his nose. So surprised was Balelin that he yelped, clutched his nose, and tumbled backwards off his box.

The Brownies darted left and right with unbelievable speed and nimbleness, sometimes disappearing under the leaves only to surface several feet away and usually behind one of the Dwarves who was their next target. They would somehow run up the back of the Dwarves, climbing up them quicker than a squirrel up a tree, getting onto their heads where they could reach down, grab their long beard and pull them back over their faces. Thus, as one dwarf ran to the aid of another, they unexpectedly found themselves blinded momentarily by their own beards, and instead of helping, they went crashing into each other. The Dwarves dived and jumped after the little Brownies but missed all of them. Instead they tripped over furs and blankets, clattered into each other, and fell over discarded shields and weapons.

One dwarf grabbed up a crossbow, took careful aim, and fired. But in doing so he had missed the other Brownie that had leapt on him from behind, grabbed his beard, and tangled it up with the crossbow string. When the dwarf fired he was firing blind, and he also let out a scream of agony. For the Brownie had tied his beard to the crossbow blot also and, as it fired, it ripped a great lump out of a once-proud beard and left the rest snarled in the crossbow's workings.

Jay had been watching the Brownies vigilantly, watching how they would disappear under the leaves, scurry under them for a few feet, then pop up again. There seemed to be a pattern to it, a design almost. Each time they disappeared they always popped up two feet behind the dwarf they had targeted. Then, as one of the Brownies darted under the leaves in front of a dwarf next to him, Jay made his move.

The Brownie disappeared; Jay dived, not at the feet of the dwarf but at a spot two feet behind him. As Jay landed, the Brownie popped up, right into Jay's hands.

Jay grabbed the Brownie round the waist, surprising the little creature as it made to jump on the dwarf's back. But the surprise was only fleeting. The Brownie twisted round quickly and punched Jay squarely in the nose. Jay's head jerked back, his eyes crossed as stars danced before them. '*Outch*,' Jay groaned, trying to blink away the tears in his eyes, but he hung on to the Brownie.

The little creature began kicking and punching for all it was worth, yet still Jay hung on. It bit him on the hand, drawing blood, and still Jay hung on. The Brownie stopped its attack on Jay, but only long enough so that it might call for aid from its fellows. It made a strange, crackling noise, like twigs snapping or dry leaves crunching under foot, but it was enough for the other three Brownies to come running. They leapt upon Jay, grabbing his hair, pulling at his face, kicking and punching with all the strength they could muster, which, despite their small size, was quite a lot. Jay did the only thing he could: he hung on to the Brownie in his hands, curled up in to a ball, and weathered the storm. 'A little help here,' Jay shouted, adding '*ouch, oww, ah*,' as the Brownies pummelled him.

Jay's action, be it foolhardy or brilliant, turned the tide. With all the Brownies now focused on Jay and getting their little companion free, they failed to see Ed and the Dwarves quickly closing in on them. In a minute it was over. The Brownies were once more prisoners, this time with their little hands and feet tied so that they couldn't cause any more trouble.

There were of course still several other things to be sorted. Grooflin was still putting out the small fire that continued to smoulder in his beard. Two Dwarves were arguing with a third about how best to cut a crossbow out of a beard. And Liz, Kate, and Grizlan were frantically trying to untie the ferocious little knots that the Brownies had tied it their hair.

'Now then,' Balelin said, sitting back down on his box and wiping the blood from his nose, 'if we have got that out of our systems, can we talk? Please.'

'Just waits tills we's gets free,' one of the Brownies shouted back. 'Then we's really gonna dos yous fuzzy face.'

'I say put them on a stick and roast them on the fire,' Grooflin sneered.

'No,' another dwarf snapped, 'not enough meat on them. Put them on hooks and we can use them for bait to fish with.'

'Well?' Balelin asked, drawing out a long knife and studying the blade thoughtfully. 'What's it to be, little ones? Shall we talk or,' he flicked the knife letting it land point first an inch from the head of one of the Brownies, 'is it to be fishing bait?'

The four Brownies looked at the knife, then each other, and then back at Balelin. '*Talks yes, we's talks, talks good verys goods,*' they all jabbered in unison.

Balelin smiled, 'Good,' he nodded then, turning to Grizlan, he asked, 'Do we have some ale, Granddaughter?'

'To drown them in?' Grooflin wondered aloud.

'No,' Balelin said reaching forward and cutting the Brownies free. 'To drink; these are our guests.'

'Guests?' Grizlan scoffed, finally giving up on the knots in her hair and cutting herself free.

Ed sank to the ground next to Liz and Kate. His wife and daughter both sat huddled up under the thick fur. They, like much of the remainder of the camp, were wrapping themselves against the cold, but watching the Brownies closely and warily.

It had taken the better part of half an hour to put the camp back together after the Brownies' little adventure. Half an hour to rebuild the fire, sort out bedding, and for everyone to find their equipment, not to mention untangling a dwarf's beard from a crossbow's bow string. Then, with all the trifling tasks associated with camping in the woods sorted out, the party sat down again. They were exhausted yes, but they didn't trust the Brownies sitting wide-eyed and smiling as they waited for their ale. Nor did the Dwarves trust the rest of the little fellows still out in the woods surrounding them enough to allow themselves to sleep. All of the Dwarves, Ed and his family also, remained awake and watchful, and especially watchful of the four little creatures currently sitting with Balelin and enjoying an ale of all things.

Balelin was once again sitting upon his little box, wrapped tightly in his fur, as he drank from a flagon. In front of him, sitting cross-legged on the ground and using both hands to drink from what appeared to be egg cups, the four Brownies seemed more disposed to talk. Perhaps because of what Balelin said, or perhaps because of the ale, the truce was holding. Even in the woods around them, where the rain that Grizlan had called forth had stopped, the other Brownies were holding back. Every now and then the other Brownies could be heard, little telltale sounds of movement, of leaves being disturbed or tiny feet stepping in muddy puddles, but they held their fire, and like the Dwarves, they watched and waited.

Everyone within the camp continued to be vigilant. If just four Brownies could cause such so much uproar, then what several dozen could do was not worth thinking about. And the truth was that but for Grizlan's ability to call forth wind and rain their camp would have been overrun. But Grizlan looked exhausted by her earlier efforts. She was had wrapped her fur around herself, slumped heavily onto the ground near Balelin, and could scarcely keep her eyes open. If she was called upon to do more it was doubtful she could manage it. So everyone stayed awake, swathed in thick furs against the night's cold, and with one eye on the four Brownies sitting with Balelin and the other on the woods.

Only Jay managed to sleep, but then, as Kate often said about him, 'Jay could sleep through an earthquake'. Whatever was happening, whatever the circumstances, Jay always managed to sleep. After the fight with the Brownies, in which he had admittedly done his part, Jay had grabbed his blanket and fur, found a nice dry spot close to Balelin, curled up and gone off to sleep just as fast as if he was in his own room back in Seattle.

Ed was alert to the danger surrounding them and also spellbound by the Brownies. He watched and listened intently as Balelin talked to the four little characters. The old dwarf was very calm and self-assured, and when he talked to the Brownies, he talked to them as equals. There was nothing in Balelin's tone to suggest a victor talking down to a vanquished. Nor was there anything to suggest threats or intimidation. Balelin was, as he repeatedly explained to the Brownies, nothing more than an old dwarf travelling through the woods with a party of his fellows on his way to his new home. He explained that, with the agreement of the Brownies, many more Dwarves might also want to travel through the woods. They would, Balelin assured them, be willing to pay a toll, it was only right and proper, so long as it was not unreasonable or excessive.

To begin with the Brownies would have none of it. Tangle Wood was their wood and nobody was allowed to pass; on that point, the Brownies that had bitten Balelin and who appeared to be some sort of leader, were adamant. Again and again the Brownies flat out refused to even consider letting anyone pass. But, when Balelin eventually mentioned a toll, the Brownies became a little more interested. In fact the very mention of a toll had the Brownies mildly excited. They suddenly stopped talking to Balelin, breaking off so that they could confer among themselves.

The Brownies went into a little huddle, noisily debating the merits or otherwise of the idea. What was said was anyone's guess, for the Brownies held their diminutive conference in their own tongue which was a strange language and yet not like a language at all. To the untrained ear, and all then present had untrained ears when it came to Brownies, the Brownies' language sounded more like a series of hissing and crackling than words. It was the sound of wind whistling in leaves, of wind whooshing and swishing in the brushwood, of the creak of a branch or the crunch of dry twigs, all the sounds of a wood in fact, and all of it impossible to understand.

Whatever else Balelin was to the Dwarves, an elder, a chief or some suchlike, the one thing he was for sure: a good negotiator. He knew how to insist, without giving offence, knew how to concede without appearing weak, but most of all he knew how to get talks started and how to keep them going. And keep them going he did, right through the night and long into the early dawn. He also knew how to wait as the Brownies discussed among themselves the proposal he was putting to them. But, and most importantly, Balelin knew that if he was going to get some agreement, then he had to find a common ground which all could agree upon. Whether he had some idea of what that should be from the beginning, or whether it came to him later, he never said, but what he did do was find the one thing all, Brownie and dwarf alike, could agree upon. Both of them had a common foe, and that foe was the Goblins and half-goblins that were fouling the land.

The very mention of the word seemed to enrage the Brownies. The very moment Balelin said 'Goblin', all four Brownies jumped to their feet. They cried out some indistinguishable curse in their own tongue, a cry that was quickly taken up by the hundreds of unseen Brownies that surrounded the camp. The wood was suddenly filled with a sound like thousands of branches shaking in a mighty wind and thousands of leaves being crushed and shredded. But there was no wind, and no branches were moving nor were any leaves being crushed: there was just the terrible and unnerving sound that caused all the Dwarves to leap to their feet and be on guard once again.

The apparent leader of the Brownies raised his arms and the woods became abruptly silent at his signal. He turned to face Balelin, his tiny face a portrait of hate. 'We's kills any Goblins comes into ours woods,' the Brownie avowed.

Balelin slowly nodded his agreement. 'And we too have fought and beaten those foul creatures many times.'

'Yous kills many,' the Brownie asked.

'Very many,' Balelin assured him.

'Goods.'

Balelin nodded towards Ed saying, 'Why this very day our friend here sent three of those fell beasts to whatever hell they call home.'

The Brownie's eyes widened as he looked at Ed. Then a smile slowly came to his thin lips. 'Goods. Verys goods,' he grinned broadly. 'Hails to yous, goblins slayer.'

'But there are always more. Sad to say,' Balelin interrupted.

'Yesssss,' the Brownie said. 'Always mores of thems, manys mores.' He sat back down with his three friends and, using both his tiny hands to lift the egg cup, took a sip of ale. 'We's is only littles, too littles to kills thems all. Theys comes and sometimes burns woods, burnings for no reasons. Not to takes trees like mens do. Mens take trees yeses. But builds. Mens puts back trees alsos, so can takes later, and so can hunt. But nots Goblins. Goblins justs hews and burns and destroys. No hunts. No builds. Justs destroys.' He looked down at his ale sadly and was silent. The other three Brownies gathered round him, placing comforting arms around his small shoulders. He spoke again, his small voice strained and quivering, 'In pasted days we hads friends. Elves is Brownie friends. And Brownies is Elves friends. Buts Elves gones now. Gones fars away. Nows Brownies haves no friends. Brownies alones. Ands Brownies toos smalls to kills all thems goblins. Can'ts kills thems, can'ts stops thems. Buts we's fight thems.'

'You still have friends,' Balelin assured the Brownie leader. He sat forward, looking the little Brownie in the eye, his face set and stern. 'Anyone that swears to kill Goblins is a friend of the Dwarves. We have no love for those fell creatures. They are a walking evil. They attack our mines. Ambush us underground and above. Steal our food and animals. No, we have no love of goblins.'

'Then Brownie and dwarf be friends ifs Dwarves kills goblins,' the leader said, drawing himself up to his full height, all two feet of it.

'I am called Balelin,' the old dwarf stated in a commanding tone. 'I can speak for all the Dwarves in Angron. We will be friends with the Brownies, if the Brownies will be friends with us.'

The little leader got to his feet, 'I ams Twiziltwig, son of Nettlestem of the Rowan Trees clan, I cans not speaks for all Brownies, that musts come for Brownies councils. But, for tonights, we wills be friends. My words on its.'

With that they toasted each other, toasted their covenant, and finally toasted to a speedy end for all goblins. In the woods surrounding the camp there was the sound of cheering, but not as Dwarves or humans understood it. It sound more like a high-pitched whistling, like a wind hissing through a tight gap, and it went around and around the camp in waves.

They had an agreement, in principle at least. The details had yet to be sorted out but Balelin seemed satisfied that the Brownies would keep their word. Twiziltwig was pleased also, even if, as he explained, he would have to take their words back to the elders of his clan, and if they agreed, then he would have to take that agreement to the chiefs of all the Brownie clans. A process that might take days. So, for the time being, Balelin and Twiziltwig agreed no dwarf would enter Tangle Wood, nor take wood from it, nor hunt in it until they held council again. For their part the Brownies agreed not to attack Dwarves but, should a dwarf enter the boundaries of the wood by accident, then the Brownies would make them leave without harming them.

With all that settled Twiziltwig got to his feet, a little unsteadily it had to be said, and held out his tiny hand. 'Yous hands on it goods, dwarf,' he said.

Balelin smiled and offered the Brownie his hand, a hand that was nearly as large as the Twiziltwig himself. Twiziltwig looked at the hand, tilting his head left and right as he attempted to size up the hand and how he should go about shaking it. Finally, with a big grin on his little face, Twiziltwig spit on his own hand and then slapped Balelin's palm.

'Yous may camp ins this wood,' Twiziltwig informed Balelin. 'or yous may travels to meets your folks. We's wills finds yous tonight. Thens, Twiziltwig will brings words for clan elders.'

Balelin nodded. 'We are agreed then.'

Shortly afterwards the four Brownies took their leave of the party. They finished off their egg cup-sized ales, got to their feet, bowed low, and staggered off into the woods.

Only Balelin and Ed were still awake when the Brownies left. Everyone else, in spite of their caution, had finally given in to sleep.

For a long while neither man nor dwarf spoke. Both sat there, wrapped tightly in their furs against the cold, and deep in their own thoughts. They watched the fire as it slowly died down and listened to the dawn song of the birds in the trees. Eventually Ed moved. He let the thick fur slip from his shoulders and, shivering against the morning chill, went and placed more wood on the still glowing embers of the camp fire.

He sat back down, momentarily getting himself tangled up with the unfamiliar sword at his side. Muttering to himself Ed unbuckled the belt and lay the sword on the ground beside his blanket. Then he made himself as comfortable as possible. He lifted the fur round his shoulders again and stared into the fire once more.

Balelin finally spoke to him. 'Something troubles you, Longshanks?' Balelin asked in a near whisper.

'Not, "something," Ed sighed, 'Everything.'

Balelin looked long and hard at Ed and asked, 'Explain?'

Ed took a deep breath before saying, 'Yesterday, sorry no, it was the day before yesterday now, but anyway, then we were just a family on vacation, enjoying ourselves and that was that. But now, now I haven't got a clue what is going on, or where we are, where we are going, and what is happening. I don't even know what is real anymore. I mean, Balelin, is this some sort of dream?'

'Does it feel like a dream, Ed?' Balelin said, avoiding giving an answer.

'No it does not,' Ed said, 'that's the strangest part. It feels all so very real, and yet it can't be.'

'How so?' Balelin tilted his head and waited for Ed to explain.

'Well, all of this,' Ed said, his hand sweeping round the camp quickly. 'Dwarves, no offence, and Brownies and goblin-men, it's just not real; it can't be.' He slumped back, his shoulders dropping fractionally as he pulled the fur tighter around himself and snorted a laugh. 'I must have hit my head really hard in that accident. Any minute now, I'm gonna wake up in some hospital bed with a lump on my head the size of a baseball.'

'Did you hit your head?' Balelin asked, looking at Ed full of anxiety.

'No,' Ed scoffed, 'leastways I don't think so. But I must have; it's the only possible explanation. This is all a dream, or a nightmare, and I am going to wake up with the strangest story to tell. Just you wait and see.'

'But if it is a dream,' Balelin softly contended, 'then when you wake up I will not be here to see. You will be in your bed and I, well, I will be no more.'

Ed thought about that for a few seconds then said, 'Well, that would be sad. What I mean, Balelin, is in the short time that I have known you and your companions, I have sort of gotten to liking you. And I have to say, as dreams go, this has been one of the strangest, fun yes, but very strange. And do you know how I know it is a dream?'

'How do you know, Ed?' Balelin smiled.

'Simple,' Ed sat up to emphasise his point. 'Because none of this can be real. Come on, me, having a fight with three guys with swords and beating them. Ten years ago and twenty pounds lighter perhaps, but now, no way. And Brownies: I'll bet that is my subconscious telling me to lay off the candy and cakes. Not that it would do me any harm; I have been putting on a few extra pounds lately.'

Balelin nodded slowly and gave Ed a reassuring look. 'In that case Longshanks, 'tis best that you sleep. I will watch the fire and wait in case our little friends return. Sleep, friend, you will feel all the better for it.'

With that Ed lay back. He covered himself in the fur, 'Wait till I tell Liz; she will never believe it.' And saying that, Ed went to sleep.

# Chapter 7

## A New Day

Ed woke slowly the next morning. He was warm if a little uncomfortable. For a long while he remained lying there, not wanting to open his eyes. His bed was not the best, and he had slept in much better. But, whatever the bed felt like, Ed simply didn't want to open his eyes. He didn't want to move, didn't want to hear anything, but above all, he just didn't want to get up.

'Ed, honey,' Liz said softly. She placed her hand gently on his brow and stroked it lovingly. 'Ed, how do you feel? We have been so worried about you. You were talking in your sleep, saying some of the weirdest things.'

'Ah sweetheart,' Ed smiled, though opening his eyes only slowly. 'I have had the most peculiar dream.' He gradually began to sit up. 'It seemed so rea…' Ed was suddenly dumbstruck. His mouth continued to move, but no words came out. Instead of waking up in a hospital bed surrounded by his family, Ed woke to find himself sleeping on the ground and surrounded by a group of Dwarves.

Balelin was sitting close by as Ed woke and began to sit up; the old dwarf glanced over, smiled, and asked, 'Am I still here, Longshanks?'

Ed, now sitting bolt upright, stared around him. Liz was sat beside him, a puzzled expression on her face. Jay was over by the camp fire, toasting some bread that he was holding on the end of a stick. Kate was standing next to one of the carts, brushing her hair and talking with Grizlan as she did so. Also, going about their business around Ed, the rest of the Dwarves began to look over at him, smile, and wish him a pleasant morning.

'No,' Ed stammered, 'it can't be. It was a dream. It has to be a dream.'

'What was?' Liz asked.

'All of this,' Ed groaned. He shook his head, attempting to dispel the mental miasma that was clouding his brain. 'But I was sure . . . I mean, I thought . . .'

Liz's profession kicked in. Without thinking about it Liz was taking Ed pulse and checking his other vitals. And with Liz still fussing over him, Ed got slowly to his feet. Part of him still refused to believe any of what was going on, and yet he could not totally dismiss the evidence of his own eyes.

'Are you OK, honey?' Liz asked, her face etched with anxiety.

In reply Ed shook his head slowly, saying, 'You know, Elizabeth.' Straight away that told her that something was genuinely wrong: Ed only ever called her Elizabeth when something was genuinely wrong. 'You know, last night I had convinced myself that this was all just some strange dream. That I had banged my head and that I was going to wake up in hospital where I would have a damn good laugh about it.' He paused, looking around him as if he might somehow find something, anything that he could latch onto in the hope of proving that it was all still somehow a dream. But there was nothing; leastways nothing to disprove that he was anywhere other than in a wood, in a camp, and a camp filled with Dwarves no less.

Perhaps it was that realisation that made Ed sway on his feet. Later Liz would maintain that it was some form of delayed shock. But perhaps, just perhaps, it was the sudden coming to terms with the facts that life, as Ed knew and understood then, had fundamentally changed, and there did appear to be any chance of changing them back.

'You all right, friend?' Grooflin asked. He had been bringing Ed some breakfast when he saw him tottering.

'Sure sure,' Ed said.

Grooflin stared intently as Ed then, quickly putting down the bowl of porridge he had been carrying, he raced back to one of the carts, grabbed a small barrel from among the several that were there, and hurried back to Ed. 'Here you go, Longshanks, something to rest yourself upon.'

Ed sat down heavily. 'I do wish you people would stop calling me that,' he groaned.

'We are not people,' Grooflin stated firmly, more than a little offended. He drew himself up to his full five feet, adding, 'We are Dwarves and proud to be such.' And then he relaxed a little, saying, 'I know it is a small point to some, but to us it is a matter of very great importance. It is not just what we are, it is who we are.'

'I am sorry,' Ed said smiling, 'I guess I will have to get used to a lot of new things and new ways.' He held out his hand to Grooflin. 'I meant no offence, friend. Will you forgive me?'

'Of course Long . . . Ed?' Grooflin replied.

'Ed will do fine.'

They shook hand and then Grooflin recovered the momentarily discarded porridge. 'Here Ed, it is not much, but in a few days we hope that we can show you true dwarf hospitality.'

'A few days?' Ed repeated Grooflin's words slowly.

'I am afraid so,' Balelin answered for the younger dwarf. Balelin had been sitting just a few short feet from Ed and had also been watching him closely.

Neither Ed nor Liz had noticed Balelin's eyes before, maybe because of all that had happened the previous day or because of the shadows from the time they had entered the woods, but Balelin had the most intense and compelling blue eyes that they had ever seen. Most of the Dwarves had brown eyes, very dark and very brown. They were warm eyes, friendly to be sure, but nothing like Balelin's eyes.

The old dwarf had a heavy brow; his eyebrows were thick and bushy and, just like his hair, grey and on the verge of being silver. His face was round and set with a long, luxuriant beard. His skin was creased with age, darkly tanned and leathery, and his nose was large and a little reddish: no doubt from the consumption of lots of ale over countless years. But his eyes were clear, conspicuously blue, and strangely piercing.

They were not the type of eyes that unnerved someone, at least not unless Balelin wanted to, in which case they had best look out. But they were the type of eyes that told all that he looked on that they would know if he was being lied to. Above that, Balelin's eyes also told those he was looking at that he was not the type to lie. In a way it could be said, and with some fair amount of certainty, that Balelin didn't need words: the old dwarf could say all he had to say with only his eyes.

And so, when Grooflin left and went about his duties, Balelin looked at Ed asking, 'You will come with us, won't you, Ed? At least as far as Bennith Dure.'

'Talk about an offer you can't refuse,' Ed laughed.

'Indeed,' Balelin laughed also, oblivious to Ed's reference.

'What is this, Bennith Dure?' Liz asked slowly, hoping that she had pronounced it correctly.

'Ah,' Balelin began, his eyes soft and tender as if recalling a fond memory. 'How should I start?' the old dwarf asked himself aloud. 'Bennith Dure is to be our new home, a real home, the type of place all Dwarves can truly be content in. It is a mine yes, but oh so much more, far more than humans can really understand.' He gazed at Liz, his eyes clearly demonstrating his deep emotion for the place. 'You see, good lady, Dwarves may sometimes live above ground, not often to be truthful, but sometimes. But we have a love for being underground, to be deep within the very bedrock of this world. That is where Dwarves dearly love to be, right in the heart of this earth. To feel it surrounding us, to hear it when it speaks to us. We understand its moods, its needs, and its desires.'

'You mean you live in caves?' Liz said bluntly, a comment that seemed to wound Balelin slightly. But the affront was fleeting and soon forgiven.

'Not caves,' Balelin said in a well-humoured tone. 'Animals live in caves, and Dwarves are not animals. Dwarves live in, well, you would call them mines. But they are more than mines, far more.' Balelin sat for a moment, his eyes closed as he recalled something long forgotten. When he spoke again it was in a manner more of someone speaking of their first true love. 'We Dwarves are not great lovers of open places; we do not feel comfortable in treeless steps or tall forests. We do not shun the light of day, as some fell creatures do; rather we love the warmth of world to enfold us. You know, the Elves used to say of us that Dwarves have hearts of stone.' Balelin smiled at that, nodding his agreement with the sentiment. 'They understand us and pay us high compliment in so saying.'

Liz stifled a giggle. 'I don't think it was meant as a compliment, Balelin.'

'No?' Balelin asked.

'No,' Liz said. 'We also say that people sometimes have a heart of stone; it means that they have no feeling. Just like a stone.'

A puzzled expression came to Balelin's face. 'But stones have feelings,' he protested sympathetically. 'Every dwarf knows this.'

'But does every Elf?' Liz replied.

'Elves? What would they know of stone?' Balelin scoffed. 'Elves think only of trees and green places.' He began to laugh softly to himself for a while then, sitting forward, he motioned for Ed and Liz to come closer. He glanced about him before whispering in a conspiratorial tone, 'We say of the Elves that the only way to get an Elf underground is when they die, and that is way they became immortal.' So saying Balelin began to chuckle at his own joke.

Liz waited for a Balelin's mirth to settle down before asking, 'And what about having a heart of stone?'

'Well it was a . . . I mean it was meant . . . When they said that it was... Those pointy-eared, pasty-skinned, skinny-legged . . .' Balelin paused, perhaps in rage, or perhaps because he had run out of insults. For a while he just huffed and puffed, his head downcast, like he was searching the ground for the next sting of abuse. But gradually Balelin's anger was replaced by amusement. He began to laugh, softly, to himself only at first, but getting louder and louder all the while until he threw his head back and bellowed his merriment for all to hear.

'Three hundred years and more I took that for a compliment,' Balelin roared. 'It would seem that that young fool has become an old fool. Oh that is good, priceless.' Balelin laughed so long and so loud that he became breathless. 'Oh those Elves, what must they have thought of me.' Again he guffawed, 'Thank you, dear lady, thank you indeed. You have shown this old fool that he still has much to learn, very much, to be sure.'

'Then you're welcome, I think,' Liz said. 'But perhaps you could do something for me.'

'Anything, My Lady,' Balelin smiled, and rising slightly from his seat, he gave a tiny bow.

'Is there anywhere round here where we could get a wash?' Liz said. 'I'd really like to have shower but I suppose that would be out of the question. And it has been over two days since we last had a shower. To be honest I am really starting to feel all yucky, Kate too. So if you might know somewhere we could, you know, do what has to be done. You know, somewhere private.' Liz was blushing a bit by the time she had finished.

'I'm not sure I understand, good lady,' Balelin said slowly. 'I mean there is a stream over there but it would be better if you stay where we can all see each other.'

Liz cleared her throat. 'There are things that I would prefer people didn't see.'

'Oh,' Balelin said; then it dawned on him. 'Oh, oh, oh, well yes, no I do see.' The old dwarf appeared a little flustered as he quickly glanced around him looking for somewhere where Liz's requirements might be met. Then, getting to his feet, he added, 'I shall speak to Grizlan; she will know.' He bowed low, 'My Lady.' And with that he left.

A short time later Grizlan came and collected Liz and Kate saying, 'We found you somewhere nice and private.'

'We found?' Kate said. 'I wonder just how private it's going to be then.'

'Shush,' Liz snapped at Kate under her breath; then turning to Grizlan and smiling, said, 'That's great, thank you very much.'

Liz and Kate collected one of the rucksacks containing their few belongings and followed Grizlan. What the dwarf had found for them was indeed a private little spot where the women could get themselves cleaned up.

A few hundred yards from the camp the little river made a bend to the east. There, on the near bank of the river, the water had washed away the top soil and made a cut into the bank. This had formed a pool, about ten feet across and a little over three feet deep. More importantly the river bank was several feet high at the bend and lined with a high gorse thicket that surrounded the pool, hiding it from view on virtually all sides. The only way into the pool was by a tiny path at the water's edge, and once inside, the tree and gorse roots that had been exposed by the water's erosion made convenient places to sit and on which to hang their clothes.

Setting the rucksack aside they removed their trainers and socks.

'My words, that's cold,' Liz gasped as she dipped her feet into the pool for the first time. She dipped them in, drew them out again twice as fast, then reluctantly, she slowly lowered them back into the water, splashed them about for a few seconds, and drew them out once more. 'I don't much fancy getting a bath in this,' Liz laughed.

Meanwhile Kate gamely plunged both feet into the water only to, seconds later, begin slashing and stomping about as she gasped, 'Cold, cold, cold, too cold, too cold.' She jumped up on to the tree root that her mother was sitting on; they both looked at each other and suddenly burst out laughing.

'What we laughing at?' Kate asked.

'I dunno,' Liz giggled. 'It's just that we both know that we got to get washed and the only way to do that is to get into that freezing water.'

'I know,' Kate said, crinkling her face, 'but they say that if you just jump in quickly it's not so cold then.'

'I see,' Liz mused. 'OK then, you go first.'

'No way. You go.'

'Your idea, you go.'

'You're the mom, you should set the example; you go.'

'You're the daughter; you should do as you're told.'

'Yeah, like that's going to happen. We go together or not at all. Deal?'

'Deal.'

They quickly stripped off their clothes, hanging them over the gorse bushes then, mentally daring each other, they plunged into the small pool.

'Seeeeee,' Liz shivered, 'it's not that bad once you get in.'

'Izzz w . . . w . . . w . . . worse,' Kate stammered back. 'Wer . . . wer . . . where's the soap?'

As quickly as their shivering bodies and numb hands would allow they washed themselves. Liz and Kate took turns washing the other's back and then, quicker than they had got into the water, they got out.

Liz grabbed the towel and began to dry herself, rubbing vigorously in an attempt to get the blood flowing again in her frozen limbs. 'Great Scot but that was cold,' Liz exclaimed as she wrapped the towel round herself.

Beside her Kate stood shivering, covering herself with her hands and arms to hide her modesty. 'Damn right it's cold,' she gasped. 'Where's my towel?'

Liz glanced at her daughter sheepishly. 'I only packed the one. Sorry, sweetheart.'

# Family Holiday

'Why'd you only pack one?' Kate groaned loudly. 'I'm damn well freezing here.'

'All right all right,' Liz said handing the towel over. 'I had kind of hoped that we would have found a hotel or something.'

'Instead of being stuck here with nothing but one towel between the two of us,' Kate moaned as she wrapped the towel round herself and sat down heavily on the bank.

'Between four of us,' Liz corrected her as she sorted through the rucksack for some clean underwear. 'You know how hopeless your dad is with packing, and Jay . . .'

'Jay never washes anyway,' Kate cut in as she pulled the towel tight round her in attempt to get warm.

Neither woman said anything for a short time. Kate was too busy shivering and Liz, once she had gone through the rucksack, was occupied with hurriedly getting dressed. Just then, unnoticed by Liz but seen by Kate, two small objects fell from the bundle of other clothes. They were black, very fine and very, very lacy, sheer and see-through, with tiny pink hearts embroidered on them and small pink bows at the hips. Looking up at her mother, Kate gave a stuttering whistle, 'Someone's been shopping at Victoria Secrets.'

Liz blushed as she dressed quickly, more quickly now that Kate had seen her delicate things. 'I bought them for your father, for . . . well you know. You're not a child anymore, Kate.'

Kate began to snigger softly. 'I can guess what for. I am just surprised that after an accident in the middle of nowhere your first thought was to pack something sexy.'

Liz continued to get dressed. 'It wasn't my first thought.' She explained, 'It was just that there was no light and I grabbed the first things to hand.'

'Yeah, sure,' Kate teased. 'Still Dad will be pleased. Ew . . . I just thought.'

'What?' Liz demanded.

'You and dad,' Kate groaned, twisting her face as if she had just swallowed foulest tasting mouthful imaginable. 'But you're so old.'

'We are not old. Just older,' Liz corrected her. 'I keep myself in shape. And your father still has a good body.'

'All right, Mom. Too much information,' Kate said. 'But still, "it's nasty".'

'What's that?' Liz said softly.

Kate shivered under her towel again; she pulled it tightly around her saying, 'I said, it's just nasty.'

'Not that,' Liz hissed in a hushed whisper. 'I heard what you said. I mean, "what was that?"' She nodded her head at something the other side of the gorse bushes then, signalling Kate to be quiet, she turned her head slowly as she tried to hear whatever sound it had been she had heard only moments before.

Liz moved as quietly as she could towards the river bank; unobtrusively as possible she glanced round the edge of the gorse bushes. There was nothing to be seen and, for a short moment, nothing to be heard. Once more Liz signalled Kate to keep quiet and to stay put. Then, very cautiously, she slipped round the edge of the gorse and back along the river bank in search for the sound she had heard.

Kate sat silently on the bank next to the tiny pool that she had used as a bath. She wrapped the towel tight about her and almost climbed in amongst the gorse in an attempt to hide, holding her breath as she waited for her mother to return.

Liz froze when she heard the noise again; she froze and hid behind a tree. The noise was closer, or she was getting closer to it? And was now much more recognizable. It was the sound of steel crashing on steel and, in between, the sound of laughter. She stood, rooted to the spot as she struggled to make sense of what she was hearing. Again Liz heard the sharp clang of steel on steel, then another sound, a duller sound that seemed to be beating out some sort of time, and then the laughter began all over again. First came the *clang clang clang*, then the dull *thud thud thud*, then again *clang clang* and then more laughter and sometimes clapping.

The wood went silent for a minute and Liz took a very careful look around. There was nothing to be seen, leastways not yet, and Liz was beginning to fear what she might see. There was only one thing that those noises could be, and the thought of what that was filled Liz with dread: it was the unmistakable sound of sword on sword, not that she was that familiar with swordplay. But she had seen enough movies to recognise the sound when she heard it. But what or who was the laughing? The possible answer to that chilled her to the very core.

Suppressing her fear Liz pressed on. She moved stealthily, moving from tree to tree in short, rapid sprints, keeping low and as unnoticed as possible. She was getting closer to the noise, and worryingly, closer to the camp.

It had only been a short while before that she and Kate had left the camp. Then everything had been peaceful. The Dwarves had been at their breakfast, or packing up and making ready to leave. Some she had passed at the river bank, washing their plates and spoons as they went about their morning routine. And now the peace of the camp was interrupted by the intermittent but unmistakeable sounds of fighting.

With her back pressed up against a tree trunk, Liz endeavoured to control her breathing, gasping for air and fearing that at any moment whoever was at the camp would hear it. She took one last deep breath and, ever so slowly, turned her body to look around the tree.

She saw Ed standing close to one of the wagons: no, not standing, more like half crouching. He was on his feet, but his feet were slightly splayed and his knees bent with his upper body arched slightly forwards. In his right hand Ed held the long, curved sword that he had taken from the goblin-man the day before; in his left hand he held a round shield. As she watched Ed raise the sword and swing it downwards, *clang*. Then, in one fluid motion to keep the blade moving, Ed swung it round and back, his arm moving like a windmill, and then down again: *clang*. And again, *clang*, and again, *clang*. A cheer went up at the camp. Suddenly the sound changed and the thudding sound began again. *Thud, thud, thud,* and with each thud she saw Ed thrust out his left arm with the shield.

Ed suddenly took a step back, stumbling and nearly falling as he did so. He regained his footing just in time to thrust out the shield again as one of the Dwarves jumped towards Ed swinging a ferocious-looking axe, *thud.* Once more the dwarf swung the axe, and once more Ed blocked the swing with his shield. Only this time Ed did not just block the swing; he also sidestepped it. The axe blow was deflected off the shield and the force of the blow carried the swing down and buried the blade into the ground. At that moment Ed spun himself round, swinging his sword in a backhanded fashion as he twisted round and planted his feet again. The blow was aimed at the dwarf's head and would have hit home had the dwarf not suddenly ducked. At the same instance as he ducked, the dwarf pulled his axe from out of the ground, hooked the back edge of the blade around the rear of Ed's ankle and, with Ed unbalanced, gave a sharp tug and upended Ed.

Ed hit the ground hard, and from behind her tree, Liz quickly covered her mouth to suppress a cry.

Ed grunted heavily as the wind was knocked out of his body. But his grunt was drowned out by a resounding cheer from the other Dwarves.

'Nice move, Longshanks,' Balelin laughed, clapping his approval. 'But you have to watch your balance.'

The dwarf put his axe to one side, leaning on it, as he extended a hand to lift Ed from the ground, offering Ed some advice as he did so. 'You have to learn not to put all your weight on the front foot, Longshanks.'

'Like a boxer,' Ed said, getting to his feet and shaking the leaves off his back.

'Like a what?' the dwarf asked.

'A better balanced sword would help,' offered Cromlin thoughtfully. 'There is far too much weight on the tip.'

'Well then, Cromlin. Why don't you fix it? Shouldn't take much for a dwarf of your skill,' Shamlin taunted, giving his younger brother Dannit a tiny nudge in the ribs and a wink as he spoke.

Cromlin waved his hand dismissively at Shamlin saying, 'I could take a palm off the tip, maybe add a bit weight to the pommel, but it wouldn't make any real difference.' He walked over to Ed and held his hand out for the sword: Ed passed it to him. Shamlin then sliced the sword through the air a few times, turned this way and that, and tested the sword's balance every which way. Finally, still staring at the blade intently, and in a most considered tone, he said, 'No, there no point. Balance is all wrong to start with, and the steel is bad, you see. Goblins just don't know how to work steel right. Look here, see, edge is too brittle, back edge too thick, not tough enough by half. "Can't make good bread with sawdust" ss I always say.' He took a deep breath and added, with all the other Dwarves joining and mocking, for they had heard Cromlin say so many times before. 'Best throw it away and start anew.'

'What on earth is going on here?' Liz demanded as she strode angrily towards the small gathering at the camp. Her hair was wet and slicked back, giving her a very stern appearance. Her body was still wet from the cold water of the pool under her clothes. She had hurriedly pulled on T-shirt and jeans without drying herself to come and investigate the noises she had heard, yet she did not feel the cold at that moment: she was far too furious. 'Somebody might have gotten hurt.'

Ed spun round to see Liz virtually stomping towards him. 'Hi, honey,' he smiled weakly.

'Don't you "Hi honey" me, Edward Deeks,' Liz snapped at him. 'What do you think you're doing?'

'Just practicing,' Ed said apologetically.

'Practicing? For what? Halloween? Clown school?' Liz walked right up to Ed and stood squarely before him. 'Have you any idea how dangerous what you were doing is?'

'Look, honey . . .'

'Don't, just don't,' Liz cut Ed off before he said any more. Around them the Dwarves were beginning to grin at Ed's discomfort but Liz wasn't about to let them off any easier than she had Ed. She swiftly turned and faced the small crowd of bearded faces, her hand firmly planted on her hips. 'And as for you lot, I would have thought you should know better. You're not playing with toys . . .' Liz's words trailed off as her eyes fixed on one of the short figures standing before her.

Dressed in a short mail coat that was too loose around his small chest, and a helmet that was far too big and was forever slipping down over his eyes, was one figure without a beard. A short sword dangled limply from the oversized belt at his waist and he held a shield up in an attempt to hide his face. 'Hi, Mom,' he said meekly as his mother's eye fell on him.

'And what, exactly, are you meant to be, young man?' Liz demanded.

'I just thought . . .' Jay started, but he never got the chance to finish.

'You just thought! You just thought you'd get dressed up like some ridiculous . . . ridiculous . . . I don't know what and get yourself injured in some stupid horseplay.'

'But, Mom,' Jay protested weakly as his mother began to strip him off his arms and armour. 'Mom, everybody is watching.'

'Well, let them watch,' Liz snapped. 'In fact let them watch while you're grounded for the week.'

'Grounded?' Jay groaned loudly. 'Grounded how? Grounded where? It's not like you can send me to my room, Mom.'

'Don't you backchat me, young man,' Liz said sharply.

Again the Dwarves began to snigger but, as Liz snapped her head round to face them, not one of them would face her eye to eye. Liz stared at each of the stout Dwarves in turn, and as she did, each dwarf seemed to wilt and turn away as they suddenly remembered that they had something else to do or somewhere else to be.

'Look, honey,' Ed said contritely, attempting to intervene on Jay's behalf. He walked towards Liz, who was then busy divesting her son of his borrowed mail shirt, but was stopped short as her arm swiftly thrust towards his chest.

Liz held Ed at arm's length, literally, saying, 'We'll talk later, *honey.*'

A distant scream rang out from the riverbank.

Nearly indistinguishable at first, and muffled by both trees and distance, but then it came again, much louder and clearer.

'Mom! Dad! Help!'

'*Kate*,' Ed gasped as he looked at Liz. He said no more but instead raced to where Kate's cries for help had come. Beside him, sprinting as fast as they could, the Dwarves also ran towards the screams, their weapons drawn and ready for use.

'Dad, Dad help, *argh!* Help!' Kate cried out again.

'Kate, Kate, where are you?' Ed called as he ran towards the riverbank.

'Here. *Aaaargh*. Dad, help.'

Ed saw the gorse bushes move, saw them shaking angrily. Then Kate screamed again and, just as he redoubled his efforts to reach her, something tripped him.

Ed went crashing to the ground. The forest floor had been nearly flat with nothing but a few leaves and the odd twig scattered around the place, yet something, as if from nowhere, a tree root had suddenly appeared before his feet and tripped him. Ed held his hands out in an effort to save himself but it was little use. One second he had been running at full tilt, the next he was sprawled out full length and face down in the dirt. His sword, that unfamiliar blade which he was far from comfortable carrying, went flying off in one direction and his shield went flying in the other. He looked up to see the Dwarves running either side of him but, just as abruptly as he had tripped, some of the Dwarves began to trip and stumble.

Dannit was closest to Ed and made the mistake of looking at Ed falling as he ran past. Then, and all of a sudden, Dannit fell over. His brother Shamlin, who had been hard on his younger heels, was left with no time to stop or to save himself. As Dannit went down Shamlin went crashing on top of him, winding them both. Polmet, who despite his sizeable girth, moved with great speed and lightness of foot and had been out in front when he was abruptly felled. One second he was racing along like some stampeding elephant, the next he was upended and rolling away like a bearded bowling ball.

From nowhere tree roots had seemingly just sprung from the ground and long, tough, prickly Bramble runners had suddenly sprouted, tangling themselves around the legs of the Dwarves.

'Brownies,' cried one of the Dwarves, which made all of the other Dwarves stop running instantly and put them on their guard. Those that had fallen quickly got to their feet, cursing the Brownies as they did so. 'Those treacherous little devils,' hissed one. 'Liars, cheats, and pilfers,' responded another. They scanned the woods, looking for any sign of their tiny attackers. But Brownies were far too adept at camouflage to be seen, especially in their own woods. The only signs were a rustle of leaves here, a disturbed branch there, and the sound of softly diminishing laughter.

'Dad. Get off me. *Get off. Dad help!*'

Ed jumped to his feet again, 'I'm coming, Kate.' He grabbed the sword he had dropped and sprinted towards the gorse.

Just then the gorse was shaken violently, sending up a cloud of the yellow pollen that filled the air like a smokescreen. At the same time Kate leaped from the edge of the bushes, her hair matted and tied in knots about her face, her arms and legs covered in scratches and, the only thing she wore, the only thing she had left, was a towel. It was torn at the edges, spotted with blood and covered in yellow spoors, but Kate hung on to it as if her life depended on it: her modesty certainly did.

Ed ran to Kate, wrapping his arm around her, offering her whatever protection he could. The Dwarves fanned out, forming a rough protective circle about the pair as they scanned the woods. They caught sight of leaves moving on the ground, or a branch shaking in the trees, but was it the breeze, or something else? As to where the Brownies had gone, no one could say. Swiftly, a single thought dawned on Ed, and a good many of the Dwarves at exactly the same moment. Everyone stood motionless for a second, then they turned and faced each other, and then, all at once, several of them said what they were all thinking: 'The wagons!'

Turning on their heels the Dwarves sprinted back to the camp, their weapons at the ready. Behind them, walking more slowly as he comforted his traumatized daughter, came Ed.

By the time Ed and Kate reached the camp the girl was in fits of tears. She was shaking, barely able to stand, let alone walk without her father's aid, and as she cried, she kept repeating, 'I couldn't stop them, Dad, there was too many; they took everything, the bag, our cells, clothes, everything. I tried, but there were too many, I just couldn't stop them. I'm so sorry, Dad.'

'It all right,' Ed told her.

Liz ran to help Kate, who was by the time they arrived at the camp on the point of collapse. 'What happened?' she demanded, wrapping her arms around her daughter, offering whatever protection she could. 'This was my fault. I left her there; it's all my fault.'

'Don't beat yourself up, Liz,' Ed said gently. 'It's nobody's fault; it's this place.'

Grizlan came towards them carrying a blanket which she offered to Kate. 'Longshanks is right,' she said to Liz. 'This wood belongs to the Brownies and we should leave it to them as soon as we can.'

'Balelin,' Ed said sharply, raising his voice to get the attention of the old dwarf who was still sitting by the fire, who had in fact remained sitting by the fire throughout the whole of the morning's events. 'Balelin, I thought you had come to some sort of arrangement with these Brownies of yours.'

Without raising himself from his seat by the fire Balelin slowly turned round to face Ed. A soft, reassuring smile played across his face. 'Brownies of mine? They are not mine; they are their own,' Balelin said slowly. 'And as to arrangements. No, not with these Brownies? With the Brownies last night, yes. But there are many tribes in these woods and it takes time for word to get around. Is that not the way of things?'

'Well, yes but,' Ed began hesitantly, 'but look at Kate, look what happened to Kate.'

Rising to his feet slowly, as slowly as only a very old dwarf can, Balelin got up and walked over to Kate. Liz was sitting with her, busy cleaning and dressing the worst of the many little cuts and scratches. He placed a hand upon her head, smoothing back the girl's hair that had been matted and tied by the Brownies. 'I am sorry, my child,' Balelin said earnestly, 'but you are strong and these cuts will heal. I ask only that you find the strength to forgive those that did this as they do not know any better. Soon we are to have council with the chiefs of all the Brownie tribes. You have been wronged, yes, attacked while under oath of safe passage. This I will tell to the council, and if you can, you shall also speak for it was you that these little fellows wronged. But do not speak with hate on your tongue or in your heart. That is not the way to build friendships or tolerance. But rather speak as what you are: one who has been wronged. Then the Brownie council will know how best to make restitution if restitution can be made.'

Liz turned and faced Balelin, her anger revealed like a flicker of fire in her eyes. 'Is that what my daughter is to you: a bargaining chip?'

'No, good lady,' Balelin protested softly.

'Yes, she is,' Liz snapped. 'You want to use her attack to get something from these Brownies. How dare you! My daughter is not some pawn to be used to get . . . well, I don't know what you expect to get.'

Balelin shook his head slowly. 'I do not expect to get anything from the Brownies,' he said softly. 'They have little if anything that we could want. Please, good lady, try and understand; this wood is their whole world, their home, and their lives. It means everything to them, and just as you or I or Ed or anyone else, they have a right to defend it.' Balelin stood and looked at the wood around him for a short moment before turning back to Liz and saying. 'All I hope is that the Brownie council will accept that we Dwarves do not want anything from them, save free passage to our new home.'

'And what about Kate?' Liz demanded.

Balelin sighed heavily, 'I am very, very sorry for what has happened to Kate, and I am sure that the council will be also, once they hear of it. But we are the trespassers in their land.' So saying Balelin turned and began to walk back to the small fire.

'I see,' Liz called after him. 'So basically all you're interested in, the only thing you are interested in is getting to your damn precious mine. Is that it, Balelin?'

Balelin paused for a second, his shoulders sagging as he breathed a long sigh. He turned slowly back to face Liz and gave his answer. 'Yes, good lady. I am sorry, but yes.'

With that Balelin walked away.

Soon the order was given to break camp. The fire was doused and the wet embers buried. Ponies were hitched to wagons and everything was loaded aboard. Ed and Jay saddled the horses and made ready to ride while Liz and Kate were helped into the one of the wagons so that Liz might tend to Kate's wounds. In short order the whole party was ready to depart, and once Balelin had been helped into the other wagon, the group set off again.

# CHAPTER 8

## Tangle Wood

The journey through Tangle Wood was long and slow. The party had set out from their overnight camp and were heading deeper into the wood. There was no road to follow, not so much as a path or trail, for no one save the Brownies ever went deep into the forest, and Brownies leave no tracks. Yet deep into the forest was exactly where the party was heading.

Their journey took them northwards to begin with, following the course of the small river besides which they had camped. They followed this course for several miles, skirting along the riverbank until they found a shallow ford. From there they travelled eastward, or as near to that direction as they could manage. But it was hard to keep a track of their bearings for, the deeper into the forest they travelled, the closer and the taller the trees became. And the taller and closer the trees became, the less the sun was able to penetrate. By midday, or what they estimated to be midday, the party was travelling through a seemingly endless mass of incredibly tall trees.

Occasionally a bright shaft of sunlight would pierce the leafy canopy, breaking through like a searchlight's beam to illuminate the forest floor for a short while before either a cloud or the turning of the world changed the angle and the light was gone again. Then, once more the little caravan was plunged back into the half-light of the forest. Earlier in their journey, in the first hour after they had left the camp site, they had passed through several small clearings. In those places the sunlight was bright and the air fresh and sweet. The party used them to fix their direction and to take short stops before setting off again. But, as they went on, the clearings became few, and much further apart, and the forest became much thicker and ever closer than before.

They came to yet another stream, one of many that twisted and turned their way through the forest. For in that part of the forest the ground seemed to be continually cut and broken by streams both large and small. Some of them were nothing more than the tiniest trickle of water, water that bubbled up from the ground or that seeped out from the soft, peaty banks and mounds that ageless erosion had formed around those tiny brooks. Even so, soon one tiny brook would join another and another till many came together and formed little streams. Some of them were slow and gentle running, like silver ribbons quietly bubbling their way along before joining an even greater flow. Other streams were fast flowing and carved deep into the soft soil until they hit bedrock. But all of the streams had one thing in common: the water in them was cool and clear and very refreshing on a hot humid day. Several times, as they travelled, they would take a short pause at one or other of the streams. They would take a few sips, refill water bottles, or let the horses and ponies drink. Then they would press on, moving still deeper into the forest until finally they came to a stream that made the party stop and think for a while.

This stream was faster running than the small stream they had camped by, much faster. All of those other tiny little streams and brooks must have been feeding into this one. In fact it was more of a small river than a large stream. It was not very deep, and the bottom was quite firm, the mass of water flowing having washed away any loose soil and stones many years ago. But the banks on both sides were steep and muddy, too steep and muddy for the wagons to get across.

The wagons had to wait by the bank while a couple of the Dwarves went north at the same time Ed and Jay rode south in an attempt to find a crossing point. Eventually a ford was located two miles south. The banks of the river there were not so steep, but they were slippery. The mud there was knee-deep, at least knee-deep to Ed as he had discovered while probing it with a long stick. But he had also discovered that there were large boulders hiding under the mud, boulders that could, if they were not careful, snap an axle or even tip the wagons over. Yet, search as they might, there was absolutely nowhere else to cross the river.

The Dwarves arranged themselves around each wagon in readiness to make the crossing, bracing their broad shoulders against the sides so as to act as both breaks and stabilisers as the wagons went down to the river ford. The first wagon hit a boulder, twisting the front axle sharply to the left and tripping it over to the right. All the Dwarves on the right quickly rammed their shoulders hard into the wagon's side, holding it up. While the Dwarves on the left raced to grab the mud-covered wheel. With hands slipping from the thick mud, they heaved at the wheel, turning it, pushing it, and lifting it over the buried rock. Once over the boulder the wheel bounced down into the mud, shooting the wagon forwards as it lurched back over to the left. The whole process had to be repeated with the wagon's rear wheel, and by the time it was done, the Dwarves were caked from head to foot in a thick, clinging layer of mud.

Then the wagon was pulled by the ponies and pushed by the Dwarves through the river ford. Grizlan, who was driving the first wagon, flicked the reins, calling to the ponies, 'Come on, little fellows.' With that the ponies seemed to launch themselves at the far bank; simultaneously all the other Dwarves jammed their shoulders into the wagon and with a cry of *'two three heave,'* the wagon was pushed up the steep bank and onto the flat ground beyond.

A little cheer went up from the Dwarves as they allowed themselves a tiny celebration: a brief moment of merriment before they faced the task of getting the second wagon across. They crossed back through the ford, laughing at and ridiculing each other as to who was covered in the greatest amount of mud. Some stopped midstream to wash the worst of the mud from their hands. Others simply splashed in the water, stamping their feet in order to clear the mud out of their boot treads and also to kick water at one another as they did so. But, once they were back at the second wagon, all the mockery and horseplay stopped.

Leaving the horses with Jay, Ed offered to lend a hand, and another shoulder, with getting the wagons across. He positioned himself on the right hand side, reasoning that, if the wagon should tip again, then that was where he could do the most good. And so, with everyone taking up position around the second wagon, they set off down the muddy slope.

Grooflin was driving and he steered the wagon further to the right, hoping to avoid the boulder that nearly toppled the first wagon. And he did avoid it, but only at the price of finding a boulder on the right that kicked the wagon up and over to the left before dropping it back into a deep mud hole on the right.

The front wheel sank in deep, almost up to the axle. Ed and the Dwarves on the right side braced themselves hard against the wagon, pushing and lifting for all they were worth. Yet still the wagon was sinking. Their feet struggled and floundered in the deep mud, the Dwarves sinking up to their knee and more as the weight of the wagon pressed down on them. For one brief moment it appeared as if the wagon might be kept moving forward as some of the Dwarves heaved against the weight while others pushed and pulled at the wheels to keep them turning. They shouted oaths and curses at the wagon, at the mud, and at each other, yet still the wagon was sinking. Then, just as it looked like the wagon would be pushed out of the mud by the colossal effort, it slowly, and inextricable, was sucked back in.

'Everybody round this side,' Ed shouted and, as quickly as they could, all the Dwarves struggled through the mud to assemble on the right hand side of the wagon. 'Jay, find a lever: quick. Right, all together now: *Heave*.'

Jay looked about him, his head turning rapidly from side to side as he tried to find something strong enough to lift the wagon. Meanwhile the Dwarves, after much slipping and sliding, had arranged themselves along the lower side of the wagon, their backs to it and their hands holding the lower timbers.

'All together now,' Hamfast shouted, 'two three heave.'

They heaved, heaved with all their strength. The wagon stayed put but the Dwarves did manage to push themselves deeper into the mud.

'Two three heave,' Hamfast shouted again, and again the Dwarves heaved, and again they sank deeper into the mud.

'Stop stop stop,' Ed called out. 'You lot heave any more and you'll be up to your necks.'

'I got my feet on something solid,' Hamfast announced.

'You got your feet on my foot,' Polmet, the fattest of the Dwarves said.

'Beg your pardon,' Hamfast said, moving his foot and sinking deeper as he did so.

'Granted,' Polmet said, then, as he watched Hamfast sink he asked, 'find anything solid down there?'

Hamfast muttered something under his breath which made the Dwarves that heard it smile despite their current predicament.

At last the wagon stopped sinking. It was up to its axles in the mud and stuck fast. At least it was no longer in danger of tipping over, but nor was it in danger of going any further until it had been dug out. Firstly, however, the Dwarves had to dig themselves out of the clawing mud that was forever threatening to suck them down.

'Nice driving, Grooflin,' Hamfast said, pulling himself out of the mud by laying back in it and slowly pulling his feet out one at a time, an action that was accompanied with some very noisy sucking, slurping, and gulping from the thick mud. It also left Hamfast stuck in the mud on his back with his feet and hands waving about in the air like some giant upturned tortoise.

'Yeah, Grooflin,' shouted Maklin, 'how's about you get your fat behind down here in the mud and start digging out what you got in.'

And so it went on as all the Dwarves struggled and strained, flopping and floundering, in their efforts to extricate themselves from the oozing mud. And as they did so, poor Grooflin, who to be fair was the only dwarf not covered in mud up to that point, was the target of their countless curses and oaths.

Once they had extracted themselves from the mud, no easy task in of itself, they got their tools out of the wagons and set about the mud with a will. No instructions were issued, other than, 'By me Gammet. Harrlin Shamlin, by the front wheel.' Yet, for all there appeared to be no one dwarf in charge, they all seemed to know where they should be and what they should be doing. And in short order every dwarf, save Grizlan and Balelin, were around the wagon and digging for all they were worth.

Spade full after spade full of mud and slime, of sodden peat and loose soil, was dug and tossed away from the river bank. It was like watching a snow blower at work, no, ten snow blowers, and all of them attacking the clinging mud that held the wagon fast. Even the hidden boulders were no match for the determined Dwarves. They simply dug down to them, then cleared the mud around them, and setting their back to them, heaved them up and out of the way.

In no appreciable time the task of digging out the wagon had been accomplished. Not only that but the Dwarves had cleared both banks and cut an easier incline on the far bank to get the wagon onto high ground again. At the end of it everyone was covered in a thick layer of sticky mud.

Finally, with the wagon dug out, a carpet of branches had been laid under its wheel. With one last effort the Dwarves and Ed again gathered round the wagon, and on a signal from Grooflin, they all pushed and heaved. Down the short slope it went, bouncing over the rough carpet of logs. It splashed into the water, across the ford and, with a 'two three heave' it was pushed up the other bank.

Ed went back over the ford, and with Jay, he led the horses over. The horses didn't like walking on the half sunken carpet of logs, but, and with only a few protesting whinnies and snorts, they too quickly crossed the ford.

The party allowed themselves a short break: some time to clean themselves up and have a drink of water before they pressed on once more. There was no time for food. Too much time had been wasted at the ford. It was getting late, already long into the afternoon, and the forest was becoming darker and less friendly with each passing moment.

From the ford they began to go uphill. To begin with it was hardly noticeable. The broken nature of the forest floor meant that the party was forever having to go up and over some enormous tree root and then down the other side. If they could they went round the massive roots, but that put upon them the risk of losing any clear sense of direction. The trees in that part of the forest stood several hundred feet high, and their girth was such that all of the Dwarves holding hands together could not stretch around their full circumference. Around each tree their roots spread out like giant fans. They lifted the soil up several feet in places, and in other places they were interlinked and twisted over and under one another so as to form an impenetrable barrier to the wagons.

In such a forest it was impossible to go in a straight line. Time and again the wagons had to be diverted several hundred feet round this tree or that. Time and again the party was pushed off course, and time and again they somehow had to find it once more or else become for ever lost in the vast forest.

In such a forest the going was slow, far too slow for anyone's liking. The Dwarves wanted to be out of the forest, and the sooner the better. For Dwarves are no lovers of forests, not even one as ancient, or as majestic, as the one they were wrestling their way through.

Yet not all of the party was unsettled by the colossal trees of Tangle Wood. Walking side by side, leading their horses, Ed and Liz were awestruck by the sheer grandeur of the forest. Even Jay, not normally noted for his appreciation of natural things, was left speechless in wonder.

'Did you ever see tree like this before, Ed?' Liz whispered, though why she was whispering she could not think: there was no one other than the Dwarves around to overhear her.

'Never,' Ed whispered his reply. 'I don't even think that the giant redwoods can match these trees.'

'How old do you think they are?' Liz asked, her head tilted well back as she gazed up at the leafy canopy high above.

Ed took a deep breath, then let it out in a long, slow stream, pursing his lips as if to whistle though not making any sound. 'I dunno know,' he said at length, 'a few hundred years, I can tell you that much.'

'More than that,' Polmet muttered cautiously. The largest of the Dwarves had been trudging along close to Ed and Liz and must have overheard their conversation.

The couple hadn't being paying much attention to the fat dwarf. He had, to all intents and purposes, appeared to be quietly walking along, keeping to himself as he picked clumps of mud from out of his beard. Now, with the majority of the beard grooming done, he joined in.

'It is the working of the Elves,' Polmet said softly, casting his arm around at the forest. 'There are many of them, Elves that is, and they loves their woods so they do. Everywhere they pass, they plants seed, and the next thing you know, another wood just springs up.'

'What's wrong with that?' Liz asked.

'Nothing I suppose,' Polmet said reluctantly. 'Just that they never seem to make home anywhere. I'm not talking about White Elves, White Elves are different all together you understand. It's just them there Green wandering fellas that starts wood like this then go off again.'

'But this is such a magnificent forest,' Ed protested. 'We should be so lucky to have forests like this at home. I mean, just look at it, such gigantic trees. I have never seen anything like it before.'

'No,' Polmet agreed, 'and I bet you have never tried to get a wagon through such a "magnificent forest".'

'Well no,' Ed was forced to admit.

'We has,' Polmet hissed. 'It's going to make digging that there wagon out today look easy. You mark my words, Longshanks.'

'I'm sure that was not their intention,' Liz said in defence of the Elves, not that she had ever met one or in fact believed that they existed.

'Perhaps not,' Polmet sighed, his expression softened for a second but soon hardened again. 'But Elves are forever meddling, meddling and interfering as if they were the only folk of this world.'

They all trudged on, Polmet walking a little ahead of Ed, who could not resist giving Liz a sidelong glance as they went. He pulled a face and nodded his head towards the fat dwarf. Liz got his meaning straight away and began to giggle: truth be told it was the first time in too long time that the couple had been able to share a joke.

There was however no joke when it came to travelling through the forest. It seemed that they had to alter course every hundred yards, and navigation in the forest was becoming harder and harder as the sun began to dip in the sky. Even when the sun had been at its zenith, on the forest floor it had been little better than twilight. Now, as the sun began to slowly set, shadows grew longer and the gloom of the woods grew ever deeper. And that only made keeping to a true course harder still.

Finally even the stoutest of the Dwarves was forced to admit that they were not going to get out of the forest that night. Ever since they had dug the wagon out their progress had been far slower, and far more tortuous, than they had hoped. They were forever having to push the wagons up and over the tree roots or dig them out of some other hollow or pit. There was only one thing left for them to do: they would have to make camp for the night and begin again early the next morning. It was not a prospect any of the party relished but, with the light failing and everyone already tired to the point of exhaustion, there was no other option. And so, for the second night, the party made camp: this time deep in the heart of Tangle Wood.

Night drew like a sudden black embrace. It came on so quickly and so completely that it left all within the party feeling unnerved: dwarf, man and beast, all of them felt the unnatural nature of the swift darkness that engulfed them.

Two giant roots from one tree stretched out to form a sort of open-sided triangle. The roots had pushed the forest floor up some eight or nine feet nearest the tree and stretched out a good forty feet before the root on the left was bisected and forced downwards by another root from another tree. At that point the roots seemed to be all tangled up in one another but, they did form a rough enclosure, about forty feet by forty, with an opening that was only ten feet wide. Within the enclosure the ground was, for the most part, flat and, more importantly, dry.

Within the camp they went about their tasks as quickly as they might. Some gathered fire wood, though finding dry wood for a fire was far from easy: the forest was simply too damp and everything seemed to be covered in thick moss. Others set about securing the animals for night, but the ground was too soft to hold a tether spike nor were there any branches low enough to which they could tie the horses and ponies. In the end they just ran a line between the two wagons and tethered the animals to that.

Their evening meal was a far from joyous affair: a bowl of barley porridge seasoned with a little salt. Along with their porridge they each drank a small tankard of ale, and this they drank in silence. For there was no cheer to be had in the forest that night, not even from the strong brew.

Around them the night was beginning to come alive, and this only unsettled the already uneasy Dwarves. High above them there was movement in the trees, perhaps birds returning to their nests, or owls leaving to hunt at night. Maybe they were the sounds of squirrels or opossums, or some other woodland creature doing whatever it was that they did at night. Whatever it was it did nothing to settle the Dwarves. Every time there was another creak or squeak or rustle of branches overhead, the Dwarves would look up sharply, straining their eyes to see in the near pitch black, as they cursed whatever it may be under their breathe. And there were other noises, besides the ones high above them, noises all around them on the forest floor.

The setting sun had been the signal for rabbits to come out of their burrows. The party had seen many of the little creatures emerging while they themselves struggled with the wagons. Now, with the sun set, all around them they could hear many more scurrying back and forth in their hunt for food. And there were not only rabbits, but things both bigger and smaller: mice, screws, deers, and all manner game. Some of it came right up to the camp, cheekily looking in as if they were checking the new neighbours.

Grooflin and Dannit went to the wagons and retrieved a pair of crossbows. 'Just a short while, friends, and we shall have us some venison for supper.' Grooflin smiled.

But Balelin forbid them saying, 'Put your weapons away. This is not our wood and that is not our game. We will just have to endure another night of hunger, my friends.'

Grooflin and Dannit grumbled quietly to themselves, their bellies grumbled, the bellies of all the Dwarves grumbled, but Balelin was right. This forest belonged to the Brownies, and he was not going to do anything that might upset the uneasy truce between them. True, a dwarf is far and away much stronger than any Brownie and much the greater warrior. But why fight when there is no reason to? Talk was much better, and Balelin had been around long enough, and seen enough, to know that.

And so the party built the best fire they could, set their guard, rolled out their blankets and furs for the night, and with their rumbling bellies adding to the other noises of the night, they tried to sleep.

Ed and Shamlin took first watch: which mainly consisted of keeping the fire well supplied with wood so that it did not die out. Ed placed some of the logs around the fire.

'Why you doing that, Longshanks?' Shamlin asked softly.

Ed sat down next to the dwarf and said, 'It helps dry the wood out. It'll still smoke a bit, but not as bad.'

Shamlin didn't reply other that to nod his head slowly as he gazed into the fire.

In the distance, somewhere far off a wolf called to the night. Both Ed and Shamlin got to their feet, turning their heads this way and that, as they attempted to locate the animal. Again it howled, and was answered by another, more distant wolf. However, either because of the distance between them, or the confusion caused by the trees, neither Ed nor Shamlin could pinpoint where the wolves were.

'That's not a good sign,' Shamlin muttered quietly.

'Just a couple of wolves,' Ed replied, in equally hushed tones.

'Perhaps,' Shamlin said, sitting himself back down by the fire, poking at it vigorously until long tongues of flame leapt high into the air. 'Still, let's just keep this fire stoked and weapons close.' He tossed the long stick that he had used to poke the fire to one side, huddled under his fur, muttering, 'I hate these woods. Hate them.'

Ed sat down next to Shamlin. He pulled the fur round his shoulders. Under the fur Ed felt for the unfamiliar hilt of the sword he carried, a sword that he was carrying all the time now. Why Ed carried the sword he really could not say; he doubted that he could do any real damage with it. Yes he had been practising with it that morning, and yes he was beginning to get a feel for it. It wasn't the best sword in the world, too heavy for one thing and, as Cromlin had pointed out, the balance was all wrong. But a sword was a sword was a sword, wasn't it? And if they should run into anymore of those goblin things, at least Ed would not be empty-handed. Then again, he had to wonder, would he be any good with the sword if push came to shove?

Shamlin's head came up sharply, 'What was that?' he asked in a brusque whisper.

Ed was at the point of asking, 'What?' when he was silenced by the sounds of some frantic commotion close by. A few moments before the only sound there had been was the rustling of leaves: most likely the sounds of rabbits going about the business of finding themselves food for the night. Then came the sound of leaves being kicked up all about the place, like someone, or something, racing aimlessly about. Then a frenetic scream cut through the night, startling both Shamlin and Ed and waking several of the others who were doing their best to sleep off the day's labours. The scream was chilling and sudden, and just as suddenly as it came, it died.

Shamlin was on his feet, axe in hand and ready for anything that might attempt to break into the camp. 'Come on then, foul creature,' he hissed. 'Come and taste the axe of Shamlin for it will be the last thing you ever taste.'

Ed was standing also. The commotion and the scream had startled him, just as it had done Shamlin. But, whereas Shamlin was readying himself to repel an assault from the night, Ed was beginning to relax momentarily. He gave a wry smile, looking down at the dwarf and saying, 'Relax Shamlin, that scream was just a rabbit. Most likely a fox or something got it.'

'A rabbit?' Shamlin whispered. 'Are you sure?'

'Fairly sure,' Ed assured him and the other Dwarves who had been alerted by the noise. 'Every sound seems to get magnified by the night, but I am sure that was just some poor rabbit.'

'Well, at least somebody got some meat tonight,' Shamlin grumbled. He sat down heavily, resting his axe on the log he was sitting on as he pulled his fur tight around his shoulders once more. 'What were all those other noises, Ed?' he asked.

Ed was at the fire, turning some of the wet logs so that they would dry more evenly. 'I don't know,' he shrugged. 'Probably just the hunt before the kill.'

Shamlin stared at him, willing him to say more.

'You know,' Ed went on, 'whatever it was that got the rabbit most likely had to chase it round a bit first.'

Shamlin seemed happy with the explanation; he didn't ask anymore questions in any case, even when similar sounds were heard later in the night. Whatever was out there hunting could stay out there hunting for all Shamlin cared. All he was worried about was keeping the fire burning and keeping himself warm.

After an hour Ed and Shamlin handed over the guard duty to Dannit and Polmet. Ed went to where Liz and his children were sleeping.

Kate was sound asleep; the attack on her that morning had left her shocked and dazed. She hadn't said much of anything to anyone the whole day, which was most unlike Kate. Even when Bromlan found a dress and shoes for Kate to wear she didn't say more than a cursory thank you. Both Ed and Liz had been expecting Kate to pass comment about the rough linen that the dress was made from, or the shapeless nature of the dress, or the lopsided pattern that was embroidered around the skirt and sleeves. But she hadn't; the girl who was always so fussy to the point of being pernickety about how she looked simply took the dwarf dress, said thank you, and put it on. True, it was large on her, very large in fact, and hung like a sack, but it covered her modesty and that was what was most important. Kate had found a short length of rope that she used as a belt; it was a tiny improvement and the best she could manage for the time being. But try as she might Kate could not get used to the woollen leggings that Grizlan gave her. They were sort of like footless tights that fit only where they touched and caused itching everywhere else. Yet, after all of that, after all her travails that day, Kate was sleeping like a lamb.

Jay, however, was another matter: he was still very much awake. He, like the others not on watch, had spread his groundsheet and blanket on the driest ground he could find, pulled the fur over himself, and tried to sleep. Yet, as Ed could see when he approached, Jay was far from asleep.

Jay was tossing and turning, kicking at the blanket and fur in frustration and even punching the ground in some futile attempt to get to sleep.

'Jay,' Ed whispered. 'You all right, Son?'

'No,' Jay groaned. 'I can't sleep.' He flopped onto his back and stared up at the branches of the trees above.

'I know, Son,' Ed said, his voice soft and sympathetic. 'Just try and ignore the sounds of the forest. We're pretty safe here. Just imagine it's like when we go camping in the Cascades.'

Jay heaved a sigh. 'It's not that, Dad. It's I got a damn tree root stuck in the middle of my back.'

'Oh,' Ed smiled to himself. 'They why not move if it's bothering you.'

'Can't,' the boy stated flatly. 'Got to stay close to Mum and Kate to protect them while you're on watch.'

'All right then,' Ed said quietly, happy that the night hid the tiny tear of pride in his son's commitment to his family.

Jay flipped himself onto his side again, kicking the blanket that once more had become entangled with his feet. He fidgeted around for a minute under the fur, lifting his hips for a second before dropping them down heavily again. Then, and much to Ed's surprise, Jay pulled one of the sword belts, with sword and dagger attached, out from under the fur.

'A tree root?' Ed said slowly.

Jay turned to face him bashfully. 'Don't tell, Mum.'

Ed smiled. 'Your secret is safe with me, Jay. Just keep it hidden under the blanket.'

'I will,' Jay mumbled. He let out a very long, exhausted yawn, and then closed his eyes. 'Night, Dad,' he muttered softly, and with that he was asleep.

It was still pitch black when Ed next woke. High above him, in the tree tops, there was a slight breeze, gently blowing, while down on the forest floor where he laid the air was motionless. The sounds of the night had faded. But there was something else, some noises that could only just be heard above the sounds of the crackling of the fire. One other thing that caught Ed's attention was Jay. The boy who would normally sleep through anything, once he was asleep of course, was sitting up, his knees pulled up to his chest under the fur, staring off at something on the other side of the camp.

Ed looked at Jay for a minute, looked at the way he had wrapped the fur round his shoulders and pulled the edges round his legs as he sat, legs balled up and stared in astonishment at whatever was going on across the camp.

Rubbing the sleep from his eyes, Ed slowly lifted his head. 'Jay, Jay,' he whispered. 'What's happening?'

Jay turned and faced him slowly. He never spoke, but rather pressed a finger to his lips and signalled his father to be quiet. Then, very slowly, he pointed at whatever it was he was watching.

Ed raised his head a little further, stared for a moment and then, once his eyes finally overcame his sleepiness and focused, he sat bolt upright.

Standing close to the fire were three of the Dwarves. Balelin was easy to identify because of his grey hair. Polmet was there also and, because of his size, also easy to recognize. Ed could not make out who the third dwarf was as he had his back to him. But it was not the Dwarves that had caught Ed's attention; it was who they were talking to. Standing in front of the Dwarves, and warming themselves at the fire, were six much smaller figures: the Brownies had returned.

But these were not the same Brownies that the group had encountered the night before. Well, perhaps one of them was, the one in front of the tiny group, the one that appeared to be doing most of the talking looked very much like Twiziltwig. Not that it was an easy task, telling one Brownie from another; they look so much alike. To make matters worse they were also in the habit of covering themselves in dirt, grass, and twigs so as to blend in with the forest. And that was also making it more difficult to identify the Brownies, not because they were camouflaged, but rather that they were not. These Brownies, the little party of six that had come to the camp in the dead of night, were not disguised at all. All of them were however dressed most curiously.

Each of the Brownies wore pants that had been cut off below their knees. They wore no shirts or jackets; rather they had on two cross belts which had a tiny gold badge of some sort that held them together in the centre of their chests. Over their shoulders they wore capes of bird feathers that had high mantles about their necks.

Two of the Brownies were standing in front of Balelin, talking. The other four were standing a little way behind, watching and listening, and holding the reins to their mounts. These Brownies had not walked to the camp; rather they had ridden there on, and it was extremely difficult to see in the half light of the fire, but they had ridden on what looked like Foxes. These were not your everyday, run-of-the-mill Foxes however; these were much bigger, more about the size and build of a domestic dog. But Foxes they most assuredly were. On their backs they carried small saddles, and around their heads, they had on a sort of bridle, though there was no bit.

Easing himself up into a seated position, just as Jay had, Ed tried to get a better view of what was happening and at the six tiny figures and their mounts. He could not hear what was being said: the conversation within the group was hushed in an attempt to not disturb the others. Not that it had had that effect for, as Ed looked around the camp, he could see that almost all of the Dwarves were awake and watching just as he was. However he, and everyone else watching, could see that there was something going on; some sort of arrangements were being made between the Brownies and the Dwarves.

At length, there appeared to agree. Balelin bowed to the Brownies, and in return, the Brownies bowed to Balelin. With that the six little figures returned to their mounts, whispering something that made the Foxes lie down. The Brownies climbed into their saddles, whispered another command, and the Foxes stood up again, turned, and sprinted off into the night.

Balelin and the other two Dwarves turned and came back to the camp. Seeing nearly everyone awake and looking at him, Balelin paused for a moment, saying, 'Get some sleep, everyone. We will have a guide in the morning but there will still be much work to get the wagons through.' And then he returned to his bed for what was left of the night.

# Chapter 9

## Brownie Council

The morning air was chilled and damp. Everyone, man, woman, and dwarf woke stiff, cramped, and cold. Some stretched their limbs, slowly and painfully forcing the cold out of their joints. Others stamped their feet, or wrapped their arms around themselves, beating themselves rapidly in a vain effort to get warm.

More wood was piled on the fire: perhaps more than was strictly necessary, but soon the fire was blazing and all of the party gathered round it. Water was boiled and tea, nettle tea, was brewed. Polmet had a great iron pot that he retrieved from one of the wagons. This was filled with porridge and water and was soon bubbling away on the fire.

Everyone was impatiently waiting around, bowls in hands, while Polmet stirred the thickening porridge. Bellies grumbled noisily, some more noisily than others, and all too soon, the Dwarves began to grumble vocally. But Polmet would not be rushed. He took his time, and great care, in the making of porridge. It had to be cooked slowly, to ensure that all of the flakes had properly dissolved. And it had to correctly seasoned, not too much salt, nor too little, or else it would be ruined. At least that was what Polmet knowledgeably informed all the other Dwarves as they attempted to hurry him along.

From time to time Polmet would take a spoon and test a little of the porridge. He would lift the steaming spoonful carefully to his lips, blowing on it gently. When he judged it to be at precisely the correct temperature, he would place the glutinous infusion into his mouth, savouring it thoughtfully as one would a fine wine. His eyes would close as he rolled the porridge round his mouth with purposeful thoroughness. 'A little more salt,' he would say considerately, still with his eyes closed as he continued to relish his latest batch. Setting aside the tasting spoon, Polmet would take out his little box of salt, extracting from it a good pinch between his fat finger and thumb. He held his hand high above the bubbling caldron, and with considerable flourish, he sprinkled the salt.

'Get on with it,' barked Shamlin.

'Yeah, Polmet, hurry up,' Cromlin said. 'It'll be nightfall before we get breakfast.'

'You can't rush porridge,' Polmet stated matter-of-factly.

'Yes, you can,' Cromlin replied. 'Unless your name is Polmet, that is. All you got to do is boil the water and hoy the porridge in.'

Polmet was unmoved. 'Peasant,' he retorted softly, adding. 'Well, you cannot rush *good* porridge, and that is the fact of it.'

Cromlin puffed his substantial chest out and squared himself to the much larger Polmet. 'But *you* cannot make *good* porridge and that is a fact also.'

Polmet looked wounded. He looked around him for support, but all he could see was the other Dwarves looking at him and eagerly waiting to hear his reply and the now much overdue breakfast. Finding no endorsements from his own party Polmet's eyes fell on Ed. 'What say you, Longshanks?'

Ed's cheeks flushed a little as all the Dwarves faced him. He took a long, deep breath before stammering, 'I, I, I really couldn't say. I am no expert on the cooking of porridge, or the eating there of.' He turned to his wife. 'Liz?' he said anxiously.

Liz simply looked at him for short while, 'A very diplomatic answer, honey.'

'Yes but what do you think?'

'I think Polmet asked you. Didn't he, honey?' Liz demurred.

'Yes. But I am asking you,' Ed protested gently.

Around them the Dwarves began to chuckle softly. Liz was acting all innocent, and was clearly not going to be drawn into the argument, while Ed was left looking a bit awkward. It might very well have gone on longer had Polmet not finally announced that the long anticipated porridge was equal to his exacting standards.

Presently everyone was stood, warming themselves by the fire, with a steaming hot bowl of porridge. And it has to be said, that no matter what had been said, or however long it had taken Polmet, the porridge was remarkably good. It was thick and creamy, without lumps or the slightest stodginess, and the seasoning was perfect. Leastways no one was complaining and all were spooning mouthful after mouthful into their hungry bellies.

Most of them even returned to Polmet's cauldron for a second helping, which he was only too glad to dole out. And with each extra helping Polmet distributed, the fat dwarf could not resist giving Cromlin a self-satisfied grin.

The only one that did not seem to take delight in the porridge, and who had in fact been somewhat withdrawn from the moment she got up, was Kate. She had been standing close to her mother, her blanket wrapped tightly round her, as she warmed herself by the fire. She had seen and heard the banter that had taken place around the pot of porridge, but she had not reacted to any of it. From the very moment she got up, while others had been stomping and slapping themselves to get warm, Kate had simply pulled the blanket round herself and walked slowly to the fire where she stood unresponsive to anything else as she stared into the flames. Everything about her, the way she walked, stood and even eat, spoke of some inner lethargy.

'You all right, sweetheart?' Liz asked, clearly concerned for her daughter.

Kate sluggishly rolled her shoulders under the blanket, 'Hmm, suppose so.'

'Are you sure?' Liz pressed gently.

Kate put her spoon in her bowl, scratched herself where the coarse material of her dwarf dress was itching. 'Yeah,' she said. 'Didn't sleep well, that's all.' Adding in a near whisper. 'Well that and this dress. It's a bit, well, you know.'

'I know, sweetheart,' Liz said, forcing a smile. 'But we'll get that sorted out soon as we can.'

'I don't know,' Jay grinned broadly. 'It's a new look for sis. You could really pull it off. I heard grunge is in this year.'

Kate did not reply. She merely shrugged her shoulder, stretched her arm out from under the blanket, reached behind her little brother, and gave him a sharp smack on the back of the head.

The Brownies returned as the Dwarves were busy packing the last of their gear into the wagon. Ed and Jay were busy with the horses, brushing them as best they could before saddling them once more. Jay had also gone and named them, giving each the name of some Greek hero, and from then on only ever referring to them, or talking to them, by their new names. Ajax was the name given to Ed's horse, or rather the horse that they had taken from the four dead goblin-men and which his father was then riding. Liz's horse was named Achilles, and Kate's was now called Paris. However the grandest name, at least as far as Jay was concerned, he saved for his own horse, and this he named Hector. All the time Jay was tending the horses he was talking to them, saying, 'Come on, Hector, time to get your bit in. Yes I know you don't like it but you have to have it so come along and be a good boy.'

Strangely the horse appeared to be responding to the boy and to the names he had given them. How they had been treated before was anyone's guess but, with the family taking care of them, not pushing them too hard, walking with them as much as riding them, and especially with Jay fussing over them, the horses seemed more at ease than they had the first day. Years ago, when Ed had first taken the family riding, he had impressed upon them that you have to take care of the horse before you take care of yourself. It was something that both Jay and Kate had grown up with and something Jay, in particular, was putting into practice. Conceivably because of Kate being attacked at the water hole, she seemed less interested in everything, let alone the horses. But, if Kate was distracted, then Jay was only too happy to make up for it, the boy positively fussing over the horses at every opportunity.

He fed and watered them, brushed their coats first thing in the morning and last thing at night. He would stand rubbing their backs when their saddles were removed and rubbing their faces after feeding them, all the time talking gently to them and calling each by their new names.

'Kate,' Jay called to his sister. 'You going to be riding Paris today?' Jay stood at the side of their camp holding the reins of two horses. He lifted his left hand, offering the reins to Kate.

'Paris?' Kate said.

Jay turned to face the horse on his left. 'Don't you worry, Paris, she'll soon remember your name, just like you have to remember your name.' He turned to the horse on his right, adding, 'Not like you, Hector, you already know your name: don't you, boy.'

Hector bowed his head, turned it towards Jay, and gently rubbed its face against Jay's body.

'I don't believe it,' Kate gasped. 'Did you see that, Mom? My brother the horse whisperer.'

Ed was with Balelin and Grizlan at that time. The three of them had gone to meet the Brownies guides that had come to the camp, and what a gathering of Brownies there was. From their conversation the previous night Balelin had assumed that there would be two or three Brownies to guide the way. But, with the Brownies tribes ripe with rumours, and Brownies being just plain noisy at the best of times, a whole army of guides had turned up to see the Dwarves and their human friends of course.

There were Brownies from several different tribes; that much you could see from their appearance. There were ten Brownies, six from the previous night, riding their large Foxes. They had on their cloaks made from motley brown and grey feathers with large mantles of black Raven feather at their necks. Another tribe wore cloaks of reddish brown, decorated with soft, white downy feathers at both collar and tail. And these Brownies rode also, but not on Foxes, they rode wild cats, an animal that looked part feral cat and part Lynx and all together ferocious.

Away off from the main group four Brownies were seated on their mounts of wild boars. These little guys wore cloaks all of shimmering black feathers and carried short spears in their hands. They held their boars back from the rest of the Brownies, and they also appeared to hold themselves aloof from everyone.

Other Brownies came to the camp, some as guides, but most only as nosy onlookers. Some rode on Foxes, Wildcats, and even Badgers, but most walked. The Dwarves, as was their custom, greeted each new arrival with, 'Welcome stranger, well met'. The Brownies however were not so courteous. They did bow politely, and even extended words of greeting, but it was all very formal, very functional, without being cordial. To anyone witnessing the exchange it was clear; to the Brownies, the Dwarves were to be tolerated, for the time being at least, but they were most assuredly not welcome.

Balelin set the example for the Dwarves and for Ed and his family to follow also. He was the pinnacle of politeness, always smiling warmly and greeting every new Brownie he met. However, with so many Brownies turning up to see the curious sight of Dwarves and humans in their woods, it would have taken all day to greet everyone formally. In the end the late arrivals to the ever growing crowd had to make do with a passing 'hi', or 'hello there', as the party made their way to the Brownie council.

It was perhaps just as well that the Brownies remained distant and standoffish for the Dwarves were soon fully occupied with the task of getting the wagons down the route that their guides had chosen.

In front were the ten Brownies riding their Foxes; following behind were those riding the Wildcats. Between these two groups were the Dwarves and the Deeks family, leading their horses and pushing and pulling the wagons over the broken ground. The Brownies had selected a route that, while not as difficult as the previous day, was both disorientating and protracted. There were still times when the Dwarves were forced to bring out their spades and build ramps over the many enormous tree roots but, as they travelled on through the day, those hurdles became few and much less difficult.

Eventually, conceivably some time around mid-afternoon, the going became far easier. They were still traversing a forest dominated by huge and ancient trees, but the trees were now much further apart and the forest floor, though still broken and bisected by the giant roots, was now more open and with a clear path.

Around the party, as there had been from the very beginning of their journey that morning, the Brownies had been gathering. There had been a few dozens at the start, which had grown to a few hundred, and as the party neared the Brownie meeting place, there were several thousands of them. All around the party, in small but constantly growing groups, the Brownies lined the route. They stood atop the great roots of the trees, as if standing in some grandstand to watch a game. They climbed the trees, using every knot or branch to gain a vantage point from which to view the Dwarves and humans in their forest.

For Tangle Wood was their forest, a Brownie forest. Dwarves would never go there, unless they were forced to do so. But there were other things in the world apart from Dwarves and humans; the Brownies knew this. And those other things cared not for the forest or for any living thing that dwelt within.

It was that that one thing which had forced the Brownies to consent to Dwarves and humans being in their heartland, and not just their heartland, but to the very centre of the Brownies world. For, although they did not know it, the Dwarves and Humans were being taken to the place that the Brownies called Naissance, in the common tongue, the place, according to Brownie legend, where the world began.

Every tree, every branch of every tree, was filled with Brownies. Thousand upon thousands more watched the party's passing. The Brownies spoke with each other, chattering away in that strange tongue of theirs, until the whole of the forest appeared to be filled with the sounds of scratching twigs and whistling in the leaves. Like some unnatural, endless static, the sound of the Brownies hissed and crackled all about them. And the closer the party came to Naissance, the louder it became.

Dwarves, being Dwarves, walked with their heads held proud and high, but it was more a case of putting on a show of their stiff, stubborn necks rather than anything else. If you watched them, watched them very closely, you would see that the eyes of the Dwarves were looking all about them, fleeting every which way at the horde of tiny figures that were surrounding them. True, twelve Dwarves could take on many times their own number, and it was also true that the Brownies had granted them safe passage. But what if things went ill? What if safe passage was nothing more than a lure? What then? Twelve Dwarves and four Humans could not possibly withstand so many. All the Dwarves could do was look proud, look strong, and hope for the best.

Eventually the party arrived at the edge of a glade. The massive trees that they had been passing all day gave way to a more open area. It was not a clearing, as such, for there were many smaller trees within the glade. The glade was a flat area, ringed by the huge trees, shielded almost, and was 300 yards across. It was circular and, on the south side, sloped gently down towards a stream. Within the circle, formed into concentric rings, were numerous smaller trees. There were willows, nearest the water's edge, and Hazel trees, Beech, Ash and Oak, along with a profusion of fruit trees. In each of the myriad of trees there were hundreds of Brownies and something else also. In each of the trees there were strange-looking wicker baskets. At first glance the Dwarves could be forgiven for thinking that they might be bee hives, for they were very much alike in size and appearance. But, on closer inspection, small door and window openings could be seen. These had to be the Brownies' homes, unless someone had placed thousands of doll's houses up in the trees simply for the fun of it.

At the entrance to the glade a party of Brownies stood guard, their bodies painted green and earthy brown, their hair matted back with mud and woven with grasses and twigs. In their tiny hands they held spears, which were tipped with sharpened flint. Around their waists were belts and, tucked into them, were blowpipes and flint daggers.

The escort of Fox-riders moved to one side and the leader of the guards stepped forward, holding up his tiny hand as he said, as loudly as he could, 'Halts. Who wishesis to enter thisss worlds.' As he said these words the line of Brownies behind him brought their spears up, holding them in both hands, and levelling them at the approaching party.

Balelin held his hand up and signalled the party to halt.

He stepped down from the wagon, walked slowly towards the Brownie guard commander and then, with several paces still between the two, Balelin stopped and gave a low and very dignified bow.

'I am Balelin of the Dwarves of Bennith Dure. I and my companions beg your leave to enter. We come as friend and mean none harm.' So saying Balelin bowed for a second time.

'Ifs you be friends what purposese bringed you heres?' the commander asked.

'We wish to speak with the Most Great and Honoured Council. To speak with them and to be nourished by their great wisdom,' Balelin replied respectfully.

Kate was next to her brother, their two horses standing side by side at the rear of the party. She leaned over towards him, whispering, 'Somebody's got an ego problem, don't you think?'

The guard commander seemed pleased with Balelin's responses, but the Brownie Fox-riders, being the acutely sharp-eared individuals that they were, shot Kate a very disapproving stare.

Seeing the Brownies looking at her, Kate bowed her head, 'Sorry,' she whispered.

'Ifs comed as friends thens Mosts Great and Honoureds Councils will meets with yous,' the homunculus commander informed Balelin. 'Buts no weaponsis may yous carrys.'

Again Balelin bowed, his hand on his chest. 'We thank you and we thank the Most Great and Honoured Council.'

With that the two, Balelin and the little commander, parted. Balelin returned to the wagons where all the others had been standing watching the exchange.

'No weapons?' Cromlin said, more than just a little suspicious.

Balelin gave him a reassuring smile. 'We must learn to trust, Cromlin my friend. Besides, what weapons do we need, we have safe passage and we have Grizlan with us.'

'Then let us hope that their honour stands a little higher than they do,' Cromlin muttered.

'Indeed,' Balelin agreed. 'Now then my friends, all weapons in the wagons. And no holding back. I have given my word.'

The expressions on the faces of the Dwarves told the truth of how they felt: none of them liked the idea one little bit. But they all, some more reluctantly, abided by Balelin's ruling and began to divest themselves of the weapons they carried. The canvases of the wagons were pulled back, and each of the Dwarves stepped forward, placing what weapons they had inside, and for some that took quite a while.

Axes were pulled from their belts and placed into the wagons. Swords were unbuckled, so too the daggers which were pulled from inside of jerkins, out of boot tops, and from up sleeves, and all other manner of hiding places. Some fished about in their pockets, pulling out knuckledusters and short stabbing knives. Even when they had finished Balelin glared at some of the Dwarves.

'Cromlin, Harrlin? Don't hold back now.'

Harrlin drew out a short-bladed knife from his left sleeve saying, 'But it's for eating with.'

'Harrlin,' Balelin insisted.

Harrlin tossed the knife into the wagon, along with another from inside his jacket. Then Cromlin, after glancing at Harrlin and back at Balelin, produced a couple more knives he had been hiding within his clothing and tossed them into the wagon.

'I don't like this,' Cromlin protested as he pitched his final weapon onto the pile. 'I feel naked.'

Balelin grinned. 'And we are all thankful that you are not.'

Finally, when all the weapons were in the wagons and the covers tied down, Balelin turned to the guard commander saying, 'We entrust our wagons to your safe keeping.'

The little commander drew himself up to his full height, all two feet of it. 'Wes guards with our lives. Follows pleases.' The guard commander bowed, turned and led the way into glade.

Balelin walked in front, flanked by his granddaughter on his left and Kate on his right. 'Please walk with me, child,' he said to Kate softly. 'You and I shall be doing the talking here.'

'I don't know if I can,' Kate muttered in reply. 'I don't know what to say, and even if I did, I don't know if I can find the right words.'

Balelin smiled sympathetically. 'What to say? That is easy, speak the truth.'

As Balelin, Kate, and Grizlan walked into the glade, the rest of the party followed in behind them. The Dwarves walked in loose pairs, with Ed and Liz bringing up the rear.

Ed looked about him for a short while, deep in thought, and scrutinising the gathering of Brownies that surrounded them. At length he turned to Liz, 'I wonder why Balelin wants Kate to speak.'

'You know, Ed, for an intelligent man you can be quite thick at times,' Liz said.

'Meaning what?'

'Meaning, Ed darling, can you not see what Balelin is up to?'

Ed shrugged, a blank expression crossing his face.

'Meaning Balelin wants Kate to say how she was unjustly attacked yesterday.'

'Well that much I know, sweetheart,' Ed said caustically.

Liz heaved a heavy sigh. 'You really don't get it, do you Ed? Balelin wants Kate to say how she was wronged by the Brownies. Just like the Brownies have been wronged many times themselves, no doubt. Don't you see? He's going after the sympathy vote.' Liz grabbed Ed's arm and held him back for a moment, turning to face him as saying, in a sharp but hushed tone, 'He's using her Ed. Balelin is using our daughter to get what he wants. I just wonder who else he is prepared to use.'

'No,' Ed dismissed Liz's comments with a shrug. 'Balelin just wants to get his people to their new home sure. But he seems all right by me.'

'You're always the same, Edward Deeks,' Liz admonished him. 'Too damn trusting by half.'

'And you are too cynical and suspicious,' Ed retorted.

Liz was silent for a moment. A tear moistened her eye. 'I seem to recall us say things like that to each more than once.'

Ed bit his lip. 'I know, sweetheart, we've said that and a whole lot more besides. I'm sorry. I shouldn't be so trusting, you're right.'

Liz shook her head slowly; no longer able to look at Ed, she cast her eyes down. 'Ed, when we get home . . . I mean when we get away from this place,'

'Don't say it, Liz. Please,' Ed cut her off. 'Let's get through this first; then we can think about what happens to us. Right now let's just try and get us all out of here, wherever here is.'

At the centre of the glade sitting about a foot high was a raised mound. On top of it was a wooden platform, planked with fine polished timbers and intricately carved posts that held up a thatched roof. For all the world it looked like an architect's model, and the six daintily carved chairs that sat upon it looked like something out of a doll's house. But this was no model or doll's house: it was the focal point, the very heart of the Brownie's world. These were the seats of the Most Great and Honoured Council. Before this mound, which while tiny to both Dwarves and humans, would have towered over all the Brownies, several logs had been placed. The party was escorted to these logs and asked to sit.

The Most Great and Honoured Council of the Brownies consisted of six diminutive figures representing the six clans. There was Nettlestem of the Rowan Tree clan and father of Twiziltwig. The next was called Holly Leaf of the Bubbling Waters clan, a very old, grey-haired Brownie who partly walked with a stick and was partly supported by a younger male Brownie that remained by his side always. Mertalberry was of the Bramble Fields clan. He appeared to be head of the council as other five bowed to him, as indeed did all the Brownies assembled. Thistlerod of the Ash Tree clan and Willow Root of the Willow Tree clan were two more. They, just like the others already mentioned, were old yet keen-eyed and possessing all their faculties. The final member of the council was however younger, and from the cape of glossy feathers he wore, they guessed he was one of the Boar-riders. This was Oakbranch of the Fern Hollow clan.

It then fell to Balelin to introduce all of his party, and with a pomp and magnificence that equalled the introductions of the Brownies, he went about it with great relish. First he presented Grooflin, son of Mayfund, and his own grandson. Next was Harrlin Quick-hammer, son of Baldren Tunnel-master and Shamlin Doubleaxe son of Gloy, not forgetting his brother Dannit. And so it went on, Balelin naming each of the Dwarves in turn, a process that took some considerable time. As their names were given, each dwarf stood, bowed to the council, and sat back down.

When Balelin had finished he had named everyone, everyone that is but Ed and his family. After naming all the Dwarves, Balelin paused for a moment, before saying to the council, 'There are four others travelling with our party. They are dwarf-friends that we met on the road and who may stay with us for as long, or as little, as they wish. I will not name them but, as they are their own people and may do as they will, I will let them name themselves.' With that Balelin looked at Ed, nodding his head to indicate that he should now speak.

Taken by surprise Ed quickly cleared his throat and stood up. He went to speak but, suddenly remembering where he was, he paused, bowed to the council, and then said. 'By your leave your honours. This is my wife, Elizabeth Deeks, Doctor Elizabeth Deeks.'

Liz rose and gave a small bow. 'Pleased to meet you, Your Honours.'

'That is my son, Jason Cameron Deeks.'

'Sirs,' Jay said as he bowed and sat down again.

'My daughter Katherine Estelle Deeks, Kate for short.'

Kate was too nervous to stand properly. She pushed herself up but, sort of half standing half sitting, she gave a little bow without saying anything.

'And I am Edward . . . Ed Deeks Your Honours.' He bowed again and sat back down. With the introductions over Ed allowed himself to relax: at least he began to relax, until Liz leaned slowly over, whispering in his ear.

'Told you, Balelin is putting some distance between us and his Dwarves.'

Ed's head spun round to look at her, but Liz didn't look at him; she was watching Balelin as he got up to speak again, watching him very intently.

'Great and Most Honoured Council members,' Balelin began. 'We come here by mischance. We are, as you can see, nothing more than a small party of Dwarves travelling to our new home. But alas, because of circumstances, we were forced to take other roads, roads that have lead us to this place. We ask nothing of this honoured council, other than to be allowed to pass in peace.'

'And yets yous comed into the world uninviteds,' snapped Oakbranch. 'Comed and stoppeds, nots one nights buts twos. Thats against laws.'

The glade erupted at that, filling the air with the sounds of hissing and scratching as the Brownies voiced their agreement with Oakbranch's words.

Holding his hand up, to still the noise around him, Balelin said, 'We were forced to seek the protection of the woods. We had no knowledge of your laws but were fugitives in a hostile land.' He fixed his eyes on Holy Leaf. 'For many days now we have been sought by our enemy, an enemy that is enemy of the Brownies also.'

Again the glade was filled with sound, but this time it was like a soft whistling in the leaves. The party could not guess what it meant, perhaps sympathy, perhaps understanding, or perhaps something much less benign. Whatever it signified it was soon silenced again as Balelin went on.

'We Dwarves do not fear our enemy. Indeed we have fought them many times and many times we have crushed them. But our charge this time prevents us from seeking open battle.'

Holy Leaf raised a frail hand and, in a low, nearly inaudible, voice said, 'Wes knows the enemies you talks offs. Wes too hads fought thems.'

'Yeses,' snapped Oakbranch brusquely. 'Ands nows theys brings more goblins follwings afters thems.'

Oakbranch's words caused another enormous gasp to escape from the Brownies and filled the air with sounds of chattering and scratching.

'We did not bring the goblins here,' Balelin protested.

'Dids,' Oakbranch protested. 'Fours time fours, and fours more comeds intos the world lasted nights.' Oakbranch waited as the sounds of shock and anguish echoed round the glade. 'Theys comed lookings for yous. Comed with swords and fires. Comed killings and burnding.'

Once more the glade erupted with angry noises, noises that chilled the stoutest of the Dwarves. Oakbranch stood for a long time, his tiny arms outstretched, as he tried to quieten the protesting Brownie crowd.

'Wes killided thems. Killided them all. Wes, the Fern Hollow clan, wes killided them alls deads.'

A great cheer went up among the Brownies. Then Oakbranch held up his hands again.

'Buts,' he said as the gathering calmed down again. 'Buts wes losts manys warrior. Evens nows, as Mosts Greats ands Honoureded Councils sits and talkings, me clans is speakings the lasts times names ofs our fallens.' He turned, facing the other members of the council, adding vehemently, 'Theys bringed this dooms. They musts pays. Its is the laws.'

Holy Leaf raised his arm for the crowd to be silent, but Oakbranch had whipped them up and it took some time before the Brownies settled down again. At length the old Brownie said to Balelin, 'Yous has bringed deaths and fires to the worlds, Dwarves, a charges that's means deaths. How says yous to thises?'

'We did not bring the goblins to the world,' Balelin began.

'Dids, dids brings thems,' Oakbranch insisted. 'Goblinses, Dwarvess, Gnomess, same same. All bads. Alls nots wanteded in worlds. All shoulds dies.'

Once more a great cheer went up from the surrounding Brownies, followed by a chanting that echoed around and around the glade.

'I guess this means we're not invited to dinner,' Shamlin muttered to Polmet.

The fat dwarf frowned, muttering a reply, 'I think we might be dinner, if we are not careful.'

'Please, please,' Balelin said and then, much louder to make himself heard over the clamour of enraged Brownies. 'Please. If I may speak.'

Mertalberry stood, holding up his hands and making an unearthly and ear-slitting screeching sound. It was a sound like nothing the Dwarves had heard before but, almost at once, the other Brownies in the glade fell silent.

With the rumpus of the chattering Brownies stilled, Mertalberry spoke, his voice clear and measured, 'Lets the dwarf says whats hes wills.'

Balelin placed a hand upon his chest as bowed his head. 'I thank you,' he began in a low, courteous tone. 'We grieve for you, Oakbranch.'

Oakbranch stared at Balelin and snorted a dismissive reply.

'We grieve for your loss and for the many who have lost kinfolk. But it was not us that brought the goblins upon you.' Balelin went on, 'Outside of your world goblins are multiplying, many times many more. And not just goblins, but other things more evil and wicked than you have yet met, I fear.'

'Thens wes killided thems too,' Oakbranch shouted.

'May be,' Balelin replied sharply. 'And may be they kill many more of your people.'

The Brownies all howled at that, perhaps in anger, perhaps in alarm: it was so difficult to understand their language. But, as Balelin went on, they quickly quietened down, listening keenly to what he was saying.

'We Dwarves do not want to harm the Brownies. We do not want anything from your world. We only want for you that which we want for ourselves: to live long lives and to live in peace.'

That brought a murmur of approval from the gathering but an expression of sheer distain from Oakbranch. 'Dwarveses not harms Brownies. Dwarveses nots wants Brownie world. Dwarveses lieds. Dwarveses just big Gnomes and Gnomes wants to takes Brownies worlds. Wes alls knows thisis,' Oakbranch hissed his reply.

'Then you know wrong,' Balelin snapped back. 'We came here by chance. Not because we had any intent against the Brownies. But because we found other roads barred to us, we were forced to take this path, and after talking with Twiziltwig, we were granted safe passage through your world.'

'Twiziltwig cannots gives safes passages,' Oakbranch cut in. 'Twiziltwig nots Brownies councils. Onlys Brownies councils mays give safes passages.'

Holly Leaf nodded in agreement. 'Oakbranch speaks trues,' he said. Then, turning to face Balelin directly, he asked, 'Whys yous nots asked Mosts Greats and Honoureds Council?'

'How do we ask?' Ed said, getting slowly to his feet.

'Musts speaks with council,' Oakbranch replied dismissively. 'Thats the laws.'

'So we cannot enter the woods unless we speak with the council?' Ed asked to clarify the matter.

'Yesis,' Oakbranch retorted. 'Isis laws.'

'But to speak with the council we have to enter the wood,' Ed argued gently.

'Cans nots,' Oakbranch snapped. 'Againsts the laws.'

'But that makes no sense,' Ed exclaimed. 'If we cannot enter the wood, then we cannot speak with the Most Great and Honoured Council, and if we cannot speak with the Most Great and Honoured Council, then how do we get permission to enter the woods?'

Oakbranch stared at Ed for a minute while he tried to puzzle out what he had been asked. Finally he spoke, spitting his words out rudely, 'Nots point. Needs nots make senses. Its laws.'

'Yes but,' Ed argued calmly, 'the law has to make sense or else what is the point of the law. For example, if the Most Great and Honoured Council made a law to say that rain may not fall on a holiday, then that would make no sense: the rain will fall when the rain will fall.'

'Ifs councils say rains no falls, thens rains no falls,' Oakbranch replied. 'Most Greats and Honourables Councils is makes laws and alls musts obeys.'

'But how can the rain obey?' Ed asked politely.

'Alls musts, laws is laws. Alls musts obeys,' Oakbranch declared. 'Ifs rains nots obeys then is punisheded.'

'And how would you do that exactly?' Ed enquired.

'Yeses,' Holly Leaf asked, 'hows exactilly, Oakbranch?'

'Mes not knows,' Oakbranch said. 'Ifs councils says is thens councils say how punishes.'

'Buts yous is councils alsos,' Holly Leaf pointed out.

'Thens . . .wells . . .ifs...' Oakbranch stammered as he glanced about him for support; seeing none to be had, he suddenly shouted, 'Nots point. The laws is the laws.'

'If I may,' Ed said tactfully, 'yes the law is the law. Oakbranch is correct in that.' A comment that made the little warrior and council member smile broadly. 'And I have no wish to embarrass him. I am sure that he is both a very brave and very wise member of this most illustrious body. However, surely a law has to make sense, and just as it would be foolish to tell the rain not to fall, it is also foolish to say only the Council might give leave for people to be in the wood when being in the wood is the only way to speak with the Most Great and Honourable Council.' Ed raised his hand and struck a most dramatic stance. 'Gentle Brownies of the Most Great and Honourable Council, I humbly submit that no law has been broken as Twiziltwig, that great and brave warrior, gave permission for our party to enter the world and in doing so he was speaking with the voice of the council. For he, Twiziltwig, was most wise and knew that we came here in peace and it was the only way that we could come to this place and speak with you, The Most Great and Honourable Council,' so saying Ed gave the council a deep bow, then sat back down.

'Well put, sweetheart,' Liz whispered in his ear.

'I only hope those guys think so,' Ed whispered back.

For a short while there was silence in the glade. Finally Holly Leaf rose and told the gathering that the council was to withdraw and consider what they had heard. In the meantime the party was to remain at the council mound and were, for the time being, prisoners of the Brownies. With that, everyone rose, bowed to each other, and the council made its way off the mound and over to an old Ash tree. A staircase had been built on the outside of the tree and this they climbed until they came to a large knot hole. The council members went inside the knot hole, into the tree, and shut the door, which filled the knot hole, behind them.

'Well done, Longshanks,' Balelin said, once all the Brownie council was cloistered behind their door. 'I am afraid that hearing of the battle between the Brownies and the Goblins last night threw me a little.'

'Me also,' Ed replied. 'The only question left is, who were the Goblins hunting, you or me?'

Balelin shrugged. 'No way of knowing that. Leastways not now with them all 'killided'. And then again there is no way to be sure that they were hunting anybody. Goblins being what Goblins are, they might just have been out for some mischief and decided to have their sport with the Brownies.'

'If that was their intention, then it would appear that they picked on the wrong Brownies,' Ed smiled.

'Indeed,' Balelin returned the smile. 'But, to the matter at hand. Ed Longshanks, it would appear that you speak as well as you fight. What say you take over negotiations with the Brownie council?'

'I don't know,' Ed said hesitantly. 'You know more about these little guys than I do. You understand them.'

'True,' Balelin agreed. 'But you yourself heard them. Brownies think of Dwarves as nothing other than big Gnomes. And they hate Gnomes more than they hate Goblins.'

'But they don't hate humans,' Ed offered.

A pained expression crossed Balelin's old and deeply creased face. 'Well they don't hate them as much.'

'Great,' Ed groaned.

'Yes,' whispered Liz, 'and if everything goes badly, everybody can just blame you.'

'So no pressure,' Ed said, forcing a smile.

As the Brownie council sat in secret conclave, food and drink was brought for the party, even if in doing so a whole new host of problems came to light.

To begin with the Brownies did not have bowls or cup big enough for the Dwarves, even the largest of the Brownie cooking pot was little more than a small cup in the hands of a dwarf. And while one small rabbit might feed an entire family of Brownies for two days, a dwarf could cheerfully consume six rabbits at one go and think of them as nothing more than his starters. Then there was the Brownie stew of roots and herbs, which whilst perfectly able to satisfy the hunger of a Brownie, was, to a dwarf's taste, only fractionally better than tea, and a very weak tea at that. Worst of all, from the dwarf's standpoint, was the Brownie bread. They were small, tiny really, about the size of a dainty biscuit, and a stale and rather tasteless biscuit at that.

In the beginning the Brownies had brought the food, set upon the ground before the Dwarves, and stood proudly beside the fare they were offering to their 'guests'. Each of the party was given large bowlful, or rather the largest bowls that the Brownies had, of stew. Beside this there were four loaves of bread, and a half rabbit.

The Dwarves thanked the Brownies; however, the expressions of their faces told the Brownies that this might not be enough. Quickly the Brownies ran off to bring more. Every large cooking pot in the glade was pressed into service. Every storage barrel and jar not already being used was brought forth and utilized as a cup for wine or stew.

It was all most confusing: on the one hand the party were prisoners of the Brownies, but prisoners treated like honoured guests.

Meanwhile Balelin had taken Ed to one side: the two sitting on their own as the old dwarf explained as much as he could about the Brownies in whatever time they might have.

At last, with the meal over, the Most Great and Honoured Council of the Brownies emerged from their conclave, and the debate began anew.

Balelin and Ed stood centre stage before the mound, and as she passed on her way back to her seat, Liz paused to wish Ed luck. She kissed him gently then, whispering in his ear, 'Nice move that, on Balelin's part; now all our lives are in your hands.'

'Liz please,' Ed gasped, shocked by how suspicious his wife had become of the old dwarf and how she could make light of it too.

Liz pulled away from him and took her seat, mouthing to Ed, 'Told you so.'

Once more the members took their seats, all that is but for Holly Leaf who stood at the edge of the platform, clearing his throat and holding up his hand. He faced the party saying, 'Wes, The Most Great and Honoured Council, have agreed.'

The whole gale fell silent as everyone, Brownie, dwarf, and human waited to hear the decision.

Holly Leaf went on, 'Twiziltwig acts right. Hes saids the party mights come into the world ifs Most Greats and Honoured Council agrees. Hes alsos askids Most Greats and Honoured Council for us agrees. Wes agrees.'

'Thank you,' Ed said, bowing to the council.

'Waits,' Holly Leaf said sharply before Ed had finished his bow. 'Wes agrees nows. Buts yous entered world before wes agrees so wes musts banished yous.'

Ed was more than a little puzzled. 'If I understand you correctly,' he said slowly, trying to comprehend what he had just been told, 'we have permission to enter the world but, we are banished from it.'

'Yeses,' Holly Leaf said as he took his seat. 'Yous are free to enters but are banished.'

'Thank you for clearing that up,' Ed said, adding to himself, 'I think.'

'Stills matters thats Dwarveses bringed Goblins,' Oakbranch shouted as he got to his feet. 'Dwarveses bringed Goblins, Dwarveses bringed deaths to Brownies. Dwarveses must paysed.'

Holly Leaf nodded his head. 'Verys serious matters. Verys serious.'

Again the Brownies gathered in the glade murmured and muttered their agreement: bringing death into the world was a very serious matter indeed.

Ed raised his hand, turning slowly to face all the gathered Brownies before he spoke. 'Most Great and Honoured Council,' Ed began. 'May I ask Oakbranch some questions?'

Holly Leaf nodded his agreement as did all the other council members.

'Brave Oakbranch,' Ed began, sure that a little flattery would not go amiss. 'You said that many of your warriors were killed in this fight.'

'Yeses, manys many.'

'Then for that, we all grieve with you, and with your loss.' Ed paused as a small murmur of agreement went round the glade. 'And this is not the first time you have fought the Goblins?'

'Nos,' Oakbranch stated proudly. 'Manys times theys comes. Manys many times wes killeds thems.'

'And do they come more often now?'

'Sometimes mores, sometimes less. Wes killeds thems all the same sames.'

'I see,' Ed said slowly. 'These Goblins must be stupid to keep coming.'

'Nots stupid nows,' Oakbranch said proudly. 'Alls deads nows.'

'And they always come from the same place?'

'Yeses,' Oakbranch laughed. 'Theys comes buts nots go backs. Alls deads. No gos back whens deads.'

The crowd of Brownies cheered at that and Oakbranch grinned broadly at the cheering for his and his warriors deeds.

Ed waited, letting the cheers die down before he said, 'But if they come from the same place, and if they come often, and attack at the same place, then surely we have no way of knowing who they were after. These Goblins might have just as much been after you as after us.'

'No,' Oakbranch shouted. 'Yous comes then Goblins comes. You bringeds them.'

'But you just said that the Goblins have come many times before,' Ed reminded Oakbranch. 'If they had come before, many times before, then last night might have just been another raid. One of many.'

'No,' Oakbranch shouted again, but the other members of the council were nodding their heads in agreement with Ed.

'Truly,' Ed said loudly, hushing the increasingly noisy Brownie crowd. 'Truly we are sorry for all the brave Brownies that have been lost fighting the Goblins. But rather than blaming each other we should be trying to come together to fight the Goblins as allies.'

Ed's comments brought another sound from the crowd. Partly they cheered at the idea, but partly they voiced their suspicion. However the crowd did not influence Oakbranch; his mind was set.

'Whats know yous ofs fighting Goblins,' Oakbranch hissed. 'Oakbranch know, Oakbranch fights manys many times.' Then his anger began to get the better of him and he turned it on the crowd of Brownies watching the council. 'Yous nots know. Its wes that fights. Mes and mys clans that fights. Wes keeps yous safe. Nots theses big gnomes, nots evens thisis councils. Wes.'

'Oakbranch,' Holly Leaf snapped loudly.

But the young Brownie would not be stilled. Oakbranch turned on the council, hissing and spitting at them as he cursed them in their own Brownie tongue. The party may not have understood the words that Oakbranch used but, from the way he pointed at the other council members, the way he hissed and crackled at them, even pulling a knife from his belt and waving it in their faces, they knew the exchange was not a pleasant one.

Finally Oakbranch spit at the feet of Holly Leaf, an action that brought a dismayed gasp from the crowd, then he turned and stormed off the platform. As he left many more Brownies joined him, jumping down from tree and branch and causing many small arguments within the crowd as they departed.

Holly Leaf was on his feet, his arms raised in an attempt to regain order. Finally, after Oakbranch and his clansmen had left, the crowd quietened down. When all was still, Holly Leaf again took his seat, asking Ed to continue with his case, which he did, at some great length.

# Chapter 10

## Grassland and Grog

Night was upon the party when they once more climbed onto their wagons and horses. The debate with the Brownies, and indeed the trial, for that was what it had descended into, had gone as well as it could have. Ed had argued with Oakbranch and the other council members skilfully, though it had taken a long time, and several conclaves by the council, before they came to their final decision. And it was a typical legal decision in that it gave a little to everyone and satisfied nobody.

The Dwarves had entered Tangle Wood without malice which, everybody agreed with, and Twiziltwig had given them permission to stay and meet with the council. But, as Twiziltwig was not a council member his permission could not stand and the party had to leave. Further, if the party wished to enter Tangle Wood, then they must ask permission of the council, and until that permission came, they would have to wait on the edge of the wood. But as the Dwarves had so clearly trespassed in the first place, intentionally or otherwise, they were to be banished from the wood and must not enter for ten winters, even with permission of the council. As to who brought the goblin attack upon the Brownies, as there were no goblins left alive to say, no one could be truly blamed for the attack. They could after all have been looking for Ed, or for the Dwarves or, and just as likely, merely out to cause havoc with the Brownies for their own sport.

Oakbranch was not at all happy with this and made his feelings known by storming off the council mound, gathering his boar-riders together and departing the glade in a most dramatic fashion.

And so it was all over. The party would have to leave Tangle Wood by the quickest paths and not return for ten years. For their part, the Brownies would not be friends with humans, and could not be friends with Dwarves, which was very much to Balelin's disappointment. Another disappointment was the council's attitude towards Kate. She had been attacked yes but, as she was trespassing at the time, the council insisted that that the attack was justified and that was the end of it.

'Sorry it didn't go better,' Ed said to Balelin.

But the old dwarf smiled at him, saying, 'You did very well, my friend.' He climbed up on to the wagon next to his granddaughter adding, 'It takes many years to undo the mistrust of ages. You have made a beginning, a very fine beginning.'

Ed gazed at the old dwarf for a long moment before saying, 'I suppose so. At least I got the dialogue started even if the outcome was not what you were hoping for.'

The Brownies led the party away from the glade. In front, Twiziltwig and his Fox-riders, behind them the Wildcat-riders, and, on either side, dozens of guards with their flint spears and knifes. Many more of the Brownies filled the woods, scampering over every tree root and climbing every branch to watch them go. The Brownies made torches to light the way as did the many Brownies in the trees beyond the party, until the wood appeared to be brimming to overflowing with thousands of tiny torch lights.

And so the party travelled until at length they came to the eastern edge of Tangle Wood. Here Twiziltwig and his riders bid the party a last farewell. He dismounted and came to the wagon carrying Balelin, bowing and saying, 'Yous must leaves the woods by firsts lights: the

Mosts Greats and Honoureds Councils saids so. Yous mays nots hunts nors takes foods from woods, nor cuts woods for fires.'

Balelin returned Twiziltwig's bow. 'We understand, my small friend. But, perhaps in the future, we may meet again and on better terms.'

'Perhapsis,' Twiziltwig replied. With that the two groups parted.

The party travelled for another hour, reaching open country shortly before sunrise. The air was chilly, and a gentle breeze blew from the north, carrying with it the faint scent of summer blossoms. Around them, as far as the eye could see, there was an ocean of tall grass, dotted everywhere with wild flowers that erupted with bright colours and sweet fragrances as the sun rose higher.

Towards the south the plains sloped down before rising again into low gentle hills. Small stands of trees dotted the low valley floor, following it eastward for some considerable way. There was also game aplenty in those sweeping grasslands, rabbits, and hares where everywhere and, with the Tangle Wood now far behind them, the Dwarves took the opportunity to replenish their depleted larder.

Pausing for a short time, the Dwarves took crossbows and quivers of bolts out from under the canvas. Then, spreading out from the wagons, they began hunting.

Every now and then the rhythmic turning and squeaking of the wagon wheels was interrupted by the abrupt twang of a crossbow and a sharp hiss as another bolt was loosed off. Not that every bolt found its mark. Often the dwarf that had shot was forced to make the fruitless walk to find his bolt again. But enough did find their marks so that the wagons soon filled with a supply of rabbits and hare sufficient to satisfy the hungriest of Dwarves.

Possibly the best shot among the Dwarves was Polmet; he had already bagged ten or more rabbits close to the wagons before venturing a little further afield. He and Dannit, after tossing two more rabbits into the wagon, set off a little to the south in search of additional game. For the remainder of the morning, till the sun was high in the sky, Polmet and Dannit hunted. They walked parallel with the wagons, but a good way off, never going as far as to be out of sight of the wagons, but far enough so that the wagons' noise did not disturb their prey. And when they returned, they brought with them twenty good-sized rabbits, enough to feed several very hungry Dwarves. They also brought back word that there was a narrow stream at the valley floor and that the fast-flowing water was both clear and refreshing.

Balelin decided then that the party, which had after all been up the whole night, would stop in the shade of the next stand of trees and there they would rest a while before pushing on, a decision that was welcomed by all.

So they made camp. Swiftly, as only seasoned travellers can, the Dwarves had every necessary task underway. Wood was gathered and a fire lit. Water was brought from the stream to fill the kettles. Rabbits were skinned and roasted. Horses and ponies were unsaddled or unharnessed and taken to the stream where they drank heartily. In a short time, a very short time, the whole of the party was sitting down to a plentiful meal. Balelin even decreed that, as they had come through Tangle Wood successfully, very much to Ed's skill as an orator, a flagon of ale each would not be inappropriate.

Again the wagons were opened; wooden flagons and a small barrel of ale were brought forth. The party gathered round the fire as the flagons were filled and passed out.

'A toast,' Grooflin called, raising his flagon high. 'A toast to our Lord Balelin.'

All the other Dwarves cheerfully concurred and raised their flagons also.

But Balelin held up his hand saying, 'No, my friends. We should drink a toast to our new friend, Ed the Longshanks. For it was he and his fine, eloquent words that delivered us from Tangle Wood.'

The Dwarves looked at each other, nodding their approval and muttering words of agreement.

'To the Longshanks,' they exclaimed as one, raising their flagons high and drinking to Ed's health.

'You're embarrassing me,' Ed laughed, adding, 'but thank you all the same.' Ed took a long, deep swig of ale as the Dwarves cheered him on. Perhaps he should have been a tiny bit more cautious, for dwarf ale is noted not just for its rich full flavour, but also for its strength, and the party was drinking a particularly intoxicating brew known as Old Noggin.

Old Noggin was renowned among both Dwarves and humans. It had the smooth creamy flavour of lightly toasted malt on first drinking, with a delicate and slightly nutty after taste. All together it was a very agreeably brew and indeed was the most popular among the Dwarves. But Old Noggin was deceptively strong, as Ed soon discovered.

Ed didn't say anything; he didn't have to: his eyes said it for him. After taking such a large draught of Old Noggin, Ed stared at the flagon as if something in it had bitten him. He rocked unsteadily on his feet as he let out a horse gasp. 'Strong that,' he croaked: a comment that made the Dwarves chuckle and toast him again.

Several toasts later and the barrel was empty. There was nothing left for the Dwarves to do but get another barrel from the wagon and start toasting each other all over again. They toasted Polmet for his skills as a hunter. They toasted Dannit for being such a good helper, and toasted Grizlan for her skill at wagon driving, and toasted Cromlin for his skill as a sword maker and Shamlin, well for being Shamlin. In fact the Dwarves toasted everyone and everything for just about any reason that sprang to mind. And three barrels of Old Noggin later, when they could neither think of who or what to toast next, and when nearly all of the Dwarves couldn't even stand anymore, it was decided that they should perhaps spend the night by the stream.

And so they did. They gathered round the fire, drinking and eating, and toasting one another all over again. By then Ed was very, very drunk. He tried to get to his feet, only to stumble back again, almost rolling off down the slope and into the stream. Why he tried to stand he could only guess at; he sure as hell could not walk. So Ed sat there, grinning like someone demented, as he drank more of the ale.

'A song,' shouted Grooflin, 'let's have a song.'

'Song, song, song, song,' the others chanted.

Then, through a drunken haze, Ed realised that the Dwarves were in fact chanting at him. Not being much of a singer, and not having the best of voices, Ed was understandably reluctant. But the Dwarves pressed him.

'A song, a song, give us a song.'

Finally Ed gave in. He held up an unsteady hand, burped noisily, then said, 'Right then, right then. I'll give you a song.' He pointed a finger at Grooflin saying, 'But you're, *hic*, next my bearded friend. Right? Right.' Ed cleared his throat. 'Here's a song some friends of mine from England taught me. Great guys. Play rugby, you know. Great, great guys. Strange game they play, but great, *hic*, guys. Its, *hic*, called, The Mayor of Bayswater. Join in when you know the words.'

It was a song that Liz had never heard Ed sing before, and the truth was, had he been sober, he would never have sang it in front of her. For, The Mayor of Bayswater, was not exactly the type of song that should be sung in polite company. But it was just the type of song that the Dwarves could appreciate, and very soon, and very noisily, they were joining Ed in the chorus.

# Chapter 11

## Factor Drayloc

Drayloc had been the factor of Guidepost for six years, factor, bailiff, and under-sheriff if we were to give him his full list of titles. As such he was a man that could do pretty much whatever he wanted to do. And what he wanted most was go right along doing as he had been doing for the past six years.

His position and title, or positions and titles, not only made him his own man, it had also made him a considerably well-off man too. He received three salaries each year, each on their own enough to live comfortably, but the three combined were bounties beyond his dreams.

Drayloc had grown fat from his four incomes: three official and one, very unofficial. Well, everybody skims a bit off the tops, don't they? He often excused himself while pocketing his percentage of the rents and taxes. Yes Drayloc had grown very fat, both figuratively and actually. So what if the odd tenant had to be leant on for more rent? It was their choice to be farmers, wasn't it? And if they couldn't pay, then they had best just learn how to be better farmers. All Drayloc was doing was enforcing the law; that was his job, what he got paid for. It was only right that he got a little extra for all the ill-will people held towards him. He didn't want to be a bad man, but the law was the law and it had to be kept.

Drayloc had only just finished his rounds. Part of his duties as under-sheriff was to make sure that the town gates were closed and bolted every night. He had to walk the town walls, check each of the gates, and check that the town guard was sober enough to do their duty for the night.

'Many people think me greedy,' Drayloc thought to himself as he walked the walls, 'but look at them. They're all tucked up in bed and I am still working; working hard to keep them safe.' Under such circumstances, who could argue with Drayloc the factor, bailiff and under-sheriff, helping himself to just that tiny little bit more?

Drayloc reached his home after his nightfall rounds. His house was on the edge of the market square, next to the Jolly Shepard, and in truth, there was little difference in size between the two buildings. It had not always been so. When Drayloc first took up his many appointments his house, gifted free of rent as long as he held office, was little more than three ground floor rooms. There was a front room, part sitting room part rent office, a bedroom, and a small kitchen at the back.

That had been six years ago, and a lot had changed since then. The first extension had been to the side. So what if it had meant knocking down that smelly old bakery? Their bread was never that good anyway. But the extension did allow Drayloc to build himself a real sitting room with a fine big open fireplace. A new bedroom was also added, along with the most expensive bed he could afford from the best craftsmen in Briloness, the main city of Brildaleshire and the seat of the Lord Marshall of the Western Marches, who was, officially, Brayloc's employer. The kitchen was also expanded, and a new, grand dining room that could seat sixteen guests but which had never seen a single one. With all the rebuilding and remodelling of the house Drayloc had been able to have himself built an in-door-privy. It was the only in-door-privy in the whole of Brildaleshire. Though many locals asked, 'Why have the privy indoors? It must stink the house up something terrible.' But others would smile, and reply that Drayloc would not part with the skin off a turd: an indoor privy proved it.

And Drayloc could be contented that it really hadn't cost that much. After all, there was a good quantity of stone going cheap: least there was once the bakery was pulled down. And labour was easily had, especially after he'd had to evict some farm tenant for not paying their taxes: plenty of out of work labour had come from there.

By the end of his second year in office Drayloc had the largest house in the shire. It was time to think about marrying: he was forty-one and not getting any younger. He also had an eye for a young girl called Gytha, the beautiful daughter of a tenant farmer.

Drayloc fell in love with her from the very first, and like so many men in love, he would do anything for her if she would only agree to be his wife. And Drayloc did; he did do anything he could to make her his. Drayloc told her father that he would lower the rent if Gytha married him. He would forget the taxes for one year. He would not call upon the farmer's sons for unpaid duty as town watch, a position that requires one year's service to the factor unless extended by special order of the local under-sheriff. But, if Gytha did not marry him, well, the law was the law and Drayloc had to uphold the law.

And so, in the second summer of his office, Drayloc married the very pretty Gytha. He was forty-one and head over heels in love, and she was in the full blossom of womanhood, ripe for children, and a very beautiful sixteen. Sadly love was not to last for Drayloc. Gytha died of an uncontrolled internal bleeding only months after her honeymoon. She was buried on her father's farm, but her father and mother were evicted for unpaid rent and taxes, and Gytha's three brothers were killed when, for no reason whatsoever, they attacked Drayloc in the town square. Luckily Drayloc had the guard with him or else things might have gone ill for the factor.

Drayloc did marry again, very shortly afterwards, to a woman called Rafendil: she was more of his age and childless.

Rafendil was already married when Drayloc first took up his positions in Guidepost. She was married to a not very successful farmer called Kendrel, a man known throughout the shire as being fonder of a drink than hard work. Rafendil's marriage was therefore not a happy one, and money was always tight.

Shortly after Drayloc took up his posts Rafendil had to go and see the factor. Kendrel was behind on his rent and Rafendil, being the forthright woman that she was, went to see the factor with the intention of having the rent reduced. Well, the poor woman must have thrown herself on the factor's mercy, not that anybody believed Drayloc had any mercy, but she managed to get an extension on the rent. The poor woman must have begged, for her knees were sore, and her skirts all dusty, by the time she left. Yet some how she managed to talk the factor round, but then many people said how she was good with her tongue.

Well, as things sometimes happen, with Drayloc having a bigger house built, and with Rafendil needing extra money, it only made sense that she should work as his housekeeper cum cleaner. It was an arrangement that suited both of them, and indeed made Drayloc very happy. Often you would see the factor, anxiously waiting for Rafendil to arrive, and getting so very fidgety. When she went to begin her day's work, Drayloc would be pleased to see her, overjoyed almost. He would take her inside the house, obviously to give Rafendil her instructions for the day, a task that could take quite some time. Afterwards Rafendil would see the factor off for his duties at the front door, her knees already dirty from where she had begun to clean the floors. But Drayloc was all smiles and had a positive spring in his step, knowing that his house was being well cared for.

Strange to relate but some species of friendship seemed to have developed between the factor and his housekeeper. At least as far as there can be a friendship between master and servant. And it must have been hard for Rafendil for, the more she did to try and support her husband, working all hours at Drayloc's house, even staying over nights to get right back to work in the morning, the more her husband drank.

Yet there were other times when Drayloc would take Rafendil out hunting: more by way of getting the unfortunate woman's mind off her drunk of a husband at home. But she wasn't a good hunter, nor was Drayloc, come to that. Neither of them ever seemed to bring back much by way of a kill. And the woman was clumsy to boot; every time she went hunting she always managed to fall over somehow and get the back of her skirts all muddy. Drayloc's knees were always dirty too: probably got them that way trying to help the poor woman up.

Gytha never got on with Rafendil. From the time of Gytha's betrothal to Drayloc, up through the wedding, and until she died shortly after, Gytha would not allow Rafendil in the house. But the girl mustn't have been any good at cleaning as Drayloc had to get Rafendil in to clean every time Gytha went to see her father and brothers. But poor Rafendil had to be out, her work done, before the flighty girl got home. Poor Rafendil was even seen having to leave her work and sneak out of Drayloc's back door because Gytha had come home early.

At least Rafendil showed what a good friend she was when Gytha died: staying the night at Drayloc's house to console the poor man in his grief.

Rafendil's misfortunes dogged her though. Shortly after Gytha died Rafendil's husband died also. It was bizarre in the extreme, though perhaps inevitable, that drink should finally do for the man. He had a fresh brew of cider on the way, his best yet; so he reckoned. But somehow, and nobody knows how exactly, but he fell head first into a barrel of the stuff and drowned. Drayloc had taken Rafendil home late after a long day's work and, being so late, stayed the night as her guest. When the two rose the following morning it was to find Rafendil's husband's feet sticking up out of the barrel and the poor man dead.

Naturally there was a full investigation into the death but, as recorded by the under-sheriff, the death was just an accident: what other explanation could there be?

With nowhere else to go, and Drayloc being the good friend that he was, Rafendil moved in to be his housekeeper. And they married two weeks later.

But they made an odd pair. Drayloc was getting fatter by the day, while Rafendil was as thin, if not thinner, than when she was a young girl. Yet they worked well together, perhaps too well when it came to collecting rents and taxes. Some unkind people said of Rafendil that she was forever looking as to how to squeeze the last penny out of every farm rent, ferreting around for every coin. Others, even more unkindly said as how she had the face for it, ferreting that is. And to be fair, Rafendil did have a rather pinched face and small eyes.

Even so, a year after they were married, Drayloc's house was rebuilt again, upwards this time. More bedrooms were added, perhaps for children, but they never came. So Drayloc and Rafendil settled in to a life together: a life of collecting taxes and rents and buying the finer things in life.

There was a never-ending caravan of tradesmen and foodstuff suppliers going to their door, a lot of them having to go more than once to get their money. And then, after that half-goblin shanty sprang up south of Guidepost, there were even more comings and goings at Drayloc's house, and a lot of it at the dead of night.

No one knew what was going on there. Drayloc, if nothing else, knew how to keep a secret. Rafendil, just like her new husband, kept her lips tight shut, a first for her. And so the people of Guidepost could only suppose what may, or may not, be going on.

Around that time Drayloc had the town watch increased: from sixteen to twenty five men. The people were warned to stay within the town walls at night, which they did. Nobody liked the idea of a goblin camp, even if they were half-goblins, on their doorstep. Word was sent to the king, Drayloc assured them, but none came back, and things began to happen.

People found dead or disappeared; livestock gone missing; homes robbed: goods and chattels carried off. Soon people were leaving Guidepost and going off to live with family outside the town. That was when farm walls got higher, and any good man with a bow or sword quickly found steady employment. It got to the stage that you either left Guidepost with everything you had or you stayed indoors and protected it. You couldn't even go a visiting for fear that you would have nothing left when you returned.

And what was the king doing about it? Nothing. And what was the factor doing about it? Getting fatter.

After his rounds Drayloc was sitting down to his meal. He had been looking forward to this: a roast chicken stuffed with sage and apples. It was getting harder to get good meats: not many merchants want to go where there are Goblins. But Rafendil had managed to get a good-size chicken, plenty of potatoes, and fresh cabbage, which she had fried with bacon fat and onions.

They were in the grand dining room: though theirs were the only two settings on a table built for many more. The room was large with fine tapestries hanging on three walls and an ornate fireplace filling most of the other wall. Yet the room was gloomy and joyless. A meagre fire was burning in the hearth, which was insufficient to provide either warmth or much light to the room. On the table, next to the food, there were two candles, and they offered the only real light by which to dine.

'Busy night, husband?' Rafendil said, setting the meal before the corpulent factor.

Drayloc sighed heavily as he planted his considerable bulk in the chair at the head of the vast and all but empty table. 'As always, sweet wife-man,' he said, ripping off a leg and placing it on a plate that he then handed to Rafendil. The rest of the chicken he placed on his own plate.

'Found two stupid sods asleep on the south gate,' Drayloc said before ripping off a leg for himself. He held the leg to his mouth, biting at it repeatedly and rotating it at one and the same time. In very short order, all the meat was stripped from the leg and in his thick-lipped mouth. 'Cant av dat: da azy uckers,' he said, his mouth overstuffed, with food and spittle flying at Rafendil on every word.

'No dear,' she replied, pressing a napkin to her check to dry off the remnants of his words.

'Azzz ay, gim en a inse ad zay take a mile,' he reached over for a silver goblet as he spoke, held it up, waving it in front of Rafendil's face. She put down her food and poured the wine. Drayloc wiped the grease from his lips on the back of his sleeve. 'Ta,' he said in a burp, 'I'll have to get me some new watchmen. This lot is a bunch of drunks.' He took a long swig of wine before burping again and saying, 'There nought but cowpats, every last one of them. Cowpats.'

'Then maybe you should find some new lads, dear,' Rafendil quietly offered.

'Ummm,' he grunted, his mouth stuffed with a potato as he ripped the breast from the chicken with his dirty fingers and lifted it to his grease smeared lips.

Drayloc opened an already full mouth to bite the chicken breast, but the bite never came. Instead Drayloc froze as a crashing sound, like a clap of thunder, came from his front door. It was a heavy door, the heaviest in Guidepost, but the second crash was quickly followed by the sound of the door splintering off its hinges and falling to the floor. Then came the sound of heavily booted feet running up his corridor, and just like the front door, the dining room door was smashed down.

Rafendil screamed, jumping to her feet in terror. Yet Drayloc remained seated, the chicken breast hovering an inch from his mouth.

Two black-cloaked figures walked into the room, trampling over the newly dislodged door. They wore black helmets on the heads and yet, even in the miserable light from fire and candles, their narrow eyes, more yellow than white, were clear to see. Both the goblin-men smiled at Drayloc, though with their sharpened teeth it was a smile that made the Factor more afraid, not less.

Behind the goblin-men, walking more slowly, and for that, more menacingly, came a tall man. He was also dressed in black, although the cloth of his cloak and his padded leather armour were of a finer craft than his companions. His hair was combed back from his face, cut short, and scented with perfumed oils. His face was thin and clean-shaven, and his lips thin with a harsh edge about them. And his eyes were dark and intimidating. As he walked he slowly and very deliberately removed his long riding gauntlets, folding them and tucking them into his sword belt. 'Drayloc, my old friend, long time, no?' he said in a tone devoid of any affinity.

Drayloc made to stand, spitting the half-chewed, mouth-filling potato into his hand as he did.

'No no, please,' the man said, holding out his hand and motioning the factor down. 'Please sit,' he said, his lips narrowing into a shadow of a smile. 'I insist.'

Rafendil moved to her husband's side as Drayloc sat slowly back in his chair, his entire immensity shaking as he did so.

The man did not give anyone the chance to speak, but then he was accustomed to being heard at any and all times.

'Had a little trouble in the square, Drayloc,' the man said slowly. 'Things got a little out of hand. So they tell me.' He nodded at the two goblin-men who were blocking the doorway with their bodies. The man went on, every bit as clam as Drayloc was afraid, 'What I cannot understand, what really vexes me, is, why did you not send word of this yourself? You are the under-sheriff, are you not?'

'I . . . I . . . I . . .' Drayloc stammered.

'I, I, I,' the man mocked. 'How many days have passed?' he asked rhetorically. 'Three. Three days and no word.' A laugh, or a poor imitation of one, was forced from his mouth. 'Now I begin to wonder why. What matter of great import could have caused such an oversight? Why, O why, I ask myself, would my good and trusted friend Drayloc not send me word? Why would he sit around, stuffing his already overstuffed face, not saying a word, when four of my best lads are dead,' his voice suddenly raised to a shout as stood over the Factor. 'And the bearded bitch was in your grasp.'

'I . . . I . . . I . . .'

'I, I, I, seems we heard that before,' he laughed, a soft chilling laugh full of derision. The two at the door joined in the laughter. And Drayloc's body began to shake even more.

'Therrrrrrre was someone with them,' Drayloc managed to splutter.

'Ah yes,' the man turned to face Drayloc again. 'The Knight. The King's man. The Paladin that is come to ride this land of Goblins. I know, I heard it from that shrivelled old crow of a kindling seller. But fear not, Drayloc. She shan't be telling her tale to anyone else. Not now.'

The two at the door began to snigger at the man's joke. Then, as the man went on, they watched him playing Drayloc like a fisherman plays a hooked trout.

'But, but he was, I mean, never did I see anyone fight as he.'

'Ohhhhh,' the man said, glancing at the two by the door. 'And what with you being such an expert in the fighting arts, as we can all see.'

Drayloc didn't reply.

'You send out the guard, of course?'

'They were of horse,' Drayloc said quickly. 'The guard followed best they could, but they made for Tangle Wood and the guard would not follow.'

'Frightened of trees, are they? Or maybe the dark?' the man mocked coldly.

'I sent twenty lads from down the road,' Drayloc protested. 'They're much better trackers, much better hunters.'

'You got no right to use my lads,' one of the two goblin-men at the door hissed.

'Golna, please,' the man said softly rebuking the goblin-man interruption.

'It's Gol-nar boss, *Gol-nar*,' he replied. Adding proudly, 'My mother called me after him she thinks was my father.'

The man stood, staring at the goblin-man for a long moment, his expression unreadable. 'Fascinating,' he said acerbically.

He turned his attentions back to Drayloc, asking, 'So then, what news of the hunt? There is news, I take it?'

Drayloc shook his head slowly. 'No word has come back yet.'

'Nor will it,' he said, his eyes narrowed as he fixed them on Drayloc. 'But you would know that if, as the under-sheriff, you and your men had followed to the wood as was your duty.'

Drayloc was perplexed and floundering. He knew what had been expected of him, the four in the square had told as much. And he knew also that he had not done it. 'But, My Lord, sir, I tried to, that is I sent men... but you do not know what I have had to contend with these last days.' Drayloc excused his inactions. 'People up in arms. Talk of the king come back and such like.'

'Really?' the man derided Drayloc. 'But you of course put them right. No?'

'It's all he's been doing these last days,' Rafendil said sharply. 'Looking after your interests, so to speak.'

The man stared at Rafendil for a moment then turned again to Drayloc saying, in a silky but disdainful tone, 'Put a muzzle on your bitch, Drayloc, lest I do it for you.'

Rafendil gasped. 'Well, I never did.' She looked at Drayloc, demanding, 'Are you going to let him talk to me like that?'

'Yes,' the man snapped sharply. 'He is.'

'Drayloc?' Rafendil snapped.

'Whist woman,' Drayloc snapped back.

'Well said,' the man smiled at Drayloc before saying, 'so, you missed the Dwarves; let them slip through your fat fingers when they were within your grasp.'

'I tried,' Drayloc protested. 'Soon as the fight began in the square I ran to have the gates closed and call out the guard.'

'You?' the man asked.

'Yes.'

'You ran? You, Drayloc, you ran? Now that I would have paid good coin to see.'

The two at the door began to laugh among themselves.

Gol-nar turned to the man saying, 'We could may be make him run a bit, now boss.'

'In good time Gol-nar my friend. All in good time.' Then once more he turned to Drayloc asking, 'So then, this knight of an absentee king, what did he look like? Describe him to me, every detail mind you, and leave nothing out.'

'Well,' Drayloc began. In truth he hadn't got a good look at the knight, but, with his own life hung on it, Drayloc gave the best description he could. How he was dressed and how his family was dressed, the bright colours they wore, and how they all looked. And what Drayloc could not recall from the briefest glimpse he had, he made up. It seemed to make no matter: the man wanted details, so details were what Drayloc gave him, and as many as he could think of. Yet it was not just the man that was taking in each detail Drayloc mentioned, the two goblin-men at the door were mentally noting every detail as it was they that would be doing the hunting.

When Drayloc finished the man asked, 'The horses, you said they were of horse but you didn't say what their horses were like.'

'Well no,' Drayloc said. 'They walked into town…'

'Walked?' the man asked. 'What sort of knight walks?'

Drayloc shrugged. 'I do not know, sir, but after the fight and your lads were dead they took their horses.'

Something in what Drayloc said stung the man. He clenched and unclenched his fists as he demanded of Drayloc, 'Are you saying now that this knight took my lad's horses.'

'Yes sir.'

'He took *my* horses?'

'Well yes,' Drayloc said, then he realised what he had said, and added, 'I am afraid so, My Lord. Sorry.'

'Sorry?' the man said slowly. 'Sorry? You lost the Dwarves, you were bested by a lone knight, and you lost my horses.'

Drayloc didn't hear much of what the man said for, as he spoke the man walked towards Drayloc, and his words, in Drayloc's mind at least, were drowned out by the sound of the long blade dagger being drawn out.

The factor, bailiff and under-sheriff was a clever man, clever enough to know that this day might come. And just like every other clever man, when that man makes a deal with treason and treachery, he knew that he would need some way out.

Faster than anyone could have imagined Drayloc made his move, a move that might well be his last. He jumped up from his chair, bravely pushing his faithful wife on to the blade of the approaching man while, at the same instance, sweeping the food and candles from the table.

The room was plunged into almost total darkness. One candle went out all together, the other spluttered and flickered as it hit the floor and rolled across the room where it finished up against the wall and beneath one of the fine tapestries. Rafendil screamed as she collided with the man, but her scream was short-lived as the dagger pieced her body below the ribs to be thrust up into her heart.

Drayloc, using the few moments of darkness, ran towards the wall. Hidden there, covered by one of the tapestries, was a secret door. He was under the tapestry and through the door before the two goblin-men could move. And just as the sound of the plates crashing to the floor covered the sound of the door opening, the sound of Rafendil's body hitting the floor covered the sound of the door closing and being barred.

Drayloc was in a dark, narrow corridor, a secret way that he had never told anyone, not even Rafendil, about. It had been built some time ago, a time before he was as fat as he was now. Drayloc was forced to turn sideways in the corridor, pushing with all his strength as his belly and butt wedged themselves against the sides of the stone corridor. He was panting with the effort; sweat dripped from his chubby face, and several times he feared that he might become jammed. That would not be a dignified way to end his days, speared while trapped like a rat in his own rat run. He gave another heave, wriggling desperately to free himself from the grip of the stone walls. Then, like cork from a bottle, Drayloc popped out into a void within the wall.

Behind him he heard the sounds of someone beating on the door. They kicked at it, hammered on it with their fists, then, from the sounds, tried smashing his best chairs against it. But the door would not yield to them. Drayloc had ensured that that door was the strongest door in the house.

Hurriedly he grabbed the items he had placed within the void: items he had thought he might one day need, but had prayed he never would. Hanging on a peg there was a belt, a sword, dagger, and coin purse filled to bursting already fixed to it. The void was black as pitch, of necessity it had to be, and Drayloc felt around for the other things hidden there. He found the travelling cloak, swung it over his shoulders, and fastened the clasp. Then he felt round for the short crossbow and quiver of bolts. Finally he located the small pack.

Someone was still trying the door, smashing at it with all their strength, and having no more luck than before. But there were other sounds, sounds of booted feet running through his house, and no doubt leaving muddy footprints everywhere as they searched for him.

Bending down, Drayloc hurriedly searched for the hidden handle to the trapdoor in the floor. When he found it he lifted the door but, rather than make a quick getaway, Drayloc felt around to ensure that the steps were where they should be. They were there, and Drayloc heaved a sigh of relief. Testing the steps to make sure that they would take his wait, he lowered his bulk through the trapdoor. Twice, his great belly and some of his gear caught on the floorboards. Drayloc wriggled and squirmed until he dropped through.

When he was down, he closed the trapdoor behind him, and when he reached the bottom of the steps, he pulled a lever. Ropes pulled above Drayloc, wedges and pegs were withdrawn and, under the force of a counter-weight, the rear wall and false floor of his private indoor privy slid back to cover the factor's escape route.

From the small pack Drayloc fished out a tinder box. He knelt on the ground of the tunnel in total darkness as he struck the flint. On the fifth strike the spark caught, and pursing his fat lips together, Drayloc gently blew on the kindling. Above him the booted feet had run into the privy. 'They must have heard the wall and floor moving,' he thought. A tiny flame flicked to life in the tinder box, and Drayloc shielded it with his body as he edged his way along the tunnel on his knees. He had a torch, but he dare not light it for fear that those above might see it through the floorboards. So he waited, holding his breath and shielding the small flame, until those above left the privy.

When they were gone Drayloc lit the torch. He closed the tinder box and stowed it back in his pack. He turned back towards the steps, pulling out the small pegs at the foot: one last surprise for anyone foolish enough to follow him. And with that he hurried off down the tunnel towards his escape.

'Would you *please* stop making so much noise, Gol-nar,' the man said sharply. Then, when the goblin finally ended its insistent, and very distracting, assault on the door, the man coolly said, 'Thank you, that's much better.' He bent down and, taking a handful of Rafendil's skirts, cleaned her blood from his blade.

The room was a little brighter now, the candle that had rolled under the tapestry had caught and tiny flickers of flames were beginning to lick up the material.

'But he's getting away, boss,' Gol-nar hissed.

'Where is the fat slug going to go?' the man asked calmly. 'We hold the gates, and does he look like he can climb the walls?'

Gol-nar chuckled, 'No, boss,' then his eyes turned to the tapestry and the growing flames that were consuming it. 'Err, boss.'

'Moreover,' the man said, the first true smile of the night coming to his thin lips, 'with his size he will not be able to run far. Most like his heart will burst before he's gone a mile.'

'Yeah, boss,' Gol-nar sniggered eyeing the flames. 'Boss?'

The man went on, ignoring his companions concerns. 'However, just in case he does manage to get beyond the walls, send two of your best men.'

'Yes, boss. Boss?'

'Yes, two should do it,' the man said quietly, thinking more aloud than talking to Gol-nar. 'But I want that fat fool alive. Make sure they understand that Gol-nar, alive mark you.'

'Sure thing, boss,' Gol-nar said adding insistently, 'But, boss.'

When Gol-nar had torn the tapestry off the wall he had thrown it on the pool of wine not realising that Drayloc preferred the stronger type: the fortified type. Now, with the heat coming from the burning tapestry, the wine began to warm and soak up through the second one. Suddenly the alcohol flashed over and the room filled with a flickering blue flame.

'*Boss?*'

'Yes yes, Gol-nar,' the man said. 'You can get at Drayloc in a minute.' He was walking back and forth in front of the fireplace, lost in deep thought.

'I am a little concerned, Gol-nar; I do not mind telling you,' the man said.

Gol-nar didn't hear him; he was watching the smashed chair legs on top of the burning tapestry begin to smoulder.

'*Boss?*'

'Yes Gol-nar you're worried too, as you should be,' the man said as he paced. 'It's the horses, right? You are thinking on them too.'

'It's not that, boss,' Gol-nar said nervously as he shifted away from the growing conflagration.

'Oh, you mean your lads,' the man said knowingly. 'The twenty that went after them into that Tangle Wood and no report back.'

'Well yeah, boss but…'

'I know I know,' the man said. He stopped pacing and stood thinking for a while. 'They should have sent word back. You don't think they were ambush do you?'

'No, boss. But, boss…'

'No. Even had they been ambush one at least would have got back,' he said thoughtfully. 'But then, if they have not been ambush, and they have not run down our quarry, then where are they?'

'Don't know, boss but…'

Gol-nar shifted away from the flames. He could feel the heat on his face and his long cloak was beginning to smoulder.

'It is a riddle, is it not?' the man said unhurriedly.

'Yes, boss, but, boss…'

'And what if that knight, if indeed he is a knight, wins through to Two Rivers. What then? Moorbe is a fool, but he is not an idiot. He will know where the horses came from and will want to know the why of it.'

'Aye, boss…'

'But if he is not a knight, Gol-nar, then that might work in my favour.'

'I don't understand, boss, but can we . . .'

'It's simple, you halfwit,' the man said, his voice as monotone as it had been almost all evening. 'If this so-called-knight is just some pretender then,' he faced Gol-nar and suddenly stopped speaking.

'Gol-nar,' he snapped, 'will you stand still while I am trying to talk to you. Stand still and stop that fidgeting.'

'But the fire, boss.'

'What about it?'

'It burns.'

'Of course it burns; it's a fire.'

'No boss. It's burning me.'

'Then what are you standing there for, you idiot. Get out.'

Gol-nar, the man, and the other goblin went outside. In the town square dozens more goblin-men were gathered. In front of them, their hands bound behind them and kneeling in the mud were sixteen men of the town watch.

The man mounted his horse, an exceptional beast, tall and powerful, and as grey as a ghost. He sat into his expensive saddle and drew his gauntlets from his belt. As he pulled them on he looked down at the men. Then, looking at Gol-nar, he said, 'Get on with it.'

Gol-nar grinned and nodded to his lads standing over the kneeling town watch. As one, the goblin-men drew their blades and set about the defenceless watch. Some had their heads pulled back and their throats opened with one quick slice. Other struggled, trying to get up and run. But a slash of a blade to their hamstrings brought them down where they were and run them through as they lay. Their screams and cries filled the town square but, if only briefly. And then the square fell silent again. The only sound came from the man's horse. The scent of blood filled the air, and the horse snorted and shook its head as the bouquet came to its nostrils.

'Easy, boy,' the man said, patting the neck of the beast, a beast bred and impatient for war. 'Soon, boy, soon.'

'And the town, boss?' Gol-nar asked, a wicked grin on his heinous face.

The man thought for a moment as he looked around him. Finally he said, 'Never much like this place, truth be told. Have your sport, lads, then burn it. But I want you on the road and after them Dwarves by sunrise. Clear?'

Gol-nar and his lads gave a great cheer and then set about their work with a joyous will. The old kindling-woman, Rafendil and the men of the town watch were but the first to die that night in Guidepost and perhaps the luckier for that: they died quickly. The remainder of the town would not be so fortunate.

Drayloc reached the end of the tunnel. He was breathless from the exertion and perspiring freely. He had travelled a mere 300 yards underground. But that had been 300 yards in a tunnel that had been built in secret and that, to keep the secret, was not well maintained. The timber props holding up the roof were dry and, in many places, beginning to crumble. The boards, sheering up the sides of the tunnel, creaked dreadfully, threatening to give way at any second and none more so than when the fat man pressed against them as he forced his way through the tunnel. Yet somehow Drayloc made his way to the end of the tunnel. He had pushed and yanked both himself and his gear through, struggling against the tightness of the tunnel that threatened to ensnare him at any moment. Several times Drayloc had feared he would become wedged in the tunnel, and several times he cursed his own great bulk that might cause him to be lodged within, leaving him trapped and at the mercy of the goblin-men or worse, buried alive in a cave-in. But that had not happened; there was no cave-in, and he was not trapped. He had made it to the tunnel's end and for that, panting frantically for air in that oppressively tight, dark place, he thank his good fortune.

There was a ladder just ahead of him and, above it, a trapdoor that led to freedom. Drayloc paused for a moment, desperately trying to catch his breath. He set his torch to one side and made ready his small crossbow. His hands were shaking uncontrollably as he fumbled to fit a bolt. Heavy beads of sweat dripped into his eyes, the salt stinging them and forcing him to rub them dry on his sleeve.

Behind Drayloc, from the distant end of the tunnel, there came a crashing noise. He looked back, panic-stricken that the goblins may have found the way in. They hadn't. But the floor of Drayloc's private privy had collapsed into the tunnel. Then, as the dust cleared, and only just visible, the first flames began to flicker in the tunnel.

Smoke drifted down towards Drayloc, slowly filling the tunnel with suffocating fumes. The walls and roof of the tunnel, already dry, began to smoulder.

'My house,' Drayloc gasped. 'My beautiful house. They've burnt my beautiful house.'

He slotted the bolt into the crossbow, his hands had stopped shaking as anger replaced fear. 'How dare they burn his house!' Drayloc thought, his house, the house he had worked so hard for, and when he had been such a faithful and honourable servant.

Drayloc thrust the torch into the earth, rubbing out the flame as he made ready to climb the ladder. His legs felt weak and he was still short of breath but, he felt for the first rung with his foot and began to climb.

Holding the crossbow in one hand, and resting his body on the ladder, Drayloc reached up to locate the bolts that held the trapdoor secure. He slid them back, his throat tightening as the first whiff of smoke reached him. He raised the crossbow, ready to loose the bolt at anything or anyone that might be waiting in ambush for him, and lifted the trapdoor. It didn't move.

Drayloc pushed again, his right hand pressing at the trapdoor with all of the strength his arm could muster. Still the trapdoor would not budge. He climbed up another rung of the ladder, putting his wide back hard against the trapdoor, and as his breath caught and he coughed from the effects of the smoke, Drayloc pushed up with his legs.

The trapdoor held. He pushed again, a rising terror and fear of the smoke giving the fat factor strength he never knew he possessed. The trapdoor yielded, it did not fly open, but it rose an inch or two.

Drayloc heard a loud scraping sound above him. He froze, wondering what the sound could be, and fearing that at any moment he would be discovered. Below and behind him the fire had taken hold in the tunnel: heat and smoke were building, and now that Drayloc had opened the tunnel exit, a draft was drawing the fire rapidly towards him.

Drayloc was sweating with both fear and the heat of the fire that was now coming towards him like the flames of a blowtorch. He pushed at the trapdoor again. Again it moved and again the scraping sound came, louder than before. Another push was followed by more scraping and a muffled crash, and the trapdoor came free.

He squeezed through the tight opening, stopping and then having to reverse when his sword belt caught on the narrow gap. The smoke was coming up around Drayloc, chocking him, as he finally popped out of the opening. Quickly Drayloc thrust the trapdoor shut, cursing himself for being so stupid as the trapdoor banged back into place. For a moment Drayloc was frozen, wanting desperately to take a lungful of fresh air, but fearing to do so in case someone had heard him.

Slowly, more slowly and far more cautiously than he had even moved before, Drayloc crept to one of the boarded windows and looked out.

The tunnel had come up in the floor of one of the many boarded-up houses in Guidepost. When the town had begun its unalterable decline at the factor's hands, the house, the nearest house to the east gate, had been abandoned. Drayloc had kept it like that, even when others had offered to take on the rent; he had kept the house empty for just such a time as this. As his own house was built Drayloc had instructed the builders to construct the tunnel in secret, which they had, for a price. And now he was standing among the dust and dirt of the abandoned house, the broken furnisher that had covered the trapdoor littered around his feet, and watching the four goblin-men guarding the east gate.

'Damn them,' Drayloc hissed under his breath. He had a crossbow, but there was no way to loose a bolt without opening the window shutters, and they were nailed securely shut. And even if he managed to get one, the other three would be on him before he could reload.

But the goblin-men were distracted. They stood by the gate, but were not truly attending to their duties. Up the street, in the centre of town, there were far more interesting things happening. Fires were burning; people were screaming and crying out. Swords were flashing in the growing red-and-orange glow. And the wicked laughter of their fellows could be heard as they went about their business of the night. The four by the gate shuffled their feet, their hands clenched and unclenched, as they chatted among themselves; they were missing out, missing out on the fun.

The house opposite Drayloc was occupied by a young couple, a young couple with a child. Something had woken the husband, Amfrid, in the middle of the night. He did not come out to take a look. Rather he had found a small gap in the shutters from which he could view part of the street outside and the gate also. What he saw was the guard being bound at sword-point, their hands tied tightly behind their backs as they were marched up to the square while four others took over the gate.

Amfrid had kept a watch at the shutter, a long knife in his hand and a cudgel tucked in his belt, just in case.

'What's happening, husband?' Emmaline, his wife, whispered in his ear. Emmaline was a beautiful, dark-haired and dark-eyed woman. She had risen silently and, just as silently, had come to stand beside him.

'I don't know,' Amfrid whispered back, but something in his tone told Emmaline that, whatever was happening, he was afraid.

She placed her hand on his; she had not seen the knife in the dark, but she felt the hilt in his hand. She looked up into his eyes, and she too was afraid. 'Curse this place,' she whispered. 'I wish we …'

Emmaline said no more as the sounds of men screaming and crying out in terror came from the square. The sounds died quickly. And Amfrid and Emmaline turned to face each other.

For a short time no sounds came from the square, but there was a strange red glow in the night and the smell of smoke in the air.

More screams came to their ears, and the smell of smoke came stronger. Amfrid wanted to open the shutters, to look and see what was causing all the commotion in the town. But Emmaline would not let him. She too had seen the goblin-men at the gate, and she knew only too well what that might mean.

'Husband,' Emmaline said softly as she fought back the tears, 'I have loved you always. Do not let them take me.' So saying she held Amfrid's hand tightly, and lifted it, and the blade he held, to her breast. 'Promise me.'

'Don't talk such, woman,' Amfrid said, pulling his hand away. He put the knife down and held her tightly in his powerful arms. 'We do not know what is happening.'

'I know,' Emmaline said, her tone resigned, 'and so do you, husband. If truth is told then we have always known what might happen. Though we believed ourselves safer within the walls. But we have always known.'

It was true. The threat of this night had hung over them like a spectre. Ever since those foul beasts had come, ever since the factor and the town watch had failed to rid them of those goblin-men, this night was inevitable. And now, as the screams, the smoke, the fire, and the sounds of death were all getting closer, Amfrid might have wanted to deny it, wanted to shield his beautiful Emmaline from it, but there was no escaping it.

Amfrid turned away from her, unable in his shame and anguish to hold her gaze any longer. Why had he not left when the others had? Why had he stayed, stayed and brought his wife and child to this end? It was their doom and his burden.

He looked out of the shutter and saw a half naked old man running down the street.

'Alarm alarm,' he cried, running as fast as his old legs would carry him. 'Alarm, we are attacked. Alarm.'

Then he froze. He had been running towards the guard at the gate but, as he neared them, he saw that the four at the gate were not the town watch. He turned on his heels, very nearly falling as he did so. 'Alarm, the gate is lost. Murder is on us alar . . .' Those were his last words.

Two of the goblin-men at the gate raced up the street, their swords drawn. They reached the old man in three rapid strides and hacked at him mercilessly.

Amfrid gasped and hurriedly drew back from the shutter. His grip tightened around the handle of his long knife as his entire body tensed.

Emmaline had left him for a few moments but now she returned. 'Husband,' she whispered softly, not the least trace of emotion in her voice.

He turned towards her and tears flooded into his eyes as he saw her holding their child.

'Please, Amfrid,' she begged tenderly, 'do not leave us to those things. We both know what they will do should they take us alive. Do not make us suffer that.'

Amfrid began to cry. 'I cannot do this,' he sobbed.

'Then give me the knife, husband,' Emmaline said softly. 'Give me the knife and please, do not cry.'

He was trembling visibly. 'I am sorry, Emmaline. Do not ask me. I have failed you.'

She stepped closer to him, placing an understanding hand lightly on his cheek. She looked up at him, smiling sweetly as she said, 'No, husband. You are a good man and I have always loved you. Never did you let us go without a roof over our heads or food on our table. No, you never failed me. Please, husband. Do not fail now.'

With that she reached up, and clutching him round the neck with one arm while holding their child in the other, she kissed him deeply. Amfrid returned her kiss, shutting his eyes against the stinging tears, as he pressed his lips to hers with all the passion he felt. He felt her warm breath upon his cheek as her tears intermingled with his own and then, for love's sake, he thrust the knife swift and deep into her heart so that she might not suffer too greatly.

Emmaline's body went limp. Her arm gripped him one last time; then her grip failed. She slid slowly from his embrace and Amfrid lowered her gently to the ground. Sibony, their daughter, gazed up at her father through sleep-filled eyes. The child could not understand what her father had done, could not comprehend why her mother was lying motionless.

Amfrid stifled the cries of anguish within his own throat. He knew what had to be done and hated himself all the more for having to do it. Kneeling down in front of his daughter and, hiding the blood-drenched knife from her gaze, he held her as he kissed her head a final time. 'Close your eyes, child and the nightmare will be over,' he tried to say, but his voice was quaking and he had no idea if she heard his words or not.

Yet Sibony did not cry. Rather she closed her eyes, hugged her father round the neck, and kissed him as her mother had done.

A thunderous banging came to Amfrid's door as he laid his daughter next to her mother. Amfrid mopped the tears from his eyes with his hand. His nostrils filled with the iron aroma of the blood. At once the tears were gone; now there was only hate and rage.

He jumped to his feet as the door burst in and the first of the goblin-men rushed at him. Too late the goblin-man saw the long knife: Amfrid thrust it into him, twisted it, then ripped it sideways.

The goblin-man screamed in agony and clutched at his stomach as his guts spilt onto the floor.

Amfrid had his cudgel out then. He ran at the second goblin-man, dodging past the point of his outstretched sword as he smashed the heavy wooden club against its skull. But the goblin-man was wearing a helmet, and the blow only stunned the creature. For a second it stood there, motionless as bells echoed noisily inside its head. Yet that was more than time enough for Amfrid to slash at its throat with the knife and release a spray of the beast's dark blood.

The other two goblin-men backed off. They had not been ready for this. A few old men, the sick lame and lazy, that was all there was in Guidepost: that was what they had been told. Yet now, two of their fellows were dead, and a madman was charging at them.

Amfrid cried out as he charged at the goblin-man standing at his door. He swung the cudgel, but the creature stepped back and his swing went wide. He thrust the knife out as he rushed on; again he missed, and he failed to see that the other creature had moved off to the side.

As Amfrid charged, the fourth goblin-man sung his sword. The blade caught Amfrid mid-chest. Then the creature quickly drew the sword across his chest, the blade rasping noisily against Amfrid's ribs as it ripped through both flesh and muscle.

For a second Amfrid stood motionless. Blood came to his throat and his eye went wide. His arms dropped to his sides; knife and cudgel fell to the ground. Amfrid slumped to his knees as his eyes rolled back in his head.

The goblin-man that had brought Amfrid down raised his sword to make sure he was dead by giving him a few more tasty cuts. He was only stopped when his companion raced past him.

'Where you going, Rath-gil?' he shouted.

'He fought too well, Blar-nig,' Rath-gil shouted back as he went through the door, 'what's he been protecting?' Then Rath-gil stopped and looked down at the dead woman on the floor. 'Ooo, that's pretty now,' he said happily, as he began to undo his belt and jerkin.

'Rath-gil,' called Blar-nig, 'she's dead as dead.'

Rath-gil didn't turn round: he was far too busy undressing. 'Still warm but warms as good as alive. Better maybe. Don't fight as much.'

## Family Holiday

'Rath-gil, you're not right; you hear me, Rath-g...' Blar-nig was abruptly stopped short by the bolt that lodged itself in his back.

Drayloc had been watching from across the street: watching as the old man had been hewn down, watching as Amfrid had dispatched two of the goblin-men before he had himself fallen. Now Drayloc made his move.

The factor moved as silently as he could, exiting the abandoned house and creeping across the street. When he was close, so close that it was impossible to miss, he loosed off a bolt from the crossbow into the back of one of the goblin-men. Blar-nig never knew what hit him.

Yet, even before Blar-nig hit the ground, Drayloc ran into the house, sword drawn. He knew there was but one other goblin-man in there: he had watched them go in. Now he found the vile creature humped over the body of a woman.

Drayloc stabbed, jabbing his sword down into the back of the half-dressed creature before it had a chance to defend itself. He twisted the blade, forcing a harsh grunt from the creature, as its body flopped down over the dead woman. Then, as he drew the blade out, Drayloc saw that the girl beside the woman had her eyes open.

The child was bleeding heavily, her breath was irregular and came in short gasps. With all the strength she had left, she lifted her hand to Drayloc saying, 'Please.'

Drayloc felt something akin to pity. It was something he had not felt for a long time, a very long time, and then he remembered what it was: an inconvenience.

He kicked a goblin blade towards the prostrate girl as he cleaned his own saying, 'Look to yourself, child. We must all look to ourselves tonight.' And with that he ran out.

By the gate the four goblin-men had left their horses tethered. Drayloc made for them, watching up the street towards the town square as he did so. He opened the gate, cursing it as it squeaked noisily upon its rusty hinges. He gathered up the reins of three horses, wrapping them round his hand as he mounted the fourth. Three times he tried to mount, and three times his legs proved too weak to lift his fat body up. Breathing heavily, and with sweat pouring down his face, he half-jumped, half-pushed, and somehow managed to flop himself onto the horse.

Drayloc found the stirrups and kicked hard into the horses' flanks. At first the beast would not move; he kicked again, even harder, and with a leap, the horse bolted out of the gate. So abrupt was the horse's response that Drayloc was very nearly wrenched out of the saddle by the reins of the other three. Yet, as soon as his mount began to run, the others quickly followed.

Drayloc stayed low, holding himself flat atop the horse as he spurred it on. Any second he expected to hear the sounds of alarm following him; any second he expected to hear the hiss and whizz of arrows over his head. Or, worse still, feel the sting of an arrow in his flesh. But it didn't happen. The only sounds behind Drayloc were the sounds of Guidepost's extinction.

He sat upright. He was over 500 paces from the gate and well beyond the reach of a bow. Again he kicked the horse's sides, pushing it harder, as he demanded every ounce of speed the beast could summon. He had no need of the other horses now, and he cast their reins to the night. But the horses kept running with him, following his mount for no other reason than that they did not know what else to do.

Drayloc was two miles from Guidepost when he passed the first walled farm. Already the men of the farm were alert. They manned the high walls and were facing to the west. A red glow was on their faces as they watched the burning of Guidepost in horror and rage. Drayloc did not stop; he did not tell them what had happened nor warn them what was soon to come their way. Again he kicked at the horse's sides, and again the beast responded with another turn of speed, and then Drayloc was gone into the night.

# CHAPTER 12

## The Day after the Night Before

'And you were in a fine state last night, Edward Deeks,' Liz scolded.

The sun was barely up on another day; his head was pounding, his throat dry, and already Liz was using his full name: Ed knew from the get go that he was in trouble.

Raising slowly, every fibre of his body aching, Ed sat up and cradled his head in his hands. 'I got a stinking head,' Ed muttered. Had he been hoping for some sympathy, he wasn't getting any.

'Serves you right, mister,' Liz snapped, 'here we are, stuck out in the middle of who knows where, and you go and get yourself drunk as a skunk.' She as good as tossed the bowl of porridge at him, adding, 'And you smell like a brewery.'

'All right, all right,' Ed groaned, 'just let me get cleaned up and have something to eat. But please, for now, don't go on about it.'

'Don't go on about it?' Liz huffed, and with that she turned on her heels and stomped away.

Ed left the porridge for the moment: in fact he couldn't really bring himself to eat it just then. He went down to the stream, washed his face, splashed water over the back of his neck, and sluiced his mouth. Feeling only fractionally better, he went and sat back down with his bowl, that and a good-sized mug of nettle tea, and ate what he could.

Around him, cheerfully going about their morning tasks, the Dwarves greeted Ed with broad smiles and knowing nods in his direction.

'Morning, Longshanks,' Balelin said as he passed, 'how we feeling this fine day?'

'Like crap,' Ed groaned. 'What was I drinking last night?'

'Just Old Noggin,' Balelin said, looking at Ed with concern. 'Do you feel ill, my friend?'

Ed would have shook his head, but that would have been too painful. 'No,' he mumbled instead, 'I feel hung-over.'

Balelin stepped closer. 'I do not understand. Hung over what?'

'You know,' Ed said, looking up at the old dwarf, 'hung over. Like when you drink too much and suffer for it the next day. Just like I did last night and am now suffering today.'

'Oh, Oh,' Balelin chuckled loudly, too loudly for Ed. 'We say "you're under the barrel."' Balelin laughed and slapped Ed on the back, an action that sent a shockwave of pain reverberating around the inside of Ed's skull. 'Fear not, Longshanks, a good bowl of porridge and a ride in the open air will see you right. We move in short time. Eat up, my friend, we still have far to go and a good day for the going.'

'Where, exactly, are we going?' Ed asked, once the world stopped spinning.

Balelin looked off towards the east, saying, 'We are making for Two Rivers, but we will not come to there before nightfall of the morrow. Still, there are farms on the way and we might be able to do a little trading, perhaps even be able to trade for something better than porridge.'

Ed forced a smile. 'No, the porridge is fine really.'

Balelin laughed loudly. 'And I am an Elfling in that case. But come now, Longshanks, time to mount up.'

The party travelled eastward that day. Grizlan and Balelin rode in the lead wagon, with Bromlan and Harrlin in the other. Either side of the wagons, as they had the day previous, the other Dwarves walked and, when game was about, hunted with their crossbows. The family rode on the horses they had acquired and were become quite accustomed to their mounts as were their mounts with them. Kate and Jay would occasionally ride off from the party a little, scouting the way sometimes, not that they actually knew where they were headed and at other times just to race one other. Had circumstances been different, had they been at home in the States, then perhaps they might have been having fun: and in some ways they were. But they were not at home, and their experiences of the last few days had already taught them that, this journey could, at any moment, be far from fun.

But, on the whole, the party was relaxed. The sun was up, the sky cloudless, and there was a light, cooling breeze blowing from the north that made the grass and wild flowers that surrounded them sway gently.

Whatever the dangers were, they appeared, at least as far as the Dwarves were concerned, to be behind them. For the now, while the day was good, they would gather what food they might find, and restock wood for a fire later. Yet the hunting was not as satisfactory as it had been yesterday. Not that there wasn't plenty of rabbits and hares about; there were. But the grass was longer, and denser, and that made it too easy for the little critters to hide.

Time and again, one of the party would get a good bead on a rabbit with their crossbows, only to see it disappear into the tall grass before a bolt could be loosed off. And it wasn't because the Dwarves were poor hunters; on the contrary, they were experts. It was the rabbits themselves that were the problem. With the sun up high, the day so warm, and the air so fresh and sweet, the rabbits, as they often do, had ideas in their heads other than eating.

'Too damn frisky,' Ed cursed under his breath, as yet another rabbit skipped out of sight. He was taking his turn at hunting and was out, away from the noise of the wagons, with Polmet.

The fat dwarf chuckled. 'You will have to be quicker, Longshanks; our little friend there have nought but passion in their heads,' he smiled broadly, adding wistfully, 'can't blame them on a day such as this.'

'Yes. Just seems a pity stifle their ardour with a bolt.' So saying Ed loosed the crossbow and bagged another rabbit.

'Good shooting,' Polmet said, slapping Ed on the back. 'Looks like you're getting the hang of a crossbow.'

Ed looked down at the weapon in his hands. 'They're not the easiest of things to master.'

'Still, not bad for a beginner,' Polmet said cheerfully.

By the time they returned to the party Ed and Polmet had bagged a grand total of fifteen rabbits: more than that day's total by the rest of the party combined. Leastways the party would eat well again that night. Other than hunt rabbits, the party had been foraging wherever they could and had been reasonably successful. There was a large selection of field mushrooms, roots, and leaves of various plants, Danny Lions and Comfrey, which made an excellent substitute for potatoes. Fresh Nettles and wild flowers had been gathered; bunches had been hung round the side boards of the wagons to dry to make tea with later. Berries, from a bramble thicket near the stream, had been picked and washed and now filled a good-sized basket. While it wasn't exactly a feast, it was better than yet another bowl of porridge. Which made everyone happy: everyone that was, but Liz.

For most of the day Liz had been riding at the rear of the party. She was very much keeping herself to herself. While the others went about hunting and foraging, Liz either rode slowly, on her own, or walked, with nothing other than her horse for company.

Several times Ed had gone to her, asking if everything was all right, and each time he'd asked, Liz merely said, 'Yeah, sure' then carried on, on her own.

It was while Liz was walking that Grizlan got down from the wagon and went to talk to her. To begin with, the conversation was more than a little awkward: Liz wasn't really in any mood to speak and Grizlan didn't quite know what to say.

Liz repeatedly assured Grizlan, saying over and over things like, 'I'm fine, thanks,' or 'No, nothings wrong,' when clearly Liz was anything but fine: there was something very wrong.

So Grizlan talked, if Liz didn't want to talk, then so be it, but Grizlan talked and hoped that, when the time was right, Liz would talk also.

'He's a fine man, that man you have there,' Grizlan said, watching Ed setting off to hunt again. 'Polmet says he will make a good hunter. Which is good. Least you and the little ones will have food on your plates each day. And that is more than can be said for some.'

'Suppose,' Liz replied without emotion.

'Brave too,' Grizlan went on. 'The way he stood his ground against them four gobs. Not many would do so, especially seeing as he was with naught but his hands.'

'Stupid. That's what it was: damn stupid,' Liz retorted sharply. 'And now look at us, running like some fugitives and getting further and further from our way home.'

'So that is it,' Grizlan said softly. 'You want to go home.'

'Of course.'

'And where is home?'

Liz stopped walking and turned to face the dwarf. She could not think of her as a woman, even if there was a softness to both her voice and manner, which was all together lacking from her male counterparts. But a woman does not have a full and, it must be said, expertly braided and bejewelled beard. Nor does a woman have shoulders wider than Ed's. Yet there was something in Grizlan's eyes, something warm and understanding and distinctly feminine. Liz found comfort in those dark brown eyes, something trustworthy, and as she looked deep into them, the wall she had built around herself crumbled away as tears filled her own eyes.

Dwarves, contrary to what some might say, are not devoid of emotion, nor are they unable to see emotion in others. So, as soon as the tears began to fill Liz's eyes, Grizlan knew at once that the woman needed a hug.

'Come on, dear,' Grizlan said, as she stepped closer and wrapped her arms around Liz.

But if Liz did indeed need a hug, she got one, and more besides. Grizlan wrapped her arms around Liz like a bear grabs a tree.

Liz felt like she was being crushed as Grizlan's arms enveloped her with all the gentility of a Python's coils. And when Grizlan patted Liz on the back, it felt as if she was trying to dislocate her spine.

'There there,' Grizlan said soothingly. She pushed Liz's head onto her strong, broad shoulder, saying, 'It will be fine. You'll see.'

Rather than feeling comforted Liz found her face compacted into the mass of Grizlan's wavy brown hair. All Liz could think about was the robust smell of Grizlan's leather jerkin, heavily polish with Linseed oil and saddle soap and no small measure of yesterday's rabbit stew. Not to mention the dirt and sweat from several weeks' travelling.

'Thanks,' Liz gasped, pushing herself free from Grizlan's bear-like embrace before she suffocated. 'It's just . . . well it's . . . look, Grizlan, please do not take this the wrong way. But I have to get home. It's not that I haven't enjoyed being with you Dwarves. Come to think about it, it's an adventure that nobody will believe when we get home. And if I do tell anybody, then most likely I will be out of a job and on the cover of the *Enquirer*. Which is not the place to be when you're a doctor, trust me on that. But, and I do not know how, but we have to get home. There are people that need me; you understand that, don't you?'

Grizlan stood silently thinking for a moment before saying, 'If we can help, we Dwarves that is, if we can find a way, then we will see you home. But, in the in-between time, there are people here that need you.' She nodded her head towards where Jay and Kate were riding.

Liz sighed heavily, 'That's not what I meant. I meant I have patients waiting, patients that depend on me. It's different. I love Kate and Jay, and I would do anything to protect them. That's another reason why we have to get home: it's too damn dangerous here. Wherever here is.'

Grizlan was puzzled. 'Why this is Wickenshire, the East Marches of Angron,' she said slowly.

Liz, grunted her frustration before saying, 'I don't mean that, Grizlan. I mean this place, this land, this whole damn world. It's not where we should be. Not you, or the other Dwarves, or the damn Brownies for that matter. I mean Ed, Kate, Jay and me; we should not be here. Now, and I don't know how it happened but, we somehow slipped into this place through, I don't know, some kind of door or something. I just want to get back to it and go home but, the further we travel, the longer we keep going east, then the further we are from that door. Grizlan, don't you see, for us anyway, we are going the wrong way.'

'I see,' Grizlan said slowly. She began walking, catching up a little with the wagons that had gone on ahead. 'As grandfather said, you are welcome to travel with us for as long or as little as you like. But, if I may advice, come with us to Two Rivers, that far at least. It is not much further; we will be there on the morrow, then, if you wish, take your leave with our best wishes only. When you are there buy some new clothes.'

'What is wrong with these clothes?' Liz asked confused. 'I know I smell a bit but . . .'

Grizlan gave Liz an understanding glance. 'After what happened at Guidepost there will be gobs hunting you. If you wish to go back there, then you will have to dress the part.' Grizlan smiled broadly, adding, 'Do you not see? Your colourful clothes stand out like a rose on a dung heap.'

Liz stopped and stared down at herself. She hadn't entertained the thought before but, now that Grizlan had said it, Ed's light blue T-shirt, her red fleece and blue jeans, and Jay's multi-coloured striped shirt, stuck out like as many sore thumbs.

'Oh my,' Liz mumbled.

Grizlan smiled again. 'Fear not, good lady. When we reach Two Rivers you may be able to buy some cloth that is less colourful.'

'More dung and less rose,' Liz smiled.

'Exactly so,' Grizlan began to laugh, and Liz joined her.

'There is one small problem,' Liz said, suppressing her mirth. 'How are we going to pay for the clothes? We have no money, least no money for here, and nothing to trade.'

Grizlan began to giggle again. 'You forget, you have three good-size purses of coin. Donations towards your wardrobe from those benevolent gobs.'

'You mean the purses Grooflin took off them dead . . . whatever they were.'

'Gobs,' Grizlan said, stressing the word with a touch of pure hate.

'Right, gobs,' Liz replied. 'No. I am sorry but I couldn't touch that.'

'Why not?' Grizlan shrugged, then, smiling, she added, 'They will not need it where they have gone.'

Drayloc was cold when he woke: chilled to the very bone in fact. The sun was high in a clear blue sky yet, in the shade of the trees, he felt frozen. 'What in the name . . .' Drayloc gasped as he sat up suddenly, too suddenly as his head was pounding and every muscle ached more than he had thought possible. 'No,' he cried, 'no, no, no, no.' He looked about him quickly as he attempted to figure out what had happened. How had he ended up in Tangle Wood and, more importantly, how had he ended up naked as the day he was born?

Slowly, and very painfully, Drayloc got to his feet. Around him, scattered here and there around the wood, were a few of his possessions. Thirty feet from where he had woken his crossbow lay. Near to it was the quiver, though all of the bolts had gone. His sword was another twenty feet away while the scabbard was fifty feet in the opposite direction. Other than an old pair of leather riding breeches, all his clothes were gone, as was his food, horse, money, and everything else.

Picking up the old breeches, Drayloc pulled them on. They were tight, too tight really, as he had had them made some years before when he was a little less round the middle. But, needing something to cover himself, he pushed, pulled, tugged, and heaved until he had them on. All that then remained was to suck in his ample gut enough to fasten them closed.

Sometime later, with his pants on and his head a little clearer, Drayloc began to pad around the wood in the hope of finding of his goods. 'Shoes would have been a good start,' he said to himself. But there were no shoes to be had, so slowly, and with sore feet smarting from the many hidden twigs under the leaves, he repeatedly stood on, Drayloc stumbled on in his vain search.

He saw a horse, a little ways off near the edge of the wood. Its head was down, grazing happily on the lush grass that grew in the lee of the wood. Drayloc didn't know if it was the horse he had ridden the night before or if it was one of the others that had followed him. All the horses looked the same to him. But after all, a horse is a horse of course, and riding was much better than walking, especially with no boots on your feet.

Slowly, and muttering soothing words the whole time, Drayloc approached the beast. Initially the horse regarded Drayloc with suspicion. It watched him carefully, leisurely chewing on the long grass in its mouth while looking as if it might bolt at any second.

'It's all right, boy,' Drayloc said softly. 'I am not going to hurt you. Just want to ride you. You're lost just like I am. What say you and I be friends and then we can be gone from this bad place?'

The horse stood still and allowed Drayloc to come closer.

'That's a boy. Been a bad night all round, hasn't it boy? First them bad men and goblins burnt the town. Very bad men. But you're a good boy, yes a good, good boy. Then none of those bad men at the farms would give us shelter. Not that made much difference; they all burnt I seem to recall. But not you and I; good boy, yes good boy.' Drayloc reached out his hand to pat and stroke the horse's neck. 'All the farms east of the town were up in flames last I saw. And, when we turned north, looked like flames in the sky there too. Easy boy, it's all right now. The flames have gone. And all them goblins running round last night have gone too. Easy boy, just me and you know, that's it easy, yes, good boy.' Drayloc pulled up a handful of long grass and offered it to the horse. 'So where do we go, boy? That's the puzzle. Can't go south, can we? Too close to Briloness; I wouldn't be welcome there. Can't go west; we know what's coming from there, don't we boy? No, no, sorry boy, easy, easy, that's it, good boy. Don't worry, boy, we are not going that way. Nor will we go north in that case if that is how you feel about those goblins. All right sorry, boy, easy; I won't say it again, easy now, easy. But I don't want to go east, not through the wood, not into that fog again and whatever it was in the fog. Besides, no point going to Two Rivers. So where to go?'

Drayloc patted the horse gently as he took hold of the reins. 'Where to go?' he asked again as he made ready to mount. 'Just a minute, boy. You got something stuck in your rump,' he said, seeing several small dart-like things lodged in the horse's rear. 'What on earth are these,' he said pulling one out, but, as he did, the horse let out a cry and reared up suddenly. The reins were ripped from Drayloc's hand. He jumped back in fear as the horse bolted off across the fields leaving him standing with the small dart in his hand.

'You stupid animal,' Drayloc shouted after the horse. 'I was only trying to help. Come back, you stupid horse, come back here…' Suddenly Drayloc went silent. It occurred to him that he was standing at the edge of the woods, shouting at the top of his lungs, with who knows who or what within earshot.

The day had been pleasant, the hunting fruitful, but the travel had been slow, slower than any of them wished. By nightfall the party was still in the wide open grasslands of Wickenshire, and the northern breeze was freshening as dark drew in around.

They made camp on the southern slope of a small ridge. The wagons were pushed together, forming a windbreak and a shelter made from spare canvas. A fire was quickly built from the supply of wood they carried with them. It was only a small fire, just big enough to cook by, but not large enough to offer much warmth. Even so the Dwarves managed to concoct a very passable supper of roasted rabbit, mushrooms, and rather tasty, if a little strange, mash.

'We shall make an early start in the morn,' Balelin said after finishing his meal. He drank a cup of the flowery tea, smiling down at the cup in a show of approval, then said, 'If I remember true, there is a wood just east of here. After that there are farms where we can trade. Then, before nightfall, Two Rivers, hot food, warm ale, and a good soft bed.'

The Dwarves all gave a small cheer at the thought of it. The family also gave a cheer, though perhaps for different reasons. But at least the thought of hot food and clean sheets buoyed everyone's spirits.

During the night a light rain fell, not enough to soak them but enough to irritate them when they took turns standing guard. There was also no fire to keep them warm and barely enough wood left to burn for tea making the following morning. What wood there remained, moreover, was damp and burnt with a low flame and far too much smoke.

They broke camp before sunrise, packed away their blankets, furs, and canvas, then, after drinking a cup of warm tea, they set off.

Ed and Jay rode ahead of the party, scouting out the land while the wagons came lumbering on behind them. The rain had stopped and the sun was rising fast. Soon it was going to be another stunning day: the morning just had that feel about it. The wind had shifted once more, coming more from the east now and bringing with it the smells of summer.

Father and son rode up onto a low ridge. Ahead of them, and a fraction to the south, they could see the woods that Balelin had spoken of the previous night. From their vantage point, when they placed their hands up to shade their eyes from the sun, they could also see a road. It was a little to the south, following for a short way, the stream they had been following themselves. It looked a bit odd, like the road simply stopped in the middle of nowhere, or more correctly, they were looking down at the eastern end of the road and, therefore, at its beginning.

Soon the wagons were on the road and making good time. They followed it to the wood where, for the first time in days, the Dwarves were welcomed.

In the wood there was a camp, a loose collection of crude huts dotted either side of the road. Outside of the huts, and around them, there were people. Women were hanging out washing, cooking on open fire, and, while they worked, gossiping with their neighbours. Children played, running after each other in an energetic game of tag; others climbed trees or chased a rather harassed-looking chicken. It was, in so many ways, a very happy scene; poor to be sure, but happy nonetheless. There were no men about this little, irregular village, but the wet stones that stood by almost every hut told the party why: it was a woodcutters' and charcoal makers' camp and the men were busy in the wood.

The Dwarves did not stop to trade at the camp. Woodcutters were transient labour and never had with them more than they needed, or more than they could carry. But the party did pause for a short time, enough to take a drink of fresh water and to spend a moment or two with the children of the camp, many of who had never seen a dwarf before and all of who were eager for news of the world outside the wood.

The party had passed through the wood before the sun was at its zenith. Following the road a little further they came to a planked bridge. It was old and not in the best state of repair. The wagons crossed one at a time for fear that their combined weight may be too much for the bridge. Even so, as the wagons and the Dwarves crossed, the bridge protested noisily, creaking and groaning like an arthritic old man getting up in the morning.

By mid-day they saw the first stone-built walls and, just a short distance away, the first farms. Outwardly, they looked very much like Braygon's farm, dry stone walls to make field boundaries and taller walls to surround and protect the house. But there were many differences also. These farms had lower walls around them and the houses were much larger; the windows of the houses were also much bigger, not the narrow slits as on Braygon's farm. In an instant you could tell that these farms were richer and, more importantly, less well protected.

The people were also quite different. Where before those people around Braygon's farm had been stand-offish and withdrawn, these people were positively friendly, waving to the party as they approached, waves which, with the biggest smiles they could muster, the party returned happily. Then, as they arrived at the gates of the first farm, they set about the commerce of the day.

It began, as it always began with Dwarves, with many 'Greetings friend well met'. Then there was much from the Dwarves, 'How is the weather for you? And how goes the harvest?' In return the farmers enquired about life on the road, the rain last night, and all the usual pleasantries. This, along with the offering and the drinking of tea, went on for some time. Questions were asked about distant places, had the Dwarves passed that way or this, did they know of so and so, or had they news of somewhere or other. Finally, with all the formalities of barter satisfied, everyone got down to the business at hand.

Deals were struck, exchanges were made, and all of it done with good-natured cries of, 'would you see the shirt off my back,' or 'for shame, you are robbing me, would you see me starve.' And it went on like that for a good while. Everything, and that did mean everything, had to be quibbled over. How many potatoes were worth how many rabbit pelts? How many carrots to a potato? If a small cooking pot was ten cauliflowers, then a big cooking pot was a side of bacon and ten cabbages, surely.

As all this was going on Ed and his family stood to one side; they had nothing to trade. But they were also amused just watching how business was done. The Dwarves were good businessmen, or should that be businessdwarves, and drove hard bargains, hard but fair. It was all very serious, but good-humoured also. Both sides protested they were being taken 'a lend' of, yet at the end, both sides got what they wanted, and for a reasonable exchange.

The party stopped at three farms that noon. Three times they went into the whole routine, and three times the farmers played along. When they had finished the Dwarves had parted with nearly all their trade goods, and in return, they had amassed a wealth of fresh produce. So much in fact that the wagons were now groaning under the strain of it all.

Balelin explained to Ed, 'We shall keep part of it and have a fine meal tonight. The rest we will sell at the market in Two Rivers. We should get a good price for all this.'

Ed laughed knowingly. 'I get it now. In other words you barter goods for produce then sell the produce. After that you buy or make more goods and so on and so forth.'

'It's a living,' Balelin shrugged.

They set off for Two Rivers. The wagon timbers groaned, and the axles squeaked with every turning of the wheels. So heavily loaded were they that it was all hands round the wagons and a good strong push to get them up even the smallest hills. Progress was slow, but there would be a good pay day at the end of it.

Ed and Jay were leading their horses off to the right of the road, but close enough to lend a hand, when they heard it. Both thought it was some new, strange sound coming from the axles, but it wasn't. They heard it again and both stopped, staring way off at a distant hill as they tried to see what it was. They heard it a third time, this time clearer: a long loud call of a horn.

High above them, and some miles distant atop a hill, a rider was standing up in his saddle. The sun was high, very bright, and behind the figure, both Ed and Jay shaded their eyes to see the man. He was, at that distance, little more than a shadow: a dark cloaked shadow on a dark horse.

# Chapter 13

## Riders in the Wild

Again the figure stood high in the saddle, and again he blew a long resounding call with his horn. From near the woods, way past the farms behind the party, came the sound of another horn, a long blast followed by two shorter notes, as if in answer to the first call from on the hill. Then, from north of the road, came yet another answering call: one long and two short. And the calls seemed to be getting closer.

Ed looked over to Balelin and the others. 'Are we being hunted?'

Balelin smiled at him, as did the other Dwarves. 'I shouldn't worry about it,' the old dwarf said calmly.

'But the dark rider,' Ed pointed towards the man on the hill, 'is he not the same as those at Guidepost?' And as he looked, he saw several more riders joining the one on the hill. It was clearer now, even with them silhouetted by the sun, that a good many of the riders carried spears, their steel points flashing in the sun's glare and the spear pennants flapping in the gentle breeze.

'Who are they?' Ed demanded breathlessly.

Balelin glanced casually towards the hill and shielded his eyes with his hand. 'Why not ask them yourself? They are coming this way,' he smiled.

Ed looked back towards the hill. Balelin was right; the riders were indeed coming, coming straight at them and blowing that infernal horn as they came. For a moment Ed was bewildered as to what he should do. There were twenty riders at least coming down the hill, far too many to fight. There were also signs of dust rising from the road behind them. They could not see the riders there, but they were coming.

Again a horn sounded in the north: a long eerie note that made Ed spin his head towards the sound. He could not see who had made that call or how many others were with him. The riders on the hill answered the northern call as did those on the road behind.

'We're surrounded,' Ed groaned.

'So it would appear,' Balelin said, as a matter of fact.

The riders came down from the hill at a fast trot. They did not charge or gallop, nor did they walk their mounts slowly down the slope. Rather they came on at a steady and constant pace, and they were coming directly towards the party. When Ed had first seen the lone rider on the hill there was something like two miles or more between them. Now, at the unvarying pace, the riders would be upon them in a matter of minutes.

'Balelin, what are we to do?' Ed asked.

'Nothing,' the old dwarf said. 'We shall just have to wait and see what these men want.'

'Grandfather, you tease so,' Grizlan laughed.

Balelin did not answer her. Instead he turned to Ed and smiled broadly saying, 'Fear not, my friend. They do not come for you or your family. They come for me.'

'For you?' But before Balelin could answer, the riders from the hill were nearly upon them.

Ed looked at them, half expecting to see the same black clothing and helmets he had seen in Guidepost. But what he saw was a troop of men, no, a troop of cavalry, coming towards the party.

Each of the men in the troop, save but one, were dressed alike. On their heads they wore helmets made of steel, open-faced with cheek and nose guards and a flared back projection to protect their necks. On top of their helmets was a raised ridge that followed down to the sweep of the neck flare, where it ended in a foot-long horsehair tail that was blue in colour. Their long cloaks were of a fine woollen cloth, dark blue in colour, and decorated with a broad pale blue band set several inches from the edge. They each wore armour, a leather cuirass over a padded leather jacket, and their leggings were also of padded leather. On the left breast of their cuirass was a herald, of a sliver eagle's head.

But one, the one riding at the head of the column, wore a much more ornate helmet. His helmet had a high crescent on the crown, faced with a silver eagle head and with folded back wings upon the sides; it gave the impression of an eagle diving on its prey. He also wore a padded jacket and cuirass, but his were partly hidden under the tabard he wore. A tabard of blue cloth, edged with finely worked silver thread and bearing a large silver eagle's head upon his chest.

The riders came nearer; the twenty from the hill were only a few short horse lengths away when a dozen more, on the road behind the party, came into view. When the column got to within a few paces, the one in the crested helmet raised his hand and, without so much as a spoken order, the column came to a halt.

For a moment, a moment that seemed to stretch out into infinity, the man in the crested helmet looked at the party, examining them closely with keen eyes. He came closer, walking his mount, a powerful grey charger, right up to the wagons until he was within a sword's length of Balelin.

Finally the man spoke, his voice strong and commanding, yet gracious also. 'My Lord Balelin?' he said, his surprise clearly apparent.

Balelin stood in the wagon and bowed. 'Well met, friend. I am at your service.'

The man leapt down from his horse, removing his helmet as he did so. A smile spread rapidly across his face, a smile that showed both pleasure and great relief.

'We feared you lost, My Lord,' he said walking to the wagon where he thrust out his right arm up and clasped Balelin's in greeting.

'Not lost,' Balelin grinned, 'just delayed.'

'We have sent riders afield these past days. Ever since the new moon when you failed to arrive.'

Balelin jumped down from the wagon, an energetic action that belied his great age. 'As you can see, my young friend, we are well and in good health, though perhaps a little thinner as our rations were shorter than our journey.'

The rider looked at the Dwarves, who themselves were now all smiles, then he looked at the wagons and the heavy load they were carrying.

'But what price this, My Lord?' the rider said turning again to Balelin. 'You have the makings of a fine feast.'

Balelin chuckled. 'We traded, young man. Pots and pans, tinker's fair, for food stuffs. And now, if you would allow us to make for Two Rivers, we shall be for the market.'

The rider looked stunned. 'But, My Lord you jest. You do not really intend to go to market.'

'Of course I do,' Balelin matter-of-factly, as if it was the most natural thing in the world. 'Why do you and your men not join us? To tell the truth we have overloaded and it is proving hard going getting these old carts up the hills even with such stout Dwarves as my companions here. So, what say, you friend? Will you join us?'

The rider was dumbstruck, and the puzzlement on his face was a sight to behold. 'But . . . but . . . My Lord. Surely you make sport of me. To market? You? I mean My Lord?'

'Well, of course, friend,' Balelin fell silent for a moment then said, 'Come now, I cannot keep calling you "friend". What is your name, young man?'

'Forgive me, My Lord,' the rider said bowing. 'I am Wolfric. Thane to King Reynfred and captain of horse.'

'Greetings then, Thane Wolfric,' Balelin said solemnly. Then, turning to his granddaughter and holding out his hand for her to take, he presented her, saying, 'Thane Wolfric, this is my granddaughter The Lady Grizlan.'

Again Wolfric looked bewildered. 'My Lady,' he said slowly, 'I have heard of you, of course, but . . . but . . . I am honoured.'

'Nonsense, Wolfric,' Grizlan giggled, blushing like a school girl under her beard.

'Imagine that,' Jay whispered loudly to his father, 'we've been travelling with royalty all this time.'

'Looks like,' Liz said dismissively. 'It explains why the old SOB never got down off the wagon to help get it through the woods.'

It was a comment that did not go unnoticed by Wolfric, and as the rider straightened up to his full height, his expression changed, from a smile to one altogether more formidable, as something briefly overlooked came racing to the forefront of his mind. He raised his hand, his finger pointing directly at Ed. 'You sir,' he said, his tone challenging, 'you are a stranger. Announce yourself and account for the king's herald you wear.'

Ed smiled, or at least tried to smile, as he said, 'It's not the king's herald. It's my football team.'

Wolfric looked suspicious, 'Foot-ball? What is foot-ball?'

'It's a game,' Ed explained, 'a sport we play in my country.'

'It sounds most interesting,' Balelin offered. 'Ed has agreed to teach us a little of it, if we have time that is.'

'A sport?' Wolfric said slowly. 'Foot-ball? Hmmm. If you say, My Lord. But I do not like that he wears the eagle head.'

Ed extended a hand to Wolfric, saying, 'Edward Deeks. Pleased to meet you. My wife Liz. Daughter, Kate. And this young man is my son Jay.'

Wolfric was not happy with Ed's explanation, not happy in the least, and it showed. Yet, as each of the family was introduced and said hello, he nodded curtly and bid them all welcome.

Wolfric was a powerful man and equal in height to Ed's six feet two. But his shoulders were wider and stronger. His hair was fair, not blond, but a very light brown, and long, coming down past his shoulders. It was tied back from his face with a band of fine blue and silver cloth. His features were stern and forthright with a resilient jaw and straight nose. When he first looked at Ed, Wolfric's eyes were narrowed, much like a predator watching its prey. But, when Ed explained the T-shirt, Wolfric's eyes relaxed a little and showed that they were a rich green colour.

'Thane Wolfric,' Balelin said, interceding on Ed's behalf. 'This man is dwarf-friend, and I believe you know what that signifies.'

'Dwarf-friend?' Wolfric said slowly turning to face Balelin. The true significance of the title may have been lost on Ed, but not on Wolfric, who now regarded Ed in a completely different light.

'Indeed,' Grizlan said, stepping over to Ed's side. 'I owe this man my life, Wolfric, a debt I will honour always but can never truly repay.'

Wolfric's mouth fell open as he regarded Ed anew. He did not yet know who this Ed Deeks was, and was no doubt still unhappy that he should be wearing what looked too much like the king's herald, but, Lord Balelin and Lady Grizlan had vouched for the man so, for the time being, that would suffice.

It was Balelin that finally put an end to the staring contest taking place between Ed and Wolfric. He cleared his throat loudly, a poorly disguised cough with which to get everyone's attention. Then he said, 'Shall we away? There may still be time to catch the market.' With that he climbed back onto the wagon and waited for Grizlan to join him.

'But, My Lord Balelin,' Wolfric protested. 'Chancellor Moorbe has bid me that I take news of you directly.'

'Then please take your news, and without delay,' Balelin replied. 'But be so good as to leave us several stout fellows to lend a hand with the wagons on the hills. We have a market to attend, ten good fletches of bacon in the wagons, and this sun is not doing them any kindness.'

Wolfric went to protest again but was hushed by Grizlan flicking the reins.

The first flick only made the ponies pull into their harnesses. Grizlan flicked the reins again; the ponies heaved at the wagons, and with a little help from the Dwarves' strong shoulders and legs, the wagons were off to the market.

Being left with little choice, as it were, Wolfric mounted his horse, replaced his helmet, and with a hand signal, had his men fall in either side of the party.

The party began to move slowly and Wolfric shook his head, saying in a tone that was partly frustrated, partly annoyed, and wholly laughable, 'Dwarves.'

And so it was, and for the only time in history, that a wagon of bacon received a regal escort to market.

The grasslands the party had travelled had entirely given way to well cultivated farms. The one road they had taken from the wild was joined by other smaller roads. They passed several more walled farmsteads before, after heaving the wagons up another grade, they stood astride a small ridge.

Below them, stretching out as far north or south as they could see, was the River Dinn. Its waters were as clear as glass, slow flowing, cool, and inviting on a hot day. It originated far to the north in the iron hills, where numerous streams, fed by the melting of winter's snow, were gathered together into this one, majestic river. It was, at the point the party was approaching, over a hundred yards wide. Two miles further to the south the River Dinn made a turn east where it joined with the River Gath, a river every bit as wide as the Dinn. Where these two great rivers met, and sitting atop a rocky outcrop, was the town of Two Rivers.

The land that the town sat on was a triangular shape, formed by the meeting of the water that surrounded it on two sides. At the southern end, the narrow end if you will, the rocky outcrop was over a hundred feet high. It was dark grey granite and rose vertically from the waters in sheer cliffs. On top of this cliff a stone wall and keep had been built. Some 300 yards back from the confluence of the rivers, the rock sloped down gently till only fifteen feet above the water level. A curtain wall, some twenty feet high, extended from the keep to a point over a mile to the north. The wall was divided by several towers and a gate house and set back a little from the river.

On the western shore of the town there was a boat landing and dock. Boats were tied up there, loading and unloading cargos of all types. Some boats were loading timber, others unloading grain. There were men all about the docks: busy, strong men carrying goods up ladders, or lowering them down with ropes.

The town was far bigger and far more prosperous than Guidepost had been. At the southern end of the town, the end nearest the keep, there were several very large houses that overlooked the wall. And as was always the way, the largest houses had taken the riverfront locations with the best views. As the eye travelled north over the town, the houses became smaller until the roof and chimneys of tiny shanties where all but hidden by the wall.

The party made their way down off the ridge, following the road as it made a slight turn to the north. They were heading towards the only bridge over the River Dinn and the only entrance into the town of Two Rivers from the west.

There was a long queue of people and wagons at the bridge, people that muttered and cursed as they milled about listlessly and waited to be allowed to cross. Their wagons were full of produce, and they wanted to get into town and to the market before things began to spoil.

Walking up and down the queue was a man dressed in scruffy brown clothes and wearing a broad-brimmed hat to keep the sun off his head. As he walked he repeatedly called out, to no one in particular, but to everyone directly, 'a penny a man or boy, two pennies a horse a penny a rider, four pennies a wagon, toll and tax. A penny a man or boy...' and so he went on, chanting the words again and again until, and looking utterly bored in doing so, he reached the end of the queue. He turned round and started chanting his way back down the line, 'two pennies a horse a penny a rider, four pennies a wagon, toll and tax.'

At the head of the queue, by the entrance to the bridge, two more men took the toll and allowed the people to cross. They were as uniformly scruffy as the disinterested chanter and wearing the same broad-brimmed hats.

Wolfric rode in front of the party. Calling out as he went, 'Make way make way, king's business, make way there.'

The chanter fell silent, spinning round angrily to see who was making all the noise when it was clearly his job to make all the noise. Upon seeing Wolfric and the riders approach, the chanter's expression changed from irritation to one of submission. He touched the brim of his hat and gave Wolfric a curt bow before quickly taking up a new chant. 'Make room there, come on, make room; king's riders coming through. Make room.' The man went down the line, shouting his new instructions, and bodily pushing the slower people aside as he went.

The queuing people stepped aside, but not without muttering their discontent as they eyed the heavily loaded dwarf wagons that trundled by with the riders.

'Somebody's kissing them on high,' one man in the queue side to another.

'And not on the lips neither, I'll wager,' the second man replied.

The riders close enough to overhear the exchange shot the two men a withering glance and the men quickly turned away and went about their business.

Wolfric and six riders went on the bridge ahead of the wagons. The other riders had to wait as the bridge was too narrow, and far too poorly built, for more than one wagon at a time. Once they were all across Wolfric again turned to Balelin saying, 'My Lord, will you not come with me to Chancellor Moorbe? He awaits news anxiously.'

Balelin looked at the captain and sighed. 'I have been on the road for many days, too many for polite company. Please convey to

Chancellor Moorbe my regards and my assurance that, once I have had a good meal, a sleep in a soft bed and a hearty breakfast, I shall be at his disposal. Until then, young man, be so good as to show me the way to market.'

'But, My Lord,' Wolfric groaned. He would have said more, he was thinking of saying more, it was as clear as his green eyes that he was thinking of saying more. But, seeing as Balelin was a dwarf, moreover a Dwarf Lord, and had made up his mind, there would be no way to steer him off the course he was set upon. It is easier, they say, to move the mountain than to move a dwarf.

'Follow this street to the water trough,' Wolfric relented. 'The market square is on the right. I will send some of my men with you.'

'Please no,' Balelin said softly. 'Your men and horses need rest. And besides, nothing put people off buying more than having soldiers standing over them.' Balelin bowed, more by way of dismissing Wolfric and his men than out of politeness. 'I shall send word of what lodging we find the night, and I shall be at Chancellor Moorbe's service on the morrow.'

The Dwarves got their wagons rolling towards the market and Ed and his family followed on behind. As they passed Wolfric, he signalled for them to stop.

'Lord Balelin has vouch for you, strangers,' he said, his eyes narrowing as he stared directly at Ed. 'But the chancellor will want to speak with you on the morrow. Do not therefore try to leave. I will send word to the guard that you are to be arrested if you should try. So, till the morrow, you are all free to move about at your will. But you must remain within the town precincts.'

'Just a minute,' Liz said sharply, staring back at Wolfric every bit as hard as he was staring at her. 'Are we prisoners?'

Wolfric straightened up in his saddle. 'That shall be determined the morrow.' He pulled at his horse's reins saying, 'Good day to you all.' And was gone before any of them could reply.

'Well, that's nice,' Liz hissed.

'What did you expect?' Ed asked, his tone non-committal. 'I guess what happened at Guidepost is about to catch up with me.'

Liz turned to Ed, her hard expression softened to one of trepidation. 'But that was self-defence; Grooflin and Grizlan are witnesses, as we are.' She turned, looking for support from Kate and Jay.

'That's right, Dad,' Kate nodded.

'They attacked you and Mum,' Jay said loudly. 'Remember, they were gonna cut Mum's finger off.'

'Yeah,' Kate agreed. 'They can't blame you for that. Everybody has the right to protect themselves; that's the law.'

Ed laughed a humourless laugh. 'At home for sure. In England also. But we are not at home or in England we are here, wherever here is.'

Liz moved her horse closer to Ed's, leaning over and whispering to him, 'Then let's make a run for it. The horses are rested and word could not have got to the guard yet.'

'Great idea, sweetheart,' Ed sighed. 'But run where? Run how far? And just how far do you think we would get? Look how we are dressed. Not to mention that running is as good as saying "yeah, I'm the guilty one".'

'There is the money Grooflin took off them things back there,' Liz offered. 'Grizlan said we could buy some new clothes at the market, something that would, you know, blend in more. Kate already looks the part.'

'Thanks for reminding me, Mom.'

'I'm sorry, dear, but you do blend in. In a good way,' Liz assured her.

'Yeah, all she has to do is put on a few pounds and she'll look like real dwarf,' Jay chuckled. He stopped chuckling when his mother shot him one of her looks and when his sister smacked him round the back of the head again. 'Mum, tell her to stop doing that.'

'Kate, don't hit your brother so hard,' Liz said indifferently.

'Is this all right?' Kate said smacking Jay again, though not noticeably any lighter than before.

'Mum, damn it,' Jay cried out.

'Will you two quit it?' Ed snapped at his children. 'For pity's sake grow up, both of you.' He turned to Liz, saying, 'I don't really want to touch those purses, but we need fresh clothes. Even if it is only to blend in. For one thing, while you have been fooling round, you haven't noticed the way people are looking at us.'

Liz glanced around at the faces watching them. 'So we are getting some new clothes?' she said.

'Yes,' Ed said. 'But we are not making a run for it. We'll go and see this chancellor fella tomorrow and explain what happened. Then, hopefully Grooflin and Grizlan will back us up, and we will get it all sorted out.'

'And what about getting home, Ed?'

'One thing at a time, Liz.'

They dismounted and led their horses to the trough Wolfric had mentioned. After allowing them to drink for a while, they set off to find the rest of their party, but it was Polmet that found them.

The fat dwarf came strolling down the middle of the street. 'Ah, friends. Come along now, come along.' Polmet came striding up to the family, smiling and talking loudly, ''tis a good market and business is brisk. Follow me.' With that he turned on his heels and, seemingly without pausing to take a breath, said, 'I'll show you to our lodgings. Nothing fancy, but clean and better than sleeping under the moon. There's stables round the rear and a good strong lad to take care of the horses. We got the ponies there already and Balelin has instructed them to prepare us a suitable meal this evening, at the lodgings not the stables that is. By way of celebrating our happy arrival and, sadly, as we may be partying company soon, our farewells. But don't let us dwell on that. Let's get you to your rooms. Get these trusty beasts into the stable and then shall we see what offerings this market has. What do you say?'

'Yeah, sure, fine,' was all the family could reply to the whirlwind that was Polmet.

'Nearly forgot,' Polmet said, without missing a rapid stride. He reached into his jerkin and pulled out the purses they had taken in Guidepost. 'You will be needing some coins while you are here. And don't let these rogues take a lend of you. Haggle, that's the way of it, haggle for everything.' He tossed the purses to Ed and Liz then suddenly turned off the road and into a lane between two inns. 'Here we are,' he announced, strolling purposefully towards the back of the building and shouting for the stable boy.

In short order the horses were being fed, watered, and brushed by the enthusiastic boy. This was his stable, his little business at the back of the inn and, for a few copper pennies a horse, the best equine lodgings in Two Rivers.

'You take real good care of them,' Jay told the boy, who was in fact taller than Jay, and considerably more stoutly built.

'Have no fear, sir,' he said to Jay. The boy was a businessman, and a businessman is always polite and smiling when he is after your money. 'I'll treat them like they're my own, sir. Have they names?'

'Of course,' Jay replied. He pointed at each horse in turn. 'That's Ajax, Achilles, Pairs, and this sweetheart is my Hector.' Jay cuddled the horse's neck, patting him firmly, and in return, Hector snorted contentedly as he pressed his face into Jay's chest.

The stable boy rubbed his head saying, 'Strange names for horses, but then you look like you have come from far. Suppose you all have strange names there; meaning no offence, strangers are always welcome.' The boy flushed with embracement and quickly added, 'I'll look after them; have no fear on that account.'

Ed paid the stable boy in advance from one of the purses though he needed Polmet's help as Ed, and the rest of them, didn't know what coin was what or how many added up to what.

# Family Holiday

Polmet had to give them a swift lesson. He opened one of the purses, tipping out the contents on a barrel top. 'That's a penny,' he said, holding up a copper coin. 'And that's a shilling. Fifty pennies make a shilling and twenty shilling make a crown. But a crown is gold, so no mistaking them.' Polmet began to count out the coins from the purse, totalling it all up and saying, 'Not bad. Seven shillings and twenty-three pennies, and that after you have paid for the stables.'

'Is that a crown?' Liz asked. She had been rooting round in the purse she held and now brought a shiny gold coin out into the light.

'Well, bless my belt buckles,' Polmet smiled joyously. 'Seems you did even better, good lady.'

Liz shrugged and looked back down into the purse. 'I wasn't sure because they all look the same.' She tipped the coins out onto the barrel. 'Here look.'

All the coins did look very much alike; that was true. They were much the same size and, in the shadow of a purse, hard to tell apart. But, when they were tipped into the daylight, everyone could see that there were four pennies, three shillings, and twenty-one gold crowns.

'Ed, what's in the other purse?' Liz asked.

'Don't know,' he said; he had been carrying the purse since the fight and had never given it much thought. He fished it out of his pocket and emptied it out on the barrel. Thirty more gold coins rolled and jingled among the small fortune already assembled.

Polmet roared with laughter. 'Bless my boot and britches,' he clapped his hands on his sizeable belly. 'You're rich. You have enough to buy a house here let alone a room for the night. Come to think, why not buy the inn?'

But Ed wasn't smiling; Liz was, a little, more out of embarrassed confusion than anything else, but not Ed.

'Is this a lot of money?' Ed asked Polmet.

Polmet grinned from ear to ear. 'Longshanks, my friend, it's a fortune.' He began to chuckle again adding, 'We expect to do well out of the market today, thirty, maybe thirty-five shillings. But you could buy and sell us ten, twenty times over with this lot.'

'And what about the other purse?' Ed said, 'Has Grizlan opened that one?'

Polmet stopped laughing and stared at Ed. 'You know, I don't think she has; she would have said so if she had.' Then, thinking for a moment, he asked, 'What are you saying, Longshanks?'

'Just this. We've got fifty-one gold crowns here and who knows how much Grizlan has in her purse. Now, am I right in thinking those things, those gobs as you call them, are little more than thugs and bully-boys?'

'It would be an insult to a thug to say as such, but yes,' Polmet spat the words out. 'I could tell you stories about gobs that would turn your hair white. Everyone in Angron knows what they are and what they are like. Killing and burning, and worse, much worse. Stealing womenfolk away and...' He suddenly stopped talking when he saw Liz looking at him.

'So not the most intelligent of creatures then?' Ed said.

'Intelligent, ha,' Polmet mocked. 'Nought but stupid base beast doing the bidding of their master. They are evil, wicked, and cruel. Pitiless to any living thing; cunning, yes, would happily stab you in the back so long as they are ten or more to one in their favour.'

'So how then did they come by all this money?'

Polmet shrugged.

'I mean,' Ed said thoughtfully, 'they don't exactly sound like thrifty savers.'

Again Polmet shrugged, 'Perhaps they stole it.'

'Perhaps,' Ed said thoughtfully. 'But from who and from where. There didn't look much to steal at Guidepost nor the farms around there. Not unless I missed something.'

Polmet shook his head and began to fiddle with his beard. 'Best we put this out of sight. Longshanks is right; someone will be missing this much and they will come looking. Curse it; I was stupid and careless, tipping it all out like that; careless and stupid, that's me.'

Ed began to gather up the coins and place them back in the purses; as he did, he looked at Polmet. 'Better go tell Balelin what we found. And tell Grizlan to check her purse also.'

'Aye, I'll do that,' Polmet said. He walked back up the lane to the street, all the while muttering to himself. 'Stupid and careless, what could you be thinking, you stupid, stupid dwarf?'

Their rooms were on the first floor of the Stubborn Donkey inn. A brightly painted shingle hung above the door. It depicted an overloaded Donkey, which had sat itself down and was steadfastly refusing to move, while its owner pushed desperately at its rear. It was a sign that made the family smile, as was its intent.

Inside they were greeted by the owner of the inn. 'Welcome, strangers,' he bellowed in the friendliest tone. 'Always happy to meet new folk from afar.' He stepped round from behind the bar and offered his hand to Ed. 'Come you in and have a rest. I'll wager it's been a long dusty road and you'll be wanting a wet for your dry throats. Finest ales in Two Rivers; brews them meself so I do.' He shook hands with Ed, slapping him on the shoulder in an overly familiar manner. 'Cenwalh Brewer, at your service, my good people.'

Cenwalh was a short round man, with a head of curly brown hair and rosy red cheeks. He wore a red waistcoat over a whitish shirt that was decorated with stains of stale ale on both sleeves. His trousers were a grubby brown, with a V-shaped panel of grey material where his trousers had been let out at the rear. And as business got better, and his girth got larger, that V-shaped panel got bigger also.

'No bags, good people?' Cenwalh asked, casting his gaze around. 'No matter, no matter. I'll have the boy show you to your rooms,' he said brightly, but then his expression changed, and his tone was positively apologetic as he added, 'Master Balelin commanded me to give you the best rooms. And I did, truly I did. They are my best rooms, overlooking the street and nice and airy. But I am sorry, good people; I have only two rooms left, what with all the new folks in town on account of the building and such like. So, I am afraid that, by your leave of course, but the young master and mistress here will have to share a room. I just hasn't got any others.'

'Yeah, that's not gonna happen,' Kate groaned.

'Not a chance,' Jay replied, for once agreeing with his sister. 'Share? With her? Don't think so.'

Ed shot them a look, a look that said shut up; it didn't work. Kate and Jay were arguing now, arguing over who was the worst to share with, who had the worst habits, but mostly just arguing because brothers and sisters are supposed to argue about anything and everything.

'It will be fine,' Liz assured Cenwalh. Then she turned to her children saying in a tone they both knew meant "be quiet and do as you're told". 'We can make do for now, can't we?'

'Yes, Mom,' The kids answered in unison.

The boy was called by Cenwalh and the lad showed the family to their rooms.

Ed and Liz opened the heavy oak door to the room. The room was large with solid oak posts, in-filled with white plaster and windows that overlooked the street. But the windows were small and made from yet smaller squares of poorly made glass held together with lead. The glass was uneven and of irregular thickness, giving a distorted view of the outside world. In the centre of one wall, and the main feature of the room, was a massive four-poster bed. It was also made of oak, stained a deep brown and craved, both on the post and base, with depictions of fruits and sheaves of wheat or barley. But the carvings were not what could be called artistic or refined, more workman-like and amateurish. It was the same for the chest at the foot of the bed and the chair and chest of drawers. It was as if someone had a grand vision of how it should look but lacked the skills and know-how to make the vision substance. The one saving grace in the room was the bed; it had a deep but firm mattress and with a duck feather quilt that was nearly a foot thick.

'It's lovely,' Liz said to the boy whose name she hadn't caught, if indeed Cenwalh had ever said it; for all anyone knew, the boy was called, "boy".

Then the boy opened the other door to show Kate and Jay their room, and immediately Kate protested, actually stamping her foot down like a petulant child in a tantrum. 'That's it. I am not sleeping in the same bed as him. Mom!'

The boy showing them the rooms blushed. 'I can get a bolster,' he stammered. 'Put it down the middle like.'

'Mom?'

'Or I can fetch up another small mattress and make up a bed on the floor.'

'Mom? Dad?'

'Another small mattress will do just fine,' Ed said to the boy.

'I'm not sleeping on the floor,' Kate whined.

'Well, I'm not,' Jay whined right back at her.

'Why don't you go and sleep with your damn Hector then?'

'I might just do that; he's a nicer person than you.'

'He's a horse butthead.'

'You're no beauty, douche bag.'

'Dork,' Kate shot.

'Dingbat,' Jay shot back.

'Will you two shut the hell *up*!' Liz shouted, and instantly both of them shut up. They had rarely heard their mother shout, and they had never heard her swear.

Ed turned to face Jay and Kate once more. 'Right, it's settled. Jay, you're on the floor, Kate you get the bed. And no arguments, clear?' Then he saw the boy watching him and his face flushed with embarrassment. He pulled one of the purses from his pocket, opened it and, without looking, tossed a coin to the boy.

The boy grabbed the coin, closing his hand tightly round it as a huge smile spread across his face. He gave a quick bow, little more than a nod of his head, and touched the tightly closed fist containing the coin to his forehead. 'I'll get the mattress right away, sir.' He said making for the stairs. 'And clean linen; best we got, sir.' Again he nodded and touched his forehead before he opened his hand, bit the coin for conformation, then skipped merrily down the stairs.

Ed stared down at the open purse, muttering to himself, 'I wonder how much I just gave him.'

# Chapter 14

## Two Rivers and the Party

The Deeks family went shopping after they had cleaned themselves up. There were no showers in the Stubborn Donkey in, not even a bath. What there was, was a large earthenware bowl and an earthenware jug of cold water standing on the chest of drawers in each room. Beside them, a single linen towel and a small bar of unperfumed soap. That was all there was to wash with, so hoping that they may find something better later, they washed and went outside.

Polmet was waiting for them out in the street, along with his wife Bromlan, Shamlin, and Hamfast. When he saw Ed and the family come out Polmet stepped close, explaining that Balelin had insisted that the Dwarves accompany the family. He spoke quietly, almost conspiratorially, as he said, 'Balelin is unsettled by the money and worries that some might take advantage of you. He sent us look after you, so to speak. Make sure that you do not get robbed by the merchants here.'

'Is that the only reason?' Liz asked.

Polmet blushed under his beard. 'Balelin is worried,' he said, 'and I will say no more.' And with that he led the family to the market square.

The market square at Two Rivers was a cobbled area some 300 feet by 200, so not really a square at all even if it was called such. At the southern end was a high stone wall, topped with castellation and with a gatehouse aligned with the main street that led to the bridge. In the centre was a round wooden building raised up on some stone steps: this was the market office. Around the building, filling the square, were line upon line of stalls and wagons. Most were selling foodstuffs, apples, pears, potatoes, turnips, and all manner of produce, while some sold fish or meat. There appeared to be some order among the mass of wagons and stalls. Insofar as the meat sellers were kept into one row, vegetables in another, and the fish sellers in one corner over by the wall. Around the square, on three sides, there were more merchant houses. They were not exactly shops, not as the family understood them, but rather a large house where the merchant plied their trade from the front room, or in the street outside.

Yet, what struck the family most was how busy the market was. Compared to the poor excuse of a market at Guidepost, or in fact to anything they had ever seen in their lives, the market at Two Rivers was an endless bustle.

There was a constant stream of wagons coming into the square and more waiting in the main street to be allowed in. The wagon drivers would report to the market office, get themselves a pitch, and begin selling whatever they had to sell. Others went to the more permanent stalls or merchant houses, offloaded, then left the square by another road. And all the while there was the noise, not just the noise of wooden wagon wheels on cobbles, which was loud enough, but the noise of the stall owners and wagon drivers hawking their wares.

Townsfolk filled the square also, hundreds of them, and every one looking for the best bargains of the day. People went from stall to stall, haggling with each and every one of the stall owners to get the best prices. Buyers would compare the price at one stall to the next, informing the seller loudly that they were overpriced. While sellers would point out the much better quality they had on offer and, at the same time, decrying the fact that they were being robbed. Sometimes it all got a little heated, or at least it appeared to. Yet it was all good-natured, if you ignored the arm waving, scowling, cursing, fist shaking, shouting, and name-calling: that just seemed to be the way business was conducted in Two Rivers market.

On the east side of the square were the meat merchant houses. Trestles were set up in front of the houses with meat and poultry either on the trestles or hanging up in the windows. Facing them, as part of the market but separated by the street, were wagons loaded with live chickens and rabbits. Sheep and cows were sold and slaughtered elsewhere with wagons bringing the meat to the merchants when needed. The east side of the square also had a very distinctive smell about it: a smell of stale blood and high meat.

The northern side of the square were the houses of the leather and cloth merchants. Here you could find every type of leather, cow, sheep, kid or what-have-you, all laid out on tables or hanging up inside. Several cloth merchants had stalls with bolts of cloth on display, and inside the front room, you could see the family feverishly working at their looms. Wagons brought them in supplies of wool or linen twine in various colours and various grades, depending on the needs of the cloth makers.

On the west side of the square were the tailors, hatters, boot and cloak makers. They were easy to spot as each had a shingle or emblem hanging above their doors. Outside, on the street, they had racks of cloaks or jackets, shirts, smocks and blouses, or boots and shoes, depending on their trade. And it was to this row of merchant houses that the family went.

Later, after much haggling, protesting, and no short measure of name-calling, the family had been outfitted like just about every one else in Two Rivers.

Each of them had new boots, leather boots that were much better for riding in, and far less conspicuous than white Nike trainers. Ed and Jay opted for supple leather riding breeches, while Liz and Kate went for linen pants with a reinforced leather seat. They got shirts and blouses, two each, linen of course, and all white, or whitish, principally because it was the only colour available. Jackets and cloaks were purchased, along with hats, belts, and waistcoats. As each of them was fitted out they would model their new clothes, promenading up and down the street, turning this way and that, swishing their cloaks, and giving bows, all to the approval and applause from the others, and the curious looks from passers-by. Travelling luggage, saddle bags for their horses, and bed rolls were also bought. Kate and Liz treated themselves to a pair of fine linen dresses and dress shoes. They did after all have to go and speak with the chancellor the following day and wanted to look their best. Besides, all their new purchases, along with the tales they have to tell, would make fantastic souvenirs when they got home, and with the expert haggling skills of the Dwarves, they did manage to get everything at very reasonable prices. All told, the family were suited and booted, for the very acceptable cost of two shillings and fifteen pennies.

They returned to their lodging house and dropped off their extra gear. Then, dressed in cloaks and travelling clothes, they went back to the market. This time they went shopping, not for themselves, but for something for the Dwarves. Polmet and the others protested, claiming that there was no need. What had been done had been done out of friendship and there was no reason for gifts or reward. But Liz, in particular, would not hear of it.

'It is our custom,' she told them gently but insistently, 'where we come from when somebody does you a good turn it is only right that you give them a little something to say thank you.'

'That's not to say that we will not do anything we can for you in the future,' Ed agreed. 'You have all been very kind, looking after us and feeding us when you have had so little for yourselves . . .'

'That will change tonight,' Polmet interrupted merrily.

'I dare say,' Ed went on, 'but you must let us get you each a little something, a forget-me-note if you like.' Ed smiled, though the Dwarves appeared unconvinced, so he looked at them a little more sternly, saying, 'We shall be insulted if you refuse.'

# Family Holiday

At that the Dwarves graciously, but reluctantly, gave way.

So the party set off again from the Stubborn Donkey, only this time to find something to give to the Dwarves, not so easy a task in Two Rivers. Had they been at home then the family would have simply gone to the mall or to one of the many gift shops in Seattle. But they were not at home, not in Seattle, so where could they go when gift shops appeared to be extremely thin on the ground. Sure there were shops, and merchant houses, of all sorts. But they were more utilitarian than anything else. And besides, what do you buy a dwarf as a gift? Then again, what about Balelin? He wasn't any old dwarf; he was a Dwarf Lord. What on earth do you buy for a Dwarf Lord?

Eventually Liz found something; it was in a large merchant house near the dock and close to the walls of the keep. It was among the more prosperous houses with a stone-built ground floor and timber-built upper floors. It had large windows, and the glass was of better quality than they had in their rooms. Inside there was a display of fine tableware, silver and pewter drinking cups and glassware.

Liz went in with Ed, telling the Dwarves that they had to wait outside or else they would spoil the surprise. They agreed, but not without warning Liz and Ed to make sure that they haggled, which is exactly what Liz planned on doing.

Most of the things they had seen in Two Rivers had been crudely made, robust no doubt, but lacking skill. This shop was different; this shop had goods on display that were finely detailed and unmistakably made by a craftsman. There were rings and brooches, cloak pins and clasps, combs for the hair, and beads of coloured glass and silver. But that was not what Liz had her eye on. Not to mention that the Dwarves had things like that already and of much better quality. No, what Liz had seen through the window, and what she was now haggling over, were twelve travelling canteens. Each one had a knife and spoon, the handles of which were made from deer antler bound with silver, a pewter plate and goblet, and a leather carrying bag. They were all nicely made and highly polished, and while not perhaps the best quality items in the shop, the Dwarves would be reminded of the family every time they ate with them.

'Six shillings,' the shop owner informed Liz as he placed the twelve canteens on the counter.

'Six? Did you say six shillings?' Liz gasped. 'My good man I want to buy them, not them and the rest of your shop besides. Two shillings.'

'Lady, please. I have a wife-man and four children to feed. Five shillings and thirty pennies.'

Liz turned to Ed repeating something she had heard in the market, 'Better strip naked now, husband, as this robber will have the shirt off your back before come to bedtime. Two shillings and ten pennies?'

'It cost me two shilling for the handles alone. And look at the workmanship: this is not your everyday peasant ware. This is quality, this is. Five shillings and my five children will go hungry if I take less.'

'You have been busy,' Liz said. 'A minute ago it was only four children.'

It went on until a price of three shillings and twenty-five pennies was agreed, which included a wrapping of brown paper and string for each canteen. At which point the man took the money and gave them their goods. Liz did feel a little guilty, perhaps she had haggled too much, but, in an odd way, she felt better when she later found out she had paid over the odds and that, in fact, she had been taken advantage of.

As they walked back to the inn Ed said, 'I think you enjoyed that, Liz.'

'You know what,' Liz beamed, 'I did. I mean I really did. Haggling's fun and I am going to do it more often.'

'Don't know how it will go down at Wall-Mart,' he chuckled.

Liz grinned a mischievous grin saying, 'I'm going to love to find out.'

They walked along the street, looking at the large merchant houses and generally just enjoying what was left of the day. Liz was certainly more relaxed than she had been for days. Even Kate and Jay had stopped their squabbling: though, perhaps, a temporary cessation of hostilities would have been a better description.

True, they had been spending someone else's money, and that did play on Ed's mind, a little. But it was a small price to pay if it kept everyone happy or at least kept their minds off thinking how they were to get home. Two Rivers wasn't such a bad place. The market was good, plenty of fresh produce, meat, and fish. And there were the shops that surrounded it. It was a little noisy and a little smelly: well, a lot smelly in fact. After all, there was an endless string of pony, and horse drawn wagons, coming and going all day long. And ponies and horses being what they were, they tended to leave their calling cards in steaming piles all over the square. There were men with barrows and shovels cleaning the mess up, but there didn't seem to be enough of them to keep pace with the supply. No sooner had they shovelled up one load and taken it away than another horse would pick the very same spot to do what horses do best. But, what could they expect? Two Rivers was a market town, and a market town supplied exclusively by horse and pony.

It wasn't such a bad place, the opposite in fact: it was quite pleasant really. So, until they could figure out how to get home, Two Rivers appeared to be as good a place as any to stay a while. You just had to watch where you walked on market day.

Ed and Liz walked in front of the others, happy with the gifts they had bought. The canteens were not decorative, that was true, but they were functional and much better than the wooden plates and earthenware cups that the Dwarves had. Behind them, and carrying their share of the canteens, Kate and Jay were also chatting away merrily.

Perhaps they should have been paying more attention to the comings and goings around them. Perhaps if they had been thinking more about their surroundings, and less about how glad they were to be out of the grasslands, perhaps, had they been less concerned with the upcoming party that night, they might have noticed the man walking a discreet distance behind them.

He had driven his wagon, loaded with kid skins from the tannery, into the market square earlier. Right around the time that the family went shopping for the Dwarves' gifts, he had just finished the task of unloading when he first saw them.

The man looked at them, stared in fact, but they did not notice him; he was just another wagon driver delivering goods. But he noticed them. It wasn't their new clothes that caught his eye, nor the new boots and fine cloaks: there were many in Two Rivers that were dressed just like them. It wasn't even the Dwarves that walked with them, though they were an odd sight in town to be sure. What caught the man's eye first was Ed, or rather Ed's hair.

Nearly every man in Two Rivers, every man in Angron come to that, had long hair. Some had it tied back, some had it in braids, while others wore head bands to stop it blowing into their eyes. But Ed's hair was short and closely cropped all over. Then the man noticed that Liz also had short hair, cut more in the manner of a young boy than like an Angronian woman. Then there was the young girl and the boy. The man noticed them all.

He left his wagon for a while, ignoring the protests of the other drivers that had to make their way around his abandoned dray. He covered his head and face with the hood of his cowl, pulling it closer around his shoulders as he followed them at a discreet distance. He followed them to the rich merchant's shop, watching from the entrance of an alleyway while Ed and Liz went inside. Then, as they walked back to their lodgings, chatting cheerfully among themselves, he ducked back into the alley unnoticed and stayed out of sight. The wagon driver hid in the gathering shadows of the early evening until the family and their dwarf friends were well past. When they were clear of the alleyway, and a fair distance ahead of him, he came out of his hiding place. He followed them again, checking all the time to see if anyone had spotted him: they hadn't. So he followed them all the way to the Stubborn Donkey inn. And without once being noticed, the hooded wagon driver followed close enough to hear them talking and laughing amongst themselves. That was when the wagon driver allowed himself to smile a little. 'Well, well, well,' the wagon driver whispered to himself as he stood in the shadows. And with that he turned and walked away, assured in his mind that he would be returning to meet the family again.

Balelin had asked for a private room in which they would have their party. He had also asked for, no, demanded, that they had the best food and ales that the Stubborn Donkey had to offer. And with the coin he was paying, Cenwalh was only too happy to oblige.

A fire had been lit in the hearth: a big fire of pine logs that filled the dining room with a sweet fragrance. A long table had been set and around the table were sixteen chairs, all made from solid oak. Candles had been placed over the hearth, lots of them, on the window ledge, around the picture rail, on corner tables and just about anywhere else that there was free space to put them. They filled the room with light, orange light that danced and flickered and bathed the room in warmth and good cheer.

The Dwarves had all assembled in the room by the time the Deeks family came down. The first tankard of ale had also been served, and already, the Dwarves were toasting their arrival in Two Rivers, toasting a good day at the markets and just about anything else they might think of.

Grizlan saw the family first. She banged her hand on the table several times, getting everyone's attention as she loudly called to Balelin. 'Grandfather, our guests.'

Balelin had his back to the fire, warming his rear as only the very, very old know how. He was laughing and cheering along with every toast, lifting his tankard high in the air before knocking back another hearty gulp.

'Come in come in,' Balelin called out merrily looking at the family at the door. 'Innkeeper, more ale,' he shouted then, as Liz and Kate entered the room, he added, 'look here you noisy rabble, we have been travelling with two rare beauties.'

All the Dwarves turned to face the family, and Liz and Kate in particular. For a short moment they were silent then, as if by some unseen signal, they all bowed and, with a wave of their hands, bid them welcome.

'To the two fairest ladies in all Angron,' Polmet said, lifting his tankard high in the air and then taking a deep swallow of ale.

'To the fairest ladies,' all the other Dwarves called out joyfully, and then they too drank an enthusiastic toast: but not before Bromlan gave her husband a sharp dig in the ribs.

Polmet coughed and spluttered into his ale. 'You are also beautiful,' he hastily said to Bromlan when he recovered.

'Am I?' she teased.

'The fairest of the fairest, my sweet,' Polmet declared. He embraced his wife and, after both wiped the ale from their beards, they kissed, which brought another loud cheer from the rest of the Dwarves.

Balelin stepped towards the family, offering his hand to Liz, and saying, 'You look stunning, my dear.' He looked at Kate, quickly adding. 'And you also, child. You both look truly lovely.'

Both Liz and Kate were blushing at the compliments by then. It was true that they were looking the best they had in days. But then it was the first time in days that they had managed to get themselves cleaned up. They had washed, a proper wash and not just a bird-bath splash of water on the road, brushed their hair and, for the first time in days, put on a little make-up. They had also put on the new dresses they had bought: fine linen dresses with long flowing sleeves and skirts that were delicately embroidered with lace around the cuffs and hem. Liz's dress was white with white lace and coloured stitching, while Kate's was lime green with white lace. Both dresses were decorated around the high necklines and set with matching belts.

Kate gave Balelin a small curtsy. She was not used to giving curtsies and was a little unsteady on her feet while doing so. 'Thank you most kindly gentlemen,' she said then, remembering herself she blushed again, 'I mean, Gentle-Dwarves.'

Liz opted to give a small bow; it was easier and besides, she didn't know if she could hold her balance in her new shoes. 'You have all been so very kind and helpful,' she said softly. 'Rescuing us as you did at Guidepost...'

'No.' Grizlan cut in, a wide smile showing through her beard. 'It was your Longshanks that rescued us.'

'*True, true,*' the Dwarves all agreed rowdily.

'To Longshanks,' Grooflin cried out, raising his tankard.

'*To Longshanks*,' the others echoed. And they all drank deeply.

Yet, for all the toasting and all the back and forth compliments, Ed and Jay were still standing in the doorway, their arms loaded with the gifts for the party, and they had not a tankard of ale between them.

Balelin soon put that right. He motioned them inside, poured them each a fresh tankard, and the toasting was repeated.

After drinking a toast Ed and Liz passed the travelling canteens around, saying that they were just a little something to remember them by. Then, as the Dwarves opened their gifts, and were quiet for the first time that evening, Liz managed to get a toast in.

'Is there any food at this party?' Polmet called out. He held up the new pewter plate he had been given. 'We got us plates. What say we get something to fill them up.'

And with a noisy cheer from all of them, they took their places at the table while Cenwalh, his boy and a great many cooks, brought the food in.

First in, and the centrepiece of the table, was a suckling pig. Its mouth stuffed with an apple and roasted till its skin was crispy while the meat was as tender as soft bread. There was roast rib of beef, rare and juicy and looking like half a cow had been placed on the table. In fact it had taken two cooks just to carry the beef and three to set the gigantic joint on the carving platter. Roast goose glazed with apricot was brought in, as were roast potatoes with garlic and thyme, roast carrots and parsnips in honey, mash potatoes and fried cabbage and bacon. Three different breads were also placed on the table: a malt barley bread, wheat bread flavoured with linseed, and dark rye bread. Then came a platter of half chickens, roasted in herbs and piled high on the big plate. Cheeses and fruits were placed on the table, and with all that food, there was barely enough room to fit several fresh flagons of ale.

As each dish was brought in the Dwarves cheered and banged their hands on the table, showing their hearty appreciation. When all was on the table Cenwalh, his boy and cooks took position by the door. They all gave a low bow as Cenwalh said, 'Please, good people, eat drink and be merry. The boy will attend you if you need more.' And with that all but the boy left.

Ed stood up, raising his tankard, and saying, 'To good friend, good health, and thanks to our host Lord Balelin, to good eating.'

'*To good eating*,' they cheered, they drank, and then they snatched at the food as if they had not eaten in weeks.

The party lasted late into the night. There was more food and more ale than even the hungriest dwarf or man could eat, though they all made a great attempt at it.

The boy was kept busy all night, fetching more ale and carrying away empty platters. But he never once complained, quite the opposite in fact. Every time Ed happened to look in the boy's direction, the boy would give a big smile, come and ask if there was anything they wanted or needed and then run off and get it. Every few minutes the boy went round the table, pouring more ale or fetching more food. Each time the boy would say something like, 'More ale, good sir,' or 'Would you like some fruit, good lady.' Though several times the boy did get confused and called both Grizlan and Bromlan 'Good sirs'. It was a mistake he made more frequently as the night went on, and from the way the boy swayed as he walked, it was clear that he too was enjoying Cenwalh's best ale.

In the bar, where the general public sat drinking, a good many heads were turned by the sounds of merriment coming from the party room. A few even asked what was the ado about. But all that Cenwalh would say was that it was a private party.

By the time the party was over it was as much as any of them could do to get their overstuffed bellies out of their chairs and off to bed.

Ed was drunk, not as badly drunk as the night he had drank Old Noggin, but drunk enough. Liz might have said something, but she was drunk herself and far too busy trying not to look it. Kate and Jay were likewise suffering the effects of too much ale. Kate was staggering in a most unladylike fashion, giggling uncontrollably every time she bumped into something or someone. While the best Jay could manage was to sit in his chair, smiling like a fool as he slowly slid off the cushions and onto the floor.

They would all be suffering in the morning; they all knew it but, for the night at least, they didn't care.

# CHAPTER 15

## Meetings and Waiting for Meetings

Lord Balelin and Lady Grizlan were up early in the morning after the party. Well before any of the others had managed to raise themselves, before they had even managed to think about raising themselves, the two noble Dwarves were up, dressed and out in the street.

Wolfric along with a small guard were there also, politely waiting to conduct the two to a meeting with Chancellor Moorbe. As Balelin and Grizlan stepped from the inn the tall thane bowed low.

'Good morning, My Lord, My Lady,' Wolfric said with all due deference. 'The Chancellor waits in his office. Would you please follow me.'

'Certainly, young man,' Balelin smiled but, as he stepped out into the full glare of the morning sun, he winced and shaded his eyes.

'Are you unwell, My Lord?' Wolfric enquired as a tiny hint of a smile played about his lips.

'Party last night,' Balelin said by way of an explanation.

'I did hear,' Wolfric said quietly, smiling as he teased, 'in fact I think the whole town heard.'

Balelin looked sternly at the thane, but his expression softened quickly as he was too far under the barrel, or hung-over if you prefer, to maintain the pretence for long. 'I suppose we may have been a little loud,' he giggled.

'A little,' Wolfric chuckled. 'Even by the standards of Dwarves, My Lord.'

'We have been on the road for several months,' Balelin explained.

'Indeed, My Lord,' Wolfric nodded.

They walked through the square and to the castle gate beyond, slowly, and remarkably quietly for a dwarf, Balelin said: either as clarification or as an excuse, 'Extraordinarily fine ale that Cenwalh's brew.'

'So I have been told,' Wolfric said as they arrived at the gate. He stepped aside and motioned for Grizlan to lead the way through. 'The Mead is good also, they say,' he said in a lowered voice, and grinning, he added, 'but you already know that, My Lord.'

'Indeed.' Balelin beamed a smile. 'But I am having a little trouble remembering just how good right now. Perhaps you will join me for a recap later.'

'I would be honoured, My Lord,' Wolfric smiled. 'When my duties allow.'

With that they stepped through the gates and walked up the hill to the tower where Chancellor Moorbe was waiting.

Several hours later, and much the worse for the night before, the family got themselves up. They dressed and, with Kate endlessly complaining about her brother being ill all night and keeping her awake, went down for something to eat.

Cenwalh was there, smiling and fussing over them like they were his most honoured guests. 'Lunch will be ready shortly, good people,' he said gaily. 'Perhaps you would like some ale, just to be getting on with, or perhaps a little mead.'

'Tea,' Ed said quietly. 'Do you have any tea?'

Liz sat at a table, resting her elbows on it as she cradled her throbbing head in her hands. 'And some water.'

Cenwalh smiled sympathetically. 'Willow tea,' he said knowingly, 'best cure for after ale. Willow tea and a spoon of honey.' With that he was gone and shouting orders at the sorry-looking boy that had served them at the party.

'Anybody hungry?' Ed asked as he sat next to Liz.

'No thanks, Dad,' Kate groaned.

'Food?' Jay grunted, then his whole body lurched in rebellion at the very thought. He had almost sat down but, as his stomach mutinied again, he raced off, desperate to reach the outside privy next to the stables.

'Again,' Kate groaned. She sat down, was silent and a strange, almost pained expression came to her face. 'Excuse me,' she said, putting her hand over her mouth, and then raced off after her brother.

Cenwalh returned, carrying a tray with four earthenware cups and a large jug of steaming willow tea. Behind him carrying a tray with plates, bread and butter, fresh fruit jams and a pot of honey, came the boy.

The boy laid out the plates, his hands shaking the whole time. He looked every bit as ill as Ed felt. His skin was pale, nearly white and waxy. His eyes were sunken with dark patches around them. And he received no compassion from his employer for what was, let's face it, entirely self-inflicted.

'Hurry up, boy,' Cenwalh berated him. 'Get the table set. And have you washed up all last night's pot? There was a big stack last I looked.'

'No sir, doing it now sir, won't be long sir,' the boy mumbled.

'Well, get on then, quick as quick.' Cenwalh clapped his hands to hurry the boy on. Something that both Ed and Liz really wished he hadn't done.

'Is he all right?' Liz asked.

Cenwalh smiled mischievously. 'He was drinking the ale that your dwarf friends paid for,' he said nodding at the boy heading back to his washing up. 'That's stealing rightly. But a bit extra work should teach him to let other people's ale alone.'

Jay was returning as Cenwalh left the table.

'Good day, young master,' the innkeeper called to him. 'Cook's got some nice eggs for lunch. Would you be liking some?'

Jay didn't answer. He stood rooted to the spot as the colour drained from his young face. Then, his body shuddering as if struck a blow by some unseen hand, he spun round and raced, with hand covering mouth, back to the privy.

'Handsome boy you have there,' Cenwalh said to Ed.

'Thank you,' Ed replied.

'Looks just like you. Same shade of green too.' Cenwalh went off, laughing at his own joke.

Later, after the whole family had managed to eat and drink something, they began to feel a little better. Cenwalh had been right, willow tea and honey really was a good cure for a hangover, so they had a second, very much needed, jug of it.

The Dwarves, they were informed, had been up for some time. Not long after Balelin and Grizlan had gone to the keep, they had been up, eaten their breakfast, and then had gone to the market again. They were not selling this time; this time they were buying, re-provisioning as they made ready for their journey north to Bennith Dure in the Cragan Hills.

Cenwalh told them all this and asked if they were going with the Dwarves. But that was something that they had not planned on. In fact they had been invited but, as yet, they had not decided. Sure, Balelin was always friendly, as were the others. And there had been mention as how the Dwarves would love to show the family their new halls under the mountain. However, and much more pressing, was how was the family to get home.

There was also the matter of Wolfric's instruction that they should not leave the town without permission of Chancellor Moorbe. When, where, and if that permission was to come was another thing all together.

As they sat, drinking their second jug of willow tea and picking at the bread and jams, they talked about what they should do next. dwarf halls were tempting: another story for them to tell that nobody would ever believe. And there were sure to be a thousand other wonders to see in this strange land. But each of them knew that they had to return home. As mesmerizing as Angron was, and it really was, in a primitive if charming way, it could also be a dangerous place.

Their discussion was interrupted by a young man that came into the inn. At first he made to speak with Cenwalh but, when he saw the family, sitting on their own, he made directly to them.

He was dressed as the riders had been dressed yesterday: quilted leather jacket and pants with a blue tabard bearing the sliver eagle's head on his chest. His long hair was dark, as were his eyes, and his round face was tanned. He had a ready smile and his manner was friendly.

'Good day to you, sir,' he said warmly to Ed. 'Are you the one Lord Balelin calls Longshanks?'

Ed nodded. 'Yes, he calls me that but I really wish he wouldn't.'

A quizzical expression flitted momentarily across the young man's face. He cleared his throat purposefully before saying, 'My Lord, Thane Wolfric has asked that I extend the chancellor's apologies to you all. He fears that he may not be able to see you today and asks that you forgive him the inconvenience he has caused you.'

'No inconvenience, err . . . what was your name?'

The young man gave a small bow. 'Hardwin sir. Esquire to Thane Wolfric and Herald of Cavalry.'

'Herald of Cavalry?' Ed said slowly.

'Was my horn on the hill yesterday,' he said proudly.

'I see, Hardwin, was it? Thank your lord for the message and we will, well, we will just have to wait on his pleasure.'

Hardwin's face became all serious again as he said, 'I am afraid that the same admonishment as yesterday applies, sir. You may walk freely but must not leave the town precincts.'

'Understood,' Ed said.

'You could always come with us,' Kate blurted out, causing everybody turn to face her. She blushed deep scarlet and stammered, 'Just to make sure we don't like, wander off somewhere.'

Hardwin smiled at Kate saying, 'I would be honoured, My Lady.' Then, turning to Ed, his expression serious again, saying, 'With your permission, sir?'

'Of course. If you are not too busy.'

'My duties are finished for the day, sir,' Hardwin smiled, directing more of his smile at Kate than to anyone else.

Liz caught enough of the smile, and Kate's response, to understand. She winked at Ed saying, 'We had best freshen up first. Say ten minutes and we shall all meet back here.'

With that they returned to their rooms, Kate apparently more eager than the others to collect her cloak for a walk round the town.

They joined Hardwin at the front door of the inn, and with the young esquire as their guide, they went to explore the rest of Two Rivers.

Hardwin took them towards the dock on the west of town. This was where all of the big warehouses and merchant houses were. Between the houses and the dock there was a road, a narrow cobbled street on which men pushed heavy barrows back and forth as they loaded and unloaded the cargos from the boats. There was a wall, between the road and the dock itself, twenty feet high and thick enough to have a walkway on the top with battlements facing over the dock. Every hundred yards there was a tower, with a double tower sitting astride the dock gate. And at the gate, the barrowmen pushed and jostled each other to get through: obviously they were paid by the number of loads carried and were racing each other to get the greatest tally for the day.

'Would you like to come on the wall?' Hardwin asked. 'There is a better view up there and less chance of getting trampled by the barrowmen.'

They all agreed that it was a much better idea, and at the next tower, with the tower sergeant's permission, they climbed the steps in the tower and went up onto the wall.

Hardwin was right: the view was indeed better from the wall. They could look down to the dock, more a narrow cobbled landing with a stone facing waterside than a real, major dock. There were several boats tied alongside the dock and, standing by the gangplanks of each boat, a man, 'The Ganger', was shouting orders, calling for more barrowmen, and generally directing the unloading of the boat. Between the boats, and the warehouses, the barrowmen toiled frantically, heaving their loaded barrows from the boats, then hurrying back after dropping off at the warehouse.

At the gate there were ten very large soldiers carrying heavy-looking walking sticks. Most of the time, the soldiers stood back, allowing the barrowmen to get on with their work. But then, two barrows would collide, or someone jumped the cue, or a load got spilled, and suddenly there was a noisy, even violent argument at the gate. At that point the soldiers would step in, break up the fights, and try to restore some sort of order.

Further along the wall they came to the gate they had used after crossing the bridge. It was not much wider than the dock gate and the traffic through it was therefore more tightly controlled. Also, as the bridge was old and much in need of repair, the traffic through the bridge gate was very slow compared to the frantic activity along the dock.

There was also a change in the town by the time they reached the bridge gate. South of that point the buildings closest to the wall were large: three storey building and either warehouses or merchant houses. They were all, with only a few exceptions, built the same: solid stone lower floors and wooden clad upper floors. The only real difference between warehouse and merchant house was the number of windows in the upper floors. But, once past the bridge gate, the houses were much smaller, mainly two storey houses, but with some single storey buildings mixed among them. They were also most timber framed with wattle and daub walls. Many had whitewashed walls that contrasted sharply with the dark timber frames. Also, unlike the merchant area, these houses were a little more spread out and many of them had little gardens at the rear where the owners grew a few vegetables.

The wall at this point ran along the river bank, with just enough room for two men to walk abreast between water and wall. Inside the wall, following on from the merchant area, there was a road between the wall and the houses. Here things were a great deal less hectic than near the dock. Here women walked along the street, carrying the ingredients for their evening meal in shopping baskets, or talked with their neighbours, or hung their washing out; or indeed did those everyday things that people did. Children played in the gardens or on the street. Some playing hide-and-seek, others playing a game of tag, or hopscotch or a game very much like it, while other just pestered their mothers for a drink or something to eat.

Often they would find themselves looking down, at either a garden or a yard, where someone was busy at their trade. At one house a furniture maker was making chairs; his wife, they assumed, was beside him and busy lacquering several more chairs that were already assembled. In another garden, a man and woman were making shoes. They had a small workshop but, as it was a sunny day, they were sitting outside and enjoying the weather as they worked.

They walked along the wall for a few more hundred feet to where it came to an abrupt end. This last section of wall was new and built a little higher than the rest. There was also a new tower at the end of the wall, and as it turned at right angles away from the river, they were looking down on gangs of men building a new wall.

'This is all new,' Hardwin said as he watched the workmen labouring away at the wall. 'The town has been growing for as long as I remember. They had to pull the old wall down to make room for more houses; now the chancellor wants the wall built again and a little further north.'

They were standing on the west wall and looking out over what was nothing more than a building site. A mile away was a tower similar to the one they stood on. Between them, already built and manned was the new gate. But between the two towers and the gate there was little in the way of a wall yet.

The houses in the area of the building work were no more than shanties: a simple roof over the heads of the workmen for the night or in bad weather. There was nothing in the way of luxury in the worker's shanty town. And by the smell, little in the way of sanitation either.

Beyond the foundations to the north of the unbuilt wall there was a wooden palisade. It was ten feet high with sharpened points on the top and a walkway half way up on the inside. Every fifty feet there was a tower, a wooden structure with a covered fighting platform that stood thirty feet high. In the centre of the palisade there was a gate, flanked by two towers and with soldiers standing close by. A cart went out of the gate, and the soldiers appeared to recoil from it and the driver, as it passed.

'Night soil wagons,' Hardwin sniggered. 'Stink up the place terrible they do. Been overworked since all the builders came for the new wall.'

'Night soil?' Kate asked. She had been walking very close to Hardwin all through their tour of the town, hanging on his every word, and watching his handsome face intently. 'What's night soil?'

'Shit,' Jay said loudly.

Hardwin smiled. 'Well, yes,' he said. He looked at Kate and blushed for her.

'And I bet with all those workmen that it's a lot of shit,' Jay smirked.

'Jason Deeks, that is quite enough young man,' Liz scolded him.

'You're right, Mum. That quite enough shit for anybody.'

'Jason.'

'Sorry, Mum,' Jay said hanging his head, but grinning all the time.

Kate moved Hardwin ahead of the others, taking his arm and saying to him, 'Little brothers, they're always such a pain.'

'Oh,' Hardwin said as he looked at Kate's upturned blue eyes. 'I am the little brother in my family. Do you think I am a pain?'

'No, no, not you. I am sure were nothing like that little brat,' Kate said, her hand lingering on his arm for longer than was strictly necessary.

Hardwin smiled then whispered to Kate. 'You're right, I was worse, much, much worse.'

They turned and headed back towards the town, all that is but for Ed. Ed was watching the work going on, watching it very closely with a professional eye. He could not help himself; it was just something he did, watch and see how things were put together. The wall, the building of fortifications in general, was something that Ed had never seen before, and he was engrossed with the work taking place.

He saw how a trench had been dug down to the bedrock. Then how the rock had been cut and flattened to give a level footing for the wall. Then, the first few courses of stones had been laid, two rows fifteen feet apart, the space between them was filled with layers of stone and mortar. The crushed stone chippings and mortar were tamped down with heavy logs. There were six men around each log, holding the handles that were fixed to them. On a signal they would lift the log and then drive it down hard onto the chippings. And these were big men, very strong men; they had to be as they would be at it all day, lifting and hammering till the stone infill was packed solid.

The old wall had been robbed of its stone when the decision was taken to expand the town. That stone was now neatly stacked in piles next to the road. As the new wall was being built, the old stone would be used but, as the new wall was to be much longer, and indeed higher and thicker, a great deal more stone would be needed.

'I know that look, Ed,' Liz said tugging on his arm.

'What look?' he asked, forcing himself to pay attention to her.

'That look,' she pointed at him. 'It's the same look you always get when you're figuring out some problem. But, Ed honey. This is not your problem. Your problem, our problem, is how do we get home.'

'You're right,' Ed said, shaking himself, and shaking off the thoughts of the building work. 'Just never seen anything like that before. It's very interesting.'

'I am sure it is, honey,' Liz said with a tiny smile. 'But so is getting home.'

Hardwin led them back along the wall until they came down at the tower past the shanty town. This tower had been the corner of the old wall, but now, where the old wall had once connected, a new staircase had been installed.

They came down these stairs and walked over to the east side of the town. There was a gate there and, just outside the gate, a landing point for a ferry that took people across the River Gath and into Gathronshire beyond.

The ferry was little more than a wooden barge with a rope and pulley system. Four men stood on the deck of the ferry, working the ropes and moving the ferry back and forth on the river. On each bank, people, some with wagons and others just on foot, waited their turn to cross.

For a short while they walked along the river bank. They went past the ferry landing and down to a small dock similar to the one on the west side of town. This was much less busy than the first one they had seen, and because there was much less chance of getting in the way, a number of children were fishing off the dock.

By the time they turned back into town it was getting late. The sun had already passed overhead and the shadows were beginning to lengthen.

Both Ed and Liz thanked Hardwin for showing them around and, very much to Kate's approval, asked if he would join them for dinner.

'Another time perhaps,' Hardwin said, as gave a hint of a bow. 'I must return to barracks and dine with my company.'

'Really?' Kate sighed.

'I am sorry,' Hardwin said. 'It is our law. Men under arms must eat all their meals together unless given permission to do otherwise by their captain.'

'What about later?' Kate said, sounding a little more insistent.

Hardwin shrugged. 'I must prepare for tomorrow. Sorry, My Lady.'

'I understand,' Ed said. 'A soldier has his duties and, when not on duty, he has to be getting ready for them.'

'Just so, sir,' Hardwin nodded. 'I must see to my horse and gear, as we must each day. But, if you would agree, sir, I shall ask permission to dine with you tomorrow night.'

Ed agreed, though Kate was disappointed. But a soldier is a soldier, no matter of the time or place, and duty must come first.

They walked back to the market square where they said their goodbyes to Hardwin. He walked off towards the gate, and they walked back to the Stubborn Donkey inn.

Inside, sitting by the fire were four of the Dwarves, Polmet, Grooflin, Cromlin, and Balelin. All were deep in thought and far from the merry band they had been the night before. They were talking among themselves in hushed, almost conspiratorial tones, and almost ignorant of the comings and goings of others around them.

Liz spoke first. 'Hey there,' she said waving to Balelin and the others as she removed her cloak. 'We just been for a lovely walk. How was your day?'

The four Dwarves were suddenly stunned out of their silence; they all jumped to their feet and returned Liz's greeting.

'It has been a fine day for a walk,' Balelin said, forcing a smile.

'A fine day indeed,' Cromlin agreed. 'Have you dined? We were about to but then got to talking, and as you can see us now, we all but forgot.'

'Very un-Dwarfish that,' Polmet muttered and patted his belly, 'Forgetting food.'

Liz folded her cloak over her arm, saying, 'How about you give us ten minutes to get cleaned up and then join us for some dinner.'

'A marvellous idea,' Polmet said loudly and, before anyone could stop him he was off. 'Innkeeper, innkeeper. Fetch us food and ale. Lots of it. There are hungry Dwarves out here. Innkeeper, where is that man? *Innkeeper.*'

Liz and the kids went upstairs but Ed hung back. There was something about Balelin's demeanour that worried him and he wanted to talk with the old dwarf, alone.

'Balelin,' he said quietly. 'Could I have your advice on a small matter?'

Balelin nodded an affirmation as the others left Ed and him to themselves. They took a seat by the fire, and when he was sure that there was no one to overhear, Ed began.

'There is something the matter, isn't there, Balelin?'

'What makes you say that, Ed?'

'You. The way you are acting. The way you seem, all out of sorts. Something is up, right?'

Balelin was silent for a long moment before he heaved a heavy sigh. 'You are right Longshanks, my friend. There are many things, as you say, up.' He was silent again, perhaps wondering how much he should tell Ed, or indeed how much he could be trusted to know. Finally, as one lessening the heavy burden they carried, Balelin said, 'I have today received ill news. Chancellor Moorbe had a great many thing to tell me. A great many important things.'

Balelin cursed himself under his breath. 'While I was playing market tinker yesterday, playing like the old fool that I am, Moorbe was pacing out time, encumbered with news that worried him greatly. News that, if I wasn't such an old fool, I should have attended to more speedily.'

'Balelin, you weren't to know,' Ed said sympathetically.

'But I should have known, Ed. I should have known by the way Wolfric bid me to attend Moorbe. I should have known because we were delayed arriving and they were out searching for us. The fact is, Ed, I should have known better than to play tinker when my kinsmen depend on me.'

Ed looked at the old dwarf for a long time. Balelin was beating himself.

'You know,' Ed said slowly. 'You cannot always be at the service of others. You have to leave a little part of each day just for yourself. If you don't, then like it as not, you will end up going mad. Give yourself over entirely to others and there is nothing left of you.'

'But I am in the service of others,' Balelin stated firmly. 'Entirely so.'

'Perhaps,' Ed smiled reassuringly. 'But a little me time is a good thing. Let's your mind unwind and helps you think clearer.'

Balelin thought on that for a moment, staring into the small fire in the hearth while sipping his ale.

'So what is the news?' Ed hesitantly asked. 'If you can tell me that is.'

Balelin took a deep breath before saying, 'There is much news, and all of it ill.' He took a deep swig of ale, wiped his beard on his sleeve and then said, 'Bears and wolves have been seen in the northern marches. They have come down from the hills searching for food.'

'I am sorry, Balelin, I don't see how bears and wolves are bad news.'

'Because, Ed, they spend the summer in the hills where there is plenty of game and only come into the low country in the winter. If they are come down in summer then what has happened to the game? That is what worries me. And I fear there can only be one reason that there is no game. I fear that the goblins have multiplied in the north and in far greater numbers than I imagined; that is why there is no game. But bears and wolves are not the only things that worry me. Chancellor Moorbe has told me that he had news from Bennith Dure some weeks past. Word came that the Dwarves had done battle with three great cave trolls.

'Trolls?' Ed interrupted.

'Yes,' Balelin nodded. 'Three of them. Great grey-skinned monsters, hides as thick as a stone wall and nearly as tough. They were three times the height of a man armed with great goblins swords.' Balelin took a long deep breath as his old eyes began to fill with tears. 'Many a good dwarf died before those fell creatures were put down, far too many. And the swords, Ed, where did the swords come from? Troll have no knowledge of working metal. So where did the swords come from?'

'Balelin,' Ed said, placing his hand on the old Dwarves' shoulder, 'you were not to know.'

'But I should have known,' Balelin growled. 'I am their lord and I was not there to stand with them and fight alongside them.'

'Balelin,' Ed said. 'How far have you travelled these past weeks? Very far, yes?'

Balelin nodded, 'Yes.'

'And could you or your friends have travelled any faster?'

'Not without much greater risk,' Balelin admitted. 'But there is more, my friend.' He reached into his jerkin and pulled out a gold coin, saying, 'Remember these?'

'How could I forget them.'

Balelin tucked the coin away and said, 'Between the four purses there were seventy gold coins. Seventy, Ed. That is more than a hundred people will see in a lifetime.'

'I got that impression from Polmet yesterday.'

'Yes but, something you did not know is where the coins came from.'

'Well, from those goblin-things right?' Ed said, suddenly confused.

'That's not what I meant,' Balelin said. He leant closer to Ed, whispering, 'The coins are Bytanthian gold, from the golden horn, a land far south of here.'

Ed nodded, though he did not understand the significance.

'And Ed, something else Moorbe told me today has put a chill into my heart.' Balelin drew his lips tight over his teeth. 'Word has reached Moorbe that a price has been placed on Grizlan's head. My Grizlan.'

'Son of a bitch,' Ed gasped. He sat up, looking round the inn to see if anyone had heard his outburst but there wasn't. There was only Balelin and he within earshot. The only other man there was sitting on the far side of the room and slumped against the wall in a deep sleep.

'You mean to say,' Ed sat forward whispering his thought to Balelin, 'are you telling me that those things, those Goblins in Guidepost were sent to kill Grizlan?'

Balelin nodded. 'If not to kill her then at least to carry the coin to whoever was to do the deed.'

'Well then, Balelin, it was just good luck that I was there. Least now you know Grizlan is safe.'

'No Ed, she is far from safe.' Balelin looked into the fire as his many troubled thoughts filled his head. 'We fled from one danger to another. Nowhere is safe for Grizlan.' Balelin faced the window, quietly saying, 'Somewhere, out there, there are blades drawn against her, and against those that travel with her. She is not safe here; anyone could be an assassin. And she may not be safe at Bennith Dure. We must go there; it is our home now. But what sort of home it might be, I do not know. The news of the trolls is weeks old, and no word has come since then.'

They sat quietly for a time, minding their own thoughts and watching the fire. Finally Balelin spoke, but so softly that it was almost to himself, 'I do not believe it was luck or mere chance that you were at Guidepost, Ed.'

'Hang on a minute,' Ed said sharply. 'You don't think that I . . . I mean you're not accusing me...'

Balelin held up his hand. 'No Ed. If you had wanted to kill my Grizlan you could have done so a number of times. No. But I think, no I believe that there was something more than chance that has brought you to here.' Balelin stared into the fire again as he ordered his thoughts before saying, 'Ed, either you, or perhaps one of your family has a purpose here. I do not know what it is or how it may come to be. I am old Ed, old to the point where my mind can be clouded. But I know that there is a purpose to everything. And that being so, there is a reason why you and your family were brought here.'

'Brought here?' Ed said. 'What do mean brought here? By who? By what?'

Balelin sighed and sat back in his chair. 'That, my friend, I simply do not know.'

The sleeping man in the corner of the inn did not stir. His eyes were closed and he breathed softly. All the while Ed and old dwarf talked he sat there, slumped in the corner of the room as his ale went flat in his tankard.

It was only after the Ed and dwarf vacated their place by the fire that the sleeping man stirred. He reached into his coin purse, tossed a penny on the table and, without a word, he left.

The innkeeper's boy came forward then, collecting the empty tankards and mopping the tables with a grubby cloth. He picked up the penny that the sleeping man had left, muttering, 'Good riddens, stinking the place up like a tannery.'

# CHAPTER 16

## Moorbe

There were bacon and eggs for breakfast. Thickly cut slices of bacon fried until crispy and golden brown, and as many eggs as they could manage. There was freshly baked barley bread, dark and rich and soft with a thick golden crust. In the middle of the table, next to bread, was freshly churned butter, clay jars of fruit jams, honey and marmalade. As the Deeks' family came down to the dining room and took their seats the boy brought them tea. A few minutes later he was back again, this time with a plate of cold meats, ham and beef and chicken. He set them on the table, asking if there was anything else they might want.

'No thanks,' Ed laughed. 'I think we got enough food here for a small army.'

Kate looked at the bacon and eggs saying, 'It's a bit full on this, isn't it? I don't suppose I could just have some cereal?'

A blank expression crossed the boy's face. 'Cereal? What's that, miss?'

'You know,' Kate sighed. 'Corn flakes, shredded wheat, cereal, get it?'

'You mean like we give the horses, miss,' the boy asked. 'I could get you some from the stable if that's what you really want.'

'No that's fine,' Liz said then, looking at Kate she added, 'I don't think they have Froot Loops here, sweetie.'

'No?' Kate sighed, 'Oh no they wouldn't have. Silly me.'

'You got that right,' Jay sniggered.

Without looking Kate reached out her arm behind her brother's head and in one swift motion: smack!

'Mum, she's hitting me again,' Jay protested.

'Sorry,' Kate smirked. 'My hand slipped.'

'Try and behave you two,' Liz said.

'Yes Mum,' they both moaned.

Ed shook his head, wondering, as any parent would, when, or indeed if, they would grow out of that.

He looked at the boy who was still fussing around their table and asked, 'Are our friends joining us for breakfast?'

The boy looked back, an almost embarrassed expression on his face, saying, 'But they have left, sir. I thought you knew.' With that the boy scampered off towards the kitchen.

'Well?' Liz said to Ed. 'And what do you make of that?'

Ed shrugged. 'I know that Balelin was worried about the news he got. But to just up and leave.'

'He is an important man, I mean dwarf, an important dwarf,' Jay offered. 'Maybe he just had to get on. Wolfric did say as how the Dwarves were very late arriving and Balelin himself said that they had been delayed.'

'True,' Ed reflected, 'but just to up and leave without a word. I think Balelin was far more worried about things than he was letting on.'

'Whatever the reason,' Liz said, 'it looks like we are on our own from here on.'

'Sure does,' Ed agreed.

'So,' Liz said facing him, her expression all serious, 'perhaps we can think about getting home now.'

Cenwalh the innkeeper came out of the kitchen and over to the table. He was wiping his hands off on his waistcoat, adding more stains on top of the countless ones already there. 'Begging your pardon, sir,' he said to Ed then, nodding at Liz, 'madam, but I clean forgot this letter, sir.' He reached into his waistcoat pocket and pulled out a folded piece of paper that was sealed with red wax. 'That old dwarf fella give me this for you sir. Sorry I did not give it to you before but I've been so busy with the breakfast and the like. Cook's not feeling her best today and we got a full house. Says she is over worked and needs help, but she always says that. In fact she has been saying that all the years I have known her.'

'The letter,' Ed said, nodding at the paper that was still very much in Cenwalh's hand.

'Oh yes sir, here you are,' Cenwalh handed over the letter adding, 'I'd thought they might have been doing a moonlight flit so I did. I mean, leaving in the dead of night like that, sneaking round like as many thieves in the dark. But then that old one, that Balelin chap, he gives me that letter and coin for your rooms for as long as you wants them.'

'I'm sorry what?' Ed said.

'Your rooms, sir,' Cenwalh explained. 'The old chap paid for your rooms. Paid me in silver too so he did. Enough for the rooms for three months, if you wants to stay that is.'

'And why would he do that?' Ed asked.

Cenwalh shrugged. 'Can't rightly say, sir. Dwarves are funny folk so they are. Do the oddest things at times. Like this morning, well last night really, just gave me the letter and the coin for the rooms then up and left. Very odd folk is Dwarves, sir, meaning no offence you understand, but very odd folk indeed.'

Ed thanked Cenwalh for the letter, and as the innkeeper returned to the kitchen still muttering something about the odd ways of Dwarves, he opened the letter and read.

*To Ed the Longshanks and Dwarf-friend,*
*I am sorry but we have to leave, and for reasons I told you last night, it is better that no one see us go.*

*I hope you understand how important it is that we must go now and please do not think that we have left you. You and your family will forever be welcome at our halls. I hope, once Chancellor Moorbe lifts the admonishment not to leave Two Rivers that you will do me the great honour of coming to our halls and experience real dwarf hospitality.*

*My friend, this is not goodbye, but we must by force go on ahead of you. I am more sure now than at any time that you yet have a part to play, and for that reason, I know that we will meet again. So, until then my friends, farewell and go in good health.*

*Balelin.*

After reading the letter Ed handed it to Liz saying, 'What do you make of that?'

Liz read it and handed the paper back. 'What did Balelin mean by "the reasons I told you last night"?'

'I'll tell you later,' Ed said in a hushed voice. 'There were things he told me which I think best we not talk about in the open.'

Liz nodded her understanding and said no more.

Hardwin called on the family shortly after breakfast. He came to their rooms, placed his hand upon his chest and bowed, by way of either greeting or salute, and, very formally said, 'My Lord, Chancellor Moorbe asks that you come with me as he has need to speak with you.'

'All of us?' Kate asked with a smile.

Hardwin returned her smile and, after another small bow, answered, 'Yes, he would speak with all of your family.' He bowed again. 'I shall wait outside.' And with that he turned and left.

'What do you think, Ed?' Liz said after Hardwin had left. 'You think this Moorbe guy can help us get home?'

Ed swung his cloak over his shoulders and fastened the clasp. 'We can hope.'

Outside the inn Hardwin was indeed waiting for them, so was the escort of six soldiers dressed in padded jackets and long cloaks that did little to hide the swords they carried. On their heads they wore open-faced helmets with blue horsehair plumes running front to back.

As the family walked out of the inn the soldiers fell in on either side of them.

Seeing the expressions on their faces Hardwin said, 'It's for your safety. The chancellor will explain.'

'For our safety?' Ed whispered to Liz. 'Then why do I feel like a prisoner?'

They walked through the market square, hardly drawing an eye from the few stall owners that were setting up. Indeed, the only person to pay them any attention was a woman sweeping the cobbles outside her shop. She had to stop sweeping to let the party pass. And as they passed, she muttered something about one of the soldiers kicking over the pile of dirt she had just swept together. The soldiers did not respond nor did they give the woman a second glance. They just walked directly to the gate at the bottom end of the market square.

Somehow Kate had managed to get herself next to Hardwin. She was chatting with him, asking about his duties and if he would be free that afternoon.

Liz saw the way Kate was behaving and the way she was staring up at the young herald as they walked. She gently elbowed Ed in his side and, without saying anything, nodded at the two in front.

Ed saw the way Kate was smiling up at the young man, saw how she was giving him those big doe eyes of hers, and how she was all but hanging off the herald's arm as they walked. He sighed and rolled his eyes skyward. Kate was obviously smitten.

Jay was behind his mother and father and hadn't seen Kate; he was too busy trying to keep in step with the very large blond-haired soldier beside him. It wasn't easy, the soldier was a good foot and half taller than Jay, and his legs were far longer too. So, while it was an easy pace for the soldier, for Jay it meant he had to stretch his pace as far as he could just to keep up with the man. Jay kind of hoped that nobody had noticed what he was doing but, as they reached the gate, the blond soldier stopped, looked down at Jay, and give him a little smile.

Hardwin led the way through the gates. Then, after the gatehouse, they walked up an inclined road that took them to the first courtyard. On the left, over by the east wall, were a row of stables. All around them soldiers were mucking out and grooming their horses. On the right there was a building that, by the look of it, must have been the barracks. It was two stories high, built of stone, and had rows of small windows. On either end there was a door and, sitting outside the doors, soldiers were busy cleaning their kit, sharpening swords, and doing all those things that soldiers do everyday.

The whole courtyard was on a slope, following as it did the gradient of the rock on which it was built.

They walked through the first courtyard to a second gatehouse: this one much taller and more stoutly built than the first. The inner wall was built on a much higher part of the slope and seemed to loom menacingly over them.

There was a ramp in the right hand corner of the courtyard. It began just after the barracks and ran part way along the west wall to the second wall. From there it turned left, following the second wall for a short way until it reached the gatehouse. The second gate was therefore set at right angles to the courtyard.

The gatehouse itself was a massive structure built out of dark grey granite, four stories high, with only arrow slits instead of windows. Inside of the gates there was a dark passage that was twenty feet long with a portcullis at the far end. After that there was yet another sloping ramp, this one flanked by smaller walls. The ramp led up to a large, grassy, triangular inner courtyard.

There were a number of buildings around the courtyard. In the north-west corner, to the right of the, gate was the main tower, four stories high with arrow slits on the two lower floors and windows above that. A heavy oak door, bound with iron bars and studded with hefty iron rivets was the only entrance to the tower.

Along by the west wall, overlooking the river below, there was another barracks that appeared to be built into the very wall itself. There as a smaller tower at the southern end of the courtyard. This tower overlooked the meeting of the two rivers and was smaller than the main keep tower as it had only three stories. Then, over by the east wall, were a small collection of buildings that appeared to have been built, rebuilt, and joined into each other: almost as if the buildings had just sprouted one from another. These were the kitchens, healing house, grain and food stores, and smithies.

Hardwin led the way to the main tower in the north-east corner. He walked towards the great oak door where, after knocking, he bid them good day.

'Thane Wolfric will take you to meet with the Chancellor,' Hardwin informed them with a bow, 'my duties for the morning take me elsewhere.'

'We'll see you later, won't we?' Kate asked quickly. She blushed at her obvious impatience and added, trying her best to appear indifferent, 'If you have time and nothing else to do that is.'

Hardwin smiled, bowed to Kate and said, 'I would like nothing better.' Then, facing Ed directly, he added, 'With your permission of course, sir.'

'Only if we are not taking you away from something important,' Ed said.

'Of course, sir,' Hardwin said, snapping to attention. He gave another small bow then turned and was gone.

A big silly grin spread across Jay's face. 'Kate and Hardwin sitting in a tree, k-i-s-s-i . . .'

Kate's arm flashed out and she cuffed him round the back of the head again.

'*Mum*,' Jay protested loudly.

'For pity's sake,' Liz groaned. 'Will you two behave? We are about to meet the chancellor, and you two are going on like three-year-olds.'

'He started it, Mum,' Kate protested lamely.

'Did not,' Jay moaned.

'Did too.'

'For pity's sake,' Liz said.

The door opened and the guard escorted them up to the second floor of the tower. Here they were met by Wolfric. He wore soft felt boots and fine linen trousers. His jacket was of velvet, dark blue in colour, with a silver eagle's head on the left breast. They had only seen Wolfric once before and that was on the road when he was under arms. Then he'd looked a very intimidating figure, all leather and armour. But now, dressed in gentler clothing and in the soft light of the small tower windows, Wolfric appeared a more friendly and approachable man. His eyes that before had been narrowed against the sun at their first meeting were now warm and gracious. He offered his hand to Ed saying, 'Good morning. I see you no longer wear the eagle's head.'

Ed had no time to respond as Wolfric turned to Liz saying, 'Morning lady, how do you find our town?'

'It's very nice,' Liz replied.

'Good, I am pleased hear that,' Wolfric said. The he was suddenly all business-like as he said, 'I shall take you to meet Chancellor Moorbe now but, before I do, I must have your word that whatever you see or hear you will show the utmost discretion.'

'Of course,' Ed replied.

Liz nodded, 'You have our word.'

Wolfric turned to the children and waited for them to also swear.

'Very well,' he said at last. 'Balelin tells me that you can be trusted so you are all on your honour.' He stepped aside, and sweeping his hand towards another door, he said, 'This way please.'

Wolfric stepped to the door, knocked, opened the door and took one step inside. 'My Lord chancellor, the strangers Lord Balelin talked about are here,' he said, giving a low bow to someone that they could not yet see.

'Very good,' said another voice, its tone a little lower and slightly gruff. 'Please ask them to come in and take a seat.'

Wolfric pushed the door open and signalled them to enter.

The room was large and a little dark. There were only two small windows to provide light, and so, there were a number of candles placed around the room to help illuminate it. It was a cross between an office and a library; by the windows, on the west wall, there was a large writing desk: books, papers and scrolls littering the top. In one corner of the desk was a tray, a layer of sawdust on the bottom, and with a hamster running round and round inside of its wheel. Next to the desk, sitting on a tall perch, was a brightly coloured parrot that was far too busy eating sunflower seeds to pay them any attention. Around the room, filling nearly every inch of the other walls, were book shelves that ran from floor to ceiling. And there were more books, stacked in piles on the floor or in open cases and chests, which covered most of the floor: so many in fact that they had to tiptoe their way between them.

In the centre of the room there was an old sofa and four chairs, and more books were stacked up next to the sides of each of them. So high were some of the book stacks that they were being used as tables and candles had been placed on top of them. Sitting on the sofa, and watching their every move as they came in, was a big, golden-haired dog.

'Please be seated,' Wolfric said as he closed the door and went to the chair at the writing desk.

The family picked their way through the mass of books and found themselves a seat, all that was but for Kate. She made her way towards the sofa, and towards the big dog sitting watching them. 'What a lovely dog,' she said to no one in particular. She reached out and patted the dog's head, ruffling its curly hair in her fingers. 'What's he called,' she asked Wolfric as she again patted the dog's head.

'Please don't do that,' the dog said, staring up at Kate. 'I have just been washed and it takes me forever to get my hair right.'

Kate's hand froze in mid pat. 'You . . . you . . . spoke,' she stammered.

'Yes I did,' the dog stated caustically, 'and you still have your hand in my hair if you don't mind, young lady.'

Kate snatched her hand back, as if she was pulling it out of a fire. She gawked at the dog flabbergasted, her mouth wide open. 'But you're a dog,' she gasped. 'You're a dog and you're talking.'

'Well, I can see there is no fooling you, young lady,' the dog said. 'Now if you will take a seat, girl, we can get down to cases.'

Kate backed away, tripping and stumbling over the scattered books several times before she got herself a seat. All the while her eyes, just like everyone else's save Wolfric, were transfixed on the talking dog.

'I am Chancellor Moorbe,' the dog said earnestly, as Kate slumped back into her seat. 'You have already met Thane Wolfric.'

The family nodded in unison, nobody saying anything as they still could not believe that a dog was talking to them.

'I would like to welcome you to Two Rivers,' the dog, or rather Chancellor Moorbe went on. 'Lord Balelin has told me how you helped the Lady Grizlan. A brave deed that, Ed, may I call you Ed?'

'Err . . . y . . . y . . . yes, that's fine,' Ed spluttered.

'Very well then, Ed it is,' Moorbe said, the tip of his tail wagging slightly. 'We welcome you but we have to ask how you came to here?'

'Well . . . we . . . err . . .,' Ed stammered, looking from Wolfric to Moorbe and back again and unsure if he should be talking to the thane or the dog. 'Well . . . err . . . just sort of . . . err . . . hitched up with the Dwarves, Balelian and the others, I mean Lord Balelin, and the others, you know, Lady Grizlian and Grooflin and, well you know who, and they . . . err . . . brought us here.' Ed paused; he was rambling so, after clearing his throat noisily, he started over: this time more slowly and more coherently. 'What I mean was that after Lady Grizlian and Grooflin were attached at Guidepost we sort of joined up. We, I mean my family and I, are lost here. We do not know where we are. We do not even know where here is. We just kinda hitched up with the dwarves hoping that we might find out how to get home.'

'That much we know already,' Moorbe said. He paused a second to quickly scratch his ear with his hind leg, then went on. 'What I was asking is how you came to be in Angron in the first place. Lord Balelin could not tell me that. Other than you met with the Lady Grizlan at Guidepost. So how exactly did you come to be here in Angron? And how did you come to be in Guidepost?'

'Well that too, we are, shall I say, unsure about,' Ed said slowly. 'A few days ago we were on holiday, driving round England. Then we got into this terrible fog, got lost, crashed the car, and had to walk in the hope we might get help. We somehow ended up here. Or rather we ended up at a farm near Guidepost. It was just a small farm, near to a bridge by Tangle Wood. Braygon they call the man that runs it, the farm I mean.'

'And his wife, Salsify,' Liz added.

'That's right,' Ed said. 'Salsify. A jolly type she is. Braygon and Salsify, it was their farm that we stumbled on.'

'Then clearly you are not local,' Wolfric said softly. 'No one in Angron would even travel in Tangle Wood during daylight least all at night. Not even with all the wolves of the north snapping at their heels.'

'Well, we did,' Ed said ruefully. 'Twice actually. Once that night, just after the accident, and then the next night after what happened in Guidepost.'

'An accident and a fight with goblins all in the same day,' Wolfric observed. 'Mischance seems to dog your steps, Ed the Longshanks.'

'I hear that,' Ed mused. 'We sure as heck seem to be having a run of bad luck.' He looked at Liz for a moment, then at Kate and Jay; all appeared to waiting for him carry on. 'The truth is Chancellor Moorbe,' Ed began again slowly, measuring his words carefully, 'and no disrespect to you or your town Thane Wolfric, but we just want to go home. We don't know how we got here, but, well, to be honest, we do not belong here, we don't fit in and frankly, I am a little bit afraid for my family.'

'Afraid,' Moorbe said. 'Why so?'

'Well, because of those things that attacked us in Guidepost for one,' Ed said sharply. 'Then Balelin's talk of Trolls in the north and who all knows what else. We are just fish out of water here and we want to get back where we belong. Please Chancellor, if you know of a way, or someone that might help us get home, we would be forever in your debt.'

'I wish that I could but help,' Moorbe said slowly. 'But, as I am as yet unsure where you came from, or how you came to here, I am at a loss as to how to advice on getting back.' Moorbe fell silent, as they all did, while he thought for some time. Finally, and very slowly, he asked, 'You said that you had an accident in Tangle Wood.'

'That right,' Ed said. 'I couldn't see a thing in all that fog and then we just hit this big rock and that was that. The car has a broken half shaft and cracked sump.'

'Could you not get your cart fixed?' Moorbe asked. 'And what happened to your horses?'

'Not *cart*,' Ed said, stressing the word deliberately, 'A *car*. There were no horses. A car does not have horses.'

'Then it was only a small cart,' Wolfric offered. 'A hand cart, was that it?'

Ed snorted a small frustrated laugh to himself. 'No, again, it's not *cart*, it's *car*. C-A-R, there is no "T" and no horses. A car. And you do not push it, you ride in it.'

'How very strange,' Moorbe stated, without appreciating that a talking dog, even if he were the Chancellor, might seem a little strange to other people. 'But if there are no horses then how does this, "car" move?'

'Easy,' Ed said with a dismissive shrug of his shoulders. 'You turn the key, start the engine, put your foot on the gas, and it goes.'

A suspicious look passed between Wolfric and Moorbe after Ed's explanation. They both looked at him distrustfully as they pressed him silently for more information.

Ed took the hint, saying, 'You put gas in, that gets mixed with air and, when the mixture is in the cylinder, a spark ignites it.' He held his hands up, trying his best to mime the actions of the piston in an engine. 'It's called a four stroke. One, the piston goes down and the fuel/air mix is injected. Two, the valves at top close and the piston come up to compress the mixture. Three, the spark plug sparks and, and, and I don't believe this, I am trying to explain the workings of an internal combustion engine to a damn fool Labradoodle.'

'I am not a fool,' Moorbe barked, he jumped up on to all four feet, baring his teeth as the hair on his back raised up, 'and I am not a Labradoodle: I just happen to have naturally curly hair.'

'My apologies,' Ed said quickly. 'I did not mean to offend. It's just that, well, I have never met a talking dog before and it is taking some getting used to.'

Moorbe stared at Ed for a moment in silence. For all the chancellor's face did not betray there was an internal debate taking place within his mind. At last, when he spoke again, his tone was softer. 'I accept your apology,' he said, his back hair once more lying flat. Then he looked over at Thane Wolfric, as if seeking approval for something. Wolfric did not say anything, but he gave the chancellor a small, almost imperceptible nod.

Moorbe went on. 'I am sorry for snapping at you like that, I was not always as you see me now,' he said slowly. 'At one time I was a man, just like you. And if I might add, considered by some to be quite handsome.' Moorbe jumped down from the sofa he had been sitting on and then stood up on his hind legs and walked across the room towards the desk. 'I am afraid that my face was too well known and I required a disguise. A disguise which has left me as I am now.'

''A disguise?' Ed said, echoing the chancellor, 'but how can you change from man to dog. It's just not possible.'

'Oh it is possible. Very much so in fact as you can see,' Moorbe said. He was standing next to the desk and turned to face the family. 'All that you need is a good sorcerer and a willingness to take the risk.'

'Well, can the sorcerer not change you back?' Kate asked.

Moorbe gave what must have been the nearest thing he could manage to a smile. His head tilted to one side as he said. 'I did say that you needed a *good* sorcerer.' Then the smile was gone and his teeth bared once more in anger. 'I needed a good sorcerer and what did I get?' Moorbe's paw came up sharply and he hit the end of the parrot's perch with his paw sending it and the bird spinning round. 'An idiot with a stutter. Not content with leaving me like this, you managed to turn yourself into a parrot and a parrot that cannot even speak. What use are you, Amalric? None, that's what.' With that he hit the perch again, causing the parrot to squawk noisily and flap its wings in panic as it was spun round and round once more.

'What about the hamster?' Kate asked, nodding towards the little animal in its cage on the desk. 'Could he not help?'

'Why ever would you think that?' Moorbe tutted. 'He's a hamster.'

Kate blushed, 'I just thought, well, seeing as you are . . . and Amaliric is a . . . you know . . . I just thought that maybe the hamster was, well, I dunno.'

Moorbe looked at Kate and shook his head. 'What a fanciful imagination you have, young lady.' With that he went back down on all four paws and walked back to the sofa. He jumped up and, after walking round in several tight circles, sat down again.

'Could you not find another sorcerer?' Ed asked. 'One that might change you back, change both of you back for that matter?'

'Sorcerers do not grow on trees,' Moorbe sighed. 'They are very uncommon and they are very secretive.'

'That is truly said,' Wolfric agreed. He had been silent for a long time, preferring to watch and listen to the conversation, but now he offered up his thoughts on the matter of the chancellor's condition. 'Amalric was the first true sorcerer to come to Angron since the days of my father's father. And even if there was another, which I doubt, there is no saying that he could undo what Amalric did.'

Moorbe nodded in agreement. 'A sorcerer's spell can really only be undone by the sorcerer himself'– Moorbe turned to face the parrot once more saying, in a raised voice, 'unless of course he is a stammering twit' – then, he turned back to face Ed, 'and, if another sorcerer should try to undo the spell and fail, well...'

Moorbe did not finish the sentence. He fell silent and just stared at the floor as he became lost in his thoughts. No one else spoke either. They were all thinking the same thing, thinking what might happen should an attempt to undo the spell go wrong, and none of them liked the answers they were giving themselves.

It was Wolfric that broke the silence. 'Tell me, Ed,' he said quietly, 'Lord Balelin tells that you and your family are all good riders. Have you done much riding?'

Ed nodded. 'We are lucky where we live, where our home is I mean, there is plenty of open country and some good stables where we can hire horses.'

'It sounds good,' Wolfric said without a trace of any emotion in his voice.

'It is,' Liz offered. 'Lots of fresh air and beautiful scenery. And sometimes, in the summer, we can go up into the Cascades and go horse-trekking.'

'But you have no horses of your own?'

'Sadly no,' Liz said. 'We just don't have the time. It's just the world we live in I fear; everybody seems to have very busy lives.'

'We got the horses in the stables behind the inn,' Jay reminded everyone.

'Yes indeed,' Wolfric said deliberately. 'And how did you come by those horses, young man?' he asked Jay directly.

'We took them after Dad seen off those four goblin things,' Jay said proudly.

'Really,' Wolfric responded slowly. He turned and faced Ed direct, his eye narrowing as he gauged Ed carefully. 'And how was that?'

'After those things were dead we sort of had to get out of there quickly,' Ed replied. 'Grooflin said that they would have horses, and we had seen them riding into Guidepost earlier . . .'

'They ran us off the road, you mean,' Liz cut in.

'That's true enough,' Ed went on. 'So anyway, Grooflin said to grab their horses, and honestly, I was so shocked at what had just happened, I just did as I was told.'

'Interesting,' Wolfric said, glancing sideways at Moorbe as he did so. 'But tell me, Ed, if you can, how is it that your horses, rather the horses you took, carry the brand of Thane Helain, Lord of Briloness?'

'Well I, I mean, well I really don't know,' Ed said. 'We had seen those things riding them shortly before, and when Grooflin said to get their horses, we just grabbed them up and started riding as quick as we could. As to whatever brand they carry I really have no idea. I can only assume that those goblin things must have stolen them, and after the fight, after they were dead, we just up and ran.'

'How do you know that they were the horses that the goblins had been riding?' Moorbe asked.

'Because they were the only horses around,' Ed said. 'Apart from the ponies hitched to Grooflin's wagon.'

Ed suddenly found himself staring at Wolfric who was staring right back at him. And being in the thane's stare, Ed quickly discovered, was not a comfortable place to be. Wolfric said nothing for a long while, said nothing but continued to examine Ed with his piercing eyes until Ed began to shift uneasily in his seat.

Finally Wolfric spoke, 'Lord Balelin informs me that you took some gold from the goblins. May I see it?' he said more as an order than a request.

Ed took the money bag from his belt and placed it in Wolfric's outstretched hand.

Wolfric opened the purse and lifted out one of the gold coins, turning it over and over in his hand as he studied it meticulously. He held it up to the light, spinning it in his fingers; then he placed it in his teeth and bit down on it. Tossing the coin several times and catching it again, to test its weight, he finally looked at Moorbe saying, 'No doubt about it, Chancellor, it is Bytanthus gold. The same as Lady Grizlan had.'

'Are you sure it is real?' Moorbe asked.

'Very sure,' Wolfric replied. He placed the coin back in the purse and handed it back to Ed.

Ed, after thanking Wolfric for the purse, asked, 'What is Bytanthus gold?'

'An assassin's wages,' Moorbe growled. He would have said more but Wolfric shot him a glance which told the chancellor to hold his tongue.

'An assassin?' Jay said. 'To kill who? And why?'

Moorbe, more composed now answered, 'Why the Lady Grizlain of course, but as to who sent the assassins we cannot be sure; we can only speculate. And I am not going to speculate openly here. All I will say is that I have my suspicions but, for now, they must remain *my* suspicions.'

The questioning went on for the greater part of the morning, and indeed into the early afternoon. It would have gone on longer but Chancellor Moorbe insisted that they all take a break for lunch.

Wolfric rose at that point and, after opening the door, called for his squire. He asked if the noon meal was readied for him and his guests. The young squire informed Wolfric that it was and, with that the young man was dismissed.

'I shall have your secretary bring your meal, sir,' Wolfric said to Chancellor Moorbe as he gave a bow. 'By your leave, sir.'

'Yes, thank you,' Moorbe replied then, turning to the family he said. 'I hope you all enjoy your meal and we shall talk again this afternoon.'

'Thank you,' Liz said, as she too gave a sort of half bow half curtsy. 'Till this afternoon.'

A bow, seemingly the correct etiquette when leaving the presence of a chancellor, was given by each of the family in turn before they left by the door Wolfric was holding open for them. Outside, after Wolfric had closed the door, Liz asked, 'Will Chancellor Moorbe not have lunch with us?'

A pained expression crossed Wolfric's face. 'The chancellor always eats alone now.' He cleared his throat before reluctantly adding, 'He prefers to eat alone: his table manners are not what they used to be.'

'I see,' Liz whispered.

After a lunch of roast chicken Wolfric invited the family to join him for a walk around the walls of the keep. The sun was bright and the air fresh, with only a hint of a breeze coming over the river from the east. As they walked, Wolfric pointed out places of interest to them, more to kill time than anything else. For he, just as they, wanted to get back to Chancellor Moorbe's office and continue where they had left off.

It was Ed that asked the question that they had all been thinking. 'Thane Wolfric, do you think the chancellor will be much longer with his lunch?'

Wolfric appeared unsettled by the question. He stopped walking and, very quietly, without looking at Ed, answered, 'Chancellor Moorbe may be a while yet. He eats alone as I said, but after his meal he will sleep for a while.' He turned to face Ed adding, 'I am afraid that the chancellor's afternoon sleeps are becoming longer and there is no way of knowing if he will see you again today. I am sorry but we shall just have to wait and see if he shall receive you again.'

'Please, Thane Wolfric, tell me if you can,' Liz said, 'is he sleeping more now than he used to?'

'He can, sometimes, but not always,' Wolfric said, obviously uncomfortable at talking about the chancellor behind his back.

'And how and where does he sleep?' Liz asked. 'I am sorry to press you but I am a doctor and am therefore curious.'

'Liz?' Ed interrupted. 'What are you getting at?'

'Just thinking out loud,' Liz said. 'Has his behaviour changed at all over time?' Liz asked the thane.

'A little,' Wolfric replied.

'I was wondering if after being changed into a dog, were there any effects on him, other than being a dog that is, which is strange enough. But it occurred to me that the longer he stays as a dog then the more like a dog he might become.'

'Ah come on, Liz,' Ed sighed.

'No, Ed,' Wolfric cut in, 'your wife-man may be correct, I fear. We had hoped to effect a change back for the chancellor but, as you saw with Amalric, things did not go as planned. I fear that the longer the chancellor remains as he is, then the more dog and the less man he will become.' Wolfric turned and looked off over the wide eastern river as he said, 'We have gathered together all the best knowledge we can find, you saw it scattered round the office, but, without a sorcerer skilled in the arts, it is nothing but so much paper.'

'I'm sorry,' Kate said, 'but do you mean all those books in Moorbe's room are about magic?'

Wolfric turned to face her saying, 'All the books in the *Chancellor's office*, yes they are the best knowledge of the magic arts in all Angron and many lands beyond.'

Before he could say any more Wolfric saw Moorbe's secretary hurrying towards them. 'It would appear that the chancellor is awake,' he said, nodding towards the man. 'Shall we?' He held out his hand, indicating that they should make their way back to the tower and the office where they could resume their talk.

As they walked back along the wall Ed glanced down towards the market square. From up on the wall of the keep the whole of Two Rivers was laid out before them. It was possible not only to look down on the stables and barracks, but also beyond the second wall to the market square and the streets leading off to the north. Closer to the tower Ed could look down at the dock, the curtain wall, and the cobbled street with the merchant houses on it. He could even see the bridge gate and the bridge across the river; and the long queue of people and carts waiting to cross.

'Is the market always this busy?' he asked Wolfric.

'Very busy these last months,' Wolfric said slowly. He paused for a moment and looked down at the bridge and the queue beyond before asking, 'Tell me, Ed, when you look down there what do you see?'

Ed stepped closer to the battlements and stood beside the thane for a few minutes before answering, 'People coming and going to the market. Over there at the bridge there are more waiting to get across, no doubt with plenty to sell, judging by the way all those carts are loaded.'

'Look again, Ed,' Wolfric said softly. 'Tell me how many people are crossing to the east and how many are crossing back to the west?'

'Well about the sa . . .' Ed stopped himself saying 'the same' for, as he looked again, looked more closely, he could see that the traffic over the bridge was almost entirely one way.

On the western bank of the river there was a long row of people and carts waiting their turn to cross. Looking over the eastern bank of the other river there was an equally long row of people and carts, but these had crossed and were then headed off towards the east. Yes there were some carts entering the market and setting up stalls, but many, many more carts simply crossed the bridge, drove straight through the town, and made directly for the ferry and the east.

'What's going on?' Ed asked. 'Why is everybody heading east? Is there something on there, another town, a bigger market, what?'

Wolfric's expression was extremely sombre. 'They are not going to something, Ed. Yes there are other towns east of here; Durren Fells Farm is north-east and, many leagues to the east, there is the city of Thessabin. But those people are not going to them, leastways not directly. They are going away from something. They are moving as fast as they can from the war they know is coming. Even the very rock this keep is built on can feel it coming.'

'War?' Ed said, 'Against who and for what?'

'Why against the goblins of course,' Wolfric said. 'I have felt it coming for a long time. It is just a matter of time before the goblins and their allies attack. It may have already begun in the north, in the dwarf halls and mines. That was why Balelin made haste to be with his people. He knows just as I know that there is war coming. Even those people down there know it is coming that is why ...'

Wolfric never finished what he was saying. Something in the west had caught his attention and his words trailed into nothing as his eyes fixed upon the small group of wagons in the far west.

The whole family was waiting for Wolfric to finish, but when he didn't, they began to wonder what he was looking at. They followed his gaze, struggling to see what he had seen. But the little group that had drawn Wolfric's attention was still too far off to make out. All that could be seen was small cloud of dust rising in the still air. Other carts and wagons coming down the road had not raised dust like that so, they safely assumed, this group was, for some reason, travelling faster. And indeed, as they got closer to the river, it could clearly be seen that the small group was pushing their carts and horses as hard as they dared.

As the group approached it was possible, even at some distance, to make out that there were three wagons with several more people round them; some were riding while others ran to keep up. When the small group reached the end of the queue waiting to cross the bridge they merely pulled off the road and went round it. An action that caused many in the queue to protest. Some of those queuing even tried to get in the way of the fast moving carts but, at the front of the group, was a very large man riding a very large horse, and few people were willing to put themselves in his path.

The big rider went down the queue waving people out of the way, and any that didn't move when he told them, he kicked them as he rode rapidly towards the bridge. Even when the toll collectors at the bridge barred his way, the big man simply jumped down from the saddle, grabbed the first collector by the shirt and tossed the man headlong into the river.

When the first toll collector went for his unplanned swim the other two just stepped aside. The big man then remounted his horse and rode over the bridge. Even when the guards at the dock saw what was happening and came running with over large walking sticks, the big man just rode his horse at them till they too jumped aside. Behind him the carts were now also on the bridge, as were the other riders and runners that made up the group.

Further back, in the queue, whatever exchanges there had been between the two parties, had had a very unsettling affect. All of a sudden the whole queue, which until that time had been waiting patiently for their turn to cross, now wanted to rush the bridge. It was as much as the dock guards could do to stop them; even with the help of the soldiers from the bridge gate it very nearly turned into a riot.

'Maullen?' Ed said astonished.

'Who?' Wolfric asked.

'The big man on the horse,' Ed said, 'that looks like that Maullen the smithy from Guidepost.'

Wolfric straightened up, his face all stern and poorly masked anger. 'Then that Maullen fellow had better have a good reason for dashing the bridge like that or I will know the why of it.'

Wolfric walked away from the family and headed towards the gate to the lower part of the keep. Ed and the family remained where they were, watching as guards and soldiers scuffled with all the others trying to cross the bridge. But, from high up on the wall of the keep, they could also see Maullen, and the all the others of his party, as they entered the town. They turned off the bridge road and made directly towards the market square but, rather than stop in the square, they made straight for the lower gate.

Only when Maullen reached the gate did he stop and dismount. Quickly he was surrounded by soldiers, weapons drawn, as he held out his arms. Yet his arms were not raised in surrender, rather his arms were extremely animated, waving this way and pointing that, as he shouted something at the soldiers.

Up on the wall they could not hear what was said but, as soon as Maullen had finished waving his arms about, the soldiers lowered their weapons. Some of the soldiers ran out of the gate towards the carts while other ran into the barracks. Moments later yet more soldiers came running out, and all of them went to the carts. The next minute the carts were being brought into the barrack square.

Some of the soldiers ran up to the gate of the keep and, all but one of them, raced towards the healing house. The one that had separated from the group ran directly towards Wolfric. Words passed between the two for a few moments before Wolfric nodded and waved his arm as he dismissed the man. The other, the one that had run directly to the healing house, was now hurrying back down to the barrack square, this time carrying litters. After them, moving as quickly as they could, was an old man and a very overweight woman dressed in a long white apron.

Wolfric began to walk slowly back towards where the family had been watching events. His face was expressionless but all the colour had been drained from it.

'Sir, Thane Wolfric,' Jay said as the tall man approached, 'what has happened, sir?'

For a moment the thane did not speak; he looked down into the barrack square as the three small carts were being delicately unloaded. At last he looked at the family and, in a flat, emotionless voice, said, 'Guidepost is destroyed, many of the farms too. That is all that is left, that handful of people down there, is all that is left from a whole shire.' He suddenly looked up at Liz as something came to his mind. 'Lord Balelin said as how you were some type of healer. Is that true, My Lady?'

'Yes, I'm a doctor, a surgeon actually,' Liz replied.

'Then there is much work for you at the healing house.'

'I'll do whatever I can,' Liz said. 'Kate, come on, you too.'

As the women left Ed looked at Wolfric and asked. 'Is there anything I can do?'

Wolfric stared at Ed and said, 'Do you have a sword?'

'Well sort of,' Ed said, 'it's one of those we took from the goblins, though I am embarrassed to say I don't know how to use it.'

'Learn,' Wolfric said.

# Chapter 17

## Wolfric's Company

Within an hour of the first survivors of the massacre at Guidepost arrived at Two Rivers, Thane Wolfric and his men were ready to depart.

Orders had been issued, word sent for all healers to make for the healing house, messages written and riders had been dispatched to Thessabin. Now, even as a few more of the survivors drifted in through the gates, the Thane and two companies of riders made their final preparations to set out.

Ed and Jay had watched all of this with interest. They had watched Wolfric make his preparations without once ever showing signs of how deeply troubled he must have been. Even as the many rumours spread throughout the town, and people gathered at the gates of the keep clamouring for news, Wolfric remained outwardly composed. He also made a point of telling, whoever it was he had just issued an order to, to walk, not run, as they carried his orders.

And so, while the people of the town were running here and there, demanding news and, if there was none, embellishing the exaggerations they had heard moments ago, Wolfric had got his two companies of riders ready for the road, doubled the guards on all the gates, called all the healers to their posts and placed the town watch on alert. In little over an hour Wolfric had turned Two Rivers from a market town into an armed camp.

Ed and Jay began to walk back to their lodgings. There was nothing for them to do. They had firstly gone to the healing house to see if they could help but, as more of the town's healers came in, they quickly found themselves getting in the way. There was nothing for them to do in the keep: both Wolfric and Moorbe were far too busy to see them any more that day. And in the barracks square they simply got underfoot of the soldiers readying themselves for either the road or guard duty. So, without any employment that afternoon, and feeling more than a little awkward because of that, they walked back through the lower gates and out into the market square.

More survivors had arrived. The first carts had been carrying those most badly wounded, and with as much speed as they dared to get them to the healing house. They had left the main party of survivors behind on the road. It was now that some of those other survivors drifted into Two Rivers. Some came in on their own or with a companion, each carrying a tiny bundle of what few possessions they had left. Others came in as part of a larger group, five or ten, maybe more. Some walked, others rode in carts or on horseback. Some were wounded, bloody, and often with dirty bandages covering their injury; these the soldiers sent immediately to the healers. Some were fit and able, others were tired and footsore, while still others were totally exhausted, both physically and mentally, from their loss and the journey. Some had nothing left, save the few clothes they stood up in, while others had cart loads of goods. But all of them had one thing in common: that expression of hopelessness that only devastation can bring to a human's face.

In the growing crowd that gathered in the market square Ed spotted someone he recognised. Maullen had his back to Ed and was pushing his way through the throng as he checked each of the new arrivals. Here and there he would stop, talk with this one or the other, before moving on again. If anyone was the leader of the survivors, it had to be Maullen. And if anyone could give clear news of what had happened at Guidepost, it had to be him also.

Ed took hold of Jay's hand, so that they would not be separated in the crowd, and pushed his way through. Three times Ed called Maullen's name but the crowd was too noisy for the big smithy to hear him. But Maullen had stopped in any case, not because of Ed's shouts, but because he had found someone he had been looking for and was standing comforting them as best he was able to.

'Maullen,' Ed shouted again, 'Maullen.'

The big smithy's head went up then. Maullen had heard someone calling him yet, as he turned his head side to side to scan the crowd, he could not see who it was.

'Maullen, here,' Ed shouted. And this time Maullen turned to face him.

But the big smithy was not alone. As he turned towards the voice shouting his name, Ed could see he was holding someone. The man's strong arms were around the shoulders of another, smaller man who was trembling uncontrollably as he cried into the smithy's chest.

'Maullen,' Ed said as he got closer to the big smithy. 'Maullen what has happened? The soldiers said the Guidepost had . . .'

Ed never finished for, as he asked Maullen for news, the smaller man turned to face him; it was Braygon and the man was inconsolable.

'Goblins,' Maullen said, the tone of his voice cursing the very word itself. 'Goblins came, hundreds of them. They took the town and the watch before anyone knew what was happening. Then they killed near every living thing they could find before burning the town and moving on the farm.'

'When did this happen?' Ed demanded.

'Four nights gone, a few days after you left,' Maullen said sharply. 'It was you as they were looking for.' Maullen would have said more but he was silenced by the sound of a horn from the keep.

Soldiers moved out into the crowd and began pushing them aside. As the soldiers pushed they repeatedly shouted at the crowd to make way. A second horn sounded, and with Wolfric at their head, a column of horsemen rode out through the gate and up towards the bridge road.

The crowd fell silent as the riders passed. Every face was turned towards them and every face showed the same mix of emotions: pride in such brave young men that were setting out to find and destroy those that had destroyed Guidepost and fear that some of them, many of them perhaps, might not return.

The faces of the riders showed a similar mix of emotions: apprehension and determination in equal measures. Yet, whatever the riders may have been feeling, they rode past the crowd with heads high, their spear points flashing in the afternoon sun, their armour gleaming, and the blue eagle head pennants fluttering from their spear shafts.

Hardwin, the young fair-skinned herald that Kate had been so smitten with, rode beside Wolfric. On some, unseen signal from the thane, Hardwin lifted his horn to his lips and blew a long, rousing call. The call was quickly answered by several other horns on the walls of the keep. And then more horns sounded from atop the bridge gate. Hardwin blew his horn again and this time all the horns in all the towers of Two Rivers joined in till the whole town was filled with the calls and echoes of horns and the clatter of horse's hoofs on the cobbled streets.

After the horsemen had disappeared down the Bridge Road, some of the crowd began to drift away. Ed took the opportunity to steer Maullen and Braygon towards the Stubborn Donkey Inn. But, as both Ed and Jay looked around the crowd of survivors for the rest of Braygon's family, they received a shock.

Close behind Braygon, and looking every bit as devastated as his father, was Boargon; the boy also had his right arm bandaged and strapped to his chest. At once it could be seen that the bandage was not the cleanest. Hargon, Braygon's youngest boy was near by, supporting his sister Poppy who was walking with the aid of a rough, homemade crutch. Poppy had a leg wound that was causing her a great deal of pain. Every step was an agony for her, and there had been countless hundreds of thousands of steps between Braygon's farm and Two Rivers.

'Braygon, where are the others?' Ed asked.

'Dead,' Braygon answered, his voice stained and crackling, 'they killed my beautiful Salsify.' He began to shake visibly and he turned his face away, burying it in Maullen's broad chest as he broke down again. 'The little ones too, they killed the little ones.' Suddenly Braygon screamed, screamed in a way Ed had never heard a man scream before. A feral scream that came from some very deep and very dark recess of a shattered soul. It filled the whole of the market square and left a menacing echo. There were no words in Braygon's scream, just an unnatural noise that stopped only long enough for the broken man to take another breath before it began all over again. And as he screamed, Braygon clawed at and beat upon Maullen's chest.

The scream was so terrifying that the crowd backed away from Braygon. Nothing like it had ever been heard in Two Rivers before, nor would it ever be again. And it only ended when, without a breath left in his body, Braygon went limp in Maullen's strong arms.

Ed stepped forward to help Maullen carry Braygon. As he did he turned to Jay saying, 'Take the children to your mother at the healing house, carry Poppy, don't let her walk. Then get yourself back to the inn.' He looked at Maullen, 'We'll carry Braygon.'

Maullen did not need help to carry Braygon; as exhausted as he was from the long journey, somehow the smithy still had enough strength to lift Braygon in his arms and carry the man to the inn.

A small crowd was gathering at the front of the inn Cenwalh; the innkeeper was there too. Some form of argument or altercation was taking place. But, as Ed and Maullen got closer, Cenwalh stopped whatever it was he had been arguing about and instead pushed the small crowd back and ushered Ed inside.

'Cenwalh,' Ed said directly, 'I need rooms for my friends here, two at least but maybe more.'

'Sorry sir,' Cenwalh shrugged, 'We haven't got no rooms. I've been trying to tell that lot out there the same thing.'

'What about the rooms my dwarf friends used?'

'Well, sir, them's only for dwarves, see. Beds too short and roof too low for regular folks as like.'

Ed's lips tightened, 'You think these people give a shit about bumping their heads or being a little cramped at night. Open the rooms man, right now.'

Cenwalh paled as he backed away from Ed. He shouted for the boy and had him fetch the keys for the dwarf rooms.

'What was all that about out there?' Ed asked after the boy left them.

'Nothing, sir really,' Cenwalh said, giving a forced but embarrassed smile, 'nothing as I can't handle. Not the first time we've had beggars round here, sir. I'll soon see them off so as they won't disturb you, sir.'

Red flashed into Ed's checks on hearing that. 'Beggars? Beggars you stupid, fat, son of bitch.'

Before the fat innkeeper knew what was happening he found himself lifted and pinned up against a wall with a very, very angry Ed holding him by the throat and shouting at him from only inches away.

'Do you know what's happened to these people? Have you even the first idea in that fat head of yours what they have lost? No you don't, because you're too fat, thick and stupid to take even the slightest interest in what is going on in this distorted, warped world of yours.' Ed released his hold on the innkeeper and let the fat man straighten himself up. 'Now,' Ed went on more coolly and in control, 'go out there and invite every single person you see to come in and eat. Give them each a drink, tea, ale, mead, whatever they want. And give them the good ale Cenwalh, not that crap you sell to the workers on the wall. I'm paying, so it better be the good stuff. Got it?'

'Yes, sir,' Cenwalh said, 'right away, sir.' He bowed quickly before hurrying to the door to invite as many of the newcomers in as wanted to come in.

Ed showed Maullen, still carrying Braygon, through to the rooms where only a few nights before the dwarves had lodged. The beds were shorter than the beds Ed's family had in their rooms, and the roof was indeed much lower. Both Ed and Maullen had to duck down, stooping over as they walked, to avoid banging their heads on the ceiling beams.

Cenwalh's boy came in carrying hot water, tea, and soup for Braygon. But the farmer was by then so deeply in shock that he was nearly catatonic. He was running a fever and, from time to time, would drift into a delirium and begin to cry out Salsify's name and those of his lost children.

There was little else that Ed could do for Braygon. But Maullen, the big smithy stayed with him, sitting next to the bed, washing his face and hands to clean away the dirt of the journey, or soothing Braygon's brow with a cool rag whenever the delirium came over him. Maullen would find a clean cloth, dip it in fresh water, and hold a damp corner to Braygon's lips so that the man, even while unconscious, could drink a little.

It seemed strange that such a large and powerful man could be so kind and gentle, yet Maullen was just that. Like a caring mother looking after an ailing child, Maullen stayed with Braygon, sat with him, tended to him, and never once asked for anything for himself.

The main room of the Stubborn Donkey was filling up quickly. Word had soon gone round that there was a free meal and drink for the survivors in the offing, and many came to collect. True, and sadly so, but some of the locals thought they might also help themselves to a free meal and ale, but these were very quickly stopped and sent on their way. And it didn't take long before they began to ask who their benefactor was. Cenwalh quickly pointed Ed out to them. Soon Ed was being surrounded with people, none of whom he knew, coming over to thank him, to bestow their blessings on him and even to kiss his hand, which Ed found both embarrassing and uncomfortable.

It didn't take long before they began to tell their stories. Stories of how the goblins came in the middle of the night and what happened to Guidepost and the surrounding farms after that.

It had been the half goblin men that came first. They somehow, whether by guile or some subterfuge, managed to get the town watch to open the gates. Then they had quickly overpowered the watch, no difficult task that as the watch was made up from the fattest and laziest of the town, people that could not find other work save what that greedy Drayloc would give them. With the watch disarmed and bound the goblins then poured into the town killing and burning everything. Some managed to put up a fight, but they were quickly overcome. Those that could fled, climbing the wall or, as a small group had managed, banding together and forcing one of the gates. Seven men had tried that, and they had taken the three goblins at the gate but lost two of their number in doing so. But they also had their wives and families with them, and once outside the gate, they found themselves hunted down like animals. Of the total of twenty that got through the gate only three had survived and made it to Two Rivers.

After Guidepost was destroyed the goblins then turned their attention to the surrounding farms, but here things went less easy for them. The flames from Guidepost had lit up the sky and could be seen for many leagues around. That had put all the farms on alert, and everyone that could, took up arms and manned their walls. The goblins tried to rush the gates of the farms, but many were cut down by bow and crossbow. When the goblins realised they could not take the farms by direct assault, they began burning everything, crops, livestock, stores, and anything that was outside of the walls.

Some of the farms, the smaller ones with few people to defend them, had been overwhelmed: there was little that five or ten men could do against a hundred goblins other than die bravely. In some farms, the smaller ones, where the family and their men had retreated into their tower house for safety, the goblins simply, and without a trace of mercy, set fire to the houses and everyone inside.

It was a story as old as war itself; the only difference was those committing the atrocities. And from everything Ed heard, these goblins and half men half goblins, had absolutely no human compassion whatsoever. If anything the exact opposite was true, especially for the goblin-men: they appeared to be even more inhuman than their goblin allies, almost as if they had to be twice as inhuman to nullify that part of them that was human.

Ed was about to leave when he noticed another man watching him. The man was dressed shabbily and looked as if he hadn't washed for a week or more, but then so did all the other survivors. Yet he did not appear to be with the other survivors. He was sitting alone, nursing a small tankard of ale while he watched and waited for all the others to finish telling their tales to Ed. Finally, as the last of the survivors left Ed, the man slowly got to his feet. He walked towards the table where Ed was sitting.

'Mind if I join you?' the man asked quietly. He sat down even before Ed replied.

It wasn't what the man asked that shocked Ed, nor was it the way he asked: it was his accent. 'You're Canadian,' Ed gasped.

'Guilty,' the man smiled. He set his small tankard down and offered Ed his hand. 'Donald McLaughlin, from Regina; at least I used to be, a few years ago now, ah.'

'But how? When? I mean how did you get here?' Ed asked.

'I could ask you the same thing, ah?' Donald smiled. 'It seems to me you and I have something in common.'

'What's that?'

'Well,' Donald said sipping his ale. 'Seems as how you and I don't know how we got here, but we both want to get home, especially now, ah.' He nodded in the direction of the survivors to make his point.

'True enough,' Ed agreed. 'So, do you know a way home? I mean, is it possible to get back?'

Donald thought for a moment, contemplating how best to say what he had to say. 'Do I know the way home? No. But, is there a way home? Yes.'

Ed gasped audibly. 'If there is a way back then why haven't you taken it?'

'Simple,' Donald said. He shrugged his shoulders and stared down at his now empty tankard. 'I haven't got what you got to make it work. Frankly, I haven't got the money.'

Ed shook his head. 'I don't understand.'

Donald leant forward over the table; he waited till Ed also leant forward, then he whispered, 'There is wizard, and yes I know that sounds crazy, and anywhere else I would think it crazy myself, but not here. But like I said, there is a wizard who, for a price, five gold crowns per person, can open a door back to our world and out of here. Now, Ed, and I don't want it to sound like blackmail but I don't have that sort of money. So, if you are willing to pay my passage I will take you to the wizard; then we can all go home.'

'And what makes you think I have that sort of money?'

Donald snorted a little laugh. 'Ed, you don't mind that I call you Ed, do you? There has been rumours about your great wealth from the first day you got here. Who else but a very wealthy man would be allowed to travel with a dwarf lord. You stay in the best rooms of the best inn in Two Rivers and dress in the finest cloth. You even have a private audience with the high and mighty chancellor, which by the way only the most highly honoured in the land get. And he has even given you and your family his own bodyguards.'

'Bodyguards? What bodyguards?'

Donald let out a short but loud laugh. 'What? You mean you haven't noticed?'

Ed shook his head.

'Take a look at the two guys sitting at the table behind me,' Donald whispered, 'and the big fellow in the green cloak by the door.' He grinned as he leant even closer to Ed saying, 'You should have seen the look of panic on their faces before when you sent your son back up the keep with them two little ones. They didn't know who should stay or who should go. It was really rather funny.'

'But,' Donald said, 'getting back to the matter at hand, do we have a deal?'

'A deal?'

'Yes a deal. I'll take you to the wizard that can get us back, and in return you pay my, what shall we call it, you pay for my passage.'

Ed thought about the offer for a minute before asking, 'And how do I know I can trust you?'

'You don't,' Donald smiled. 'But ask yourself this: who can you trust round here?'

The two men sat looking at each for a while without talking. Then Ed glanced over at the men Donald had pointed out. It was true: they were watching Ed, though trying their best not to look like they were. The question was, were they watching him to protect him or for some other reason? Had they been sent by the chancellor as his bodyguard or perhaps to spy on him, or maybe Donald had put them up to it as part of some elaborate con to get his hands on the gold. Whatever the reason, whatever was going on, Ed was not to be drawn.

'Donald,' Ed began, 'at this point I am not saying yes or no. True, getting myself and my family home is the most important thing to me and for that I would gladly pay for you to come too. But, and this is a big but, massive in fact, my wife is a doctor and right now she is up at the healing house doing what she can for the wounded. If I know her, and I think I do, there is no way she is going to leave until she is sure that all of those people are on the road to recovery.'

'That may take some time,' Donald said shaking his head.

'Look, I'll talk it over with her,' Ed said finally. 'And anyway, you say you have been here a few years, surely a few more days wouldn't make any difference?'

'It might,' Donald said getting up. 'If those damn goblins get here first.'

As Donald left Cenwalh marched directly to Ed's table saying, 'Cook's not happy, sir, not happy at all. She likes to have a lay down in the afternoon; she's getting on you see, sir. And she says that there little food left, didn't know that there be this many.'

'Well if there is not enough food you had better send someone to get more,' Ed said, stating what to him was the obvious.

'And who's to pay, sir,' Cenwalh moaned. 'There's a right fine bill as is, so who's to pay.'

'For pity's sake,' Ed groaned. He reached for the heavy coin purse at his belt but then, thinking about what Donald had been saying, he thought better of paying in public. 'Cenwalh, listen, I am sorry about grabbing you before, I should not have done that. You've been a good and understanding host, and you have made my family and me very welcome. Will you accept my apologies?'

'Of course, sir,' Cenwalh said; he smiled broadly and offered Ed a hand of friendship saying, 'Understandable on a day like today. I thinks the whole town is in a shock at the news. And I am sure there have been many a crossed word today that'll be forgotten by nightfall. Think nought of it, sir. But as to the bill, sir.'

'Certainly,' Ed said, returning the innkeeper's smile. 'But not here, have you an office or a back room.'

'Aye, sir. I quite understand. This way please, sir.'

Ed went to the dwarf room to check on Maullen and Braygon. Braygon was still in a deep sleep, perhaps the best thing for him, while Maullen sat on a bed facing the sleeping man. A large bowl of mutton stew had been sent from the kitchen for him, but the smithy had not touched any of it. What he had done was wash Braygon, place him in the bed, and place a cooling cloth on the unconscious man's brow. After that Maullen had sat facing his friend and waited to see if he would wake.

When Ed entered the room it was to see Maullen's head nodding. The big smithy had watched his friend so long, watched him until he could not keep his own eyes open, and sleep began to steal upon him.

Ed could only guess how long the big man had been awake. From everything he had been told it had been Maullen that had collected them together. It was Maullen that had led a small group back to Guidepost to see if there was anyone left alive. And it was Maullen that had brought out the few that there was. It was also Maullen that had buried many of the bodies that they found, and also led those left to Two Rivers. He had stood watch every night and rode at the head to make sure their route was secure. Now, after all the big man had been through, he was close to worn out.

'Maullen,' Ed said softly, reluctantly waking the big man. 'Why not get yourself some sleep? I'll sit with Braygon for a while.'

Maullen grunted some unintelligible word as he looked up at Ed through half-closed, bloodshot eyes. Then he lay back on the bed, and because he was six three on a five six bed, he pulled his feet up, curled up in a ball, and was asleep in seconds.

Ed sat there for a long time, watching the two men sleep and every so often taking the cloth from Braygon's brow, rinsing it in fresh water, and replacing it. Maullen slept soundly, though when Braygon would suddenly cry out in his delirium, he would stir a little, shift around on the bed, and then go back into a deep sleep again.

It was late afternoon when Cenwalh gently knocked on the door. He opened it without being asked saying, 'I brought you some candles, sir, and something to eat.' He placed a bowl of stew on a chair which he had turned to face Ed, using it as a makeshift table, and then placed the candle on the small chest of draws. From his pocket he brought out more candles which he lit off the first and placed them round the room. 'I remembered, sir as you fed all them other but didn't eat nought yourself. So I was thinking you'd be wanting something, it being late and all.'

'Thank you, Cenwalh, that's very kind of you,' Ed said. 'By the way, has my wife or the children come back yet?'

'Aye sir. The little one's been back an hour, sir,' Cenwalh said. 'But I told them they best wait for you to come out. Don't worry though, sir, they's all been fed. Cook took them in the back with her. Made a right old fuss of them she did too, your boy and two other boys also,' he said nodding towards Braygon.

'Thank you, Cenwalh,' Ed replied. 'But I think if Braygon's boys are here they might want to see their father and maybe have some sleep themselves.'

'Already done, sir,' Cenwalh smiled. 'Your young lady insisted that I give them her bed. And your boy, Jay is it? He's sitting out front by the fire.' He went to turn and leave then stopped. 'Nearly forgot, sir, cook's sister has come over. Said she's willing to sit with these two if you want her too. Not inside, you understand, that wouldn't be proper. She'll sit outside, by the door like, but don't worry sir, if they stir she hear them, ears like an Elf that one, face like a half-plucked chicken, but ears like an Elf.'

'That would be good,' Ed said. 'How soon could she start?'

'Right now, sir,'

'Well in that case I'll eat by the fire with Jay.'

Ed took the bowl of stew from the chair and followed Cenwalh out the door. They walked through into the main room, passing cook's sister on the way. The innkeeper had been right about her. She had two great moles on her right cheek, both of which were sprouting dozens of long dark hairs, hairs on her top lip, the beginnings of a good beard and bushiest eyebrows that have ever been seen on man or woman. And sad to relate, they were her most attractive features.

Jay was sitting by the fire, warming his outstretched hands and looking very deep in thought. He had taken off his jacket and cloak and hung them over the back of the chair but, as Ed got closer, he could see that Jay's rolled-up sleeves, and his trousers, were stained with blood.

'Jay, are you all right?' Ed asked on seeing the blood.

'Yeah I'm fine, Dad. It's not my blood.'

'Then whose?'

Jay shrugged. 'Don't rightly know. Could have been any number of people's, or maybe some of all of them.' Jay looked up at his father, his eyes moist with tears. 'It's horrible up there, Dad, truly grotesque. I don't know how Mum can be in a place like that let alone work there. Oh, and Poppy, Mum said not to tell the boys this, Dad, but Poppy's leg is badly infected. Mum said she doesn't know if she can save it. She might have to lose the leg or...' Jay never finished; he couldn't. Rather, he bit his trembling lip and turned his face away.

Ed placed his arm round Jay saying, 'I know, Son, I know. That's what happens in war. It's always the innocent that suffer the most.'

Jay shrugged his father's arm away. 'That's not war. You don't make war on children. There are rules.'

Ed shook his head. 'I wish that were so, Jay. Somebody might write things down on a bit of paper with the best intentions in the world. But then that paper means little to nothing when the crap hits the fan. Besides, rules only apply to civilised people, and civilised people don't start wars. And do you think those goblin thing are the least bit civilised?'

'So what you saying; we're civilised therefore we shouldn't fight?'

'No I'm saying that civilised people don't start wars; they may fight in them, but they don't start them. It's those that start the wars that throw the rules away.'

'Well, then I'm going to fight,' Jay said sternly.

'The hell you are,' Ed replied just as sternly.

'Why not, Dad?' Jay demanded. 'Boargon fought; he got three goblins for sure, and Horgon got one, and he's only ten. If he can fight so can I.'

'Jay,' Ed said slowly. 'There is a world of difference between defending your home when it's attacked and going out looking to be a part of a war.'

'Dad, get real will you?' Jay hissed. 'We're stuck here; this is where we are going to have to make our home now. And when the goblins come, everybody is going to have to fight.'

'You think it's that easy,' Ed scoffed. 'You forget, Jay, I've already been to war; I know what it's like.'

'Come on, Dad,' Jay moaned. 'You said it yourself. You built bridges and cleared a few minefields.'

Ed placed the bowl of stew aside. 'You're right, Jay, that's what I told you and your mother, but that's not all I did. And no, don't ask.' With that Ed walked out of the inn.

Ed walked for a while without direction; he did have anywhere to go, he just needed to clear his head. Several times he turned round to see if that big fellow in the green cloak was following him as Donald had said: he was. About twenty paces back and, despite his large size, trying his best to keep out of sight in the shadows.

A tiny smile came to Ed's lips as he walked up past the bridge gate. There was less light there, and the streets were narrower. As Ed got to the corner of two small streets he quickly ducked round the corner and hide in a doorway. Seconds later he heard the sound of feet running on the cobbles, then the green cloaked man running past Ed, stopped, and began to frantically search the dark street to see where he had gone.

Ed suppressed a chuckle as he stepped out of the shadows. 'Did you lose something, friend?'

The man spun round on his heel so quickly that his cloak flew out horizontal. He stared at Ed and was perhaps thankful that the street was so dark that his blushing and embarrassed face could not be seen clearly.

'If you are going to go everywhere I go then why don't you walk with me?' Ed offered. 'That way you would be more like company and less like a stalker.'

'Sorry, stranger,' the green cloaked man said. 'I was looking for something and just got a bit lost.'

'Sure you were,' Ed sniggered. 'I take it Chancellor Moorbe sent you to make certain no harm came to me.'

'You must have me confused with someone else, sir.'

'Really?' Ed smiled. 'In that case you have my apologies.'

'These are bad times, sir, and people are suspicious. Your apology is accepted, friend.'

'Very gracious of you, friend. I was just going to the gate,' Ed said waving his arm in the vague direction of the bridge gate that he had just passed.

'By a coincidence I was heading for the Bridge Gate also,' the man smiled.

'Oh sorry,' Ed said, trying his best to hide his grin. 'Is that the Bridge Gate that way? I meant the Ferry Gate. So it looks like we are going in opposite directions. Perhaps I shall see you later, friend. Goodbye.' Ed stood motionless for a while, smiling warmly, as he waited for the man to move off. But the man didn't move; rather he shifted his feet nervously, almost like he was dancing, but without the music. 'It was the Bridge Gate you said, wasn't it, and it is that way, right?' Ed said pointing down the street.

'Yeah that's right, sir,' the man said, but still didn't move.

'I'm not keeping you, am I?' Ed asked, now unable to hide his grin any longer.

'No, sir,' he said. 'I was just ah . . . I mean I was just. Ah curse it all, sir. I said as how I was not cut out for a spy. Told 'm as how I didn't want the duty. I should be out there, hunting goblins, instead of ducking in and out of shadows.'

Ed laughed loudly. 'Don't beat yourself up, young man. If you hadn't been pointed out to me I wouldn't have known you were there.'

'Still sir, it doesn't sit right. Being a spy and all.'

'No I suppose not,' Ed agreed.

'I mean, sir. I would rather be out in the wilds hunting them fell beasts that did for Guidepost than following you. No offence.'

'None taken.'

'Give me a good spear and sword, put me on a horse, and I'll bring you back a tally of goblins the like you have never seen.'

'I don't doubt it.'

'Is it true what they say about you, sir?'

'That depends on what they have been saying.'

'They say that you brought down twenty or more goblins with nought but your bare hands. They say as how you tore them up so bad as they couldn't tell which arm went to which body.'

'They have been saying a lot, haven't they?'

'Aye, sir they have,' the man said. 'So tell me, sir, how many was it, twenty or twenty-five? People are not sure cause you tore them up so.'

'Three.'

'Twenty-three, that's still some tally without a sword in your hand.'

'Not twenty-three. Three, just three. One, two, three.'

Neither of them had noticed that they had been walking till the cloaked man stopped suddenly. 'But they said...'

'Like I said,' Ed smiled. 'They have been saying a lot. It was three, that's all. There was a fourth, and if Lady Grizlan hadn't got him with her crossbow, then he would have cut me a new one.'

The cloaked man thought for a second then asked, 'A new one what, sir?'

'A new one, you know; it's not very nice and would make sitting on a horse very painful.'

'You mean your back gate, sir?' he said with a smile, a smile that quickly vanished. 'You're right, sir; that would be painful.'

They continued walking for some time, not going anywhere in particular but just walking and talking for the sake of it. Cenfus, son of Ceolwulf, as the cloaked man turned out to be called, was excellent company and easy to talk to. He was also a good talker in his own right, and unlike Moorbe and Wolfric, who had always seemed guarded in their speech, Cenfus spoke freely.

He told Ed a lot about goblins, and none of it was in the least comforting. According to Cenfus, who had by his own account fought them many times, goblins were sly, cunning, devious, and underhand. They were without pity or mercy yet cowardly when cornered or when equally matched in numbers. They preferred to ambush than fight in the open, and when they did fight, they preferred to fight at night, as they could see in the dark nearly as good as in the daylight. The goblin men, or half-goblins, were another matter. They were much stronger, though not as fast, much more likely to fight in the open, and a whole lot more intelligent, though a lot more curl also.

'When it comes to battle,' Cenfus said, summing up. 'The goblins are really just a rabble. They need the half-goblins to lead them and to push them on with whips. You see, otherwise, a pack of goblins on their own, if they were to overrun one company say, wouldn't press on to fight the next. No they would be happy to just hack at the body or have their sport with any wounded.'

'They don't sound very bright,' Ed offered.

'They're not, sir. That's why they need the half-goblins with them. You see, sir, goblins on their own can make weapons, but they're very crude. Now the half-goblins, their weapons are another matter altogether. Not nearly as good as our sword smiths make mind you, but better than what goblins on their own can do. And another thing, goblins cannot ride. Well, truth is no horse will suffer one on its back. In fact most horses would happily trample one before it got the chance.'

'Sound like even the horses don't like them.'

'Trust me, sir, there's none that don't hate them, and with many a good reason.'

They found themselves at the market gate to the keep. They hadn't planned it; it just happened. The market itself was packing up for the night, and just inside the gate, the night guard of the town watch were assembling for their duties.

Ed and Cenfus walked past the guard and on up to the upper courtyard where the healing house was.

Liz was standing outside, drinking tea while she talked with some of the other healers. Her clothes were covered by a long, wrap-round apron that was marked with blood. Her hair was also covered by a scarf, pulling her hair back to reveal a tired and drained face.

'You all right, Liz,' Ed asked as he went over to his exhausted-looking wife.

'Sure, nothing that twenty-four hours sleep wouldn't put right,' she said forcing a smile. 'First time I've stopped all day. Just having some tea before I go and check on a few things.'

'Have you eaten?' Ed asked, 'I know what you're like when you get really busy. You think about everyone else and forget yourself.'

'I'll be fine, honey,' Liz said. 'I've been drinking this beef tea or what ever it is that brew up in here. It's not that bad when you get used to it. They say it helps the sick recover. Don't know about that but it keeps you going, that's for sure. Haven't a clue what's in it though.'

'Just good things,' Cenfus offered. 'I can get the recipe for you if you would like.'

Liz looked up at the big, cloaked figure who, until then, she hadn't really noticed. There were so many cloaked men going about the keep and the barracks that she had stopped noticing any of them.

'Liz, this is Cenfus,' Ed said, 'my bodyguard and watchman.'

Liz offer her hand cautiously asking, 'Do you need a bodyguard?'

'Not me, Liz, us,' Ed said. 'I'm sure that there will be one around here looking after you.'

Liz thought for a minute then said, 'There was a guy here earlier. Every time I turned round he was getting in my way. Finally one of the healing women took a broom to him and chased him out of the ward, sorry, I mean healing house.'

Both Ed and Cenfus smiled at the thought of it: a woman chasing a big bodyguard off with a broom.

Finally Ed asked, 'Do you need anything? Should I get some food sent up for you, may be for the others too.'

'No, food we got,' Liz said nodding towards the little kitchen at the end of the row of building that made up the healing house. 'There's a couple of things I could use though, a fully equipped ER with proper light, a fully staffed trauma team. Oh, and a well-stocked pharmacy.'

'Sorry, Liz,' Ed said checking his pockets. 'I seem to be fresh out.'

Liz shrugged. 'Just have to go with what we have here then. Maggots, moss and morphine, poppy sap they call it; that's the cure-all round here.'

'Sorry I don't get you.'

'They got an apothecary in here that, whatever the wound, be it a burn or a cut or what-have-you, you just get maggots, moss, and morphine in differing proportions to treat the injury. Mind you, they some times mix a little honey in with it or a few other herbs. Though what good they are I have no idea. Infection, Ed; that's what's going to kill most of these people. It's like those septic wards a hundred years ago. Once the infection sets in, it's going to be over for more than half of them. At least they will have the morphine, or the poppy sap, so they shouldn't suffer too greatly.'

Liz drained her cup saying, 'Look, sweetheart, I'm going to be here a good while longer. There's still a lot to do.' She leant up to Ed and gave him a kiss on the cheek. 'Thanks for coming up. And Kate's in the tower with Moorbe; be a dear and collect her. I am sure the chancellor has better things to do than sit talking with her all night.'

'Consider it done,' Ed said as he began to walk away from the healing house. 'And Liz,' he called back to her, 'I'll have Cenwalh put some coldcuts to one side for when you get back.'

Ed collected Kate from Moorbe's tower. The girl was full of apologies for not being able to help her mother in the healing house.

'I just couldn't face it, Dad,' Kate said. 'All them poor people cut up like that, and the burns. It was just awful.'

'War is never a pretty thing,' Ed said as they walked. 'Try not to think about it.'

'Don't think I will be able to think of anything else,' Kate said. 'You know, Dad there was a guy in there, big guy; looked like someone had tried to cut him in two. Half his chest was literally sliced open and the wound was full of maggots. That did it for me, Dad, seeing all them maggots crawling round inside the guy, yuck!'

Ed placed his arm round Kate's shoulders to comfort her. 'I know, sweetheart. But, believe it or not, those maggots might just help clean the wound out. It's horrible to look at but it works.'

'I know, Dad,' Kate said. 'Mum told me the same thing. But it doesn't make it any easier to look at. And anyway, the poor guy is badly burnt too. Both his arms and his face. Nobody knows how he is still alive and something else. Mum didn't say as much, but I don't think she thinks he will live much longer. Infection has set in, you see.'

'I see,' Ed said softly.

They walked out from the gate and into the market square. For a while they were all silent: partly keeping their thoughts to themselves, and partly because there were the night soil workers cleaning up the square after the market. They didn't want to talk in front of them lest they carry rumours round the town.

Ed was watching the men working, and they were all watching him very closely. Near the entrance to the square, not far from the Stubborn Donkey Inn, three workers stood next to their cart. One was holding a burning torch so that the other two could see as they swept up the rotten fruit and vegetables that had been discarded by the market traders. And there was a lot of it about but, just as Ed, Kate and Cenfus passed, they were not sweeping. Rather they were leaning on their brooms, watching them, and muttering something among themselves.

Abruptly Ed stopped. They had just passed the workmen when, as if struck by a lightning bolt, Ed pulled up and was rooted to the spot. 'Holy crap,' Ed gasped loudly. 'That's it. That's damn well it.'

'Dad?'

'Sir?'

As suddenly as he had stopped Ed became very animated. First he turned on his heels, took a couple of quick paces towards the night soil workers, then stopped, just as quickly and turned back. 'Cenfus,' Ed said sharply, 'do me a favour, take Kate indoors, then come back here as quick as you can.' He turned away once more then back again. 'And bring some more torches. And see if that Cenwalh is up and about. I will need him.'

'Sir?' Cenfus asked as Ed turned away again.

'I got an idea,' Ed called out as he walked towards the workmen. 'It's a bit far out, but it might just work.'

'Very good, sir,' Cenfus said, though what Ed was up to he had no idea. He took Kate back to the Inn, saw that Cenwalh was still very much up and about, collected more torches, then returned to where Ed and the workmen were then walking round the market square kicking over the refuse of the day.

# CHAPTER 18

## Into the Wilds

Wolfric and his riders headed west at a quick pace. Before the sun had begun to set in the sky they had passed the last of the farms that dotted the hills around Two Rivers.

Many folks had come out to see them, to cheer them on as they rode to do battle with goblins. Yet, even as they cheered, they knew what the riders themselves must know: that there may be too few of them. The people knew it, the riders knew it, and Wolfric knew it. Goblins never attacked unless the numbers were decisively in their favour. And for a goblin band to attack a town, there must be some hundreds of them. All Wolfric had with him were two companies, 120 men, and too many of them young and untested.

Yet Wolfric pushed on. He pushed passed the last of the farms and on into the open grasslands. By nightfall he and his riders had reached the woods and the woodcutters camp.

Most of them had already left and the rest were leaving. When the news of what had happened at Guidepost came in, the woodcutters had begun to pack up their camp. What chance did they have in an open wood when the walled town and farms of Guidepost could not stand? So, and as quickly as they could, they packed up their belongings and began the trek east. Some would stop at Two Rivers while others, most of them in fact, wanted to keep moving to somewhere safer. 'What chance did Two Rivers have with only a wooden wall when a goblin horde came?' Many asked. 'And it would come.'

The riders rest a while in the wood. It had been very late by the time Wolfric and his men reached the wood. And by the time they reached the western edge, the moon was past its zenith. But both men and horses were in need of rest, so while still under the shelter of the trees, Wolfric called a halt and allowed everyone to rest.

Before dawn Wolfric had his men moving again; they were up, saddled and riding even before breakfast. Men can eat in the saddle if they have to when time is pressing, and time was pressing.

As they neared Tangle Wood, Wolfric split his column in two. He did not want to but, in spite of having only a few men, he needed to know which way the goblins had gone. If he took all his men with him in one column he would be stronger, but he might end up chasing the goblins round the woods like two children chasing each other round a table. It was a hard judgment to make but, hopefully, he could cover more ground quicker and, once the goblins were found, bring his men back together and strike them down.

And so, as Wolfric led one company to the south of Tangle Wood Saelred, that old campaigner and Wolfric's trusted lieutenant took the second company to the north.

'We shall meet at Guidepost on the night of the morrow,' Wolfric said. 'And Saelred, just find them and report. I want information not heroes. There shall be time enough for heroes later.'

'Why, My Lord, do you think I would make a fool's charge for glory?' Saelred said.

'You would,' Wolfric smiled, 'and you have, more than once. But not this time, old friend. This time I forbid. Just find them and report.'

'Very well, My Lord,' Saelred sighed. He turned from Wolfric and to his men and called out, 'Did you all hear that? We scout and report, understand, men? Scout and report.'

'Yes, sir,' his men shouted back as one. And Saelred turned back to Wolfric saying, 'There you are, My Lord.' He gave a lopsided smile and nod of the head, by way of a bow, to Wolfric.

'Very well, Saelred,' Wolfric smiled, knowing full well that all his admonishments would be of little restraint to Saelred, if the old warrior saw a chance to kill goblins. 'Till the morrow.' With that the two columns parted.

Wolfric led his column to the south-west and very soon Saelred and his column were out of sight. All that there was, all that any of Wolfric's column could see, was the tall grass of the wilderness, and like a scare on the landscape, the trampled path made by the survivors who had travelled east only days before.

He followed the path: his men riding a short distance off on either side of it. They were looking for any other survivors that may have been left behind, but they found none. They were also looking for any signs of the pursuit: signs that the goblins may have followed the survivors or, more importantly, that the goblins may be waiting somewhere in ambush. Yet the riders found neither. All they found, the only thing they found, were the signs left by desperate survivors as they made for the safety of Two Rivers and, here and there along the trail, the graves of those too weak or too badly injured to finish the journey.

By nightfall they had reached the southern edge of Tangle Wood. Wolfric had pushed his riders all day, and with the sun long since down, both men and horses were near exhausted.

He halted the column, making camp for the night on the gentle slope where a fast flowing stream emerged from the wood. But, while they made their camp on that chilled night, Wolfric forbade them any fires. Fires would only serve to inform the goblins of their presence. So, with the horses watered and fed, the guard set for the night, and the men eating cold rations, they made their camp. Those that could managed to steal a few short, uncomfortable, hours' sleep. But for most the idea of sleep, with goblins about them, was the furthest thing from their minds. Most of the men chose to wrap a blanket around themselves and sit back to back with one of their fellows, with swords and shields at the ready. And so they spent the night, exhausted, but ever watchful.

The next morning, even before the sun had shown itself over the eastern rim of the world, Wolfric had his riders break camp.

The horses were saddled and their gear was stowed. The riders took the reins of their mounts and led them, on foot, through the frigid water of the stream. They walked for two miles or more, for it was still too dark to risk riding. Only when the first glow of the sun in the east began to drive back the black of night did Wolfric give the order to mount. And when they had mounted, Wolfric set off at a rapid pace.

Thane Wolfric made not for Guidepost, as many had assumed he would. Rather he made for an area south of the town where he had been told that the goblin men had built their shanties.

For two hours Wolfric pressed his column, pushing them, and himself, until they came to a ridge that overlooked the goblin shanties.

He brought his column to a halt on the east side of the ridge, keeping them out of sight from the shanties. There he allowed his men to dismount and rest for a while as he crept forward to get a better look at the enemy camp. But what he saw there was not what he had expected.

Rather than a shanty town, with who knew how many goblin men milling about, there was nothing but piles of ashes and charred timbers. Small wisps of smoke were still rising from the ashes, and after spending some time watching the surrounds, Wolfric could see that there was no one about.

He returned to his men and gathered them round him. His voice was lowered as he informed them, 'Over there, less than two miles off is the goblin shanty.' His words made all the men stiffen in readiness for the coming fight. 'But it looks like someone got there first. The whole place has been razed to the ground. The question is, by who?

And from the way the ashes are still smouldering, it looks like the goblin camp was fired last night: yesterday afternoon at the outside. So, keep your eyes open and weapons at the ready. Whoever set that fire might still be around and they may not be friendly. It could be that the goblins set the fire themselves, in which case they will still be close.'

Wolfric went to his horse and unfastened his shield. 'Look sharp, men; we got goblins to hunt.'

Quickly the riders went to their mounts. They removed their cloaks so as not to be encumbered by them in a fight. The cloaks were round and fastened to their saddles. Bows were unpacked, strung, and the tension tested while quivers of arrows were placed at the ready. Shields were unhitched from packs and slung over their backs, ready to be swung round onto their arms when needed.

In very short time every rider was ready, and every rider was armed for the fight.

'Mount up,' Wolfric ordered. 'Form a line. Forward.'

As one the riders crested the ridge at a trot. They swept down the western side, picking up the pace a little as they went. All along the line spears, swords, bows, and axes were readied. Yet there was no one in sight. They closed with the shanty town, looking every way for sign of ambush, but there was nothing to be seen.

Closer and closer they rode to the shanty town, but still there was no sign of goblins. All there was, all any of them could see, was the burnt out remains of where the goblins had once been.

Finally the riders reached the town. And it was, as they had seen, abandoned. Every building, every piece of wood, every table, chair, bed and cot was burnt and smashed. Here and there smoke rose from the ashes, and when prodded with a spear point, tiny hot embers would be flicked up into the air.

One of the riders rode quickly up to Wolfric. 'My Lord, there are signs of many riders to the east,' he said, pointing to where he had seen the tracks. 'Some number sir, perhaps over a hundred.'

'Can you follow the tracks?' Wolfric asked.

The rider smiled broadly. 'A blind man could follow them in dead of night, My Lord.'

'Which way do they go?'

'North, My Lord, and at some pace.'

'Then lead on,' Wolfric ordered.

The rest of the riders fell in behind their thane while, this one rider, set off tracking the marks left by whoever had been at the shanty before them. And the signs were easy to track. A hundred or more horses moving at speed over the open plains left a path anyone could follow.

They travelled north in a near straight line towards Guidepost. Whoever had made the tracks must have been moving at a gallop. For the tall grass had been flattened, and the ground was churned up over a wide path. But, as the riders got closer to Guidepost, the country around them changed dramatically.

Gone was the tall, lush grass of the plain. Now the grass was flattened and scorched. All about them there were signs of destruction. Crops had been burnt in the fields. Animals slaughtered, and their carcasses left to bloat and blacken in the sun. Black swarms of fat files hung around each carcass that, if the riders came to close, would spring into the air like some angry black cloud. The tower houses were all burnt, many collapsing in on themselves, and any poor soul that had been in them. The walls around the farms had been pulled down in places, no doubt where the goblins had stormed them. And within the courtyards, every barn, sty, and stable was now nothing more than a blackened, charred skeleton of the former building.

In some of the courtyards there were freshly, if hastily, dug graves: the only sign of their former owners. But at least they had had a decent burial. Someone, perhaps Maullen and his party, or perhaps some others, had seen to it that the dead were given all proper respect.

Wolfric and his riders crested a small rise and before them, still some miles off, was Guidepost. Other than a smoking heap of ruins it was impossible, at that distance, to make out much of the town. What the riders could see however, even as soon as they crested the rise, was a large fire near the south gate.

Near the fire there were several, cloaked figures moving: some of them mounted and some on foot. Wolfric pressed his men faster for, as soon as they had spotted the figures, they had also been spotted.

Even at a distance Wolfric could see one of the figures stand up in the saddle: stand and blow a loud call on his horn.

In seconds more horns sounded from within the walls of Guidepost. Moments later, the distance now no more than a mile between them, Wolfric saw dozens of riders pouring out of the broken gates. These riders, just as Wolfric's own riders, were armed with spears, bows, swords and shields, and they were ready for Wolfric's charge.

'They're ours,' Hardwin cried out joyfully, his young eyes able to see clearly even at that distance.

'Then give them a call,' Wolfric smiled. 'And let them hear how a herald should really sound.'

The young herald lifted his horn to his lips, sucked in a long deep breath and blew three loud sharp notes that spread across the fields like an eagle's cry and echoed off the walls of the town.

Immediately the answering call came from the gate: three sharp and one long note. Then, as the rest of the riders at the gate formed a line, three riders came forward. One was the rider with the horn, another carrying a large green banner bearing a silver gauntlet grasping lightning bolts. The third carried neither horn nor banner but was dressed in a polished mailed shirt and wore a tall crested helmet that shone like burnished sliver. He raised his right hand in greeting as he halted in front of Wolfric. Seeing the banner that was carried by one of Wolfric's men the young man bowed.

'My Lord,' the young rider said, 'what brings the Thane of Two Rivers here?'

'The same thing as brought you, I venture,' Wolfric said. 'But you have me at an advantage, young man.'

'I am sorry, My Lord,' the man said as he removed his polished helmet. 'I have grown some since we last met.' The man had long blond hair tied back from his face with a green cloth band embroidered with silver-and-gold thread. His eyes were keen and bright blue in colour. His skin was fair though a little grimy from several days' hard riding. He had no beard, and when he smiled, deep dimples appeared in his cheeks.

'Halneth?' Wolfric gasped in disbelief, 'Little Halneth that used to follow me round at the hunt. The same little Halneth that was always getting into trouble by stealing his brother's horses or climbing trees and filching apples.'

'The very same, My Lord,' the younger man laughed.

Both men jumped down from their mounts and embraced. 'You speak right well, my young friend. You have grown,' Wolfric declared. And indeed the younger man had. When last they met Halneth had been but a boy of nine years. Now he was a man of twenty, and several inches taller than Wolfric, and broader in the shoulders also.

The young man stepped back and regarded Wolfric. 'You have not changed, My Lord. Your beard may be a little greyer but you are still the man I remember at the hunt.'

'Now you flatter me with untruths,' Wolfric grinned. 'I take twice as long to get up in the morning, twice as long to mount a saddle, and I am nought but aches and pains after a long day's ride.' Wolfric looked round at his riders, adding, 'Speaking of a long day's ride, my men and their horses are in need of rest and water. I take it there is a well in this town.'

Halneth's face paled. 'There is a well, My Lord, but the goblins had despoiled it.'

'How so?' asked Wolfric quietly.

'My men are now trying to clear it but…' Halneth lowered his eyes and took a deep breath.

'Go on.'

'The town watch, My Lord,' Halneth said slowly. 'The goblins killed them and threw their bodies down the well. But . . . that is not all, My Lord . . . they cut off their heads also. So far we have brought out eleven bodies but only eight heads. The well is too deep I fear to find the rest. There may be more in the bottom but we have no way of knowing.'

'Or some half-goblin may be riding with a head or two decorating his saddle?' Wolfric hissed.

'Indeed so, My Lord,' Halneth nodded. 'There is however water north of the town: a small stream. It is not much, slow running and shallow, but it is clean and enough for both men and horse.'

'Good,' Wolfric nodded. 'Will you have one of your men show my riders where it is? Then pray, my young friend, show me what you have found here. And please Halneth, you have no reason to call me My Lord. I rode with your father many times; he was a friend, a very dear friend, as I hope you will be.'

'I hope so too, my lo . . . I mean, I hope so.'

Wolfric smiled and, with a gesture of his hand, invited the younger man to lead the way into Guidepost. 'So tell me, Halneth, how sits your father these days? It has been too long since I was in Briloness, too long since I saw the old rouge.'

Halneth's face saddened. 'He is not well, I am afraid. It happened last winter. One moment he was riding to a hunt, the next he slid from his horse unable to move or speak. The healers say they are doing all they can do, a corruption of the blood in the brain or some such. I do not know of these things but they have bled him frequently yet still the corruption has not left him. He cannot speak nor move his right leg or arm. His face is twisted, as if in pain and yet he feels nothing, or, if he does, he cannot tell us so.'

'I did not know,' Wolfric said in a low voice. 'I am truly sorry to hear such ill news.' Both men were quiet for a while, walking side by side through the ruins of Guidepost and towards the market square where the well was situated. Before they reached the square, and the bloated bodies that Halneth's men were pulling from the well, Wolfric placed his hand on the younger man's arm. 'Tell me,' he said stopping the younger man and facing him, 'if your father is so indisposed, who then is governing Briloness? Your brother Waldwin? He is the oldest, I recall.'

'He is,' Halneth said then shrugged his shoulders. 'Father made him master of horse some time back but, after father was struck down, Waldwin took my father's place but for only a short time. He has no liking for papers and laws, taxes and petitions. He has not the patience for it. Only weeks after taking up the post he handed over the running of the city to Cynrical, my other brother. No, Wladwin is happiest when in the saddle and at the hunt, which is where he will be.'

'How so?' Wolfric said.

Halneth sighed heavily. 'This past year there have been many raids in the West Marches. Farms have fallen to goblins and a lot of horses have been stolen. Waldwin has taken it as a personal affront: he is Master of Horse after all. He and fifty picked riders have been scouring the western lands for goblins; they can be gone for weeks at a time.'

'And yet there was a goblin shanty only a few leagues from here.'

'I know,' Halneth said. 'I mean, I know now. But we had no idea it was there. Some people have said that the factor of the town was in confederation with them . . .'

'Some people?'

'A few of the survivors,' Halneth said. 'Not that there was many. But they said as how the goblins, or rather the half-goblins, would come and go as they pleased and that the factor was more a friend to them than the people of the town.'

'And even less of a friend to your father; Thane Helain is still lord of these parts.' Wolfric added.

'Indeed so,' Halneth said bitterly. 'Not that it did him any good; the factor I mean. People said as his house was the first to burn.'

Halneth pointed to a pile of charred timber and broken stone. 'That's all that is left of his lodging. We found the burnt remains of one body there, a woman by the size, at least we think so. But the factor was a big man, fat by all accounts. We have not found him yet, but then he may be in the well. We just don't know.'

Wolfric shrugged his shoulders. 'We may never know indeed.'

He began again towards the square with Halneth close by his side. 'Tell me,' Wolfric said, 'how many survivors made it to Briloness?'

'Twenty,' Halneth said. 'As soon as word reached Cynrical he ordered me to take every rider I could muster and make all haste. I hoped that I might find more folk on the road but alas we found only three: two men, one very old and one not more than a boy. The boy was helping the old man walk; both were injured and they had been left behind by the others.'

'And the third?'

'A child, more dead than alive,' Halneth said, his voice stained. 'I have some men who are skilled in the healing arts. I sent one, with five other riders as escort, with the three. I only hope that they make it to Briloness in time. The little girl was badly wounded. If the old man speaks right it would seem that when the killing began, a small party, about ten or so, somehow managed to force the south gate. Two of the party, two men, were cut down there but the rest made it outside. But, as you have seen, there is no cover south of the town and nowhere to hide. The goblins brought them down with bows. The old man said as how the arrow that killed the girl's mother had gone right through her and into the child. Then the goblins made doubly sure by stabbing all that they had brought down where they lay, the child included.'

Wolfric could not be sure, as Halneth had turned away from him at that point, but he thought that the young man was crying. He could neither blame him nor condemn him if he was. So Wolfric placed his hand on the young man's strong, yet trembling shoulder and said nothing.

In the market square Halneth's men had brought the last of the bodies out of the well. They laid them on blankets; the heads they laid beside. No one knew which head went with which body as none of Halneth's men knew who had been in the town watch of Guidepost. Yet, strangers or not, or whether the men had been good watchmen or bad, they did not deserve to die as they had: slaughtered and beheaded with their hands tied behind their backs. Whatever the men had been in life, Halneth's men ensured that they at least had a good burial.

After the funeral Halneth took Wolfric aside, asking him, 'Tell me, sir, what news from the king? I assume you sent word to Thessabin.'

'I did,' Wolfric replied. 'But I left Two Rivers before any word could come back. Chancellor Moorbe is there however and he shall see to things.'

'Chancellor Moorbe?' Halneth said slowly. 'When did that happen? I thought Oshern was still chancellor.'

'Not for some two years now. Old Oshern retired after many years service. Spends most of his time fishing now; so I hear,' Wolfric said. He looked at the younger man closely. 'Does news not reach you in Briloness?'

'It would appear it does not,' Halneth sighed, 'either that or my father and brothers still think of me as the naughty boy flitching apples and tell me nothing.'

By late afternoon, as the last of the human remains had been interred in a mass grave outside the east gate, horns were heard to the north of the town. Immediately Halneth's men were on alert, but Wolfric calmed them.

'That will be Saelred,' he said. 'I sent them to scout north of Tangle Wood. They have made good time.' And indeed they had.

Wolfric had thought that it would be nightfall before Saelred and his company arrived in Guidepost but Saelred, the old campaigner, had pressed his men hard and brought them in with several hours of daylight remaining. He also brought them in cheering and in high spirits.

'We met some goblins on the road, My Lord,' Saelred announced as he dismounted. 'A lookout party I think, just ten of them, no more.' Then he gave a big grin. 'And they are no more now either.'

'My instructions were to scout and not to fight,' Wolfric reminded the old captain.

Saelred shrugged, saying, 'Couldn't help it, My Lord. We came upon them by accident so to speak. Early this morning. I guess they were just late risers as they all looked to be asleep when we rode up. One tried to sound a horn but, just as he got the horn to his lips, one of my lads shot an arrow right through its throat. Beautiful shot it was too, My Lord, 200 paces at least and from the back of a galloping horse. Dare say that goblin won't be blowing any more horns, not in this world at least.'

'I dare say not,' Wolfric smiled. 'But did any escape?'

Saelred's grin got even wide. 'Not a chance. I got one with my spear before the rest were ridden over by my lads.' His grin faded as he recalled something of that brief fight. 'Funny thing though,' he said thoughtfully. 'Them goblin could have got away. They were camped on the edge of the wood, yet when we rode up on them, they made to run into the woods only to stop, all a sudden like, then they turned to face us. Biggest mistake they made, and their last.'

'Why do you suppose they did that?' Halneth asked.

Saelred shrugged again. 'Suppose they were more afraid of the woods than of us.' He turned again to Wolfric saying, 'Something else, be funny really any other time, but, after we saw those goblins off, one of my men thought he saw a half naked man running round in the woods. Thinks it was some fat man, but we went looking for him yet could not find him anywhere. Couldn't have been that fat though to disappear like that. We did find two horses about three leagues north of here, both of them still saddled, yet no sign of their riders.'

For a short time the three men, Wolfric, Halneth, and Saelred talked. They took themselves away from all the other riders as they held a small council. After only a few minutes Wolfric said, 'Saelred, your men and horses need some rest. You and your men are to stay here for at least two hours. Then you are to follow us. Halneth's men have found the goblin's tracks. They made off to the north-west. We will set off now and give chase; you will be our rear guard, and if you discover any of those creatures following us, you know what to do.'

'Indeed, My Lord,' Saelred grinned.

'Halneth. There is a small ford north of here as I recall,' Wolfric went on.

'That's right, near a crossroad.'

Wolfric nodded. 'I would like you to send one company to that ford. Have them scout the area then head west following the north bank of the stream till we meet up again. You and I shall take the rest of the men and follow the tracks.'

'It will be done, My Lord,' Halneth said.

'Very well then,' Wolfric said, straightening himself up. 'Gentlemen, what say that we go hunt some goblin?'

North of Guidepost, near the big farm that had three tower houses and several more watch towers upon its walls, the northern column broke away; they took the north road while Wolfric and Halneth set off across open country.

Soon the ruined farms were behind them while ahead of them were the goblins and a clear path some fifty yards wide through the grasslands to show exactly where the foul creatures had gone.

Both Wolfric and Halneth had good trackers with them, men that could spot the tiniest of signs left by who or whatever they were hunting. But on this hunt they were not needed. The goblin tracks were wide and plain for all to see. There were tracks of some thirty horses and the unmistakable footprints of several hundred goblins. And all along the trail, were discarded items of plunder that they had taken, but which they now cast away in order to speed up their escape. It was also possible to distinguish where the creatures had stopped to rest, for their trail became wider at these points, like they had spread out while they paused in their flight. Around these areas there were discarded flasks of water and that stinking brown grog that they drank and piles of their waste.

Yet the riders did not stay long to look at these places, nor did they look to see what loot the goblins had left behind; rather they pressed on as fast as their horses could carry them through the afternoon and on into the night. It was only after the sun had gone down did Wolfric call a halt to the pursuit.

The men were only allowed a few small fires to warm themselves by and to cook whatever rations they had with them. The fires would also allow the other riders to find them in the dark. And if the other riders could find them by the fires, then so too could the goblins, so Wolfric set a strong guard around the camp for the night.

Dawn saw both Wolfric's and Halneth's men in the saddle again and riding as hard, if not harder, than they had the day before. The signs on the trail were fresher, the trackers agreed, and therefore the goblins could not be too far ahead of them. But, as the day wore on, the trackers reported that the goblin tracks showed that they had speeded up.

'Good,' Wolfric said, urging the men on. 'They know we are coming for them and now they flee before us. Press on, men. Press on and let us close with our prey. I want to see goblin blood before nightfall.'

The column of riders cheered at that, cheered and spurred on their mounts.

By midday it was clear that the goblins had turned north, turned and quickened their pace as they raced for the hills.

'They are running for their rat holes,' Halneth grinned as he shouted to Wolfric over the noise of the horses.

'Then let us catch them before they do,' Wolfric shouted back. 'I have no wish to have to smoke them out of their lair. It's too dangerous. Get them in the open, then we will have an end to them.' With that he gave a signal and the 300 riders at his back spurred their horses on to even greater speed.

On and on they rode, pushing themselves and their horses to the very limits of endurance. The trail they followed was littered, not just with cast-off booty but with heavy and surplus gear of war. To begin with it was an occasional shield or a coarsely made helmet. Then, as the riders pressed on, they saw iron breastplates, spears, club, and cudgels.

'Look, My Lord,' Saelred smiled. 'They are shedding their gear in the hope of quickening their pace.'

'Good,' Halneth added. 'It will make them easier to kill.'

Yet Wolfric was unsure. For two days they had been riding hard, two days in pursuit, and still there was no sign of their prey. Their trail was broad and easy to follow, yet the goblins were always out of sight. The goblins were on foot and Wolfric's men on horseback, but still they could not catch them.

On they rode, till night closed in and they were forced to halt for fear of ambush in the dark. They made camp, but no fires were allowed and silence was the order of the night. Men took it in turns to stand guard or eat a cheerless meal of dry rations.

Wolfric sat on his saddle, which had been placed on the ground as a makeshift seat, his cloak and blanket wrapped round his shoulders against the chill. He was alone with his thoughts, chewing on some dried meat, as he stared off into the black of night. Close by, resting but not sleeping, lay Saelred.

'My Lord,' the old campaigner said softly. 'In all my years I have never seen goblins like these.'

'What, my friend?' Wolfric said. He had been too deep in thought and had not heard Saelred.

'These goblins, My Lord. I have never see them move this fast. It is as if they have grown wings. Always they are just out of sight. Always just out of reach of our spears.'

'Then we shall just have to put them to spear point on the morrow,' Halneth said. He came and joined the two other men, placing his saddle on the ground, and after wrapping himself in cloak and blanket, lay down, using it as a pillow. 'The goblins cannot be but a few leagues ahead of us. We will catch them soon; I am sure of it.'

'We can hope,' Wolfric said, more to himself than to anyone. He turned to Halneth and asked, 'How are the men?'

'Disappointed,' Halneth said, 'but more eager than ever to bring this quarry to bay. They are also on full alert, My Lord. Every man paired and taking turns and turn about on watch.'

'Good,' Wolfric said. 'You two get some sleep, I shall take first watch.' With that he bit off another mouthful of dry meat and began to chew slowly on it as his thoughts once more took hold.

# CHAPTER 19

# Cooper Kettles and Rotting Fruits

'All I am saying is that there is a lot of strange goings on,' Cenwalh said as he pointlessly polished a tankard with a dirty cloth. 'I means, day after day that stranger has been coming and going at all times both day and night. Then there's them night soil men, coming and bringing all that rotten fruit and such like to my back door and asking if the stranger wants it. I mean honestly. What's any decent person want with rotten fruit anyway?' He looked at the group of faces that were on the other side of his bar, hoping to find an answer in one of them and, if not an answer, at least some support.

'Well, I don't know,' said one, holding up a tankard and shacking it to show that it was empty. 'I hear tell as how he's been round the town buying up every sweet syrup he can find. Perhaps he got a real sweet tooth.'

'He'll have no teeth at all if he keeps eating that syrup,' another said, 'just like old Aluurad over there.'

A grey-haired man that was leaning on the bar at the edge of the group gave a toothless smile. He had round cheeks and an even rounder belly.

'Well, I don't rightly know what he's doing with it all,' Cenwalh said as filled the empty tankard. 'What I do know is that he's brewing something up in my cellar.' He placed the tankard on the counter and held out his hand. 'That's two pennies, Ernulf. And he's got that boy of mine running round after him. Fetching and carrying things, running one errand after another; I mean, who's the boy working for? Not to mention that he's had my best kettle all tied up for days now. I'll never be able to get the stink out of it.'

Ernulf tossed two copper pennies on the bar saying, 'You're getting paid for the uses, aren't you?'

'Be getting paid for more than the use will our Cenwalh,' another added.

'Not the point. Not the point at all,' Cenwalh moaned. 'I can't even get in my own cellar. That big fellow, that Cenfus is always about.'

'Want to watch him,' the toothless man said. 'I hears he's more than handy with a sword.'

'More than handy with his fists too,' Ernulf added, a comment that the others in the group agreed with judging from the much nodding of heads.

'I got's me a good mind to tell them to clear off,' Cenwalh said as he twisted the dirty cloth in his hands. 'It's my inn and my cellar; I got ale to brew and I needs my kettle back, and they got no right to go walking all over me.'

'Aye, Cenwalh. You go and tell that Cenfus that,' Ernulf said, lifting his tankard to his mouth to hide his big grin.

'I will,' Cenwalh said, 'you mark my words. I'll tell them both in the morning.'

'Of course you will, Cenwalh,' Aluurad smiled. 'And I'll come and watch.'

'No you won't,' Cenwalh said coyly. 'Matters of this nature have to be handled with tact like. Best if I speak to him quietly like on my own.'

'Sure, with tact,' the small group at the bar said in unison.

'You just wait, you'll see,' Cenwalh said without much conviction.

'Well, just be sure to be tactful,' Ernulf said. 'And not just because of Cenfus.'

'Meaning?' Cenwalh asked.

Ernulf leant forward and, in a low conspiratorial tone, said, 'Meaning I've seen that stranger's daughter up at the keep nearly every day.'

'Aye, helping her mother in the healing house,' Cenwalh offered.

Ernulf shook his head. 'No. Going into the tower where the chancellor is hold up.'

'Well, there's a thing,' Cenwalh said softly. 'What do you suppose they be doing?'

'Not for me to say,' Ernulf said. He lifted his tankard to his mouth and, half turning away from Cenwalh, winked at the others that were lining the bar. 'Alls I know is that she goes there every morning. Straight through the gates and up into the tower to see his high-up-ness. And she can be there all day. Mind you, it has to be said, she is a pretty young thing. The type that would turn many a man's head.'

'Well, there is a thing indeed,' Cenwalh said as he looked off into the distance and began rubbing his dirty cloth over the bar top aimlessly while the rest of the group grinned at each other.

'What do you make of that?' Aluurad asked, trying his best to hind his smirk behind his own tankard.

'Well, I err . . .,' Cenwalh said before clearing his throat dramatically. 'Not my place to say, is it? Seeing as how they are guests under my roof an' all.'

'All I know,' Ernulf said, 'is that being a friend of a friend of the chancellor could make that friend someone of importance in this town. Especially if that friend's friend is a close friend, or indeed a very close friend of the chancellor, if you get my meaning.'

'Indeed it could,' Cenwalh whispered to himself. 'Yes, it very well could.'

Before another word was said Ed, Cenfus, and Donald, the tanner, came into the inn. Each of them was carrying a large box that appeared to be quite heavy. Many people in the inn, particularly those at the bar who had been talking with Cenwalh, fell silent and turned to look at the stranger. Stories and rumours had been circulating round the town these past few days, stories about what the stranger was up to and what he might be brewing in Cenwalh's cellar. Then, after the three men passed carrying their boxes, the rumours began all over again. However, whatever was being said, whatever rumours were being spread, Ed and his two companions were far too busy to be bothered by them.

The three men walked quickly through the inn, out through the rear door, and then down to the cellar, only stopping long enough to close the door behind them.

'You see what I mean?' Cenwalh moaned. 'It's like I am no longer master of my own house.'

'Strange folk from strange lands have strange ways,' Aluurad muttered.

'Right said,' agreed Ernulf. 'Now how about some more ale? Whose round is it?'

Ed, Cenfus, and Donald were in the cellar for some time. What they were doing down there was a matter of much speculation among the clientele of the Stubborn Donkey. But, whatever it was, it took until late that evening before the three men once more emerged from the cellar. And when they did, the boxes that they had carried in were then much heavier.

There were too few people in the inn to help carry the boxes, and even if there had been more, they all looked too full of Cenwalh's ale to be of any real help. So, Ed and Donald carried the boxes up and placed them at the door while Cenfus went and brought the town watch.

'Be very careful with these,' Ed told the men Cenfus had brought. 'Two men to a box and, whatever you do, don't drop them.'

'We won't, sir,' one of the watch said as they picked up the boxes. Yet, despite taking great care, lifting the boxes with all the delicacy with which they would lift a newborn child, whatever was inside clinked and chinked noisily and made Ed wince when he heard it.

'Carefully,' Ed said sharply, then adding in a softer tone. 'Please gentlemen, be very careful.'

And the men of the watch were careful. They lifted the boxes, carried them outside and into the street. Ahead of them Cenfus walked, carrying a torch to show the way. They walked down the street, across the market square and to the gates of the keep. From there they went up to the inner wall and through the second gate. Finally they reached the healing house where, after they placed the boxes down near the door, Ed thanked them before Cenfus sent them back to their duties.

Ed went inside and brought Liz out a few minutes later. She looked drained and, in reality, she must have been. Ever since the survivors had come in Liz had spent most of her time at the healing house. She had not been back to the inn for more than a few hours, not had a proper night's sleep nor eaten a proper meal. After four full days Liz appeared as if she was ready to drop.

Outside the healing house Ed asked her how her patients were; his question only seemed to make Liz pale even more.

In a voice that sounded every bit as exhausted as she looked, Liz said, 'Some of them are doing better but we had another two go down with septicaemia today. That makes eight now, and there is nothing I can do for them: nothing.'

'Well maybe I can,' Ed said softly. He opened one of the boxes and brought out a bottle that he handed to Liz. 'Here you go, Liz: penicillin. Now I don't know how strong it is, nor just how pure. I tried to make it as close to the recipe as I could remember. There may be some impurities in it but nothing that should do them any harm.'

Liz looked at the bottle in her hand then back at Ed. 'Are you mad?' she gasped.

'No, Liz, I am very serious,' he replied.

'Ed honey,' Liz said, 'I know you want to help, but I can't give them this: it could kill them.'

'They will most likely die anyway,' Ed said. 'You said it yourself that there was nothing you could do for them.' He placed his arms round her saying, 'Look, I have been very, very careful. Everything has been sterilised, not once but three times. The water, salts and corn syrup were all boiled for twenty minutes then cooled in a sealed container with a pasture tube. Only then did we add the spores, and I made doubly sure that it was only the blue-green spores from the cantaloupes. I was very careful about fermenting them; it's all been done in sealed containers that were sterilised first.' Ed stood back and placed his hands on her shoulders. 'Liz honey, I know how desperate you are to help those people in there. I also know how not being able to is tearing you apart. You're a doctor, and a damned good one but here, in this place, you've got none of the aids you're used to. Now, this penicillin might not be the best, but it's all that you got. You are just going to have to trust me when I tell you that I made it as close to the formula that I learnt in college.'

Liz looked at the bottle for several minutes before asking, 'And how am I supposed to administer it? I cannot have them drink it; you should remember that it passes through the digestive system too quickly to be of any use.'

'I know,' Ed said. 'But I thought of that too.' He brought out a short length of hose that had sharp, hollow needles at each end. 'It's the best we could do to make a drip.'

'What the hell is this hose?' Liz asked examining the drip tub. 'It's not rubber.'

'No it's not. It's goldbeaters skin,' Ed smiled.

'It's what?' Liz stared at him.

'Goldbeaters skin,' Ed repeated. 'It's the outer lining of a cow's intestine. Don't worry, we have had it in a salt solution for three days to kill the germs. It's airtight and watertight, and once you wash the salt off in fresh water, it sticks to itself: it's what they used to make the gas bags out of on the old airships.'

'How did you think of all this, Ed?'

'Despite what some people think, I didn't just play football in college. I was listening, some of the time. And anyway, it was your idea.'

'Mine? How?'

'What you said the other night, the first night you were here,' Ed smiled. 'You said that all you had to treat them with was maggots, moss, and morphine.'

'And from that you come up with this?' she said holding up the bottle.

'Well, yes,' Ed shrugged.

Liz looked down at the bottle and drip Ed had given her. Questions began to form in her mind. 'How did you filter it?'

'Through eight layers of linen,' Ed said. 'All of which were cleaned, washed and sterilised.'

'How long did you ferment the solution for?'

'Three days at about seventy degrees, or as near as I could figure it. And I built a small air pump to agitate the solution as it was fermenting.' Ed nodded towards the others adding. 'We, and Cenwalh's lad, have been taking it in turns to pump the air through it day and night.'

'But the air could have carried germs into the mix.'

Ed shook his head. 'I made an air filter out of charcoal and lamb's wool.' He sighed deeply. 'Look, Liz, I know it's not perfect. I know I don't have a fully equipped lab where everything can be 100 per cent sterile. But what other hope have you got to save them?'

'None,' Liz whispered.

'Well then?'

'All right I'll try it,' she said at last. 'The big guy with the chest wound won't mind; he won't live through the night anyway.'

After carrying the boxes inside the healing house the three men made their way slowly back to the inn.

'I think we can allow ourselves a night off, gents,' Ed said as they walked. 'In the morning we'll begin brewing up another batch.'

'But will that not be enough?' Cenfus asked.

Ed shook his head. 'If it were pure, if I had some way of testing it, then maybe, just maybe, it might be enough. But, as we don't know how strong it is, or how pure, and those people up there are very sick, we will just keep brewing more and more of the stuff till everyone of them is well. I know it's a bit like making a sledgehammer to crack a nut, but what else can we do?'

'Ed sir,' Cenfus said slowly. 'What, exactly does it do?'

'Liz could explain it better,' Ed said to the big man. 'But basically, right now, their blood is turning septic. In other words, their blood is turning to poison and killing them. What penicillin does is mix with the blood, find the germs that turn the blood to poison, and kill them before they can kill the patient, hopefully.'

'But if the blood is corrupted,' Cenfus mused, 'then a letting would be best.'

Ed shook his head and smiled up at Cenfus. 'No, my friend. Whatever happens, and in all cases, the best place for the blood is on the inside. All that a letting will do is kill you quicker.'

Cenfus seemed happy with the answer. He didn't ask anymore questions anyway. Rather he, Ed, and Donald returned to the Stubborn Donkey inn, ate a cold supper, then went to bed ready to begin brew again the next morning.

# CHAPTER 20

## The Hunt

'Tis time, My Lord,' Halneth said as woke Wolfric: it was before dawn and the sky still very dark. He handing him some hard baked bread and cured meat. 'Sorry it could not be better but it is all we have in our rations.'

Wolfric stretched his arms and legs, groaning audibly as the cramps and chills were forced out of them. He shook himself, yawned and rubbed face then took the offered food and thanked Halneth, 'It's not the first time I have had to live on rations, and I fear it will not be the last.' He eased himself up awkwardly and sat on the saddle he had used as a pillow then, stretching his body upright and making his back crack noisily, he smiled at Halneth. 'I told you I am getting old. These bones of mine complain at every occasion.'

Around them the rest of the men were going about their business. Their horses had been fed, and even as the men were eating their rations, they began to saddle their mounts for the day's hunt. Soon Wolfric too was saddling his mount. He had washed the dry rations down with a little water, rolled his blanket, and buckled on his sword belt. Then, after every man had filled their water bottles from the small stream by which they had camped, the riders were ready.

'Speed is needed this day I fear,' Halneth said.

'Indeed,' Wolfric agreed. 'We have to run those goblins to ground before they make their holds in the hills. If we do not do it by nightfall they will be beyond our reach.'

'Then what are we waiting for?' Saelred said, grinning broadly.

Wolfric mounted and raised his right arm. 'At speed men. Forward.' And as one the column of riders surged northwards.

They set off at a fast trot, moving as quickly as the light would allow. Yet, even in that darkest hour before the dawn, it was possible to see the goblin trail: a wide trampled path among an otherwise pristine and unspoiled grassland. As the sun rose higher the path was easier to see, and the riders' pace quickened even more.

Scouting parties moved out from the column, taking position left, right, and ahead. In the centre the main body was formed in four long columns, clouds of dust raising high behind them as they pursued the goblin raiders.

The ground began to change, raising slightly from the flat grasslands as they neared the foothills. The column pressed on faster, not one man willing to permit the escape of their prey.

It was mid morning, and the riders had been in the saddle for four testing hours. The sun was nearing its full height and beating down on man and beast, making both sweat heavily under its relentless heat. Then the first horns sounded ahead of the column. It was directly to the north of the column; a long shrill note that rolled across the plains and made the head of every rider lift up. Then came a second and third horn call, then other horns to both left and right.

'At last we have them,' cried Saelred.

Wolfric's face showed not the slightest emotion: whatever he was thinking at that moment no one could tell. But he pressed his horse until he crested the rise and there, with a clear view of the plains beyond, he halted the column.

Ahead of the riders they could see the mass of goblins: they were more than a league distant and running with all the speed their legs could muster. As they ran they cast aside anything that might slow them down; they had heard the horns sounding behind them and now, as the riders looked on, they made their last desperate bid for the safety of the hills and their deep, dark holes.

'Saelred, take your company to the right and flank them,' Wolfric ordered quickly. 'I will take my company left. But stay out of shot of their bows and use your archers to thin them out. Halneth.'

'Sir,' the young captain replied, his eyes fixed on the fleeing goblins.

'You go straight at them, archers in the fore, and force them to make a stand.'

'Very good, My Lord,' Halneth shouted then, turning to his men he called out, 'Form two lines, archers at the front.'

'Good hunting, gentlemen,' Wolfric called out as he set off with his company.

'I got a heavy purse for the lad that gets the highest tally,' Saelred called out to his company, 'who's going to win it off me?' And his men gave a great cheer and war cry as they surged forward after their captain.

Either side of the goblins there were riders: black-cloaked figures in black leather armour. They carried swords and long curved daggers and, of more use at that moment, long raw hide whips.

'Move it, you slugs,' shouted one of the black riders: a one-eyed half goblin whose face bore a scare from above his empty eye socket to the tip of his chin. He cracked his whip over the heads of the panting goblins, causing many to duck as they ran. 'Run scum, run for the hills, there's horsemen coming so run less you want them to skewer you. *Run.*'

Around the goblins other half goblins began to shout and crack their whips also. 'Get moving. Run, you maggots, *run.*' And as the whips cracked loudly, the shouting became more and more frantic. The goblins did run: as hard, and even harder, than they had for these days past.

But, as much as the black riders whipped and shouted at the mass of goblins, they soon started to become strung out. There are many types of goblins: some are tall, nearly as tall a man and can run just as fast when they have to. But others are short, bow-legged with long lolloping arms and look more like misshapen apes than anything else: these creatures are much slower. And so, even as the black riders pressed them, whipping them to try and keep them together, the fugitive group of goblins split up into smaller groups that were each more desperate than the next to escape the horsemen coming for them.

The taller ones began to push through the rest, pushing through them and disrupting the others as they ran on ahead. Even with the black riders whipping them to get them back into the main group, they began to separate from the smaller and much slower of their fellows. The bandy-legged goblins kept themselves together as best they could, knowing that their only hope was in numbers. At the very rear of the group, older or fatter goblins were lagging far behind. They had cast off their armour, thrown their helmets away, and even their weapons, in a desperate attempt to keep up, but as they fell further and further behind, they became easy pickings for Halneth's men as they closed with the group.

Riding in fast and letting loose their arrows at close range, and with deadly effect, Halneth's men made contact with the stragglers. Many of the goblins cried out in agony as the archers brought them down, while others fell to the ground wounded and were ridden over and trampled into the grass by the horsemen.

One of Halneth's riders, a stocky man armed with a long-handled axe, rode forward on his own. He brought the axe down on a goblin as it ran, splitting the creature from the crown of its ugly head to mid chest: it made no sound as it fell.

But the cries of the dying goblins had alerted the rest of the group. The black riders looked back and saw just how close the horsemen were: saw and knew that there was nowhere to run any longer.

'Halt, halt, you useless maggot. Form ranks facing them, spears in front and archers behind.'

The orders only confused the goblins: which way was front and which behind? They got themselves all mixed up, pushing, cursing, and shouting at each other till the black riders were forced to dismount to sort them out with their whips.

'That way, you thick scum. Turn to rear and spears in front.'

Yet still the mass of goblins could not get themselves in position.

Halneth's men charged forward again, taking advantage of the confusion to ride in close and let fly another devastating volley.

Dozens more goblins fell as arrows ripped into their flesh. One goblin took an arrow in the chest, the razor-sharp point tearing through its flesh and breaking ribs before burying itself into the brute's dark heart. It fell dead without making a sound. Another was hit in the face by an arrow, ripping through its mouth and slashing cheek wide open. While yet another was hit in the foot, causing it to yell ferociously as it hopped and stumbled around. Still others were hit in arms, legs, and bellies, their screaming and dying cries causing even more confusion in the already disordered ranks. The taller goblins, the faster ones that had already pulled ahead of the main group decided, saying as how they were some good way in front of the others, that they should just keep going for the hills, which they did as fast as they could.

Several of the half goblin riders called after them, shouting and cursing them as cowards in an attempt to make them rejoin the rest. But their shouts were cut short as Saelred's men suddenly swooped in on the end of the disordered goblin ranks.

Saelred's archers targeted the half goblins: shooting them would cause even more confusion in the goblin ranks. At the same moment, the goblins that had run off north came running back screaming as Wolfric charged in from that quarter. Wolfric had not just got round the goblin flank but had managed to get ahead of them and was then herding them back with arrows and spears. And of the fifty or so goblins that had tried to make their escape, only five made it back to the main group.

'Circle, circle,' the one-eyed half goblin shouted, seeing they were surrounded. 'Form a circle you sc...' an arrow in his chest and another in his throat cut short his orders.

The horsemen paused then. They had ridden hard to catch up with the goblins, pushing themselves and their mounts nearly to the limit, but now they had their quarry and they were going nowhere. For a long while the horsemen stood, watching and waiting as the goblins desperately formed themselves into a circle. Wolfric, Saelred, and Halneth would have ridden in and broken up the group, would have disrupted the circle before it could have been formed but for one thing: the goblins, in their attempt to get away, had shed most of their armour and shields. So they waited, letting the goblins form their circle for, without shield or armour, the tighter the circle, the easier a target it would make for the archers.

Finally the goblins formed a tight circle with every spear remaining to them thrust outwards, while around them, and facing in on them, the horsemen patrolled: like wolves around a flock of doomed sheep.

Saelred was the first to give the signal. A short blast from his horn sent his riders forward. They rode to within 200 paces of the circle, stopped and let fly a volley of arrows before returning as quickly as they had come.

The goblin returned with a volley of their own. But those armed with spears at the front edge of the circle cowed back, trying to escape the arrows, and jostled the goblin archers behind them, ruining their aim. Most of the arrows went wide or fell short while only two found their mark and both caused only very light wounds to the unfortunate riders.

As soon as Saelred's men were clear, Wolfric rode in with his archers, and as he was riding back, Halneth was already closing with his men from the south.

So it went on for some time, each of the captains probing at the circle with their archers repeatedly and cutting down many of the goblins every time they did so. It was not however an all one-sided fight. Even though goblin bows lack the power of the bows carried by the horsemen, and goblin arrows are rudely made, the mass of goblin archers, and the sheer number of arrows they put into the air, meant some of the men were bound to be hit. Several horsemen mistimed their charge and turn, while others strayed too close to the circle, and these the goblin brought down. A number of the horses were also hit, causing them to unseat their riders as they reared up in pain.

Saelred had made his way round the circle to where Wolfric was watching the battle unfold. His men continued to probe the circle, bring down more of the goblins with each feint till the ground was littered with their dead and the circle was only half its original size.

'My Lord,' Saelred said as he rode up to Wolfric, 'we must attack soon. My archers have but five arrows each, some less. We cannot keep this up much longer.'

Wolfric studied the goblin circle for a moment as Halneth's men sent another volley into the shrinking ranks. 'I know,' he said quietly. 'My men also are running short.' He sat upright and, without taking his eyes off the circle, said, 'Return to your men, old friend, but watch me and wait on your chance.'

As Saelred departed, Wolfric called his men together. All the remaining arrows were given to his best twenty archers; every other man was to form on him.

Saelred and Halneth watched as Wolfric raised his spear high. As he did his men fell in behind him, forming a large, dense wedge with their captain at the tip. The outer edges were made up of those armed with spears, those with swords and axes formed in the middle.

'Shields,' Wolfric cried out, and every man took up their shields, placed it on the left arm and levelled their spears towards the circle of goblins.

Inside the circle the goblins had seen Wolfric's men form up. 'Archers, over here quickly, form up here, those fools are going to charge. Spears, brace yourselves.'

The goblins stripped their archers away from round the circle till all of them were facing Wolfric's men. Then, as they strung the few remaining arrows to their bows, they saw the wedge begin its slow advance towards them.

Wolfric held his men in check, walking slowly at first to keep the formation tight together. His riders drew in close, so close that each rider's knee was pressed hard into the flanks of the horse just ahead of them. They neared the circle, breaking into a trot and then a gallop as their momentum grew. Either side of the wedge the archers rode, losing every arrow they had in order to weaken the circle ready for the charge.

From within the circle every goblin bow let fly, and as they did, a horn blew within the wedge. Suddenly the wedge split, wheeling left and right as the great mass of arrows zoomed skywards and landed harmlessly in the ground where the middle of the wedge had been. Some riders fell but most turned away in time.

The goblins were dismayed, and more so when Saelred's men smashed into the other side of the circle.

Saelred had not formed his men up in a wedge, had not made a show for the goblins to see; rather he and his men had come forward in what looked like just another feint: only this time, after they loosed their arrows, the archers slugged their bows, drew swords, and charged home with the rest of the company.

With his long spear couched tightly under his arm, and standing in his stirrups as he leant into the charge, Saelred was the first to make contact with the goblin circle. To begin with the goblins had just stood and watched the horsemen approach: more concerned were they with avoiding the arrows that had been loosed at them. But then, as the war cry went up from Saelred and his men, the goblins were struck with panic. They frantically looked both left and right, struggling to find courage in their fellows, or themselves, and finding none, they began to tremble. They held out their spears, but the strength left their hands and the spears began to fall to the ground. Some managed to steel themselves to receive the charge, but they were few in number and were soon left stranded as others fled around them.

Saelred lowered his spear at one of the goblins that had stood firm: the fear and dread were plain to see in its callused eyes. With his hand holding tight the reins, his knees pressed around his horse's side, Saelred leant forward and lunged at the creature with his spear. The sharp steel point tore into the goblin's chest, ripping through its black heart before bursting out its back. At the same instant Saelred's horse was speared in its breast, mortally wounding the proud beast beneath him.

The horse went down heavily, its fore legs buckling, as it went cartwheeling over and throwing Saelred from the saddle. One second he was spearing a goblin, the next he was propelled through the air and into the very centre of the goblin circle. The horse was not killed outright: it hit the ground hard where it began kicking out frantically in its dying agony. Every kick of the animal's powerful legs seemed to strike one of the goblins, disrupting their ranks and forcing them to move clear of the dying beast. Saelred's horse may have died but, in doing so, it had cleared a small gap in the goblin ranks: a gap that more horsemen were then pouring through.

Saelred had been unhorsed but, by pure luck, he had been thrown into the very centre of the goblin circle where he had collided with one of the few surviving goblin-men. He landed on the creature, knocking it over and knocking the very breath out of its body.

Quickly Saelred scrabbled to his feet, drawing his sword and stabbing down into the prostrate body of the goblin-man at his feet. He spun round, surveying the host of goblins that now surround him. To Saelred's left, and rushing towards him with its sword raised in both hands ready to strike, was another of the goblin-men. Saelred faced it, blocking the strike with his own sword before he spun out of the way. Then, as he planted his feet again, Saelred swung his sword and struck the goblin-man a heavy blow across its back as its own momentum carried it past him. The half goblin went down, its spin cut through: Saelred finished it with another downwards thrust of his sword before looking for his next opponent.

And by the time he had sought out another goblin within the circle, more of his horsemen had arrived. The first Saelred knew of it was as a goblin thrust its spear towards him, but the spear never found him; rather the goblin itself was knocked from its feet by a spear thrust of a galloping horseman. Saelred would had thanked the rider, but he did not stop; rather the rider pulled on his spear, ripping it out of the dead goblin's chest, before lunging it once more into the throat of another of those vile creatures.

By then almost all of Saelred's men were in the circle, stabbing, slashing and hacking at anything within. Some had, like Saelred himself, been unhorsed and these formed up with their captain to attack the goblin ranks from the inside. The rest of the horsemen were stabbing down at the goblins and using their horses to break apart the circle.

So sudden had the charge been that Halneth didn't even realise it was happening until it had. But, once he saw Saelred's men among the goblins, he quickly ordered his men to charge also.

Halneth charged in, his men close behind as a great war cry went up from the horsemen. Spears points were lowered, swords drawn and thrust towards the breaking circle of goblins. Saelred and his men were already in the centre of the circle, hacking and stabbing at every living thing and causing great confusion and carnage among the goblins. Some tried to make a run for it, but Wolfric's men were waiting for just that moment; they rode them down, stabbing with spears and slashing with sword and axe at any that tried to escape. Then Halneth's men joined the fray, smashing into those goblins that had turned inward to fight Saelred.

The goblins tried to fight back, the half goblin men especially so, but with horsemen surrounding them and horsemen among them, their circle was shattered as was their morale and they broke and ran.

It was then nothing more than a slaughter. The goblins ran in every direction, some on their own, others in small groups, but whichever way they ran and however many there were, the horsemen were hard on them.

Horsemen lunged with their spears, skewering goblins in the back and ripping open their flesh. Other men used axes and swords, chopping off limbs and heads of every goblin they could find.

Some of the goblin stopped, throwing away their weapons and begging for mercy and the horsemen gave them mercy – the mercy of a quick death, which was more than the goblins had given those they had killed at Guidepost.

Finally it was over and close to 500 goblins lay dead on the field. The horsemen had dismounted then, walking round the field, leading their mounts as they inspected the bodies of the goblins. But the men took no chances with those deceitful creatures; they stabbed each and every one where they lay before checking them.

It was victory, but the battle had not been without cost. Of the 120 men Wolfric had rode with from Two Rivers, fifteen were dead and another thirty wounded. Halneth had also lost twenty-four men dead and fifty wounded. Yet, for that, for all they had lost many a good man the band of goblins that had raided Guidepost had been destroyed and the dead of the town and farms had been avenged. The horsemen were satisfied with the day's work.

Not that the day's work was over, not by a long way. There were wounded to be tended, and as soon as the last of the goblins had been run down, the healers set about their forbidding task. Arrows had to be extracted from flesh, wounds had to be cleaned and bound, and cuts had to be sewn shut and dressed, and not just on the men. Many of their horses had also been wounded, and they, unlike the men, had to be rounded up first.

Some of the horses stood still, as if waiting their turn, as the men approached them. Arrows and spears had pierced their flesh, they were hurt and bleeding, and yet, they seemed to know that the men coming towards them were there to help. But others were in too much pain, too fearful of further injury to be approached. No matter how calming the words, nor how soothing the tone the men used, these poor beasts would run when the men got too close. It was heartbreaking for the men to see their horses like that, to see the once majestic mounts that had carried them into battle reduced to frightened, hobbling creatures that had been driven half mad by their agony.

When at last all the horses had all been rounded up, the healers set to work on them. Some, too many really, were past the healers' arts, and they were quickly dispatched so that they did not suffer any more. While others were tended for as best they could be in the field. Their wounds were dressed, and while they could not be ridden, a man was placed with horse to look after it and walk it back the way they had come.

At the same time as the horses were being rounded up other men had been detailed to collect the bodies of the fallen riders.

Each of the dead men was brought to an area away from the battle. Their bodies were washed and then wrapped in their cloaks. Other men had dug a grave, and when all of the fallen of the battle had been tended to, they were placed into the grave and a mound was raised over them. But, unlike if the men had died close to their homes, they were not buried with their swords and shields: all the horsemen knew from bitter experience that the goblins would only dig up the dead again if there was a chance of a good sword. So, for all it was not their custom, the dead were buried without arms or armour in the hope that the goblins would leave them to rest in their long sleep.

As for the dead goblins, their bodies were gathered together and piled high. A fire was set among their corpses: not a great fire, for there was no wood near about with which to build one. So, with any rag, broken spear shaft, splintered shield even the smallest bit of brushwood close at hand, the men built a fire. It was not much and it would burn only slowly, yet the men were satisfied with that: it would serve as a warning to any other goblins what would be their fate should they come south to raid into Angron.

While all of this had been taking place, Wolfric, Halneth, and Saelred had been watching the surrounds. They stood together, holding council as they watched their tired men go about their work.

'I want all the men ready to move again as soon as is possible,' Wolfric said. He was looking to the north, his eyes narrowing as he scanned the hills that were but a few miles away.

'The men are very weary, My Lord,' Halneth said. 'They could use a good night's sleep, as could the horses.'

'I know,' Wolfric said, turning to face the younger captain, 'but those creatures led us too far north. I fear that if we sleep the night here it may be our last night on this earth.'

'I agree,' Saelred said. 'Something's been bothering me from the start of this hunt, and now, looking on them hills, it's bothering me all the more.'

'What is?' Wolfric said.

'That trail,' Saelred said nodding back the way they had come. 'It was like the goblins wanted to make sure we were following them, like they wanted to be found.'

'The same thought is in my mind,' Wolfric said, turning again to look at the northern hills. 'Goblin don't like being out in the open and never far from the holds. Yet those things raided far to the south, and when they should have been days ahead of us, we caught them on a trail that a blind man on a galloping horse could not have missed.'

'Perhaps it was because Saelred killed their scouts,' Halneth offered. 'Perhaps they just didn't get a warning in time. That's why we caught them.'

'Perhaps,' Wolfric mused. 'But Saelred old friend, tell me, how many goblin hunts have you been on?'

'Too many, My Lord.'

'And how many times have you known them to set scouts?'

'After a raid,' Saelred said slowly, 'never. Before a raid, always. Or when they are drawing you into . . .' his words trailed off into nothing.

'An ambush,' Wolfric said as turned to face his two companions again.

'Aye, My Lord,' Saelred said. 'You think we were drawn here for that purpose?'

'I think,' Wolfric stated firmly, 'I think those hills are watching us more keenly than we are watching them.'

Halneth looked on the hills then with more cautious eyes. 'I shall have the men hurry their work, My Lord. But My Lord, there is little daylight left.'

'I know,' Wolfric said then in a near whisper, 'I know.'

# Chapter 21

## The Magic of Books and Books of Magic

Kate sat at the desk in Chancellor Moorbe's office. She looked out of the window, resting her eyes for a few moments as she let her gaze wander over the river and open fields beyond. For a short while her mind drifted off, her thoughts lost as she studied the swaying of the long grass in the gentle breeze. It was another beautifully sunny day, and after brief rain showers the night before, the scent of wild flowers came sweeping over the river to fill the castle courtyard.

Kate shook her shoulders and rubbed her eyes as she brought herself back to the task before her.

A large leather-bound book lay open on the desk. It was just one of many, of seemingly hundreds in fact, that filled every corner of Moorbe's office. The binding was of red leather that was scuffed and nicked in many places; it was old, very old and very faded. Two heavy brass locking clasps were used to close the book, but on this book, as on some of the others, the locks had been forced so that Kate could read it. The pages were not of paper but rather made of velum, and the writing on the pages was in a bold, heavy hand.

Over the past few days Kate had read many books like the one in front of her. She had not planned on reading them, nothing could have been further from her mind, but after she had gone to the healing house to help her mother, and after she had discovered that she could not stomach being in there, Moorbe had taken her in.

It was strange but, in just a few short minutes in the healing house, Kate had discovered a whole new level of respect for her mother. Liz was a doctor, and a good one; everybody said so. They even said that the proof of just how good she was showed in that she got sued less than most other doctors. Yet Kate had never seen her mother at work; after all, a busy emergency room is not really the place for a 'bring your daughter to work day'.

What had surprised Kate the most was how her mother could put up with what was there: the smell of blood and vomit, that awful cheesy stink from badly infected wounds. At first Kate had been given the task of helping clean up the wounded, of removing their dirty clothes and washing them ready for her mother or one of the other healers to treat them. But then Kate was given the job of helping Poppy, Braygon's daughter, but when Kate removed the rag that covered a deep cut on the girl's leg she saw the maggots crawling around inside the wound and it was too much.

Kate ran from the healing house, her eyes full of tears and her hand covering her mouth to hold back the vomit. Once outside she had thrown up, not once but several times until there was nothing left to come up and she was left dry retching and feeling faint. After that she could not go back in. She could not face the smell, nor seeing those maggots again, nor look at someone's face that was all twisted and blackened where it had been burnt. Just how her mother could face it Kate didn't know; she just knew that she never could.

Shortly after that Moorbe's messenger came for her. Whether the chancellor had seen Kate from his window or somehow word had got to him, she never found out. What she did find out however was that the chancellor wanted to speak with her. So, after letting her mother know where she was going, Kate went with the messenger and returned to Moorbe's office.

At the beginning Moorbe simply wanted to know what was going on. Wolfric had of course informed the chancellor about the raid on Guidepost and about the many wounded and homeless people that had fled to Two Rivers. But Moorbe wanted to know more, wanted information regarding the extent of the wounds and also to the welfare of the homeless. So, for two days at least, Kate became Moorbe's eyes and ears in the town. She was not the only one of course, for Moorbe, it was often truly said, had eyes everywhere and ears in even more places. And yet, even if she was not the only one, it gave Kate something to do, something that made her feel she was helping in some small way.

Everything changed on the third day. Kate went to make her morning report, as she had done each day, but while she was making her report, Moorbe settled himself down on the big, soft sofa, and promptly fell asleep. This left Kate not knowing what to do. She couldn't very well walk out; she hadn't finished her report. Nor could she walk over and shake Moorbe back to consciousness; at the very least that would be a breach of etiquette. So what could she do other than wait for the chancellor to wake up again? And while she waited, perhaps out of curiosity or sheer nosiness, Kate began to thumb through some of the many books that littered every flat surface of Moorbe's office.

Kate was sitting at his desk reading, reading a receipt for a hair restoring potion of all things, when the chancellor finally woke up.

'What you doing, girl?' Moorbe snapped at her.

'Sorry,' Kate said sharply, jumping up from the chair. She had not seen Moorbe open his eyes, nor seen the way his head shot up when he had realised she was looking in the books. But, when he snapped at her loudly, Kate had gotten a fright and she jumped to her feet then faced Moorbe and apologised, 'I didn't think it would do any harm, sir. I am really sorry for reading the books; it's just . . .'

'Reading?' Moorbe said, his tilting to one side.

'Yes sir, sorry sir,' Kate stammered. 'I only read a few pages, nothing important I'm sure. Just while you were sleeping, sir.'

'You can read?' Moorbe asked, ignoring Kate's apologies.

'Well,' Kate began slowly. 'We can all read, sir.'

'But you're a girl,' Moorbe said.

'And you're a dog, but you can talk,' Kate replied, reminding the chancellor of their first exchange.

Moorbe jumped down from the sofa and walked slowly towards Kate. Standing up on his hind legs Moorbe was nearly eye to eye with the girl as he asked her, 'When you say "we can all read", do you mean your family or everyone where you come from?'

'Well yes and yes,' Kate said. 'All my family can read, and nearly everybody where we come from can read also. It's one of the first things we learn to do in school.'

'Really?' Moorbe said thoughtfully. He glanced down at the open book on his desk saying, 'Read me something.'

Kate shrugged then turned her attention back to the book. She flipped the pages, and taking her time to decipher the rather scrawling hand in which the words were written, she began to read aloud, 'Potion for the removal of warts, bunions, and other carbuncles. In a two-pebble pot place one pebble of boiled dew that was collected after the full moon. Add a penny-mound of the dried droppings of a white rat that has been fed on honey bread and cabbage hearts. Yuck, rat droppings. Sorry sir, I'll go on. Add a tritch of fresh brown slug slime, err, again, yuck.'

'That's all right,' Moorbe said, baring his teeth in what Kate could only assume was a smile. 'You really can read.'

'Of course I can,' Kate said. 'But, if you don't mind. What is a tritch?'

Moorbe made a strange noise, somewhere between a growl and a giggle. 'Why everybody knows that. A tritch is one quarter of a penny-mound.'

'And what exactly is a penny-mound?' Kate asked.

'Well, it's as much as you can get on a penny without any falling off the sides of course.' Moorbe smiled again.

'Really?' Kate said slowly. 'And I thought the metric system was confusing.'

'Metric what?' Moorbe said, his head tilting once more. 'Look, never mind that. What else have you read?'

'Not much really,' Kate said truthfully. 'I mean like it's totally nonsense, right?'

Moorbe shook his head. 'Far from it, dear girl.' He stepped back and looked round his room saying, 'What you see here is the sum total of all the magical knowledge of Angron, and many other parts of this world also.'

'Awesome,' Kate gasped. 'Least it would be if it was for real.'

'But it is for real,' Moorbe said sitting down. 'How else do you explain me?'

'Point taken.'

'Kate,' Moorbe went on, 'how would you like a different task from the one you currently have?'

'Depends.'

Moorbe thought for a minute, watching Kate intently the whole while, and then he made her an offer. 'Your mother has her work with the healers. Your father is busy with something, though I have no idea what. And your brother is spending his time with the town watch.'

'Is he now?' Kate interrupted. 'Wait till Mother finds out.'

'Please, Kate,' Moorbe said, 'he asked that no one be told. He is only helping out, as are many of the older boys in the town.'

'OK then. My lips are sealed,' she said. Kate mimicked zipping her lips shut, locking them and throwing away the key. 'Well, they are sealed till I need him to do something for me. It's a sibling thing.'

'Understood,' Moorbe smiled. 'But, as I was saying, now that things have settled down in the town, how would you feel about coming here and reading through some of these books?'

'Why?' Kate asked. 'You looking for a cure for warts? Maybe a love potion, or I did see a forgetful potion. That would be cool. I could smack my little brat of a brother round the head, give him the potion, and he wouldn't know where the headache had come from.'

Moorbe began to chuckle at that. 'I don't think that was what magic was meant for even if I do understand the sentiment.'

'Sorry,' Kate smiled, 'only fooling.'

Moorbe made a strange hacking sound as he cleared his throat. 'Kate, if you do this there must be no fooling. The book you have been reading there is about potions; that is very low level magic, important yes, but low level. Many of the books you see here are about much more powerful magic and some, not many but a few, cover the darker arts, and that is very dangerous magic in the wrong hands.'

'How do you mean, dangerous?'

'I mean magic that can kill a man a thousand leagues away with but a thought,' Moorbe said. Then he looked directly into Kate's eyes, adding, 'But that type of magic needs great skill to control. If you tried to use it without the full skills needed it could very well rebound on you.'

'That's not good,' Kate gasped.

'Indeed not,' Moorbe agreed. 'But that is not what I want you to do. What I want is for you find something for me. It is in one of these books but someone,' he said glancing up at Amalric the parrot, 'someone forgot which book it was in.'

'What is it you want me to find?' Kate asked.

'The transmutation and metamorphosis of living things,' Moorbe said. 'Then perhaps we can somehow change Amalric back to his former self and he can change me back to how I should be.' Moorbe walked over to Amalric's perch and stood up on his hind legs. 'Perhaps then I won't have to hide away up here for the rest of my life. Though I may have young Kate here find something all together more suitable for you Amalric, my little feathered friend.'

The parrot recoiled from Moorbe, flapping its wings and squawking noisily.

Moorbe turned away from the panicking parrot and approached Kate, and for a brief second, she could have sworn that he winked at her.

'Will you do it?'

'Yes but one question.' Kate said. 'Why me?'

'Because there some people that may try to use the power and knowledge in these books to raise themselves up and become overlord of these lands. These books have a power, Kate, a very real and very frightening power. They have the power to heal, and the power to kill, if they are used for evil. They also have the power to corrupt the hearts of men unless they themselves be pure and true.

'What makes you think that they will not corrupt me?' Kate asked.

'Because I have been watching you,' Moorbe said sitting down, his tail giving several small flicks as it wagged behind him. 'I think no; I sense that you have a good heart. You are honest, most of the time even if only reluctantly like when you are caught reading things you should not be reading. But I do feel that you will do this thing for me, and more importantly, you will do it without any ill effect on yourself. After all Kate, the only women that use magic that I know of are witches, and you do not seem like a witch to me.'

'My brother might disagree with you there though he would pronounce it a little differently,' Kate smiled.

Moorbe cocked his head to one side again asking, 'The sibling thing again?'

'Can I think about it?' Kate asked. 'Just for tonight. I'll let you know in the morning.'

'Agreed,' Moorbe said. 'But not a word to anyone. This must be kept a secret even from your mother and father.'

'Agreed.'

The next morning Kate returned and informed Moorbe that she would help, if she could. And so, for the next few days, Kate would, after breakfast, walk from the inn to the castle and on up to the tower where she would spend her day searching the books of magic in the hope of discovering the way to undo the spell on Amalric.

Her father hadn't noticed what Kate was doing: he was far too busy with his new friends doing who-knew-what in Cenwalh's cellar. Her mother hadn't noticed either; she was, just like back home, far too busy seeing to the sick to even ask Kate how her day had been. In fact Liz was spending most, if not nearly all, of her time in the healing house and when Kate thought about it, it was hard to remember the last time she had seen her mother spend a night at the inn.

Most mornings it was just Kate and Jay sitting together for breakfast, and occasionally they might be joined by Braygon's children. Her father might grab a bite before heading off to do whatever he was doing, but her mother was never there. Even Jay didn't seem overly interested in what his sister was doing or where she might be going. If anything Jay appeared more interested in stuffing food into his mouth as quickly as he could, then going out the back of the inn to see how the horses were. After that Jay somehow managed to perform a vanishing act for the remainder of the day.

In a way it all suited Kate quite nicely. Everybody seemed to have things to do, places to be, and that meant that they left Kate alone and never asked her any questions.

So after finishing her breakfast alone, Kate would take a slow walk up to Moorbe's tower where, after a short talk with the chancellor, who at least was considerate enough to ask her how her day was, she would set about the task of trying to find the spell Moorbe had told her about.

It was by no means an easy task though. There were hundreds of books; some, very few though, were only a couple of dozen pages, while others were enormous volumes running into hundreds of handwritten pages. In fact all of the books were handwritten, which only made the task all the harder. For some were written in a clear, free-flowing hand that was easy to read, while others were little more than a scribble written in a shaky, trembling hand that took a considerable time to decipher. Kate also discovered that some of the books had been written in one form of code or another: these books she put to one side in the hope that they may be decoded later.

Yet, for all the difficulties of her task, Kate also found it to be somewhat entertaining. For Kate soon found that within the pages of those books, there was a spell for every conceivable occasion; that is, if what was written on the pages was to be believed.

Kate found books full of potions and ointments for every type of ailment, both real and imagined. Potions for the treatment of everything from pimples to piles, hives to heart attacks, and not the cures for but also for the infliction of the same. Another volume that made Kate smile was a massive work covering every possible type of cure and curse. This book had been put together so that the cures were on the left hand pages and the appropriate curse on the right. Flipping through, Kate found the cure for ill luck on one side, while on the other was the curse of ill luck. Shortly after that was the cure for ugliness and the curse of ugliness. On the next two pages was the cure for beauty, which seemed odd to Kate: odd in so far as to why anyone would want to be cured of being beautiful. But on the next page, as Kate was to read, was the reason why. It was a curse that made the accursed person so beautiful that she would be resented by every other woman who saw her. More than that, not only would she be resented, but every woman would become so envious of the accursed that they would be able to do nothing other than plot to bring about her downfall. And, if it was a man so cursed, then no man would ever take him seriously, or trust him near their womenfolk, and all men would eventually do their utmost to harm him and drive him away.

'Whoever wrote this must have had a twisted mind,' Kate chuckled to herself.

'What was that?' Moorbe asked sleepily. He had been curled up on the sofa but Kate's mumbling had roused him momentarily.

'Nothing,' Kate said over her shoulder. 'Just thinking about a girl I know at school.' She returned to the book and flipped the page, 'Cure for the expulsion of belly gases' it read while, on the next page, 'Curse of belly gases'. Kate smiled and began to read again.

And Kate did read, all through the morning and on till lunch time, then after a short break while Moorbe eat alone and she walked round the keep's courtyard, she would return and read through the afternoon and on till nightfall. Only then, long after the sun was down and her eyes felt strained from reading by candlelight, did she call it a night.

Kate would leave Moorbe, saying her goodnights and walk back to the inn. Beside the desk, where she had worked all day, were two piles of books: those she had read through and those she had yet to read. She wasn't reading every word, that would have been a near impossible task with all the books that filled the chancellor's office; Kate was simply skimming through them as she tried to find the spell Moorbe had asked her for. Even so, even just skimming, she knew it would take her some time to get through all the books. And then there was the problem of coded books. Kate had tried to break some of the codes: the desk was littered with sheets of scribbled paper where she had attempted and failed to crack the codes. So until someone could crack the codes, those books would just have to wait.

Kate, just as she had the night before, and the one before that, was sitting at Moorbe's desk. She rubbed her eyes, pinching the bridge of her nose then rubbing her so very tired eyes once more. She had been at the books all day and was near worn out: if nothing else her eyes felt worn out. And, now that the sun was dipping into the west, every word Kate read was a pure strain on her pupils.

'A little more light wouldn't go amiss,' Kate sighed as she again massaged her tired eyes. She was beginning to get a headache so, with her eyes still closed, she gently massaged her temples. 'Light the candles please.'

When next Kate opened her eyes it was to see the desk, and the room for that matter, bathed in light: every candle in the room had been lit.

'Thanks for that,' Kate said to Moorbe. 'I don't think my eyes could have taken much more.'

Moorbe was sitting on his sofa, staring at Kate with his head tilted over to the right. He glanced round the room for a second then returned his gaze to Kate.

'How?'

'How what?'

'How did you do that?'

'Do what?'

'The candles?'

'What about them?'

'How?'

'We're back to that. How what?'

Moorbe jumped down from his sofa and, on his hind legs, walked over to Kate. He stood facing her, his eyes level with hers as he again asked, 'Kate, how did you do that with the candles?'

Kate gave the chancellor a puzzled look. She quickly looked round the room: every candle there had been lit, even some that were lying on their side on a small table next to the door. 'I didn't light the candles; you did,' she said facing Moorbe once again.

Moorbe shook his head. 'Not me, girl. You said something about needing light, then, just when I was about to strike the tinder box, you said "light the candles" and all of a sudden, the candles were lit.'

'No,' Kate said, sitting back slowly in her chair, 'you got to be mistaken. Candles don't just light themselves.'

'Indeed they do not,' Moorbe agreed, 'not unless you lit them.'

Kate shook her head. 'Not me, sir. I've been sitting here the whole time.'

'Exactly so,' Moorbe said excitedly. 'You have been sitting here, reading book after book on magic, and now, just when you need light,

light suddenly appears.' He unexpectedly lunged forward, nearly knocking Kate out of her chair, as he looked down at the book she had been reading. 'What spells have you been reading, quickly now, what magic is in this book?'

'That's the Polaxus spell,' Kate said hesitantly. 'It's not the one you were looking for. I haven't found that yet.'

'Polaxus?' Moorbe asked.

'Yeah, it's like a spell to stun an enemy. Stop them in their tracks before they have a chance to hit you,' Kate explained. 'In fact the whole book is all about using magic to fight with. All really far out stuff like.'

'What about illumination spells?' Moorbe demanded. 'Is there an illumination spell in this book?'

Kate shook her head. 'No. Just things like that Polaxus spell or then there was that other one, the Porposish spell.'

'Porposish spell?'

'Yeah you know, like you can totally knock an enemy over or move objects just by thinking about them and,' Kate held up her hand to demonstrate, 'with a flick of the wrist, over they go.' As she said the words she flicked her hand through the air and sent a stack of books next to the sofa, and some ten feet away, tumbled to the floor.

Amalric began flapping his wings franticly and squawking at the top of his lungs.

'Cripes,' Kate gasped. 'How'd that happen?'

'You made it happen, Kate,' Moorbe said slowly.

'No way,' Kate said, 'all I did was wave my hand like . . .'

Moorbe grabbed her hand in his paws. 'Careful, girl,' he said, pulling her hand down and placing it on her lap. He patted her hand, adding, 'You do not know it but you have magic in you.'

Kate laughed. 'Get real. Magic? I mean, come on.'

But Moorbe's face was serious and his eyes were fixed on hers. 'I mean exactly what I say, girl. You have magic in you, whether you had it before and reading these books has awakened it or it has come to you from these books I don't know, but it is there just the same. My only fear is that you are young and as yet untrained. You have a power, but you do not yet have control. And power without control is a very dangerous brew. If you are not careful you may cast a spell that could backfire on you or, again if you are not careful, you could injure or even kill someone by mistake.'

'Way to put a bummer on it, sir,' Kate moaned as she slumped back in her chair. 'I was totally looking forward trying it out.'

Moorbe looked deeply into her eyes, looked so long and so deep that it began to make Kate feel uncomfortable. 'Magic is not like a new pair of boots,' he said at last. 'It is not something you can just pull on and then run down the street with. You must learn how to use it, when to use it, and where. You must control it lest it controls you like it did . . .' Moorbe's voice trailed off into nothing.

'Like it did who?' Kate asked.

'It was nothing.'

'No, you were about to say something,' Kate said. 'You were about to say somebody's name.'

'I will not say it here,' Moorbe said in a low tone.

'Say what?' Kate demanded. 'Who are you talking about and what happened to them? Did they use magic before they were ready?' Then a thought struck Kate and she stared directly into Moorbe's eyes, making him feel just as uncomfortable as she had felt moments before. 'Did you have someone else read these books for you? Is that it? You did, didn't you? You had someone else read these books and the magic backfired on them. That's what happened, isn't it? Tell me.'

Moorbe had been backing away from Kate but, at her demanding, her commanding word, he stopped. Suddenly he stood bolt upright, his back, back legs and fore legs stiff as if frozen rigidly in place. He tried to look away from Kate, but he could not turn his head. 'Please, Kate,' Moorbe gasped breathlessly, 'release me and I shall tell you.'

Suddenly Kate was aware that it was she that was holding Moorbe: holding him with only the power of her words. She jumped to her feet, 'Sorry, I didn't mean to,' she said as she ran towards the stricken chancellor. As she jumped up Moorbe seemed to crumble before her. His once frozen body buckled and he let out a yelp like a kicked dog as he fell to the floor gasping for breath.

'Please, sir,' Kate said as she bent down and took Moorbe's head in her hands. 'I didn't mean to do it; I don't even know how I did it; it just happened.'

Moorbe got to his feet slowly, testing his legs painfully before climbing back onto his sofa. Slowly he sat down, facing Kate and saying, 'I told you, you must learn to control this thing for, if you do not, you may kill someone.'

Kate lowered her eyes and apologised again.

Finally Moorbe said, 'Sit beside me, girl, sit and I will tell you what you want to know.'

She sat on the sofa next to the chancellor and he began.

'It was a long time ago, a very long time ago, when Blaecca first appeared; perhaps a thousand years ago now, it is hard to be sure as the tails are confused, and I cannot even be sure that that was his real name, but it was the name he used at the time. I do not even think that there is any who truly knows either where he came from or how old he was. All I do know is that a young man turned up in a small village called Cornstead near the town of Apollous at the mouth of the river Lous.

'According to legend he was half starved, dressed in rags, and looked as if he had been beaten to within an inch of his lift. And it was just as well for him that he did wash up at Cornstead, though it would have been better for all if he had not, for in the village there was but one place of importance, and that was the tower of a minor wizard called Griftald. You see Griftald was then very old himself and, unlike many wizards, he no longer wandered the lands searching for more knowledge. No, Griftald had settled down and made Cornstead his home. He built a small tower and healing house, which of course made the people of the village happy. They had not had a true healer in their village before and, with Griftald living among them, they would not have to take their sick or injured to Apollous. Also, Griftald was not unenthusiastic with helping out with their crops, not the planting and the gathering you understand, but he would use his magic to ensure that there was just the right amount of rain and sun so that every year was a bumper year.

'The truth was that Griftald and the villagers got along splendidly. They got a good crop every year and a healer to boot. And what if the old wizard did have a tower? The villagers did not object, even when Griftald spent his nights at the top of the tower watching the stars and thing and doing whatever it was he was doing up there. It was, you could say, a very opportune arrangement for them both. But that was before Blaecca pitched up on their doors.

'Griftald had the young man taken into the healing house where he tended to his wounds and fed him till he was strong enough to walk again. I presume it was Griftald's intent to make Blaecca well enough to work and then send him on his way, but it did not turn out that way. It is told that Blaecca did not want to leave the wizard's house that he asked, even begged, to be allowed to stay and work for Griftald, even to become his apprentice as a means of repaying Griftald. Of Griftald it is said that he did not want the Blaecca around, mayhap he did not trust him; if so he was right-minded. Yet Blaecca would not leave; for a year or more they say, he simply would not leave.

'Finally Griftald relented; he allowed Blaecca to stay on condition that he applied himself only to the healing house and to no other tasks. But, and this is where the story is a little unclear, Blaecca seems to have been stealing into the tower when Griftald was sleeping or about the village and there, Blaecca began to nose about in Griftald's books, books very much like these ones, Kate.

'Shortly after that Blaecca must have killed old Griftald. Nobody knows for sure how or when it happened. All they could say was that one day Griftald was out and about, the next he was nowhere to be seen. Whether Griftald caught Blaecca in his books or just suspected him and ordered him to leave, we don't know. Nor do we know exactly how Griftald died: a pillow smothering him as he slept, a knife in the back one dark night, or perhaps strangled with the cord from his own dressing gown, we just don't know. What we do know is that Blaecca tried, at first anyway, to pretend that the wizard was still alive. But, when people began asking to see Griftald, Blaecca would tell them the old wizard was sleeping, or at his studies, and could not be disturbed. Which everyone knew was untrue. You see Griftald, unlike many wizards, liked the people of the village. He was not aloof and stand-offish, not like some I could name; no, Griftald liked people and was never too busy or tired to help.

'Well, Blaecca could only put the villagers off for so long, and he must have known they would figure out what had happened sooner or later. So, one night while the village slept, Blaecca made off. He set a fire in the tower to cover his tracks and to dispose of Griftald's body. But it was not a good fire and was easily put out. That is how we know the old wizard was murdered. We also know that Griftald had been moderately wealthy but, after the fire, all of the wizard's coins had gone, and so had his books.

'What happened to Blaecca after that is a little of a mystery. We can guess that he found himself somewhere to hide, on doubt paid for with the wizard's stolen coin, and there he must have spent his time studying magic. But, and this is the important but Kate, Blaecca heart was corrupt from the beginning. He did not care to learn healing spells, when there were spells that could bend another will to do his bidding. No, Blaecca only wanted power, and with Griftald's books to aid him, he soon began to gain power.

'Just a second,' Kate interrupted, 'surely there were people looking for this Blaecca. He did commit murder after all.'

'Indeed he did. But, a change of name and a change of appearance, helped no doubt by the magic in the books he stole, and a few coins to quieten any questions, and Blaecca vanished as mysteriously as he had appeared. You know, I sometimes wonder if the wounds and bruises he suffered before he got to Cornstead had not been at the hands of another wizard who was less trusting than old Griftald. But, as I said, Blaecca just up and vanished: at least he did for a long time.

'Many years later some strange things happened, and not just near Apollous but all over. Little things to begin with, like too dry a summer or a sudden thunder storm right before harvest, but vastly important to peasant folk. And, just as strangely, there always seemed to be a wizard around who could put things to rights again: for a price of course.

'Didn't somebody put two and two together?' Kate asked.

Moorbe tilted his head. 'Put two and two together... ah I see what you mean. Put two and two together, I like that, but no, they didn't. You see, Kate in those days these things happened far apart and also wandering wizards were quite common back then. And Blaecca was far too cunning to repeat his little tricks close together. A dry season would happen in one place one year but the next year it was a hundred or more leagues away. But it wasn't just the weather; other things happened: goblins began to reappear for one and many of the wizards that used to roam these lands disappeared.

Moorbe shuffled round on the sofa, getting himself more comfortable then spoke again. 'You must understand, Kate that this land was not always as you see it today. Now it is a lush and fertile land with good soil, great forests, and rivers teeming with fish. But before it was a wasteland ruled by the goblins. From Two Rivers west as far as the Lomrit Mountains and everywhere north from the River Bril, through the Marches and into the Dragon Back Mountains and as far as the icy waste of the Duerogs and the northern Tundra, it was all goblin lands. But that was before the Great Alliance.

'The Great Alliance?' Kate said.

'Indeed,' Moorbe replied. 'The Great alliance was formed between Dwarves, Elves, and men. You see, we had each suffered at the hands of goblins. There were many raids and many small battles. Towns, woods, and mines were overrun. Crops burnt, animals driven off, and homes destroyed. That was when the Great Alliance was formed and formed with but one goal in mind: the destruction of the goblins once and for all. Naturally it was not easy to get the Elves to agree to such a thing. They hate the goblins as much as any but, as is their nature, they do not like to kill any living thing if it can be avoided.

'What, even goblins?'

Moorbe shook his head, 'Even goblins.'

'But if the goblins were attacking the Elves…'

Raising his paw Moorbe said, 'It is one thing to kill a goblin that is attacking you or your home, but to arm yourself and go to war, that is altogether something else. However, after far too many raids, and a great deal of negotiation, the Elves, under their King Ellinda, joined the alliance; that was over 3,000 years ago.

'Three thousand years,' Kate gasped. 'So what has all of that to do with this Blaecca guy?'

Moorbe looked at her sternly, 'Am I telling the story or are you going to continually interrupt?'

'Sorry,' Kate said, slumping back into the sofa.

'Very well then,' Moorbe said then cleared his throat, which sounded a little like a bark. King Ellinda for the Elves, King Broomlin for the Dwarves, and King Ailnoth of the Gold Horn for men all signed to destroy the goblins and drive them from these lands. I should mention that we were ruled from the Golden Horn in those days. And so a war was begun on the goblins: at least by men and Elves; the Dwarves had been at war with them for many years already in and under the Lomrit Mountains.

'Ailnoth struck first. He set out from the Golden Horn with a host of 10,000. More rallied to his banners as he marched north till he reached the river Bril. Now the Bril is both deep and fast flowing and there are few places to cross. But there is an island mid river where a causeway connects to the southern shore: it was here that Ailnoth set his aim. Several times on his march north, Ailnoth came upon goblin war bands, and several times he defeated them. Finally the goblin realised that they must gather all their strength if they were to overcome Ailnoth and his men. And so, as Ailnoth marched north, the goblins pulled back and watched. Then, when Ailnoth set up camp on the island, the island where Briloness now stands, the goblins closed in.

'They must have thought that they had Ailnoth trapped on the island, had him trapped, and could sit back and watch his army starve. But that was what the Alliance wanted them to think. As the goblins closed in around Ailnoth, they pulled more and more of their troops from both east and west. When they did that both the Dwarves and the Elves marched out with their armies. Instead of having Ailnoth trapped on the island it was the goblins that found themselves trapped between three armies.

'When news reached the goblin commander, he must have been paralysed with doubt. If he turned east or west, to face the armies come on him, then Ailnoth could strike him in the rear. If he tried to take Ailnoth, and the island, he would have to overcome the defences that he had watched Ailnoth's men build: defences that he knew would cost him many of his army and perhaps so many that he would not have the strength to face the other two armies come at him.

'Now the very worst decision is no decision at all, and that is what the goblins decided. In fact more than that, they began to fight among themselves, and not just an argument but a full-blooded, swords drawn, daggers out battle. Ailnoth and his men even sat on the island cheering one faction of goblins on against another as the whole of the goblin camp erupted in bloodletting. But the cheering only enraged the goblins more until, at some point that bloody night, one faction must have worn out and, without thinking, they charged the causeway. Which suited Ailnoth just fine.

'The causeway is much wider now, but back then, it was only wide enough for four men to walk side by side if they were very close together. So, as the goblins charged, they came under a hail of arrows from the island, cutting them down long before they made it to the island. Ten or more times they charged, and ten or times they were cut down in their hundreds. And each time they were repulsed, they became more enraged than the last, for the men on the island just laughed and jeered at the goblins.

'The battle of the causeway lasted a whole day and a night. By which time the supply of arrows was running low and so the goblins forced their way across the causeway where the fighting was hand to hand. Even then Ailnoth and his men were in a good position as his defences were strong and the goblins could not bring all their numbers to bear. What they did do was to crowd together as a mass on the southern end of the causeway in a great push in the hope of getting at the men on the island. That was how the Dwarves and Elves found them on the dawn of the second day of the battle. Their camp was unguarded; they had not placed lookouts: in fact there was no one watching the surrounds. By the time the Dwarves sounded their horns, rank upon rank of elven archers had taken position overlooking them and the first volleys were in the air.

'At that point in the battle there was no order in the goblin ranks: war band was mixed up with war band and all of them were pressed together at the entrance to the causeway. Needless to say it was a great slaughter, and while it broke the main power of the goblins, it was not the last battle of the war. That would be over ten years in coming.

'Now, at the end of those ten years of war, the goblins had been pushed out of these lands, pushed back and scattered till the only place for them to run was into the far north of the frozen tundra. And that is where they stayed; at least they stayed there for nearly 2,000 years. That is not to say that there were not raids by small bands of goblins or that there were not skirmishes from time to time; there were. But on the whole it was a time of peace; you could say it was even a golden age. The Great Alliance had fought the goblins and won them, for the greater part at least; with the goblins routed, Elves, Dwarves, and men enjoyed prosperity and free trade between each other.

'The great fortress town of Briloness was built and the city of Thessabin as were smaller towns and forts such as here at Two Rivers. The Elves, I cannot really say built, but rather planted the Mist Woods and Tangle Wood, to name but two. But everywhere it was a good time, and so it was for many centuries. But that was before the coming of Blaecca, though he has used many names to deceive and mislead as is his way.

'As I said, in the beginning it was small things: cheap wizard's tricks to make himself money. But then, and how it came to be no one rightwise knows, but Blaecca was befriended by Prince Heaccin who was half-brother of the then King Regna the Fourth known as Regna the builder.

'You see, Regna was in the north, spending most of his time in Thessabin and overseeing the expansion of the city and the port while Heaccin was in the capital, Bytanthus, in the Golden Horn. And so, with so many leagues between them, it was all too easy for Blaecca to begin planting the seeds of discord between the half brothers. But, while Heaccin trusted Blaecca enough to make the wizard his council, Regna distrusted him. And, as it happened, this rift between brothers grew at the same time as the goblins began to raid the north again in greater numbers. The real rupture however happened when the goblins attacked the fort of Oargathion in the Iron Hills.

'The goblin took the small garrison there by surprise, killing everyone within the wall before they even knew what was upon them. Only a tiny band survived, a small patrol that had been in the hills and that returned to find the goblins had overrun the defences and ... well I will not tell you what the goblins had done to the men inside. But that patrol got word back to King Regna, which took several weeks in of itself. And, once Regna heard that the goblins were marching south again, he set out with all the forces he could muster at Thessabin. He also sent word to both Briloness and Bytanthus for them to send every man in arms to meet him at Durren.

'What happened then is unclear. Heaccin was to maintain that no such message ever came to him while the supporters of King Regna maintain that they saw the riders set out carrying the messages. What we do know for sure was that the messages reached Briloness and Two Rivers and indeed many other northern towns; and troops were sent from all of them. But no troops were ever sent from Bytanthus, which at that time had the greater part of the army. And indeed, troops in Iilyan were sent south instead of north and that order came from Heaccin himself.'

Kate raised her hand, signalling Moorbe to stop for a moment. 'Sorry to interrupt, but why would Heaccin do that, turn on his brother, or at least turn against him anyway?'

'Because Blaecca counselled him it was the wisest move,' Moorbe said blankly. 'You must understand, Kate that Blaecca had spent many months, years perhaps with Heaccin, worming into his mind with honey-sweet words and false praise. You must understand Kate that we cannot be entirely sure how long Blaecca spent misleading Heaccin with his honeyed words. Nor can we know what Blaecca promised Heaccin. What we can be sure of, however, is what he was after, and that was to depose the line of the true kings of Angron and claim lordship over the land for himself.

'So, with Heaccin deserting the king, Regna was left to fight a great host of goblins with the forces he had. And what a battle it was, or rather battles, for it was fought the length of Bromin Moore, from the foot hills of the Iron Hills to Dinndelby Woods.' Moorbe suddenly looked up and quickly turned his head both left and right. 'I have a book here somewhere with an account of the wars; you should read it.'

'That's more my brother's sort of reading,' Kate said. 'Please go on with your story though.'

Moorbe relaxed and turned to face Kate again. 'Well the final battle took place at Durren Fell Farm: that's two days ride north of here. Regna had fought a masterful campaign, picking his ground carefully, never letting the goblins corner his troops, always inflicting far more casualties on his enemy than he himself suffered, and most importantly, always pulling out of battle before the goblins could really get to grips with him. But he was fighting his battle in the belief that Heaccin was sending the main army to help him. But Heaccin had no such plans, and every message asking for aid from Regna was ignored. Eventually, with his army, or what was left of it, camped at Durrin Fell Farm, Regna realised he had been betrayed.

'It is told that on that night before the battle Regna had a dream in which he saw the fall of his house and the end of his kingdom, and so it was to be. Thus, knowing that the forthcoming battle was to be his last, he dressed in his armour, mounted his horse, and addressed his men. It was a great speech, an inspiring speech and is fully recorded in the book of histories, which is around here somewhere. But, in it he foretold that he, along with many who were standing with him, would not live to see the evening. He told how they had been betrayed and that they were being left to fight on their own. You can imagine how it was a bitter brew for his army to take. But, he told them, if they were to die then they should die as free men. All bonds of service were considered fulfilled, all pledges of allegiance to crown and king met, and all debts of loyalty discharged. He said that any man or lord that wished to leave the field could go with his blessing. Any man that wished to return to his home to defend his family could go, and he forbid anyone to say a word against them as all obligations had been paid. And do you know, Kate, not one man stepped out of line, no lord, no knight, or bondsman or peasant: not a single one of them left. Rather they all took a knee and once again pledged themselves to their true king, only this time they all pledged as free men.

'Regna then stood up in his stirrups, raised his sword and cut his palm, making a blood curse on his half brother Heaccin and Blaecca. And every one of the 4,000 men in his army did likewise. Then, after so cursing the betrayers, Regna and his men faced the goblins for the last time.

'The battle lasted all day and long into the night. No quarter was asked or given and no mercy was shown by either side. Regna was facing five, perhaps six, times his number, but he did not hold back as he had before. This time Regna and his men charged. Durren Fell Farm is on a small hill, and even as the goblins were trying to surround Regna and his men, they charged down from the hill and were among them before the goblins knew what was happening. It was one of the bloodiest battles seen in Angron, and as he had foreseen, King Regna fell. Many of his nobles fell also, but in the very end, there were 500 men still standing when the goblins fled.

'So what happened to Heaccin and Blaecca?' Kate asked.

'Heaccin was dead within the month,' Moorbe smiled. 'I would like to think it was the blood curse sworn by Regna's men but the truth, even if it is less fascinating, was that Blaecca, who had been poisoning Heaccin's mind for so long had seen fit to also begin slowly poisoning his body. With the king dead all Blaecca had to do was get rid of Heaccin and lordship of Bytanthus would have been his. Rather it would have been but for an overly ambitious noble called Galppa. He used the news of the king's death to bring about a revolt of the army and stormed the palace. He quickly overcame the palace guards and, finding Heaccin sick in bed, had him beheaded where he lay. Blaecca would have also suffered the same doom but the wizard fled the city only a pace or two before the axe man.

'Galppa then set himself up a tyrant and demanded loyalty from all the lords of land. But remember Regna had freed all men, even if they did pledge themselves to him again; they were free to follow however they wished. And, the man they chose to follow was a young knight called Eanfirth, who also happened to be related to Regan by marriage to the late king's cousin. Also, at the battle of Durren Fell Farm, Eanfirth had been seen standing over the late king's body defending it so that no goblin could touch the fallen Regna. It is said he alone killed over a hundred goblins before more men came and carried off the king's body.

'Well, Eanfirth was made king by the nobles and lords of the north while Galppa was tyrant in the south. Neither one would bow to the other and the civil war that soon followed covered the land with yet more dead. And, while the north was weak, and still fighting goblin war bands, Galppa could not march north because he could never wholly trust his army. He did try, several times in fact, but each time his army was riven by desertion: seems his men liked more the idea of being freemen in the north than slaves in the south. And the only officers that Galppa could trust were those heavily in his pay or with family held hostage in his dungeons, and there were many more of the later I can tell you.

'So a truce was signed: Galppa got to keep Bytanthus, and part of the golden horn, while Eanfirth was king in Thessabin ruling over Angron and the northern marches. Blaecca finally showed himself, claiming lordship over Iron Hills and setting up at Oargathion, where the war with the goblins had begun.

'Sadly Eanfirth was never to know a day of peace while he was king. For thirty-five years he fought against the goblins and against Blaecca. But the wizard's magic had grown strong, very strong, and his goblins multiplied faster than ever before. It was not until the reign of Aethelfirth, Eanfirth's son, that the goblins were finally defeated, and then only after the Dwarves came to our aid.

'What about the Elves?' Kate asked. 'They were part of the great alliance also, weren't they?'

'Indeed they were,' Moorbe nodded. 'But the civil war between Galppa and Eanfirth had them convinced that men only wanted to fight wars for the sake of war. At least that is what they said at the time. But in truth the Elves had greater problems which they hid from the world for a very long time. For before Blaecca had come to Bytanthus, he had been among the Elves. And, just as he had with Heaccin, he had twisted the minds of many of the Elves. No one knew it at the time but the Elves had been at war with themselves for far longer than we had.

'It is truly said that Blaecca came upon the folks of this world as a friend but only left after sowing the seeds of division and destruction.'

'But Eanfirth beat him in battle, you said,' Kate said. 'Besides, this all happened, what, a thousand years ago; he'll be well dead by now.'

Moorbe shook his head. 'Wizards do not die so easy. They have ways of putting their souls into some place or thing that can prolong the years. Eanfirth beat Blaeeca's army, destroying all the goblins he could find, but he did not find Blaecca. And, the longer Blaecca lives, which I am sure he still does, the more powerful he becomes, and the more malicious his sprit becomes. It is but a matter of time before he raises another army and before that storm breaks upon us.

'And you think the raid on Guidepost was his doing?' Kate said softly.

'I think that Guidepost was raided by a goblin war band and that we should be on our guard less more come.'

Moorbe yawned, stretched himself then shook his head violently. He sat back down and looked out of the window. 'It is very late, Kate, I shall have one of my guards take you back to your lodgings.'

Suddenly feeling very tired Kate simply nodded her agreement and then wished Moorbe a good night. With that she left the chancellor and returned to the Stubborn Donkey and bed.

# Chapter 22

## Walls, Wiglaf, and the Watch

The defences of Two Rivers left a lot to be desired. The walls that ran along both rivers were good, high, solid walls with a number of towers and strong gates. The keep, and the curtain wall covering the barracks, were equally solid. But, with a partly built wall and only a wooden palisade beyond, the northern side of town was exposed to a determined attack; and everyone, though none said as much, knew it.

Ed had discussed the matter with Cenfus, who in turn arranged that Ed should put his ideas to Chancellor Moorbe. And the idea was a simple one. Rather than build solid stone walls, for which they didn't have sufficient stone anyway, not if the walls were to be the same height as the river walls, they would build an outer and inner façade of stone, then fill the gap between them with concrete.

The surprising thing was that everything was so readily to hand for the job. Three miles north of Two Rivers there was a limestone quarry and kiln: quick lime was after all one of the main cargos shipped from the dock at Two Rivers on account of the people of Tessabin's habit of lime-washing the walls of their houses. There was also a good supply of pug lime in the warehouses near the docks with which to make mortar. Also, every day, the night soil men took their wagons out of the town removing all the waste that the population produced. Several miles north of the town they had dug pits into which all the waste was tipped, and to make it easier on themselves, they had chosen an area that was made up of a fine, soft sand with black-and-grey flecks that appeared to be ash. Ed realised at once what it was: silica sand from igneous rock. For all they never knew it, the night soil men could not have picked a better place in which to dig their pits.

In a few short days, between Ed and the master mason in charge of the new wall, the whole building site was transformed. The night soil men took out the town's waste in the morning and brought back wagon loads of sand and rock in the afternoon. This also meant that the night soil men were now getting paid twice a day: once for taking a load out and again for bringing the sand and rock back in. In fact several of them soon found that by investing in a second team of horses, so they could make two return trips in a day without exhausting the horses, they could make even more money. Being a night soil man wasn't such a bad occupation, after all, it would seem.

At the wall itself, teams of masons cut the stones for the outer and inner walls, and following behind them, labourers mixed batches of concrete which they poured into the space between. But here again the stone they were using had come from the old wall and most of it only needed cleaning up before being placed into the new wall. That being so the masons were able to get the first few courses of stone, making one wall four feet high, laid in a week. That initial building spurt could not be maintained however. For one thing all the best stones had been used to build the outer façade; the stone for the inner façade needed more cleaning up, and then there was the time needed to mix and pour the concrete. It was not going to be a quick job; everyone accepted that. Indeed the wall would take several more months to be at the full designed height, but it was going up much quicker than before.

A small crowd were gathering round Ed, Donald, and Cenfus as they worked on their latest mad contraption near the wall. Ed had realised that, while there were over a hundred labourers mixing concrete by hand, they really weren't mixing it quickly enough. The night soil men were bringing in plenty of sand and stone; there just weren't enough men to mix it. What was needed was a powered concrete mixer, but how. To begin with the only power source available was good old-fashioned horse power, and even then, how do you make a mixing drum when there were no smithies able to make steel drums of the size you needed? It was Donald that came up with the answer. Why make a drum when you can simply make a trough, a circular trough to be more accurate? Then, from a central pivot a beam extended out over the trough to a harness for a horse. And, suspended from the beam into the trough, was an old plough blade. As the horse walked round the trough the plough turned and mixed the concrete. Very soon five men and one horse working on the mixer were doing the work of thirty, and the concrete fill in the wall was going up faster than ever.

The three men stood back and, along with the rest of the crowd, watched as the first team worked the new concrete mixer. There was some discussion about the merits or otherwise of such a contraption, but no one could refute the fact that the mixer was quicker than doing everything by hand. Ed didn't really take part in the discussion as his attention had been drawn elsewhere.

On the road, leading from the town to the new gatehouse, a body of men were moving. They marched at something near a run: their pace rapid but even. Beside them, shouting out the time and keeping them in step ran one of the older sergeants from the barracks. There were sixty men in the little formation, sixty men and the sergeant and all of them pounding noisily along the cobbled road from the town and out through the gate to the fields beyond the wooden palisade.

'The town watch,' Cenfus said, answering Ed's unasked question as they both watched the formation pass by. 'That's Sergeant Wiglaf with them; he hates them. Old Wiglaf's been running them round something rotten ever since he got handed the job of training the new volunteers to the watch.' Cenfus turned to Ed and smiled. 'Then again Wiglaf is a bastard and hates everybody, so they shouldn't feel hard done to.'

Ed returned the smile. 'I guess a drill sergeant is a drill sergeant in any army.' He watched as the men jogged past before adding, 'They don't look like much, do they?'

Ed's words were true: the town watch didn't look like much. They were all shapes and sizes, from the very tall, one of whom Ed recognised as Maullen, to the very short: that could have been Boargon, Draygon's eldest son who had joined the watch with his father. And there were the very fat, who looked like they could hardly keep up with the pace set by the sergeant, to the very thin that were barely able to carry the shields they were required to run with. Their equipment was also a total mishmash. Some had padded leather jerkins while others wore thick linen ones. Some had helmets with full cheek, nose, and neck guards, while others had what looked more like conical pots stuck on their head, and still others had nothing at all.

'I know what you mean,' Cenfus said. 'We got too many volunteers. Scarcely enough weapons and armour to go round. Ever since the people came in from Guidepost, men have been volunteering for both the watch and the army. Thane Wolfric left word that all who volunteered were to be taken, equipped, and trained; but there just isn't the equipment for them all.'

The two men began to walk towards the gate, following the path the watch had taken.

'You have smithies in town, don't you?' Ed said.

'Aye we do,' Cenfus said, 'and very good ones too. But it takes time to make swords and helmets and shields and all the other gear men need for battle. Take a walk round and you will see, Ed; the smithies are working day and night, as are the fletchers and the bowyers. Word has also been sent to the tanners for more leather to make armour; but it all takes time.'

They passed out of the new gate and walked towards the gate in the palisade, following the route the watch had taken.

'Well, at least they are getting some training,' Ed said, 'better than that fat lazy lot at Guidepost.'

Cenfus stopped and turned to face Ed. 'I fear those men paid dearly for their laziness.'

Ed lowered his eyes. 'I am sorry, you're right,' he said softly.

Outside the palisade, either side of the road, there were fields of lush green grass that stretched on for miles between the two divagating rivers. To the right hand side of the road, targets had been erected and before them archers were at practice. On the left hand side the men of the watch were being drilled. Wiglaf, the old sergeant, was shouting orders, marching the men one way then back again. He marched and counter marched them, had them wheel, turn and turn about and all the time harangued them if any man was out of step or allowed their formation to relax.

But, when it came time to train with weapons, the shortages Cenfus had talked about became all too apparent. Most of the men had spears, but only few had a good, well-crafted sword, in Cenfus's opinion.

Cenfus stood close to Ed and said, in a hushed tone, 'I pray that My Lord Wolfric and his riders return soon. If the goblins attack us now it will go ill. These men will fight, but they have nothing to fight with. Untrained and unequipped men are no more an army than a pile of lumber is a house.'

'That's so very true,' Ed agreed as he eyed the watch closely.

Wiglaf called the watch into a battle formation of three ranks deep. Quickly the men closed up, forming a solid wall as they locked their shields together. The old sergeant then went along the wall, beating on it with the flat of his sword and throwing himself at it, all the time shouting at the men of the watch to brace themselves and the wall properly.

'Lock you shield,' Wiglaf cried out in a harsh gravelly voice, 'my old mum could push through these gaps. Lock 'em tight, tighter; this wall's slacker than a Bytanthus whore.'

'Colourful turn of phrase your Sergeant Wiglaf got,' Ed chuckled.

Cenfus smiled broadly. 'He's just getting warmed up. You wait and see.'

And Cenfus's word was true. Wiglaf went along the line, beating on it, barging at it with his shoulder and all the time berating the men of the watch. He shouted every insult Ed had ever heard at the men, and a fair few he'd never imagined. The only man Wiglaf didn't shout at was Maullen. Not because the smithy was bigger than him but simply because no matter how hard Wiglaf beat on his shield, or threw himself at the man, Maullen's shield never moved. Wiglaf had the ranks rotate then began the same process all over again.

Ed had been watching this for quite some time when he began to notice something. The third rank was then at the front and Wiglaf was going along them, beating on their shields and barging against them. Most of the men in this rank were the shortest of the company, and Wiglaf was having little trouble pushing them back and breaking their shield wall.

'It's a bit unfair, don't you think?' Ed asked Cenfus.

Cenfus didn't answer; his attention had been drawn elsewhere.

Then Ed noticed something in the shield wall, or rather noticed someone. He walked quickly towards the watchmen as he called to Wiglaf, 'Sergeant Wiglaf, sergeant, a moment please.'

Wiglaf stopped what he was doing and turned to face Ed. The sergeant recognised Ed right off. Ed had only been in Two Rivers a short time but Wiglaf knew who he was and knew that Ed had the ear of the chancellor. 'Yes sir, how can I help?'

Ed walked up to Wiglaf saying, 'May I have a word with your men, sergeant? Well, one of them anyway.' With that he turned towards the shield wall and his eyes fell on a short figure near its middle. The helmet was over large and almost covering the eyes of the wearer. Likewise the grubby padded linen jacket was far too big, with sleeves too long and the waist ending mid-thigh. And, as Ed eyed the small figure, it lifted its shield in a vain attempt to hide its face. 'Jason Deeks, what on earth do you think you're all got up for?'

'I am training, Dad,' Jay answered reluctantly.

'The hell you are.'

'But, Dad.'

'But Dad nothing,' Ed snapped. 'What's your mother going to say? She's going to kill you and kill me for letting you play at soldiers.'

'Dad,' Jay groaned, 'you're embarrassing me.' And it was true. Around them the shield wall had relaxed their stance and was now grinning as they watched Jay's discomfort.

'Well, it's going to get a whole lot more embarrassing when I tan your hide,' Ed said.

'Dad, you wouldn't.'

'Try me,' Ed said sharply. 'Now get that stupid gear off and get back to the inn.'

'Dad.'

'Dad nothing. Move it, lad.'

'Yes, sir.'

Cenfus ran up to Ed and grabbed his shoulder. 'Leave that for now, Ed.'

'Just a minute, Cen . . .' Ed would have said more but there was something in Cenfus's expression that told him not to.

Cenfus hurried towards the gate, motioning that Ed should follow him, which he did though without knowing why.

At the gate Cenfus sought out the guard commander. Hurried, whispered words were exchanged between the two men: words that neither Ed nor anyone else overheard.

'Cenfus,' Ed said finally, 'what on earth is wrong?'

Cenfus took Ed away from listening ears before saying, 'While you were talking with your son I saw something over the river. Look there, to the north on the west bank, up on the hill left of the small wood.'

Ed turned to where Cenfus had indicated. At first he saw nothing but then, just where Cenfus had said were three tiny figures. They were moving slowly and grouped tightly together. From time to time they appeared to drop down to hide in the grass, but looking more closely, it could be seen that they were not ducking down but rather falling. They walked as if they were drunk, holding each other up as best they could before stumbling and falling once again. And then and nearly impossible to see at that distance, one or other of them would raise a feeble arm and try to wave.

'Who are they?' Ed asked, his tone as hushed as Cenfus's own.

'I do not know,' Cenfus said, his expression pained and drawn. 'But I feel ill news has come.'

The two men walked back through the palisade, through the new gates and past the masons and labours as they worked on the wall. Both men wanted to run, but both resisted the impulse to do so. They made their way to the bridge gate and were there met by a party of ten riders. The riders had brought horses for them, and once mounted and with Cenfus in the lead, they set off over the bridge.

The bridge had been empty for some days now, and there was only the guard on the walls and the three sorry-looking toll collectors to witness the riders as they set out.

Immediately they were over the bridge Cenfus wheeled northwards, ignoring the road as he cut across the fields, to where he had seen the men. They did not gallop but moved swiftly all the same. They rode up the gentle slope of the hill, and as they reached the crest, they saw the three men stagger and fall once more; and this time none of them tried to rise again.

The three men lay hidden among the long grass, even as the riders approached them; it was nearly impossible to see where the men had fallen. Yet somehow, by some instinct, Cenfus appeared to know their location. He rode directly to them, and when he found the men, Cenfus leapt from his horse without waiting for the animal to stop. At once he bent down to them and straightway he recognised one of the three.

'My Lord Wolfric,' Cenfus said in astonishment then he looked at the approaching riders and cried out, 'It is our captain; Lord Wolfric has returned and in greatest need. Fetch water and someone ride back and bring a healer.'

For a moment all the other riders were frozen. They looked down at the three men lying next to Cenfus. All three were badly cut about, their clothes were bloody and torn, their tabards and armour ripped and slashed in many places. Their cloaks, such as was left of them, had been cut up into strips to bandage the many wounds that each of them bore. They were all desperate for water after having wandered for days as hunted fugitives in their own land. For, it had only been by some miracle, that, at the very end of all endurance, they had made it back to within sight of Two Rivers.

As one rider turned and raced back to the town, the others dismounted and swiftly began giving what aid they could to the three exhausted men. They gave them tiny sips of water. Wolfric and his two companions would drink the whole canteens if they had had the chance. But the men knew that could do more harm, and so they limited the three to just small sips. And, while some men administered water, others began checking their wounds: of these there were many. Wolfric alone bore fifteen cuts upon his body, and that was what could be seen while he was still dressed: other cuts might well be hidden by what was left of his armour. Of his companions one, a man called Ceoda, had but two cuts that could be seen: one on his right leg and the other a deep wound to the left side of his head that had torn away a lump of flesh right down to the skull. The other man, Ethelblad, carried nearly as many cuts on him as Wolfric, including a broken right arm and the loss of three fingers from his left hand.

As Wolfric lay on the ground Cenfus cradled his head and gave him sips of water. 'My Lord,' he said softly, 'what news of the men? What happened to the others?'

Wolfric could not answer. He turned his face away from Cenfus, his eyes screwing up tight as the bitter memory brought an avalanche of pain that washed over his body. Finally he turned back to Cenfus, his eyes red-rimmed and his lips trembling. 'Gone,' he whispered. 'Ambushed. Five days since.'

'What of Captain Saelred and the other company?' Cenfus demanded.

Wolfric shook his head as he screwed his eyes up again, but while his lips moved, he could not make breath enough to answer.

Then it was Cenfus who had tears in his eyes. 'Curse those goblins. I swear on the graves of all my fathers, I will hunt them down and kill every last one. If I have to dig them up from their deep holes, I will kill all of them.'

'Not goblins,' Ethelblad said, his voice hoarse and near breaking. 'Orks, the orks have come down from the hills again. It was the orks that ambushed us: many hundreds of them.' And so saying Ethelblad lay back and closed his eyes.

'Not a word of this,' Cenfus said sharply to the others. 'Chancellor Moorbe will know what to do; until then, not a word, understand?'

Whatever discussion there might have been was cut short by the sound of horses approaching. The first to arrive was the rider Cenfus had sent back, and he carried Liz on his horse behind him. Quickly she jumped down and ran towards where the three men lay. She flipped open the large shoulder bag of supplies she was carrying but then stopped when she saw that Wolfric was one of the three. Momentarily her eyes went to Ed, as if asking for some explanation, but then, and without asking how this had happened, she pushed her way through the group of riders and began examining the men. A short distance behind the rider and Liz a wagon was coming also. In it, along with the driver, there were three women, each dressed in the green frocks of the healers. They also, just as Liz had done, suddenly hesitated when they saw who it was they had been called to attend.

As soon as Liz had examined the men she had them lifted gently into the wagon. She and the other healers climbed in also, tending to the men as they were carried back to the healing house as swiftly as it was safe to do so.

Near the bridge Cenfus insisted that Wolfric and the others should be covered so as not to alarm the town. But his efforts were to no avail. Word had, as word has a tendency to, already got out. The people of Two Rivers knew that there was something very wrong. They did not yet know who was injured or who the three men were, but they knew that ill news had come, and doubtless more would be coming.

Even as the wagon passed through the market square the crowd was gathering. By the time they reached the gates to the keep, voices were calling out the riders, demanding what news there was. But, just as Cenfus had told them, the riders said nothing. They rode either side of the wagon, keeping crowd and prying eyes away from whom they carried. As they passed into the keep Cenfus dismounted his men and sent the wagon on to the healing house. He also called the sergeant of the guard to call out his men.

Rumour was spreading in the town as more and more people were gathering at the gates. But, while the guard may have been able to bar the gate, they could do little to stop the spread of rumours. With the knowledge of what had happened at Guidepost, and most people already guessing the fate of the two companies, fear was stirring in the crowd. That fear would surely spread until it had infected the whole of the town. And when it did, which it would, panic and riot would soon follow.

'Cenfus,' Ed said, calling to the big man as he was issuing orders to the guard. 'Cenfus,' he called again, louder this time as he grabbed the man's arm to get his attention. 'Cenfus, we have to tell the people something. Look at them; they're scared and afraid right now, but if we do not tell them something, this could get very ugly very fast.'

Cenfus looked at Ed and then out of the gate at the crowd that was pressing in at the gate. They had stopped asking the guard what had happened and were instead talking noisily among themselves and getting noisier all the time.

'You are right,' Cenfus said slowly. 'But we must not say anything until we have told Chancellor Moorbe what has happened.'

'Then you go and tell the chancellor and I'll try and calm this lot down,' Ed said quickly.

'Very well,' Cenfus agreed. 'But say nothing of Thane Wolfric and nothing of orks.'

'I'll try,' Ed said.

They parted company and Cenfus went up towards the tower while Ed mounted his horse and pushed his way out into the market square. Almost at once the crowd closed in about him and he could make little headway.

A thousand questions were being shouted at Ed all at once: Who was in the wagon? What had happened to the riders? Where was Lord Wolfric? Was the thane dead? On and on it went. Ed shouted for them to be quiet. But the crowd kept shouting their questions without waiting for answers.

It took a long blast of a horn from on top the keep gate to silence the crowd and even then there were murmuring voices from within it. Finally Ed spoke. In a loud, clear voice he said, 'I know you are all fearful that there is bad news. You have a right to be afraid; I am too. But there is very little I can tell you.' Another murmur ran through the crowd, louder than before. Ed held up his hand and waited quietly until the noise around him stopped. 'I can tell you this,' he said as the crowd fell silent again. 'Most of you have guessed that those injured men were part of the column that rode out of here some days ago.' The crowd grew louder and Ed had to shout, 'but, but,' he repeated several times till the noise died down again. 'But,' he went on more calmly, 'just now we have no news of the rest of the column and those men were too badly injured to be able to tell us much.'

A woman stepped close to Ed and began tugging on his leg. 'Sir, sir, what are their names?' she asked her eyes full of tears and her face creased with anxiety. She wiped her eyes on the back of her sleeve then, looking up at Ed, asked, 'Please sir, if you know their names. My husband and son rode out with the column; they are all I have, sir.'

Hearing that, Ed felt a shudder run through him. He dismounted and placed his hand on the woman's shoulder. 'I am sorry but I cannot give you their names,' he said softly. 'I am very much a stranger here and as yet I know very few people. What I do know, what I have seen in the short time I have been here, is that you people are strong, much stronger than you realise. Yes, I fear that there is bad news coming but also know that whatever that news may be you people are strong enough to take it.'

Ed began to walk slowly through the crowd, looking each and everyone of them in the eyes. 'Take a look at yourselves; take a good look. And take a look at the people standing around you, your family, your friend, and your neighbours. Take a look at them and ask yourself this: who will defend them if you do not defend them? You each have a part to play in defending this city, and if you are not doing your part, why not? We need more workers on the new north wall; we need more swords, spears, bows and arrows. Who will make them if you do not pitch in and make them? There is ill news coming, you are right in that. But what are you going to do about it? Are you going to cry about it? Are you going to gather in a mob and shout at the soldiers who are already defending you or are you going to ante up and chip in? You are faced with a choice right here, right now. You can either stand around shouting to no good end or you can do something to help defend the very people standing here in this market square.'

Ed stopped and turned to face a round-faced man in the crowd. 'You there,' he pointed directly at the man. 'What do you do?'

'I'm a baker, sir,' the man said proudly.

'And have you signed up for the watch?' Ed demanded.

'Me, sir? No, sir. I'm too old for that sort of thing,' the baker replied.

'And too fat,' someone in the crowd shouted making everyone laugh.

Ed ignored the laughter and looked the man up and down. 'Do you have a sword?'

'Aye, sir, somewhere from my younger days.'

'Then give your sword to someone in the watch that needs it and bake your bread, master baker, only make sure that you give an extra loaf to them that are working for the defence of the city.'

Ed looked at another man. 'What do you do?'

'I am a silversmith, sir; that's my place there,' he said, pointing at the large building on the west side of the market square.

'Do you make knives?'

'Yes sir, the finest cutlery in Two Rivers.'

'Then you can make daggers and arrow heads,' Ed replied.

He looked at another man. 'And you, what do you do?'

This man stood up proudly saying, 'I am a butcher by day and in the watch by night, sir.'

Ed smiled, 'Then bless you, sir,' he said and shook the man's hand.

'Please, good people,' Ed said loudly, 'go to your homes; when there is news I will bring it to you, but until then, go home and think; think about what you can do to help in the defence of the city. Thank you for your patience, your concern, and good wishes for the wounded. But please now, go back about your business.'

With that Ed began to walk slowly back towards the gates. Most of the crowd began to slowly drift away, most, but not all. Here and there small groups gathered, chatting among themselves or simply watching Ed. Some talked as they made their way to one or other of the inns in town while some stood in shop doorways discussing what they had just seen and heard. There was however one other group, a group of twenty men, barrow men by the look of them, that gathered in the middle of the square after Ed had left. They stood talking among themselves for a while, then after a few minutes, they all headed directly towards the guard at the gate.

The sergeant of the guard saw them approaching; they were a rough-looking mob and looked about ready for a fight. At once the sergeant had the guard stand ready. But as they neared the gate a big man stepped out from the group and looked at the sergeant. 'Where do we sign on for the watch?' he asked.

In the healing house Liz and the healers were hard at work. The three men had been stripped of their slashed armour and tattered garments, and their wounds were being carefully exposed and examined.

In one end of the healing house a large stove was stoked and pans of water put on to boil. One of the women healers, her white apron already stained red from the blood of the three men, was mixing different herbs into the pans: one for the men to drink and the other to wash them with. Liz was with the men, examining their wounds while telling the other healers to 'put pressure on this' or 'get that cleaned up' and, as she did, Liz called for soap, water, needle, and thread.

Of the three both Wolfric and Ethelblad were in great pain while Ceoda, the man with the head wound, lay unconscious on his bed as the healers tended him. Liz told the healers to bring the men a brew of herbs and poppy sap to ease their pain. But, while Ethelblad drank the brew, and began to take some relief from it, Wolfric refused the brew but instead insisted on keeping a clear mind.

'This is no time for heroics,' Liz said, washing her hands.

Wolfric tried to sit up saying, 'I must speak with the chancellor.'

Liz placed her hand on his shoulder and, as gently as she could, pushed Wolfric back on the bed. 'Right now, My Lord, you are going to do exactly what I tell you to do. And I am telling you to stay still, shut up, and let me get on with my work. Got it?'

The other women healers gasped in surprise and astonishment at the way Liz spoke to Wolfric. He was a Thane, and the Lord of Two Rivers, after all, and no one, save the king, could speak to such a man in such a manner.

Wolfric was also surprised and he looked up at her angularly. But his anger quickly passed and a half smile came to his face. 'Very well, good lady,' he said softly.

'Right then,' Liz said. She held up a long, heavy needle as she looked into Wolfric's eyes. 'Sure you don't want the poppy sap. This is going to hurt like hell.'

Wolfric shook his head. He lay back, his eyes staring at the ceiling, his hand clutching the sides of the bed as he readied himself for the ordeal that was to come. 'Proceed, good lady,' he said then took a deep breath.

The work of the healers took several hours. All the wounds the men had suffered had to be cleaned, stitched, providing there were no signs of infection, and dressed. But some of both Wolfric's and Ethelblad's wounds did show signs of infection and these had to be left open. Fresh maggots were placed in them to clean out the dead tissue, and to keep the maggots in place, clean dressings were placed over them. Liz also sent one of the other women fetch two bottle of the penicillin that Ed had made.

The other healers had initially doubted the effectiveness of this strange liquid, but so far everyone that had been administered the penicillin had recovered. In fact Braygon's daughter Poppy had not only recovered but she had kept her leg and was beginning to walk around a little. It was only the big man that had been brought in from Guidepost with the bad wound across his chest that had not fully recovered. His wounds had healed, but even after the most tender care from the healers, all the man did was stare at the ceiling with those empty, almost dead, eyes of his.

'You are not putting that in me,' Wolfric protested when he saw Liz preparing the bottle of penicillin.

'You bet your sweet ass I am,' Liz said. 'Now shut up and stop being a baby.'

Wolfric was speechless, and more so when he saw the other women turning their faces away from him to hide their grins.

'If you insist I must have it, then at least tell me what it is.'

'Penicillin,' Liz said as she gently pushed the needle into Wolfric's arm. 'It's a drug to help fight the infection, and judging from the track marks on your body, it's not a moment too soon.'

Wolfric winced as the needle went in then, and in a very gentle tone, asked, 'Good lady, if I am not being too much a baby, what, in the name of all my fathers, is a drug?'

Liz gave Wolfric a reassuring smile. 'It's a healing potion of sorts: something Ed whipped up. Now, you be a good patient and lay still. Get some rest and let the potion do its work.'

Wolfric did as Liz told him and not because he was the sort of man accustomed to following orders but more because he was too exhausted to do anything else. Ethelblad however never said anything, nor complained while the healers tended and stitched his wounds: he was too far gone on the effects of the poppies to care.

Of the three men it was Ceoda that gave the healers the deepest worry. He had the least number of wounds but the worst also. The cut to his left arm was deep but clean and easily mended. But the blow that had carried away part of his scalp had also fractured his skull. It was only when the healers examined him carefully that the true extent of the injury was known, and with the infection already in his brain, even Liz could do little for the young man.

High in the tower inside the keep, Moorbe and Kate had heard the commotion in the market square: heard it and looked out to see what was happening. Even before they saw Ed ride out to speak with the crowd there came a heavy, frenetic knocking on the stout door to the chancellor's chambers.

'My Lord chancellor,' a page shouted through the door, 'My Lord, lord Wolfric has returned grievously wounded. And My Lord, all save two of the riders are lost.'

Moorbe's head snapped round to look at the door. He looked at it, then at Kate then back at the door again. 'Open that please, young lady, and usher that loud-mouthed fool inside,' he hissed.

Kate ran and opened the door; telling the page to enter quickly before closing the door behind him.

'My Lord Chancellor,' the page gasped, his face flushed with excitement and alarm.

'Be silent, man,' Moorbe snapped, the hair standing up on his back showing his anger. 'Pull yourself together and speak calmly, man. You know better than to shout such ill news for all to hear.'

'I'm sorry, My Lord,' the page replied as he bowed his head. 'I was shocked and overcome. I shall not let it happen again.'

Moorbe relaxed a little then, with a deliberate slowness, walked over to and sat down on the sofa. 'See that it does not. Now, what news of Thane Wolfric?'

The page bowed, stood upright and cleared his throat. 'My Lord,' he said, his voice calm and controlled. 'Thane Wolfric has returned on foot with two others. All three are wounded and have been taken to the healing house. Cenfus and the stranger Ed saw them at some distance and sent for riders and a wagon to bring them in. But My Lord, Cenfus said that Thane Wolfric informed him that the two companies of riders were lost to ambush.'

Kate gasped loudly at that. 'What? All of them?' she demanded.

'I fear so, lady,' the page said to Kate. He turned back to Moorbe. 'Have you instructions, My Lord?'

'Yes,' Moorbe said. 'Kate my dear, would you mind leaving us for a while? Please go down to the guard and ask them, from me, to have riders made ready to go to Thessabin at once.' Moorbe turned to the page adding, 'Get pen and ink, I have letters to write.'

Taking her leave of Moorbe Kate made her way down to the keep's courtyard. On the far side she could see the healing house and, just outside of it, one of the women in her green dress and white apron. Kate disliked the place; the smell, the sights and everything about it turned her stomach. Yet, despite that, she made her way over the house and to the woman.

'Hi,' Kate said weakly, giving the woman a small but friendly wave.

The woman looked up from her task of disposing of the clothes so recently cut off the three wounded men. 'Hello, young Kate,' she smiled. 'Your mother is very busy just now if you have come to see her.'

'No. It's OK,' Kate said quietly. 'Just come to see how the three men are.'

The smile fell from healing woman's face. 'Not good, I am afraid. But they are in the best place now and we are doing what we can.'

'That's good,' Kate said then, hesitated for a moment before saying, 'I know that Lord Wolfric was one of them. I heard the page tell Chancellor Moorbe so. But the other two, do you know if one of them is a herald, a young man called Hardwin?'

The healing woman looked at Kate closely and saw how her eyes moistened as she said the young herald's name. 'No, he is not one of them. Is he a friend of yours?'

'Sort of,' Kate said as a small tear appeared on her cheek.

The woman came close to Kate and placed her arm around her shoulder. 'Take heart, Kate. These three made it back and there may be others out there.'

Kate could not speak. She wiped the tear away and forced a smile, and with a small unconvinced nod, she made her way back towards the inn.

In the hour before dawn, the darkest hour of the night, Ceoda died. He had made it back to Two Rivers only to succumb to his wounds within the wall of the healing house.

Wolfric took the news hard; he had ridden out with 120 men and returned with only one other alive. He realised then that his best intentions to avenge the massacre at Guidepost now meant that Two Rivers had lost all chance of defence.

# Chapter 23

## Work for Willing Hands

A small party of riders set out over the bridge from Two Rivers at first light. They were gloomy, grim-faced men that never spoke to anyone as they rode from the keep and through the gates. Their orders had come directly from the chancellor: to ride out and look for survivors and, if they could find none, then find the dead and bury them with honour.

Not long after the riders had departed a page came to the Stubborn Donkey and summoned Ed. The reason became apparent as soon as Ed stepped out of the inn's door.

In the market square a large crowd was gathered. Not a noisy mob as they had been the day before, but rather an assembly of volunteers all of whom were waiting to be assigned their tasks. Every able-bodied man, woman, and strong lad was there and all of them carrying whatever weapons they had. Others had come too: the very old, those too old to carry sword and spear, had come and given their weapons to those young enough, and strong enough, to put them to good use.

Cenfus was also there, waiting at the edge of the square and smiling at Ed as he walked towards the crowd.

'Well, Ed,' Cenfus grinned broadly, 'you asked them to come and here they are. What would you have them do?'

And what to do with them indeed?

Ed began to make his way through the crowd with Cenfus and Donald falling in beside him. As they walked they thanked the people for coming, shaking hands with as many as they could while making for the centre of the market square. He mounted the steps of the small office there and faced the crowd.

'Thank you,' Ed began. 'Thank you all for coming. There is a lot of work to be done and little time to do it. But, and I know this just from looking at your faces here today, Two Rivers is not going to go the way of Guidepost. We are not going to be overrun by the goblins when they come. Instead we are going to reek such slaughter on them that they will never even think of attacking this town.' The crowd cheered loudly and Ed was forced to wait for a moment before he went on. 'To do that however we have got to improve our defences. The wall, the north wall, as we all know, is far from finished. So we must build other defences to make up for that. And the first thing we have to do is to build a ditch outside of the palisade. Therefore I want all them that can dig or push a barrow full of earth to go home and fetch their spades, picks, and shovels and report to the north wall within the hour. Second, all those who can make arms and armour should go back to their place of work and do what you do best. We need swords, spears, shields, bows, and arrows every bit as much as we need the wall and ditch. I will go and speak with Chancellor Moorbe and the captains to the troops and we will draw up a list of what we have and what we need.'

Ed looked over the crowd again and at the many heads nodding their agreement. 'Right then,' Ed went on, 'all those making weapons please get back to work now. All those ready to begin digging the ditch, please go and collect your tools now. And, if there any either too old or unfit for the hard labour needed at the ditch, please come back here at noon where there will be work assignments for all willing hands.'

The crowd began to disperse, going to the task that Ed had outlined. Donald and Cenfus came and stood next to Ed then.

'You really think we got a chance?' Donald asked in a whisper.

'Perhaps,' Ed said. 'But the worst thing to do when you are about to be attacked is do nothing. At least if they are doing something they will have less time to worry about what might be coming this way.'

Donald stepped closer to Ed. 'You know, Ed,' he said, turning away from the crowd so that none could see what he was saying. 'There is still time for us and your family to get out of here. We could get our horses and make for that wizard's tower I told you about.'

Ed looked at Donald long and hard. 'No, it's too late for that. Besides, I know my Liz and there is no way she would leave while she has a patient under her care. And honestly, I wouldn't feel right leaving all these people. I've never run from a fight yet and I am not about to begin now.'

Donald nodded that he understood. 'So long as you know what this fight means.'

Ed sighed, 'I do. And that reminds me. How far along is the latest batch of penicillin? We better get that finished and start another batch straight away. I got a feeling that we are going to need it.'

'I'll get right on it, Ed,' Donald smiled and began to walk back to the Stubborn Donkey inn.

Ed and Cenfus turned towards the keep, but before they could move, their path was blocked by a small group of elderly ladies.

'Sir,' one of the old dears said to Ed, 'is there anything for us to do? We cannot be digging and such as you can see.'

Ed smiled at them, 'I got the perfect job for you.' He looked over to where Donald was and shouted for the man to stop. 'Donald, Donald. Here you go, I got you some help.' And then, to the old ladies he said, 'You go along with that man and he will show you what to do. And pay attention mind you, in the days to come you may be saving many lives.'

That pleased the old ladies no end, and they went along with Donald happy to do whatever it was they had to do.

The meeting with Moorbe was brief but to the point and productive. While Ed would supervise the defensive works the chancellor and his staff would draw up the requirements for the town. It was clear that the enemy would be coming towards Two Rivers but when they would come was another question. Scouts had to be sent out, and sent as soon as was possible. Also, once the enemy came it would mean a siege, and Two Rivers was not yet prepared for one. So, the most immediate needs were the defences of the town, scouting out the enemy's location, weapons with which to withstand an attack, and food to withstand a siege.

With all of that agreed Ed went to the north wall while Moorbe issued orders that would ready the town for a siege.

The limestone quarry and kilns would have to be shut down, and so would the tannery, as they both lay outside the walls of the town, and there was no way to defend them. Likewise all the nearby farms were ordered to pack up and move into the town. And foodstuff and livestock was also ordered to be brought within the walls. All the gates of the town were to be closed and no one was to be allowed in or out without written orders from the chancellor's office. There was however one exception to this and that exception concerned the night soil men. Because of the fear of disease in a crowded city the night soil still had to be got rid of. For that reason, once a day the gate in the north wall would be opened to allow the town's waste to be taken out, but only as long as it was safe to do so and only with an armed guard of soldiers.

One other concession was agreed, and it was Kate that put the idea forward. There were two boats that remained at the docks. They were half filled with timber to be shipped to Thessabin. Kate suggested that the timber would be better used to help build the defences and that the boats could be used to take away the very old and the children of the town. It was true that neither the very old nor the children would be able to offer much for the defence of the town, and there would only be more mouths to feed if it came to a siege. While everyone knew that splitting up families would be hard on many, evacuating the old and the children offered them the best hope.

A short time later Ed was working north of the palisade when he saw the first scouting parties set out on their patrols. These were made up of just four riders to a patrol and set out from Two Rivers through every gate. A little later some wagons went out of the north gate: wagons with orders to bring into town all those working at both the quarry and tannery.

By lunch time the word had gone round town about the evacuation, and it was very much talked about. Who should go? Who should stay? Why just the old? Would it not be better to get all the womenfolk out? Yet, despite all the debate, the people realised that there were only two small boats and, at best, they could only carry 100 people, maybe 120 if it was only the children.

By evening, as the last of the livestock was being brought in from the hills and the final loads of lime carried through the gates from the kilns, a large and pitiful crowd was gathering at the dock. Children cried at being separated from their parents. Mothers cried also as their children were loaded into the two small boats. Fathers tried to be strong, telling their wives and children it was only for a short while, but the tears in their eyes betrayed their lies. In the boats the old did what they could, offering words of comfort and inventing games to keep the children entertained. Yet all knew, mothers, fathers, children, and the old alike, though no one would admit it, that this may be the very last time that they would see the other alive.

Finally, amid a gathering mist on the river, the boats pushed off and a whispered wail went up from both boat and shore. Then, as the current and the oarsmen began to take the boats down the river, all those on the dock began moving, following the slow progress of the boats and waving to those onboard until they were swallowed by mist and night. Even then, even after the boats were far away and out of sight, many could not tear themselves away from the dock.

For three days after Two Rivers was very much changed town. It had become a quiet town, a gloomy town. The sounds of children playing in the streets had been replaced by the sounds of shovels digging, of hammers hitting on nails, of swords being sharpened and everywhere the sound of feet drilling.

The strangest thing was that the goblins had not attacked yet. Scouts had come and gone, but as yet, they had not seen sign of the goblins. Word of the orks had also got out, but just like the goblins, nothing had been seen of them either.

On the fourth day a horn sounded in the north-west tower of the wall shortly after dawn. The party of riders Moorbe had sent out to search for survivors had returned.

People flocked to the wall, pushing past the guards so that they might gain a vantage point from which to see what news there was; it was not good. The party had found but four men alive and all of them in greatest need of the healer's arts. On the wall, and from the west bank of the river, the people watched the riders approach in silence. They knew then, if they had not known before, they were on their own.

Two more days passed before the ditch was finished. It stretched from bank to bank and was both carefully designed and fiendish in construction. The ditch was ten feet deep on the side nearest the wall and cut in an almost vertical slope. It was also eight feet wide at the bottom and, on the far side, sloped up at sixty degrees. All the spoils from the ditch had been piled on the far side of the ditch to form a large mound that hid the ditch from any attacker. Another little surprise was that in the bottom of the ditch, multi-armed branches had been buried, the limbs of which had been sharpened to form an abatis ready for anyone or anything that fell into the ditch.

The time had also been used to build an awning atop the palisade. It raised the height of the palisade by five feet and gave those fighting on the wall overhead cover and arrow slits through which to fire. The stone wall had also gone up another course, but it was still only six feet high. Yet, with the fighting platform behind that, it gave a second line of defence and meant those defending it would be above the attackers. Behind that Ed was busy with a gang of carpenters.

They were building several weapons, hand-powered trebuchets that would be able to throw stones clear over the wall and palisade. Each of the trebuchets was manned by a team of eight men, two to load it and six to pull at the swinging arm. And the men picked for this task were those same men Ed had seen working the pile hammers. They were big men, strong men, men accustomed to long hours of arduous labour. Nearby Cenfus was filling a large number of clay pots with a sticky mess of oil and pitch.

Behind that, where the shanty town for the builders had stood, the area had been cleared. In its place a line of sharpened stakes had been planted in the ground and angled ready to impale any that might make it over the two walls. Further back, where the first stone houses stood, all the roads bar one had been barricaded with overturned wagons.

'When was the last time you slept, Ed?' Donald asked as he came wandering through the maze of stakes.

Ed looked up and shrugged. 'Got a few hours shuteye last night,' he said, 'but then it could have been the night before.'

Donald placed his hand on Ed's shoulder. 'Well, you'll have to leave that for now; you've been summoned by the chancellor.'

'Tell him I'll not be long,' Ed replied. 'Just got a bit to finish up here first.'

'Ed,' Donald said, almost pulling him away from the trebuchets. 'You've done enough here. Besides, these men have your drawings; they know what they are doing, so let them get on with it.'

Ed nodded and started to walk towards the keep with Donald. 'How you getting on with the last batch of penicillin?' he asked as they walked.

Donald smiled. 'All finished, bottled, and in cold storage behind the healing house. And by the way, we have closed up the inn and moved everything up to the keep also. You and your family will be staying in the tower from now on: the chancellor has had rooms made ready for you.'

Ed nodded again. 'Well, that will be the safest place when the crap hits the fan. Least if we are in the tower it might stop Jay from trying to join the town watch. I caught him again yesterday, you know.'

Donald gave a sharp cough in an attempt to disguise a laugh.

'Ah crap,' Ed groaned. 'Again?'

'That Sergeant Wiglaf caught him about an hour ago,' Donald said, a smile playing across his face. 'Got to admire the boy's spirit, though. Right now he is sitting up at the healing house where your good lady is keeping an eye on him. And pretty pissed off he looks too.'

'I bet he does,' Ed laughed. 'What I should do is what my old dad did to me. I should make him go outside and cut a switch from a tree and bring it back so I can beat him with it.'

'It was the belt with us,' Donald grinned. 'Big thing it was too, and heavy. Hurt like hell it did; trust me, I got it enough.'

Ed began to laugh loudly as they walked. 'Why do you think parents used to do that? Not just to hit you but make you go and get the instrument of punishment yourself?'

'Just the way they did things back in the good old days,' Donald chuckled.

The two men exchanged stories as they walked back through the town. Through streets that were empty save the ever vigilant patrols of the town watch. Every window had been boarded up and every door barred, giving Two Rivers the appearance of a ghost town. Where once before there had been light and the sounds of gaiety, of people enjoying their lives, now there was only darkness and an ever present gloom.

Chancellor Moorbe was sitting on the sofa when Ed entered the room. As he did, Kate, who had been reading at the desk, marked the page and closed the book before wishing them both a good night. Once the door closed, Moorbe got straight down to business.

'Ed, please be seated and tell me, how are our defences?'

Ed sat down in a chair facing the sofa and began, 'Much better than they were yesterday. The ditch and palisade are ready, I wish the wall was higher, but there is little we can do about that. As for the trebuchets they will be ready by morning and every man in the guard and the watch are properly armed.'

'And how long do you think our defences might hold?' Moorbe asked.

'Hard to say,' Ed answered truthfully. 'I tried to build it like a layered defence so that . . .' Ed fell silent for a moment and eyed Moorbe closely. 'Just a minute. Has news come back from the scouts?'

Moorbe nodded his head slowly. 'They have crossed the river at a ford to the north. A great host the scouts say, perhaps 10,000. Mainly goblins but with many of those half goblins on horse and a good number of orks to stiffen their ranks.'

'How long have we got?' Ed asked.

'Two days, perhaps three,' Moorbe said softly. 'It depends on how fast they travel. Right now they seem happy to take their time: stopping at every farm and building to loot and burn as they go. But there is not much left for them to loot: everything and everyone that could be brought in is in. So, it comes down to how fast they move down from the north now that there is nothing for them to plunder.'

'Have you told the other officers yet?'

Moorbe shook his head. 'I will inform them in the morning. I intend to call a war council after breakfast. Until then, Ed, I wanted to speak with you alone. I need to know how strong our defences are and how long they might hold.'

It was a question that had Ed and Moorbe in conversation long into the night.

# CHAPTER 24

## A Glimer of Hope

The room Ed had been given in the tower was nowhere near as comfortable as that which he was leaving in the Stubborn Donkey. The bed was hard and lumpy, making him feel like he was sleeping on a bag of loose gravel. The blankets were too thin, rough and hairy, causing an itch everywhere they touched without once giving any warmth. And, worst of all, the bare stone walls of the tower were cold and more than a little damp. Even with a large fire in the hearth the temperature in the room was only just above freezing.

Ed washed himself as best he could in the basin of cold water that stood on the rough wooden table that was in front of the tiny opening in the wall that passed for a window. Shivering from both the cold and fatigue, Ed stripped off his clothes and slipped into the bed. As he wrapped the coarse blanket around himself he wondered two things. Firstly, did any of the merchants in town still have any linen sheets for sale? And secondly, who had he pissed off so much that he was being subjected to a blanket that no self-respecting horse would allow across its back?

Linen sheets, Ed thought, that would be heaven. A hot shower then slipping into bed between fresh, crisp, sweet-smelling and just laundered white linen sheets. With that one thought in mind Ed fell asleep. So tired was he, and so deeply did he sleep, that Ed never stirred despite all the turmoil and commotion that night. He slept through Liz's return: even though she talked to him as she undressed, washed, and got into bed beside him. Nor did he stir when she cuddled in behind him to get warm. He slept right through the all the noisy footsteps running up to, and then back down from, Moorbe's office during the night; he also slept through the commotion that took place outside his door when news arrived of two more of Wolfric's riders that had somehow managed to get back. In fact the only time Ed stirred was when Liz began to shake him, and shake him violently.

'Ed? Ed, did you hear that?'

'Hear what?'

'Hear that?'

'And once again, hear what?' Ed rolled over and curled his legs up. 'Linen sheets are so soft.'

'Ed? Are you sleeping?'

'Just a minute, I'll check,'

'Ed, stop messing about and wake up,' Liz said in a harsh whisper.

'All right all right I'm awake,' Ed mumbled, 'hang on a second. No I am still sleeping.'

'For pity's sake Ed, stop messing and wake up. Listen, there it is again.'

'All right I'll play along. There's what again.'

Liz didn't have to say anything: she never got the chance for there was a very loud, and very sudden, blast of a horn from somewhere within the keep.

'What the crap?' Ed shouted as he leapt from the bed.

Liz lay in the bed giggling as Ed hopped round the room desperately trying to pull his pants on. He stumbled, stubbed his toe on the leg of the heavy wooden table that held the wash basin, cursed loudly, before nearly falling on to the bed in his attempt to pull on his boot.

Again the horn sounded in the keep and this time Ed heard the sound of an answering horn in the far distance.

'There,' said Liz, 'that's what I heard: that other horn.' And satisfied with that Liz pulled the covers back over herself and proceeded to go back to sleep.

'Unbelievable,' Ed shook his head. He was still very tired but, as he was up, and more or less dressed, he figured that he might as well go see what all the noise was about.

Ed left his room, and his sleeping wife, and down the two flights of stairs to the entrance of the tower and out into the courtyard. It was still dark outside though the first light of a new day was edging over the far horizon. A good many of the guards were milling about, chatting among themselves and looking far more relaxed than they had in many days: some were even smiling and they greeted Ed cheerfully as he stepped out into the cold morning air.

Ed was puzzled by the obvious excitement; he looked from guard to guard in the hope of an explanation. Finally one of the men walked up to him and, with broad grin on his face said, 'Good news sir, riders are coming in. The king has sent us aid.'

'Where?' Ed demanded, feeling now almost as excited as the guards.

The man pointed towards the rising sun. 'Over there, sir, on the east bank.'

Thanking the man, Ed walked quickly to the east wall of the keep. He ran up the stairs to the battlements and looked towards the far bank. Still to the south, but moving rapidly towards the ferry landing, he could see a double line of torches. The torches flickered, and their flames appeared flattened backwards, as the riders on the far bank made best time towards the landing.

More and more men began to line the walls. From high up in the keep, lower down in the barracks and down to the curtain wall of the town, men lined up atop the walls, and as the riders came closer, the men began cheering. As the men on the walls cheered, the riders answered with loud blasts from many horns. They raised their torches in the air, waving them high above their heads and sending showers of sparks and burning embers into the predawn darkness. Without waiting for orders the men of the east gate guard had opened their gates and were busy unchaining the ferry. They had it free in seconds and pulled for the far bank ready to greet the relief riders as soon as they reached the landing.

Yet, even as the men cheered and opened the gates, Ed was staring at the column. It was hard, very hard to see them clearly. They were between Ed and the rising sun, lower down and very much in shadow but, for all that, Ed was able to count them.

'Fifty,' he whispered to himself. 'Only fifty.'

'That's not good, is it, Dad?' Kate asked in an equally quiet whisper.

Ed was a little surprised to find her there. He had not seen nor heard her approach, but there she was standing beside him and looking out at the riders as they came in.

'It's not going to be enough, is it, Dad?' Kate said as she watched.

'I don't know, sweetheart,' Ed said at length, trying his best to hide his own doubts.

'Dad,' Kate said slowly, 'can I tell you something?'

'Sure, anything.'

'I'm scared, Dad,' Kate said, her voice trembling and heavy with emotion.

Ed turned to her, placing his strong hands on her shoulders as he looked deep into her eyes. 'Can I tell you something, Kate?' he said slowly. 'I'm scared too. It's only natural before a battle. In fact I'll wager every man in Two Rivers is scared right now. Just do me one favour, sweetheart; stay up here, within the walls of the keep; no matter what happens, stay in the keep: it's the safest place.'

'I will, Dad,' Kate assured him.

Ed went to turn away, to watch the men crossing the river when he suddenly remembered something. 'One more thing, Kate,' he said with a forced smile. 'Try and keep that fool brother of yours up here too.'

Kate snorted a laugh, 'Easier said than done, Dad, but I'll try.'

As soon as the men had crossed the river and entered the gates they were engulfed in a sea of welcoming townsfolk. The riders were given bread, salt, and cheese by the people milling round them, but as the gates were again closed, the people began to ask if this was all.

After dismounting, the riders walked through the market square and into the lower gate of the keep. All, save one, led their horses to the stables. That one, as Ed observed, strode purposefully towards the upper gate. Moments later, and accompanied by the guard commander, the man entered the courtyard and made directly for the tower.

His name, as Ed was to discover at the small council called by the chancellor, was call Lord Beohrtric, Thane and Captain of the King's Horse. He was a short, stocky man with broad shoulders and a thick neck. His hair was as red as flame as was his beard and he had bright green eyes. He had a presence about him that was both commanding and cordial, and it was a presence that appeared to give heart to all those at the council.

The council was held in Moorbe's office. In attendance were Ed, Beohrtric, and Moorbe plus the captains of the guard, the town watch, and the scouts. Chancellor Moorbe quickly outlined the situation for Boehrtric.

'I wish I could give you better news Lord Beohrtric,' Moorbe said. 'We have some 300 men of the guard, men at arms and archers, and another 150 men in the watch. After our losses we have but thirty horses and those mainly scouts and not heavy horse.'

Beohrtric listened to this in silence before saying, 'I brought fifty heavy horses with me, but we are just the vanguard. There are another 150 horses and 500 men at arms following.'

It was news that cheered the council; rather it did until Moorbe asked the most pressing question, 'How soon till they arrive?'

'The day after tomorrow,' Beohrtric said assuredly.

Moorbe gave a deep sigh. 'Then I fear they may be too late, Lord Beohrtric.' Moorbe sat forward on his sofa and looked directly into

Beohrtric's bright green eyes. 'Our scouts have seen a large force of goblins and orks moving towards us. They put them not more than a day away now.'

'Then it would appear that we are in a foot race,' Beohrtric said. 'Chancellor, give me a rider with a fresh horse to carry a message to my men. If they are ordered they will increase their pace and march without rest.'

'And if they do I fear they will be in no state to fight when they arrive,' Moorbe said.

'I know my men,' Beohrtric said firmly. 'If I order them to force their march they will, and they will be able to fight when they get here.'

'Are you sure of that?' Moorbe asked.

Beohrtric grinned broadly. 'I am sure. I know these men; I know how they can fight and how they can march when needs must. They will be here in time but I ask only one thing: we must hold the ferry crossing and gate at all cost so that they may cross when they arrive. If we lose the crossing then my men may as well be at home in bed. We must therefore hold the crossing no matter what. Agreed?'

'Agreed,' the whole of the council answered.

'Very well,' Beohrtric said. 'Now, chancellor, gentlemen, it seems that the enemy draws near and time is fleeing from us. If I have your leave, chancellor, I would like to speak with Lord Wolfric and then, Ed is it, I would have you show me these defences the chancellor speaks of.'

Ed stood up then. 'I'd be happy to take you to Lord Wolfric, then we can take a look at the defences.'

'Agreed,' Beohrtric said, 'if you will pardon us, My Lord chancellor.'

'Please,' Moorbe said, waving a paw to dismiss them. 'And I shall have a messenger readied and placed at your pleasure at once.'

'Thank you, chancellor,' Beohrtric said, giving Moorbe a low bow. 'Now Ed, if you lead the way.' And with that the two men left the council and made their way to the healing house.

Outside, in the courtyard, Ed saw Kate running towards the tower with an anxious expression on her face. Seeing her father she stopped suddenly, throwing her hands up and sighed heavily. 'I'm sorry, Dad, he's done it again. I was taking Mum something to eat and when I turned round he was gone.'

'Blast that boy,' Ed hissed. 'Don't worry about it now, Kate. I think the chancellor will have need of you so you had better go up. No doubt your ever-loving brother is playing at soldiers again. I'll have the watch bring him back.'

'A family problem?' Beohrtric asked quietly.

Ed shook his head. 'My son, he is just a boy but he thinks it will be some sort of adventure to be with the town watch.'

'And you think other,' Beohrtric said sympathetically.

'He is far too young to be fighting,' Ed said grimly. 'When those, those things come, I want him up here in the keep where it is safest.'

Beohrtric took hold of Ed's arm and turned to face him. His bright green eyes were now narrowed and resolute. 'Your have not fought goblins and orks before, have you Ed?'

Ed shook his head no.

'Then allow me to tell you something. If your defences fail, if my men do not get here in time, if the goblins overrun this town, there will be nowhere safe. "Those things", as you call them, will not stop at killing every man. If your son is able to carry a sword then he should do so. And I would suggest that your pretty daughter should also carry a sharp dagger.'

'I am not having my Kate carrying a dagger to fight those things,' Ed asserted.

Beohrtric's expression softened as he looked at Ed. 'The dagger is not to fight the goblins with, friend but to save herself from them.'

Ed gasped. 'You're not suggesting . . .'

Beohrtric nodded. 'It is better than being taken by them,' he said then, leaving Ed, he continued to the healing house alone.

In the healing house, Wolfric was sitting up in bed. One of the healing women was spoon-feeding the good thane his breakfast of thick barley porridge washed down with herb tea: neither of which Wolfric liked judging from his expression. But, putting his dislikes aside, the past few days had seen a marked improvement in his condition. His wounds while still tender and far from mended, were healing. He was also more alert, and while not yet able to get out of bed, he was being kept up to date with all the happenings in the town.

'Lord Wolfric,' Beohrtric bellowed loudly as he entered the healing house and walked towards the stricken thane. 'I heard you were dead, or at the very least not long for this world. Yet here you are reclining in comfort like some king at a banquet.'

'Some banquet,' Wolfric scoffed. 'You know how I hate barley porridge. I would give silver for some good roast beef but none of these good ladies will take my money.'

The two men laughed as they clasped hands in greeting.

'I shall have my men bring you the best roast we can find for lunch,' Beohrtric said. 'Something juicy and tender and a good-sized flagon of ale to wash it down with.'

'You'll do no such thing,' Liz insisted as she came striding over. 'Thane Wolfric is far from well and he is certainly not going to be having any ale.'

The two thanes looked at each other and began to laugh. 'Yes, good lady,' they answered in unison, sounding like two schoolboys. 'As you say, good lady.'

Liz shook her head. 'Men,' she groaned, adding, as she walked away, 'just keep the noise down.'

Both men nodded but, as Liz turned her back, they smirked at each other. Beohrtric pulled a face and nodded in Liz's direction. 'Fiery that one, but good to look at. I can see why you allow yourself to be imprisoned here.'

Wolfric shook his head as he looked up at his old friend. 'You never change, do you, Beohrtric?'

'And why should I?' Beohrtric protested. 'Good food, good ale, a soft bed, and a beautiful woman to warm it; what more does a soldier need?' He came closer to Wolfric and lowered his voice. 'Come on, old friend, introduce me, unless you have designs upon that fine lady yourself.'

'No, I have no designs,' Wolfric said dismissively and smiled. He sat up, calling to Liz as he motioned her to come back. As she did Beohrtric stood upright, straightening his cloak and tabard as he struck a manly pose.

'Good lady,' Wolfric said nodding towards Beohrtric. 'Liz, I have the honour of introducing Lord Beohrtric, Thane and Captain of the King's Horse.' Beohrtric bowed but, as he did so, Wolfric added, 'He is a very dear friend, one of my oldest friends, in spite of being a womaniser and seducer of the worst sort, not forgetting an over puffed peacock. Beohrtric, old friend, this is Doctor Elizabeth Deeks. Did I say that correctly, Liz?'

'You did, My Lord,' Liz said and gave a small curtsy.

'Yes, Doctor Elizabeth Deeks, wife-man of Ed Deeks, healer and dwarf-friend both.'

Beohrtric looked at Liz and then back at a broadly grinning Wolfric. Suddenly he burst out laughing. 'Ambushed,' he roared, 'the man is sick in bed and I am ambushed.'

Liz could only tut as she walked away from the two men.

'I tell you, Beohrtric, one of these days you will let some pretty thing turn your head once too often and it will screw right off.'

The two men stayed together for some time, talking in hushed tones as they each passed to the other what news they had. Wolfric told of the attack on Guidepost, the pursuit of the goblins, and their destruction. Finally he told of the ambush, the loss of his men, and of the enemy host that was, even as they talked, coming nearer to the town. For his part Beohrtric told the news from Thessabin, and most of it was not good. The king's forces were stretched by constant pirate raiders up and down the coast. There was rumour that the pirates were in the pay of Bytanthus or, if not, they were at least being given safe haven by them. On hearing this Wolfric sent for Ed, and when he arrived, he asked if he still carried his purse and the gold taken from the goblin men at Guidepost.

'It is worse than I feared,' Beohrtric said after seeing the gold coins. 'Worse than even the king fears. Pirates on the coast, goblins and orks attacking both us and the dwarves, and always the hand of Bytanthus stirring every pot.'

'But,' Wolfric said, 'as yet they have not shown their hand.'

'They need not do so but their design is clear,' Beohrtric said. 'They use their gold to pay others to fight in their place while they sit back and wait. Once we have exhausted all our strength fighting each other then they will move. Wolfric old friend, word has come from the dwarves. Goblins and orks have besieged their mines and trolls are within. They are hard pressed and in need of aid. The men of the Nordhod will not move: they are holding their strength behind the mountains lest they themselves are attacked. The Elves of the woods will not help. We all know how they feel towards the dwarves. So that leaves us and, right now, we are being pressed on all sides so we cannot go to the Dwarves' aid.'

'And if Two Rivers should fall, then the enemy will have cut Angron in two,' Wolfric observed. 'Beohrtric, we must hold. For the sake of the kingdom, we must hold.'

Beohrtric took Wolfric's hand, saying, 'So long as there is breath in my body and a sword in my hand, old friend, we will hold; I swear it.'

With that Wolfric lay back in his bed and fell into a restless sleep. Seeing that, Beohrtric motioned that he and Ed should leave.

Outside Beohrtric asked that Ed show him the defences, which Ed agreed to do, but as they walked down through the gate to the barrack square, Ed asked, 'Lord Beohrtric, what do you think of our chances?'

Beohrtric smiled. 'I will know that when I have seen the defences, and I will know better when my men arrive.'

'Sir, sir,' a guard called to Ed. The man had tight hold of the collar of Jay's padded jacket and was nearly carrying the boy by it as he pushed him along. 'Sir, we found Little Boots drilling with the watch near the wall.'

'Little Boots?' Ed said, somewhat puzzled.

'That's what the watch call him, sir,' the guard explained. 'It's sort of a nickname, like he's their talisman, sir.'

Jay was twisting and squirming every which way in a desperate attempt to get free of the guard. 'Dad, tell him to get off me.'

Ed shook his head. 'You want to go fighting goblins and you can't even escape a guard's grasp. Jay, for once in your life just do as you are told and stay in the keep.'

'But, Dad.'

'But nothing,' Ed snapped. He looked at the guard saying, 'Thank you for finding him but, if you will, take him up to the tower and have the guard there put him in his room, lock him in if they have to, and get him out of that stupid jacket.'

Jay was half lifted half pushed up towards the tower: and he protested noisily the whole way.

'Spirited boy that,' Beohrtric said.

'Takes after me, I'm afraid,' Ed said. 'I was just the same at his age; must have put my parents through hell. Sometimes I think Jay was sent as some sort of payback for what I did as a youngster.'

'Do you really mean that?' Beohrtric asked.

'No,' Ed said, his tone more conciliatory. 'I am just worried he's going to get himself into some real trouble.'

Beohrtric and Ed stood on the old tower of east wall looking down on the defences. All the major work had been completed with only small details remaining. There were more stakes to be hammered into the ground and sharpened. The ammunition for the trebuchets needed to be stacked so that it was closer to hand. But, overall, the defences of Two Rivers were as ready as Ed could get them in the short time he'd had.

'Not too bad,' Beohrtric said, after casting a critical eye over everything. 'I would have liked the wall higher but, all in all, not too bad.'

'I don't understand why the wall was pulled down before the new one was built,' Ed said, more to himself than anyone in particular.

Beohrtric looked sideways at Ed with an unfathomable expression on his face. 'You are not the first one to wonder that.'

Ed shrugged. 'I am sure that Wolfric had his reasons.'

'It was not Wolfric that had the wall pulled down,' Beohrtric said slowly. 'Waldwin was lord of Two Rivers before Wolfric. It was he that gave the order to have the old wall demolished. And he did precious little to have the new wall built afterwards: too busy riding and hawking that one.' Beohrtric was silent for a while, deep in thought, as he looked down at the wall. The end towers and the gatehouse were tall and solid, he could see that. But between them, the curtain walls were little over eight feet high. 'You know, Ed,' he said thoughtfully, 'that wall will only slow down a determined goblin attack.'

'I know,' Ed replied. 'But I have tried to design the defences like several barriers. Any attacker will have to spend a good bit of his strength to take each line. As they do, we fall back to the next. Hopefully the goblins will wear themselves out as they come on and will give up.'

Beohrtric smiled at that. 'You really don't know about our enemy, do you Ed? Oh I know about your little scrap at Guidepost with the four goblin-men, but you have never been in a real battle with those fell creatures.'

'No,' Ed said truthfully.

'Then trust me on this,' Beohrtric said, a gentle smile playing on his lips. 'When they come, and they will come, they will not stop until either all of them are dead or all of us.'

'Well, then we will just have to hope your men . . .' Ed never finished.

Beohrtric's hand fell from his shoulder and his attention was drawn elsewhere. The smile fell from his face; his eyes narrowed, and he turned to face the north.

'Sounds like thunder,' Ed whispered. 'Far off though.' He said, listening harder as he stood silently beside the equally silent thane. Several long minutes they stood there, stood listening and waiting. 'There it is again.'

'Aye,' Beohrtric grinned. 'But that's not thunder. It's drums.'

'I'm sick of everybody treating me like a child,' Jay protested as he lay on his bed.

'They treat you like a child because you are a child,' Kate replied, her tone matter of fact, with a generous hint of condescension.

'I'm not a child,' Jay said, jumping to his feet and facing off against his sister.

'Oh sit down,' Kate hissed as she flicked her hand in Jay's direction.

Jay sat down all right, sat down hard like someone had just punched him in the stomach. 'You hit me,' he shouted.

'No, I didn't,' Kate said. She walked over to the small window pretending to look out as she tried to hide the smirk on her face.

'Yes, you did,' Jay said a little confused. 'You just hit me but, but how? You're all the way over there. How did you do that?'

'I didn't do anything; you fell, that was all.'

'Fell hell. You did something and I want to know what,' Jay said, then his eyes narrowed and he stared at Kate. 'What you been doing up in Moorbe's office? What's he been teaching you?'

'I told you,' Kate said calmly, 'I've just been helping him with a few things.'

'You've been doing something and I'm gonna tell Mum,' Jay said. He jumped to his feet and ran towards the door, but before he could put his hand on the handle, Kate had turned, looked at his feet, and flicked her hand again. Jay went crashing to the floor like some unseen person had kicked his feet from under him.

'Will you damn well stop doing that,' Jay shouted.

Kate smiled innocently, 'I told you I am not doing anything. You must just be at that awkward age and, like, getting clumsy.'

'Clumsy be damned,' Jay said as he picked himself off the floor.

'Please, Jay,' Kate said, trying to sound more considerate. 'Dad wants' you where it's safe...' her words trailed off as she heard the horn. For a second there was only silence then another horn picked up the call, and another and another till every horn in Two Rivers was blasting out the same call of five sharp beats. 'That must be the other soldiers coming in,' Kate said happily.

'No,' said Jay, already half way out the door. 'That's the alarm.'

Jay slammed the door behind him and took off down the tower stairs as fast as he could run. On the ground floor the tower guards were standing at the door looking out. The first they knew that Jay was there was as he thrust his way between them, nearly knocking both men off the feet.

They would have made a grab for Jay but they were too stunned. And then Kate came charging down the stairs shouting after her brother and pushing the two men out of the way again.

'Jay, Jay, you come back here right now,' Kate shouted. She drew back her hand and then suddenly thrust it forward as if throwing something or skipping a stone over water. But Jay was already at the top of the ramp heading down to the barrack square and, at that range Kate's aim was a little off. Kate missed Jay altogether but a group of four soldiers that were running close by unexpectedly found themselves crashing face first into the dirt. One second they were running, the next they were knocked off their feet and face down in the dirt, swords, shields and spears flying every which way.

'Get up, you lazy lot, this is no time for laying about,' shouted their sergeant.

'Sorry,' Kate said to the sergeant as she went after Jay.

The sergeant gave her a quizzical look, shook his head, then went back to shouting at the four unfortunate men. 'Come on, you dopy lot, get your gear, now move it.'

By the time Kate got down to the barrack square Jay had vanished. And it was easy for him to do. For there were people moving in every direction. Soldiers were grabbing their gear and heading towards the walls. The men of the watch were gathering together and running to their positions and all the time there was a stream of women coming in from the town as they made their way to the upper courtyard.

Kate looked around the barrack square, desperately trying to see her brother. All the while she was being jostled from every side by the tide of people coming into and going out off the gates. She tried shouting, but her words were quickly drowned out by the sergeants shouting orders and the cries of frightened people. And, above it, above the shouts and the cries, there were the endless blasts of the horns.

Cenfus came running towards Ed and Beohrtric. He carried a shield on each arm, a spear in his right hand, a sword in his left and another on his belt.

'Begging you pardon, Lord Beohrtric,' Cenfus said with a quick bow. Then he turned to Ed and held out the sword in his hand. 'Here Ed, I have carried this sword for fifteen years and it has served me well. I hope it will serve you just as well. Moreover it is better than that lump of goblin iron you were carrying before.'

Ed looked at the sword, turning it over several times and drawing it part way from the scabbard: it was a beautiful and finely crafted weapon. The pommel was set with a silver clasp and a fire red jewel. The handle was leather and covered with twisted silver treads. The hilt was in the form of two rearing stallions, their heads facing towards the blade that was inscribed with the words 'Fear Nought.'

'Cenfus, my friend, it is a fine sword but . . .' Ed stopped abruptly when he felt Beohrtric grab his arm.

'It would be a great insult to refuse such a gift,' Beohrtric whispered to Ed.

Ed nodded and turned back to Cenfus saying, 'Thank you, Cenfus, I hope I may do the sword justice.' With that they clasped each other's arm and shook it.

Ed placed the sword belt round his waist and adjusted it to get it comfortable. 'We never did get round to doing any training, did we?' Ed smiled.

Cenfus returned the smile and nodded towards the north. 'I think you will get all the training you need by the end of the day.' With that he handed Ed the second shield he was carrying.

With Ed armed Beohrtric asked, 'Where do you want my men?'

Ed looked over the defences; everything was in place and every man was standing at their post. 'Hold them in the market square: there are too many obstacles for them here. But be ready to charge any of the enemy that get past us. And, if we have to fall back that far, your men will have to cover our retreat until we can get into the barracks.'

'Very well,' Beohrtric said. He clasped arms with both men saying, 'Good luck to you both but remember, we must hold the ferry gate.'

The second company of the town watch had come to a halt. They were in their assigned position behind the barricade that blocked the road next to the west wall. Above them on the wall, men at arms and archers were taking up their positions. As the last of them moved along the wall, the guards in the towers closed and barred the doors.

The second company was in something of an open position as the houses on that side of town all had small gardens. For that reason Ed had placed two companies there and extra archers on the tower just ahead of them.

'That's it, men,' Sergeant Wiglaf said once he was happy that the lines were straight. 'Stand at rest for now. It's going to take them some time to get through, if they get through. So stand at rest but keep alert.'

With Wiglaf watching what was going on in front of him on the wall and palisade, he didn't see the small commotion that was taking place behind him. And there were too many orders being shouted for him to hear the men of the second company as they passed the message between themselves.

'Have a look, Little Boots is back,' said one.

'Managed to escape that big bad guardsman did y',' laughed another.

Jay blushed and signalled them to be quiet as he slipped into a position in the middle rank. Once he was settled in, as an afterthought, he swapped helmets with Boargon so as to add to his disguise.

# Chapter 25

## The Battle of Two Rivers

From on the wall and palisade, from up on the towers, after hurrying to their positions, the men stood ready and looked out to the north. Still some way off and looking like some otherworldly giant black snake meandered menacingly across the plain, came the host of goblins and orks.

As they watched the enemy approach, the men made their final and some times unnecessary adjustments to their gear. Men at arms pulled their helmets on, twisting them this way and that to ensure they were properly seated, before tightening their chin straps. They fastened, unfastened, and refastened their sword belt ensuring that their swords were right where they needed them, working their swords in and out of the scabbards several times to check they could be drawn freely. Archers laced up and twisted their arm guards so that their bowstrings would not be obstructed. They checked over the bundles of arrows that had been placed on the palisade for them, lifting several out and checking the sharpness of the points and, holding them up to their eyes, turning them in their fingers to ensure they were straight and that the flights were true.

Cenfus walked along the fighting platform of the palisade. He wore a brightly polished steel helmet with a high crest that was faced with a large eagle's head of silver. From the crest, and running half way down his back, was a plume of blue horse hair. His helmet had thick, deep cheek guards and a nose guard that was shaped like a pair of goggles so that only his eyes and mouth could be seen. Yet, for all that most of Cenfus's face was hidden, everyone knew him, for while most men wore their leather armour or thick padded jackets, Cenfus was resplendent in steel studded leather armour over which he wore a bright blue cloak trimmed in sliver and an eagle head tabard.

'Relax, lads,' Cenfus said as he walked along the platform. 'We still got plenty of time.' He stopped at a nervous-looking archer and slapped the man on the back. 'Take a look, friend, the goblins are not even formed up yet. You'll soon be able to pick them off when they discover our ditch.'

The archer forced a smile as Cenfus carried on along the platform.

Ed climbed one of the towers to get a better look. It was a tight squeeze as the platform at the top was already filled with five archers. Once on the platform, Ed looked out northwards. He could see the long column as it approached. He could also see the many black banners they carried fluttering in the breeze, and all the time as they came on, there was that endless, rhythmless pounding of drums.

'Not much in the way of musicians, are they?' Ed said to the archers crammed into the fighting top of the tower. 'That lot couldn't carry a tune in a bucket if you ask me.'

The archers smiled at Ed and one, flexing his bowstring grinned, 'We'll make them sing a different tune soon enough, sir.'

'That we will,' Ed replied. He turned his attention back to the goblin column. It appeared to have stopped, though their drums never did. It was over a mile off but, Ed could clearly see that they had stopped their advance, at least for the moment. Then Ed saw that the column had turned right as the goblins began to form up for their attack. Other units marched to the left, arranging themselves in blocks of some fifty wide and ten or twenty deep. On either flank he could see mounted figures taking position, but these did not look like horsemen: these were something altogether different.

'Ork Boar-riders,' one of the archers hissed.

Ed looked at the man and waited for an explanation; he got it but didn't like it.

The archer came closer, nearly whispering, as he told Ed, 'The orks take the boars and feed them on the human flesh of their captives. They use dark spells to shape the beast into something much larger and far more evil. They are bigger than any horse and three times the weight. And, for all they feed them human flesh, before they go into battle they starve the beasts so that they are hungry for their favourite meat. Even if you kill the rider the boar will still attack as it wants to feast.'

'That's dang unsporting,' Ed quipped. He faced the archers and, with his expression more serious, said, 'Just make sure that if those things come close enough you bring them down.'

'We will,' the five archers replied as one.

Ed began to climb down from the tower. 'What I wouldn't give for some on call air right now,' he said, a comment that puzzled the archers and had them looking skyward as they discussed what he might have meant.

The goblins had formed their battle lines. They stood motionless for a moment, staring at the palisade with pitiless eyes, while their drums pounded out an awful tumult.

Cenfus was waiting at the bottom of the tower as Ed came down. 'There are formed up. Not as many as the scouts reported, 5,000, six at most,' he said, adding quietly, 'On their flanks they have...'

'I know,' Ed interrupted. 'One of the guys up there gave me the good news.'

Cenfus nodded that he understood. 'Any change in orders?'

Ed shook his head. 'No, we stand, kill as many as we can before they take each line, then we fall back and do the same again.'

'I like that plan,' Cenfus grinned. 'Especially the part about killing as many as we can.'

And still there was the endless racket of the drums.

'It must be getting on for midday,' Cenfus said as he looked skyward shading his eyes. Then he lowered his eyes and looked at Ed. 'You had lunch yet?'

'What?' Ed asked, taken aback by Cenfus's seemingly out of place remark.

'Lunch,' Cenfus emphasized. He reached into the back of his tabard and pulled out a small linen wrapped bundle. 'It must be getting close to lunch time and I was beginning to feel a little hungry,' he said, unwrapping the bundle. Inside he had a small round loaf of bread, some cheese, and cured meat. He offered the bread to Ed saying, 'It's not much but better than nothing.'

Ed was staring at Cenfus in disbelief, as were many of the archers that stood close by. 'Are you for real?' Ed demanded. 'There is an army out there and you brought lunch?'

Cenfus looked out of one of the arrow slits in the awning, shrugged, then looked back at Ed. 'I hope they brought their own lunch. I didn't bring enough for that lot. Want some cheese? It's very good.'

'You're a class act, Cenfus,' Ed chuckled. He took the bread, tore off a chunk, and handed it back.

'Don't rightly know what that means, Ed,' Cenfus said. 'Is it a good thing or bad?'

'In your case it's good,' Ed replied. Then the two men walked slowly along the platform eating their lunch and chatting together.

Cenfus looked at the faces of the men on the platform. They were smiling now, passing word down the line about how Cenfus had brought lunch.

'I hope you men brought yourselves something,' Cenfus said to a group that were watching him and Ed.

'No,' said a young archer. He pointed towards the goblin host saying, 'We had other things on our minds.'

Cenfus took another quick look through an arrow slit and shrugged. 'They're going to be a while yet. They got to fill themselves up with grog, then work themselves up with crazy dancing and shouting before they do anything. It could take all day, maybe even into the night. I suggest that one man in five goes and gets some food and water.'

'Are you sure about that?' Ed asked quietly.

Cenfus nodded. 'They will work themselves up into frenzy, drinking that black grog of theirs and pounding the drums. They'll dance, jump about, shout, shriek, and holler every insult their little brains can think of. Trust me, Ed, you haven't heard anything yet. It's all put on, mark you, to try and break your spirit. But don't worry, Ed, we'll know when they're coming.'

Cenfus's assessment of the goblins proved to be unfortunately correct. All day long they banged their drums, shouted insults, and curses at the men on the palisade. They drank, danced, beat their fists on their chest, and howled like mad dogs. Even at a distance of a mile the noise was deafening and intimidating.

Most of the men took their lead from Cenfus. They tried to relax and ignore the noise as best they could. Some ate, others sat and took sharpening stones to their swords and spears, while others, like Donald and his band around the trebuchets, were sitting about playing a dice game and gambling away what little coin they had left to them. But there were still others that were beginning to be affected by the uproar from beyond the palisade. Their nerves were starting to show and, some of them at least, looked like they might run when the attack finally came.

Somehow Cenfus had an eye that could pick out these men and, any that he spotted showing signs of their courage failing them, he would take time to speak with. What he said Ed never heard. Yet Cenfus seemed to have an instinct for just the right thing to say to each man. Some he spoke quietly with, others he joked and laughed with but, whomever the man, and whatever Cenfus said to them, his words appeared to steel them for the task at hand. Whatever else

Cenfus may or may not have been one thing was certain about him: his courage was boundless.

High up in the keep Kate was walking on the wall. In the courtyard, all the women of the town had been gathered. Some were helping at the healing house, rolling bandages or making up beds ready for the wounded that would surely come. Others took refuge in the buildings that surrounded the courtyard while still others walked or stood on the walls looking out at the army that was gathered before the walls.

They could all hear the goblin drums, and their shouts and shrieks, and many of the women seemed terrified by it. It was the waiting that was the worst: the inability to do anything other than listen to the infernal racket coming from beyond the walls. Many of the women, as Kate noticed, were carrying weapons: knifes hidden in their purses or tucked up their sleeves but kept ready for use so that they would not be taken alive. Kate also saw a number of the women going to the apothecary where, as she discovered, they were being given small phials of poison.

Seeing all this something inside Kate snapped, 'What's the matter with you all?' she shouted. 'You act as if the end has come. You think getting ready to kill yourselves is what your men want to hear.'

'My dear,' some middle-aged woman said to Kate, 'you don't know what they will do with you if they take you.'

'Well, shit on that,' Kate shouted back at the woman. 'If they want me they are going to have to kill me first. And I am not going to go down without a fight. Now who's with me?'

The middle-aged woman stared at Kate with an open mouth as did many others. 'You cannot fight,' she said. 'The men fight; we must wait.'

'Balls,' Kate shouted. 'There are only ten men guarding the walls of the keep. All the rest are up at the palisade.' She looked round at the blank faces staring back at her. 'Well then? Are you just going stand there or are you going to do something. There are weapons in the guardroom, bows, swords, spears, and everything; let's go and get them.'

Kate turned to make for the guardroom but the middle-aged woman was standing in her way. 'You cannot go,' the woman insisted, 'the men will fight; we must wait upon our fate.'

'Shit on your fate,' Kate said loudly. 'Either lead follow or get the crap out of my way.' With that Kate pushed the woman aside and made directly for the guardroom.

The women in the courtyard didn't know what to do. They looked at Kate, then at each other, and then at Kate again. Fighting, it wasn't done, it was not their place. But then they saw Kate at the guardroom door, arguing with the sergeant of the guard. At first he held Kate back but then, and shocking the women when it happened, the sergeant went flying, knocked off his feet and thrown to the side before slamming into the wall. After that Kate went inside and emerged minutes later armed with bow, arrows, and sword.

Kate held the bow aloft. 'Well, come on then,' she shouted.

Again the women could only stare: never had they seen of such a thing nor had they ever heard of it. But then one woman stepped forward, a very large heavy-set woman that was married to a butcher. Once she stepped forwards then so did another, and another, and more after that until the trickle became a flood.

The next thing the sergeant of the guard knew, after he picked himself off the floor, was that he was confronted by a marching column of very irate women that were bent on breaking into his guardroom and stripping it of every weapon they could lay hand to.

A short time later there were 200 heavily armed women marching through the barrack square and taking up position on the walls.

All day the drums had been pounding. All day the goblins and orks had been drinking and shouting insults. The sun was beginning to set and still the enemy had done nothing but chant, shriek, curse, drink, and dance. Sure they had made a great play of thrusting weapons towards the men on the palisade. But they had not as yet come close enough to do any damage, other than unnerve some of the soldiers.

Suddenly the drums stopped. They had been hammering away all day but then abruptly fell silent. For a long moment there was nothing, no sound other than the sound of the men on the walls taking a sharp collective breath.

A shrill horn sounded from somewhere within the enemy host. Dozens more answered it. And then the drums burst into a frenzied, hasty beat.

'That's it,' Cenfus said to Ed. He strode into the middle of the defences, drew himself up to his full height and, in loud clear voice called out, 'Soldiers, men of the watch, outside the enemy is coming, behind you are your womenfolk. All eyes are on you now, do not fail. The order is: kill all that come this way.'

A great cheer went up from the men that echoed throughout the town.

'Let none pass,' Cenfus shouted. 'Now sound the horns.'

And from every tower, every wall and barricade, from the palisade to the highest point of the keep, defiant horns sounded out long and loud.

Ed and Cenfus ran to the palisade and climbed up onto the fighting platform. All along the platform archers were fitting arrows into their bowstrings. The enemy was still a good way off but they were advancing, first at a walk then, as their shrill horns sounded and the drums beat faster and faster, they began to run.

'Draw your bows,' Cenfus commanded. And the archers drew back their bowstrings and took aim. Behind the palisade two more lines of archers were drawn up; they too had readied their arrows and were then aiming high over the palisade. Further back Donald and the men working the trebuchets made ready, fire pots were placed in the slings and, on each of the trebuchets six of the biggest and strongest labours took up the tension on the ropes.

The goblins were now charging forwards, shrieking and howling as they came on. It was dusk then and, even though goblin eyes were more accustomed to the dark, they came charging forward without seeing the deep ditch that awaited them. So hell-bent were they with getting at and killing the men of Two Rivers they failed to see the trap they were heading directly for.

The men on the palisade waited, waited and watched as the goblins charged towards them. They watched as the enemy crested the small rise in the ground, a rise built up from the spoil of the ditch. Finally, but too late, the first ranks of the goblins saw the trap. They tried to stop, to hold themselves back from the doom they saw before them. But the press of those following forced them over the edge.

The goblins were running, unable to stop themselves once they were pushed over the edge and down the steep slope. Their shrieks, curses, and war cries turned to screams of fear as they tumbled into the trap and onto the waiting stakes below. Two, three, or even four full ranks of goblins fell into the trap before those behind halted. From within the ditch there came the agonising cries of the dying goblins as they were impaled on the countless points of the abatis.

'Loose,' Cenfus shouted, choosing the moment when all of the goblins were bunched up in a startled mass on the edge of the ditch.

'Fire,' Ed shouted to Donald and the men heaved on the ropes of the trebuchets.

The first volley of arrows from the palisade and the towers were shot directly at the goblins as they stood staring in surprise and shock at the ditch. It caught them unawares and killed many of them. Quickly they held their shields up to cover themselves but without seeing the second volley that was arcing high through the air before plunging down on them.

So tightly packed had the goblins been that it was impossible for the arrows to miss them. Just as the air had been rent by the cries and screams of the front ranks as they died in the ditch, now it was filled again by the cries of the rear ranks as hundreds of arrows fell among them.

Then many of the enemy were stunned to see what looked like three lanterns flying through the air. They were just small flickers of flame drifting lazily towards the massed goblins. But, when they landed on top of them, they burst open showering great sheets of fire that engulfed any that were close by.

Instantly many of the goblins were transformed into screaming torches. The fire stuck to them spitting and hissing as they ran madly about in a pointless attempt to escape the burning. Every other goblin they ran into was likewise set on fire as the pitch stuck to them and, any that tried to beat out the flames found that it stuck to their hands and burnt them also. The only way to stop the spread of the fire was to kill any of their fellows hit by the flames, and this they did. But by then their ranks were disorganised and confused and easy targets for the archers that kept up a relentless and deadly barrage.

The first assault of the goblins had stalled and between the archers and the trebuchets they had taken a heavy toll of them. Many of the goblins were cowering behind their small shield, and as the storm of fire and arrows rained down on them, they began to fall back from the ditch.

Several archers began jeering and shouting abuse at the goblins: so easy had it been to stop them. But older heads knew better: Cenfus knew better.

'Shut up, you fools,' Cenfus shouted at the men. He walked along the palisade passing instructions to the archers as he went, 'Pick your targets carefully, conserve your arrows. The enemy is far from finished yet.'

That settled the men down and their shooting became more deliberate though equally deadly.

Ed had been watching the goblins closely. Yes their initial encounter with the ditch had checked them but, as he watched, he saw several taller, black-cloaked figures moving behind the first wave.

As the fire pot burst near these figures, Ed could see that they were taking control of the wavering goblins: pushing and herding them back into the assault with whips and the flats of their swords.

'In the towers there,' Ed shouted to the men above. 'Can you see the goblin men dressed in black?' The archers in the towers acknowledged they could. 'Target them. Shoot them if you get the chance.'

And the archers in the towers began picking off the targets Ed had given them.

Cenfus asked Ed why target the goblin men. 'Because,' Ed said, 'they look like they're in charge, the officers or master or whatever goblins have. Cut off the head and the body is useless.' Cenfus nodded that he understood and went back along the platform getting the archers there to target the black-cloaked figures also.

Ed was close to the gate of the palisade when one of the archers called to him. 'Sir, sir, you have to look at this.' The man stepped back from the arrow slit so that Ed might see.

The goblins had changed tactics. Where before they had been in loose lines attempting to charge forward now they had formed a solid shield wall three shields high and with their own archers behind that. As Ed watched he heard hundreds of arrows come whistling towards the palisade. Most struck the awning, lodging into the thick wooden wall without harming the men behind. But others had been aimed at the men in the towers. They were more exposed and began to take casualties. And, the arrows that missed them were beginning to fall among the men to the rear of the palisade.

The order was given to abandon the towers, which the men did as quickly as they could. But there were wounded among them and getting them down was both difficult and costly in lives as more men trying to help the injured were hit by goblin arrows.

As soon as they were down, the labours, who had been formed into a sort of militia and pressed into secondary rolls, ran forward and picked up the injured. They loaded them on the hand barrows that had been taken from the docks and pushed the injured back through the town to the healing house.

Cenfus was again moving along the palisade issuing orders. He directed the archers to target a group of goblins he had seen close to the ditch. When he reached Ed's position he stopped. 'Take a look there; the goblins are throwing the bodies of their dead into the ditch.'

Ed looked to where Cenfus had indicated. It was true: the goblins were tossing their dead into the ditch, and not just their dead but their badly wounded also, judging from the way some of those tossed in were struggling.

'They're using their dead to build a bridge over the ditch,' Cenfus pointed out.

'Unbelievable,' Ed gasped. But it was true. And, looking along the length of the ditch, Ed could see that the goblins were doing the same thing in three different places. It would not be much longer before the ditch was full then the real assault would begin.

The women of the healing house had been waiting, filling in their time by making every preparation they could. They knew what would be coming, knew what they should expect, but it was still a shock as they heard the calls of 'make way make way, wounded coming through'.

For a long time there had been a relative calm at the healing house; yes they could hear the drums pounding all day and, if they stood outside, they could hear the sounds of battle. But whatever calm there had been was shattered when the first of the hand barrows arrived.

Immediately the women of the healing house went to work. The wounded were unloaded and carried into the house. Pressure applied to wounds until the arrow heads could be withdrawn. Those with minor wounds were set to one side while the worst cases were sent directly to Liz to be operated on.

A small commotion broke out in the healing house. As one of the healing women was helping an injured man to a bed she saw Wolfric getting out of his.

'Get you back in to bed, My Lord,' the healer told the thane. 'You are not strong enough to be up yet.'

Wolfric winced visibly from the effort and pain as he stood upright. He faced the woman and, in a polite but determined tone, said, 'Good woman, leave me be. I am not about to lie abed when my men are dying out there.' With that he brushed past the woman and made for the keep's tower. Shortly thereafter he was seen walking towards the barrack, his armour covering his bandaged wounds, sword in hand.

'Well, really,' the woman moaned to another of the healers. 'Lord Wolfric should not be up. The man can barely walk.'

The second healer agreed. She cast her eyes round the healing house cheeking that none of the others from Wolfric's two companies of riders had followed their lord and then her eyes fell on an empty bed. 'Where is that big fellow? That one from Guidepost that never speaks.'

The big man's bed was empty, but no one had seen him leave.

'Here they come,' Cenfus cried out loudly. He drew his sword and brought his shield up ready. Seeing that, Ed did likewise, though he was unsure what good he would be.

All along the palisade, men at arms drew their swords and made ready while the archers loosed off a final volley before falling back to join the two ranks that stood behind the palisade.

Outside the palisade the goblin drums began beating rapidly, their shrill horns filling the night with blood chilling calls. Hundreds of arrows came thudding into the awning, some even squeezing through the arrow slits to strike the men behind.

'Ladders,' someone shouted on the platform to Ed's right. He risked a quick glance out of an arrow slit and only just got his head out of the way as a goblin arrow whistled past his left cheek.

The man next to Ed was looking directly at him and grinning widely. 'Watch it, sir, they nearly had you there.'

Ed smiled back. 'I know. Somebody should get that goblin's name; he's going to hurt somebody if he not careful.'

The men around Ed smiled at that, but only for a moment. Seconds later the awning was struck by another volley of arrows, and it was much heavier than before. After the arrows struck home there came a long pause when the only sound was that of the shrieking and snarling goblins as they ran towards the palisade, and then the thudding sounds as their ladders were thrust up against the awning.

Quickly the men took up position at the arrow slit, not even goblins would risk hitting their own kind as they climbed up the ladders. The men waited swords and spears held ready till a goblin head appeared at the tops of the ladders. As soon as they did the men thrust their weapons out, stabbing anything that moved. From the other side of the awning they could hear the cries and screams of the goblins as they fell bleeding from the ladders. But still they came on. Their ladders were too short: they could not reach the top of the awning and, yet as many as the men killed, more and more kept climbing in a desperate attempt to reach the men.

Hundreds more of the creatures came pouring across the bridges they had built over the ditch. Among them were many orks, larger and much stronger than the goblin. The first orks to cross the ditch wore breastplates of iron and broad-rimmed helmets. They carried large two-headed axes and made directly for the ladders, pushing any goblin in their way aside.

The orks climbed the ladders and began hacking at the awning with their axes. Their axes were crudely made but heavy and at once they began to splinter the timbers of the awning. Gaps started to appear and the waiting goblins below started to cheer and chant as the orks rained blow after blow on the yielding timber.

Men tried to stab down at the orks. But the orks were too low on the ladders to get a good thrust at. Their broad helmets and iron armours were also too thick. Most of the men's thrusts were easily deflected and the few orks that were killed were quickly replaced by more of their type. One man reached out through the awning intent on driving his spear into the ork below. But the ork saw the spear, and the arm, and with one swift swing of its axe took the man's arm off at the elbow.

Goblin archers had also moved closer to the palisade. They were sending their volleys high into the air to rain down on the ranks of archers inside. Ten archers fell under the first goblin volley, eight more under their second. The sergeant in charge of the archers ordered them back behind the wall as anything between wall and palisade was then at risk.

The archers fell back quickly, carrying their dead and wounded with them. The labourers again came forward, risking their own lives to collect the injured.

On the palisade the awning was nearly being torn apart by the ork axes. Large holes were appearing everywhere and, as the holes appeared, the orks made their first attempt to climb through.

Ed saw a great axe burst through the timber beside him. It wasn't withdrawn but rather hooked into the timber and used by the ork to pull itself up. A second later, Ed saw the broad-rimmed helmet come through the hole and, as the ork's head appeared, he swung his sword with all the force he could muster. The ork's head was parted from its body and its black blood sprayed into Ed's face. But he had no time to think about the blood that soaked him for as soon as the dead ork fell another came scrambling through the gap. Ed stabbed at it but the ork caught Ed's blade in its hand. Ed yanked the sword back, taking the ork's fingers in the process, and stabbed again. This time the sword point went into the neck and Ed twisted the blade before pulling it free. The ork fell dead where it was, blocking the very hole it had tried to get through.

Several orks had managed to force their way onto the platform and were then swinging their axes at any man within reach. So heavy were the ork axes that a single blow would splinter a shield and shatter the arm holding it.

The men on that section of the palisade began to waver, giving ground and allowing more orks to climb through the gaps. It was very possible that the palisade would have fallen then had not Cenfus seen what was happening and raced into the fight himself. He ran past the men who were falling back shouting, 'With me, let none pass,' and with that he threw himself at the first ork. He raised his shield, charging at the ork and went crashing into the ork shoulder fist. The ork was knocked backwards momentarily. But then it planted its feet and swung its axe intent on parting Cenfus's head from his body. Cenfus ducked down, dropping to one knee as he thrust his sword up into the creature's guts.

The ork fell from the platform and was dead before it hit the ground. Another ork came at Cenfus, its axe raised high above its head ready to split Cenfus in two but before it could swing the blow, Cenfus rolled forward and swung his blade cutting off both the ork's legs. He jumped to his feet, stepped back a pace and stabbed down into the ork's neck. A third ork stared at Cenfus in surprise; it had just climbed through the gap, and just seen two of its type killed quickly. It roared at Cenfus, raising its axe to take a swing. But Cenfus was too fast. He leapt over the fallen ork and thrust his sword into the mouth of the roaring ork, killing it instantly.

By then Cenfus was at the gap in the awning and more men had followed him. Cenfus moved on, taking down the next ork with a slashing blow to its spin. Behind him the men began plugging the gap, hacking and stabbing at any ork that tried to climb through. As they did Cenfus pushed on killing four more orks before he had cleared the platform.

For all that, for all the bravery of Cenfus and of many other men, the orks were tearing the awning apart. More and more gaps were appearing, and there were fewer and fewer men to defend them. In the end Ed had to face it: the palisade was lost.

'Fall back,' Ed called out. 'Fall back to the wall, fall back.'

High in the gatehouse of the new wall a horn sounded the retreat. It echoed off the walls and was heard throughout the town; everyone knew what that call meant: the palisade was lost.

Hearing the horn the men on the palisade leapt from the platform and ran for the wall. They had done all they could to defend the palisade, and many of them had died doing so. But for every man that had fallen many time many more goblins and orks had fallen also. Their bodies lay both inside and out of the palisade. And yet, for all the goblins and orks that had been killed, there were thousands more to replace them. The very instant that the men abandoned the palisade the goblins and orks began to swarm over it.

The last man to leave the palisade was Cenfus. The moment he heard the horn he began getting the men near him off the platform and ordering them back. But he could not leave without taking one last stab at some goblin as it showed its head through the awning. Only then did Cenfus jump down from the platform and run back to the wall.

On the wall the archers loosed off a volley to cover the retreating men. Dozens of goblins and orks that had seconds before climbed through the gaps, thinking they had won the day, were cut down by the volley. The second volley from the archers was different however. It was Ed's second little surprise for the goblins. It was a volley of fire arrows.

Dozens more goblins were pouring through the gaps in the wall then. They gathered themselves together, forming a shield wall to cover the breaches as yet more of their fellows clambered through. They saw the volley of fire arrows and huddled down behind their shields. But the volley missed them and for that they laughed. Not one of the goblins on the palisade had been hit by a single fire arrow. In fact every arrow had gone under the platform and never even came close to hitting the goblin shield wall.

The goblins began jeering and laughing at the archers for having such poor aim. They danced upon the platform, daring the archers to try again. And all the while the goblins were blissfully unaware of the fire pot suspended below the platform only inches beneath their feet.

The archer took aim again with fire arrows. Their first volley had already gone into the wooden palisade or the piles of straw that had been placed under it. Their second volley was aimed at the pots.

Again the goblins formed their shield wall, still daring the archers to hit. And, when they saw that the arrows had gone beneath them again, they began to cheer. But that was before the first pots erupted under their feet. As one pot exploded, it set off the pots next to it and so on and so on till there was a chain reaction of exploding fire along the whole length of the palisade. Some of the goblins jumped off the platform, but they were jumping into a spreading fire and being showered by the spitting flame. Those that made it out of the fire were easy targets for the archers.

Other goblins on the platform tried to get back through the gaps in the awning but they were blocked by the others still attempting to get on to it. Desperation and panic set in. They fought among themselves, slaying each other as they tried to get away from the flames. They killed those climbing the ladders to get in and killed each other as they tried to get out. In minutes the palisade was a wall of flames and a funeral pyre for hundreds of goblins and orks.

'Do you hear that, Ed?' Cenfus asked, wiping his sword and grinning from ear to ear.

Ed listened for a moment and shook his head. 'I don't hear anything.'

'Exactly,' Cenfus grinned. 'They stopped those infernal drums. Must have come as a real surprise to them.'

'I like to keep my audience entertained,' Ed smiled.

Cenfus took a water bottle and offered it to Ed. 'Better wash your face, friend, you got ork blood all over it. How many did you get?'

'Four and a half,' Ed replied.

'A half?'

'Me and the guy next to me both stabbed it at the same time, so only a half. What about you?'

'Twenty-three so far,' Cenfus said proudly. He lifted his sword up and turned it over in his hand. 'This was my father's sword and his father before that; it is called Truesteel, his helmet also. I thought I would carry them today so that if I was killed they would know me in the afterlife.' He gave the sword an affectionate rub adding, 'but I think I will put off the afterlife for a while yet. Truesteel and I have a bit of work to do before I join my fathers.'

Ed washed his face and took a drink of water. He handed the bottle back to Cenfus who, after taking a drink himself, looked over the men on the wall.

Cenfus removed his helmet and sat next to Ed. 'What say you that we go round the men?' he said quietly so as not to be overheard. 'They look downcast and in need of some cheer.'

'You go, my friend,' Ed said softly. 'You are much better at that than me. I want to check on our defences. That fire will not last forever and, when it is out…'

Cenfus nodded. 'Very well then,' he stood up and began to walk away only to turn back after a few short paces. 'See if you can find us some food, Ed, the smell of burning ork always gives me a hunger.'

Ed went to speak with the sergeant of the archers first. They had loosed off many arrows and taken a great toll of the enemy but now their quivers were running low. So Ed had the sergeant get his men to collect as many goblin arrows as they could from the thousands that had been sent over the palisade. Goblin arrows were not as well made or flighted as correctly as their own arrows, but they would be better than nothing when it came to the push.

After that Ed was making for the trebuchets but stopped when two riders came forwards.

'My Lords,' Ed said surprised. 'What bring you here?'

'Well, that bonfire for one thing,' Beohrtric smiled. Then he nodded towards his riding partner, adding, 'And Lord Wolfric, the fool that he is, insisted on coming.'

Wolfric looked at Beohrtric and then at Ed. 'My place is with my men,' he said, his voice sounding as weak as he looked.

'Your place is in the healing house lest you bust open every stitch that good lady put in you,' Beohrtric admonished him.

'Lord Beohrtric is right, sir,' Ed agreed. 'You should be in bed. Honestly Lord Wolfric, you are no use to anybody in your condition.'

Wolfric was stung by that. He sat bolt upright in his saddle and looked down on Ed saying, 'I am still lord of Two Rivers and will not be abed in its time of need.' But no sooner had he spoken those words than he slumped back, nearly falling from his horse.

Wolfric's complexion was pale and waxy; he was sweating heavily to the point where the orange glow of the burning palisade was reflected in the beads that poured down his brow.

'Sir,' Ed said, 'please go back. We have everything in hand here.'

Wolfric never heard Ed's words. He collapsed forward in the saddle and Ed had to rush to his side to prevent the man from falling to the ground. As Wolfric was eased down, Ed called for a barrow to be brought.

'Take him back to the healing house and tell my wife to make sure he stays there. Tie him to his bed if you have to but make sure he stays there this time.'

Beohrtric had also dismounted and helped place Wolfric on the barrow. As the thane was wheeled away he turned to Ed asking, 'Is it true what you said? Is everything in hand?'

'For now, yes,' Ed began, 'but how long the fire will keep them out I cannot say.'

'Well let us hope that my men arrive before that,' Beohrtric said.

'Let's hope that indeed,' Ed said.

Beohrtric looked at Ed long and hard before saying, 'There is something that perplexes you, what is it?'

Ed was silent for a while but then, very slowly said, 'The ladders. That's what's bothering me, those bam ladders.'

Boehrtric gave Ed a warm smile. 'Don't let that vex you. They built them too short from what I'm told.'

'But they would have been the exact right length had we not built the awning on top of the palisade,' Ed pointed out. 'Then when they did attack they were stalled until they could bring up those orks with the axes.'

'And all the better for us,' Beohrtric laughed. 'You worry too much, man.'

'I'm worried because I want to know how they knew the exact height of the palisade,' Ed said. 'Cenfus tells me that orks and goblins don't see too well in daylight; that why they attack at night. And I think, standing back as they did while firing themselves up, they couldn't make out just how much higher the palisade was. That's why they lost so many waiting for the orks to get to the palisade with axes.'

Beohrtric looked deep into Ed eyes and asked, 'What exactly are you getting at?'

'Exactly,' Ed said, 'exactly I don't know. But I am wondering how they knew the height of our palisade. Was it the same way they knew where and when to ambush Lord Wolfric and his riders?'

Beohrtric grasped Ed arm and stood close to him. 'You know what you are saying, man?'

Ed nodded. 'I am saying that there has been a spy in our camp.'

'And what makes you think that they are not here right now?'

'Because the ladders were too short,' Ed pointed out. 'Had the spy still been here they would have told the enemy to build longer ladders. And they would have warned them about the fire pots under the platform. No sir, the spy isn't here now, but there sure as hell has been one.'

'Say no more of this now,' Beohrtric told Ed. 'Let us first make it through this night and hope my men arrive. Let us hope for victory and then, then we shall speak of this again.'

With that the two men wished each other well and parted.

Gol-nar spurred his horse up the slope to the small group that was assembled there. One, a black-cloaked figure, was slightly ahead of the rest of the group and sitting upon a powerful stallion that appeared restless and ready to charge at any moment. It was to this one, lone figure that Gol-nar galloped. He halted, gave a curt bow in the saddle, and said, 'They set fire to the wooden wall, boss.'

The lone figure sighed heavily then slowly turned to Gol-nar. 'Really, it's just that we cannot see that from here.'

Gol-nar stared at the boss for a moment and then turned his horse back the way he had come. He was puzzled: the fire on the palisade was plain enough. The land between them and the town was flat and without obstruction. Gol-nar could see it clearly, could see the fire; in fact he could see what was left of his lads as they ran from the flames. 'I can see the fire, boss, it's right there.'

'I know, you damn fool,' the boss hissed. 'What do you think I've been looking at these past minutes.'

'Sorry, boss,' Gol-nar said, 'you were being ironic again, weren't you?'

The boss looked at Gol-nar, his expression one of utter contempt.

'What should we do, boss?' Gol-nar asked. 'You want that we should put the fire out?'

'Well, let me think,' the boss mused. He turned in the saddle and looked at the other riders behind him. 'Should we put the fire out, lads? Anybody bring a bucket with them?'

The riders shook their heads, sniggering at how the boss was sporting with Gol-nar yet again.

'What about you, Gol-nar? You got a bucket with you?'

'Errr . . . no, boss,' Gol-nar said. 'Didn't think about it.'

'Then how on earth do you plan putting the fire out, you fool?'

'Errrrrr.'

'Err, is right,' the boss snapped. 'Let the thing burn but be ready for a full attack once it's burnt to the ground.'

'Yes, boss,' Gol-nar grinned.

'Gazzrag,' the boss shouted, calling over one of the ork commanders.

'Aye, boss,' Gazzrag, a tall, thick-set ork with extremely long arms and finger nails like talons came running over.

'These goblin scum have been as good as useless,' the boss said loudly, loudly enough that Gol-nar could hear him clearly. 'When that wooden wall burns out I want your orks to lead the attack, your boar-riders in front. Full attack, mark you, and leave none alive.'

'You can count on us, boss,' Gazzrag sneered. 'What about the women, boss? Do we get the women?'

The boss thought for a moment. 'You and your lads can have your sport with them. Kill them afterwards. I want people to know what happens when they try and stand against us.'

'Yes, boss,' Gazzrag grinned. 'Just as you like, boss.'

'We got a bit of a problem, Ed,' Donald said quietly. He led him over to the trebuchets, talking quietly with him as he explained. 'We fired off far more fire pots than I thought. As we are we got only twenty left. After that we are down to throwing rock and stones.'

Ed looked around. The men that had been manning the trebuchets were sitting on the ground. They were tired, very tired, but in good spirits. The men that had been on the palisade had told them that their fire pots had nearly all landed in the thick of the enemy, which cheered them despite how hard they had worked. But, during the battle they had used up almost all of their fire pots. There were other clay jars stacked up behind them, but they were empty as there had not been enough oil and pitch in the town to fill them all.

Ed thought for a few moments before saying to Donald, 'When the next attack comes, use stones. Keep the last of the fire pots for the boar-riders. If we can hit a few of them they might disrupt the attack a bit.'

'We can hope,' Donald sighed.

One of the men sitting by the trebuchets looked up at Ed saying, 'Don't you worry, we'll do you proud. In't that right, lads?' The men around him all voiced their agreement loudly.

'Thank you, men,' Ed said. 'I know you are all tired but best you gather any stone you can find and stack them ready.'

The men got to their feet and began piling up stones near the trebuchets. One of them picked up a large stone near a stack of barrels; he tapped one of the barrels with his foot asking, 'Shouldn't we move these? Do fancy having them about when the goblins come.'

Ed and Donald walked over to the man. 'What's in them?' Donald asked.

'Qiuck lime,' the man said. 'Part of the last shipment from the kilns before it got shut down. Nasty stuff that when it dry. Get that in your eyes and you'll know about it.'

Ed and Donald looked at the barrels, then at the man, and finally each other. They began to smile. 'Quick lime ay,' Donald chuckled. 'Now how about that.'

'You thinking what I'm thinking?' Ed asked.

'You bet y',' Donald grinned.

Ed woke up with a start. He had gone round the men earlier and then, just for a few minutes, sat down with his back resting against the new gatehouse wall. He was tired sure, but he had only closed his eyes for a few seconds. Then something woke him, something loud, something very loud. He jumped to his feet and looked round but all he could see was the fire and Cenfus standing passively by his side.

'What was that noise?' Ed demanded.

Cenfus folded his arms and rested them on the top of the wall. 'Just the palisade beginning to fall,' he said before resting his chin on his folded arms.

'I'm sorry about that,' Ed said softly. 'Falling asleep, I mean.'

Cenfus continued to stare at the burning palisade saying. 'Don't worry about it, Ed, you needed some sleep. I've had the men take turns in getting some rest too. That fire isn't going to last much longer then we will all need our strength. By the way, there's some food there for you. A nice meat pie, honey and bread, and some water.'

'Thanks,' Ed said, picking up the bundle Cenfus had left for him. 'Have the men eaten?'

'Yes,' Cenfus replied.

'What about you?'

'Had my earlier,' he said his eyes fixed on the fire. 'You should have the pie; best I've tasted in a long time.'

'It looks good,' Ed said. 'What about sleep? You get any sleep?'

Cenfus shook his head, lifting his cheek from its resting place. 'I'll sleep when this is all over, one way or the other.'

Ed was about to say something but was stopped by the sound of timbers splitting and breaking. He looked towards where the sound had come and saw another large section of the palisade crumbling to the ground. There was little of the palisade left, little save a few blackened tree trucks and piles of smouldering embers.

'Best eat your pie. Don't want the goblins to get it, do you?' Cenfus said softly. He stood up and slowly pulled on his helmet. 'It won't be long now.' With that Cenfus tied his chin strap and began walking along the men waiting at the wall. As he passed each man he told them, 'Make ready, brother.'

All around the men got themselves ready and took their places. On the walls, either side of the town, archers and soldiers lined up. Beside them, blocking the roads into town, the men of the watch stood and formed their ranks. Just to their fronts, in the centre and behind angled stakes, were the rest of the archers. Formed up with them were the bulk of the labours that had, until then, been carrying the wounded to the healing house. Now they stood ready, arming themselves with anything that came to hand. They had shovels, the edges of which they had sharpened like razors, axes, and large hammers. In the very centre of the defence was the new gate house, a huge and imposing structure that was bristling with the armed men and archers. And, from both sides of the gatehouse, was the low wall. Every able man that could carry arms manned the wall and some who were already scarred and bandaged from the earlier fight.

That was all of them, a few hundred men to defend the town against the thousands of enemy that were only waiting for the last of the burning palisade to collapse.

The drums began to beat again in the north. Slowly at first but quickly building in tempo.

A horn sounded in the gatehouse above Ed. He looked up at man looking down at him. 'The enemy is moving, sir,' the man shouted, adding seconds later, 'Boar-riders at their front.'

Ed signalled that he understood to the man in the gatehouse then he turned to Donald. Donald had already heard and gave Ed a thumbs up as the men on the trebuchets loaded the newly filled pots into the slings.

Cenfus came striding back towards Ed, his sword drawn. 'What are your orders, men?' he cried out raising his sword high.

As one, every man, every archer, every guards in the gatehouse, every soldier on the walls called at the top of their lungs. 'Let none pass.'

'Again,' Cenfus called out.

'Let none pass,' they answered.

'Again,'

'Let none pass. Let none pass. Let none pass.'

The chanting of the men echoed round the walls and up through the town. Horns joined in the clamour till the noise drowned out the sounds of goblin drums. Spears were thrust in the air, swords drawn and struck on shield, and all the time the war cry went up: 'Let none pass. Let none pass.'

'Here they come.'

From high in the gatehouse the men could see the enemy forming up. They watched as the boar-riders lined up in front of battalions of orks. Behind the orks the goblins formed in dense blocks, and all of them were moving towards the smouldering remains of the burnt-out palisade.

One man in the gatehouse signalled for the trebuchets to get ready. He held his hand up, ready to drop it as soon as the boars reached the edge of the ditch. On the wall the men raised their shields, spears, and swords held ready to strike. Archers drew their bows, aiming high so that their arrows would plunge down into the enemy.

All eyes were on the man in the tower. For a second it was as if the whole of Two Rivers held its breath waiting for his hand to fall. Then it did.

'Trebuchets heave,' Donald called out.

'Archers loose.'

Clay pots and arrows arced up into the air. Through the veil of smoke that rose from the embers they could see the enemy approaching. They watched as the boars began drawing together to cross over the bridges of dead goblins. Before they were all the way across the ditch the first clay pots landed.

The pots struck the ground and burst open. Clouds of white dust sprang up in the air. The clouds of dust were still a good way ahead of the boar-riders but, even as the first pots had landed, more pots were being sent up from the trebuchets.

The orks ignored the clouds of dust in front of them; instead they reformed their line ready to charge. Arrows began to fall among them, killing some of the riders and wounding the boars. But, even as the riders fell from their mounts, the boars, now wounded and enraged, broke from the formation and charged on the own. And they charged directly through the clouds of dust hanging in the air.

Emerging from the dust cloud the boars continued their charge, but now they began shaking and nodding the heads franticly. They started snorting loudly, sneezing and coughing and their charge became erratic. One boar stopped completely, burying its face in the dirt and rubbing it furiously. Other boards drifted from side to side, weaving and banging into one another and, when they did, they roared, snapped and bit at whatever was close by.

The boar-riders had pushed their mounts through the dust cloud, charging towards the town and, as they imagined, an easy victory. But as they came out of the cloud the riders were coughing and desperately rubbing their eyes. Their mounts too were likewise blinded by the lime causing some of them to stumble and throw their riders. One riderless boar ran into a ridden beast. The rider kicked out at it, trying to get it away. The boar bit the rider's legs, dragging the ork from his mount and shaking him like a rag doll till he was dead. Another boar and rider came charging through the burnt-out palisade, kicking up great showers of sparks as it raced towards the wall. But both boar and rider were blind from the dust and the boar ran full tilt into the wall, knocking itself out and throwing its rider.

Donald and his men kept up the barrage, thickening and spreading the dust cloud all the time. But the truth was that there were too few trebuchets and too many orks. The dust cloud may have blinded and disorientated a lot of ork and boar-riders, but it could never stop all of them. And the rest came charging through the burnt-out palisade focussed on one thing only: the destruction of Two Rivers and everything in it.

The boar-riders charged in, faltering only briefly when they saw the wall. Some of them attempted to jump the wall, but boars were never meant for jumping and almost all of them landed half on the wall and half off it. Behind the wall the men thrust their spears into the exposed necks and chests of the beasts, killing them and dragging the riders off their mounts.

Yet several of the boars did manage to clear the wall. One, still half blind from the dust charged directly at the archers behind the wall without seeing the stakes planted in the ground. But another that had also charged the archers avoided the stakes and began biting and goring any man it could reach. The rider on its back was slashing at the archers with his scimitar and doubling the carnage being wrought among the line of archers.

It was only the speedy intervention of the brave labours that rescued the situation. The raced forward to help the archers, stabbing, slashing, and hitting out at the boar and rider with every improvised weapon they had. Despite the fact they did not have sword or spear and despite the fact they did not had shield or armour to protect them. The labours raced at every boar that made it over the wall, bringing them down regardless of their own casualties.

Only seconds after the boars had burst through, and even as the men were fighting them and driving them back from the wall, the orks charged at the wall. Hundreds of them came, shouting their war cries and shrieking as they threw themselves at the wall. Behind the wall the men had an advantage: they were thrusting down at the orks while they had to fight someone higher than them. Also the archers in the towers and the gatehouse could pick the orks off from above, shooting down into their massed ranks as they pressed against the wall.

The men stood firm, protecting themselves with their shields and stabbing, slashing, cutting, and hacking at any ork that tried to scramble over the wall. But every ork they killed piled up in front of the wall and the orks that followed were using them like stepping stones to get to grips with the men.

The pressure was becoming too great. The men had the advantage of height but the orks had far greater numbers. The orks might lose fifty, a hundred, two hundred, and never notice, yet each man that fell left a gap in the wall that was harder and harder to fill. Again the labours came forward, filling gaps as they happened. But without shield and armour they were easy meat for ork spears.

Finally the orks forced a toehold over the wall. Brushing the labourers aside and clambering over the wall, they formed up in knots, forcing the gap wider and wider as they attacked the defenders from both the side and rear.

Cenfus ran directly at the centre of the ork toehold, his sword flashing in the sun as he brought down one ork after the next. But even Cenfus, as great a swordsman as he was, could not stem the tide.

'Fall back,' Ed shouted, 'fall back.'

All along the wall the cry was taken up and the men abandoned the wall and ran as quickly as they could to their final defence: the rows of sharpened stakes.

Some men fell as they turned, hacked down from behind by the orks. The archers in the towers and gatehouse loosed off volley after volley to cover the retreat. But the orks were coming over the wall in massed waves that could not be stopped.

'It's out turn now, men,' Sergeant Wiglaf said.

# Chapter 26

Gazzrag rode up to the boss. Both his face and that of the great black beast he sat astride was white from the lime dust. The boar also had sods of turf on its tusks from where it had been rubbing its face in the earth in a desperate but vain attempt to remove the irritation. Gassrag's face had red patches round his eyes where he had been rubbing them and streaks where he had poured water, or perhaps grog, to wash the lime away. Yet neither, ork nor boar, were free from the dust. Both were still half blind, and both found breathing harder and the lime continued to burn their mouths and throats.

Gazzrag got down from the boar, nearly falling in the process, and staggered towards the boss. 'You said they had no wall; you promised they had no wall.'

The boss looked down at the distressed and clearly enraged ork. 'They have no wall,' he insisted, but then a doubt formed in his mind. 'They could not have a wall; they have had no time to build a wall.'

Gazzrag coughed, squinting his burning eyes up and saying, 'Well, they got a wall. I lost nearly all my lads on it. You lied. You lied and said it would be easy. Said they had no defences. No wall. You lied and the big boss is going to hear about it. Blaecca going to hear about it and how you lost all my best lads.'

The boss climbed down from his horse slowly. 'Gazzrag, my friend,' he said passing the reins of his horse to another of the small party that

# Family Holiday

were with him. He walked towards Gazzrag, his arms open in welcome and kinship. 'It was one small setback,' he said embracing the ork captain. 'We are winning the battle and, besides,' the boss said as he reached for the dagger in the back of his belt which he drew quickly and thrust into Gazzrag's gut, ripping the blade upwards, 'besides, no filthy ork is going to be saying anything to Lord Blaecca. I shall inform him of your failure myself.' And with that he let Gazzrag's lifeless body fall.

Gol-nar, who had been riding towards the boss and his party of riders, saw Gazzrag fall; he also saw the blade in the boss's hand though he had not heard the words exchanged between them. He halted a few feet from the boss, looked at him and at the dead body of Gazzrag, and for a moment he was speechless.

'You have a report for me?' the boss asked, wiping the blood from his dagger on Gazzrag's body.

Gol-nar bowed while staying in the saddle. 'Yes, boss,' the goblin man said slowly, 'we have taken their defences and are moving into the town.'

'Good,' said the boss walking back to his horse. 'Very good indeed. Gol-nar, you take charge here. And remember Gol-nar, leave none alive.' With that he turned to his fellow riders saying, 'Gentlemen, shall we return to camp and have breakfast? Victory always gives me an appetite.'

Kate was walking nervously back and forth on the battlements overlooking the town. She had been watching the wounded being carried in and saw quickly patched-up men running back to the fight. She could hear the sounds of battle coming from the northern end of town. And, with the sun coming up and the men being pushed from one defence to the next, she began to see how close the enemy was.

There was still much fighting going on, and the cries of men, the shrieks of orks and goblins, and the sounds of sword striking shield gave testament to the desperate struggle taking place. She paused, looking across the market square and down along the street in the centre of town. As she looked, staring at the mêlée taking place at the far end of town, her hand clenched and unclenched repeatedly around the grip of the bow she was carrying. Somewhere, down there not a mile away at the end of the street, her father, and no doubt her impetuous little brother, were fighting for their lives and for the lives of every soul in Two Rivers. All Kate could do, all any of the women that had taken up position on the wall could do, was hope that their men returned safely. And that is what they did. They stood, watching, waiting and hoping.

They hoped the men could stop the orks and goblins, and if they had to fall back, they hoped that Beohrtric and his riders could buy the men time to get back to the keep. They hoped that the rest of Beohrtric men would arrive in time, and if they did not, they hoped that the walls of the keep could withstand the onslaught that was surely to come. But, above all, they just hoped that they would make it through alive.

'Is there any news of Beohrtric's forces?' Moorbe asked in a whisper as he looked over the wall next to Kate.

Kate was surprised. She had never seen the chancellor come out of his tower in all the time she had been there. Yet now, with the enemy battering its way into the very streets of Two Rivers, Moorbe had removed his chain of office and come down to take a look for himself.

'No news yet, My Lord,' Kate whispered to Moorbe, trying her best to disguise the fact that she was talking to a dog from the others on the battlements. 'Should you be out? It is not safe.'

Moorbe looked up at her. 'It is not safe anywhere, I fear,' he whispered. 'And if Beohrtric's men do not come . . .' he did not finish, he did not have to: they both knew what would happen.

'Please, chancellor,' Kate implored quietly, 'go back to your office. I will bring you news when we have some.'

Moorbe shook his head. 'No, Kate, our men are being pushed back and I need to see what is happening. I am going down.'

With that Moorbe turned and headed towards the gatehouse and the stairs down to the barrack square.

Kate chased after him, calling for him to come back. Moorbe ignored her calls and disappeared through the gatehouse door. By the time Kate got there Moorbe was already half way down the stairs. And when Kate got to the bottom of the stairs Moorbe was out the gate and running across the market square.

The gate guard tried to stop Kate but she pushed past them. Out in the market square Beohrtric and his riders were drawn up ready to charge when the call came. Beohrtric saw Moorbe run past but was too surprised to say anything. Then he saw Kate chasing after the chancellor. 'Girl, girl, stop this instant and get back inside,' he shouted.

Kate hesitated for a moment, turning towards Beohrtric as she ran sideways. She pointed at Moorbe, held her arms out wide and shrugged, giving Beohrtric a look that said, 'What can I do?'

Beohrtric understood and, then, calling ten of his men forward, he began following Kate and the chancellor.

Moorbe went to the middle street of the town. He stopped, took a quick look around him, and then stood up on his back legs so that he might see what was happening better. Ahead of him the archers were formed up at the rear of the men at arms, sending volley after volley of arrows over their heads and into the enemy beyond.

Kate caught up with Moorbe there. 'Will you get back inside the . . .' before she had finished Moorbe was off again. He dropped back down on to all fours and, using a side street, ran off towards the ferry gate.

The street there was narrow, much narrower than the street near the river gate. Again Moorbe stopped, looked round and stood up. At the end of the street the men of the watch were holding back the enemy. Also, at the end of the street, was the old tower that made up the bend in the wall that covered the ferry landing. From the top of the tower men were throwing down large stones onto the heads of orks and goblins. Archers were shooting them from the arrow slits. And, for the time being at least, they were holding.

Beohrtric rode up in time to see Moorbe drop to all fours again and run off towards the river gate. 'My Lord,' Beohrtric called. 'Damn it, My Lord, I have no time for games.'

If either Moorbe or Kate heard Beohrtric's call it did not stop them nor slow them down as they raced towards the river gate.

'It's our turn now, men,' Sergeant Wiglaf said.

Jay could only catch glimpses of the enemy as they rushed towards the men of the watch. He was not tall enough to see over the shoulders of the men in the front rank so it was only when one of the men moved their shields that Jay could see through the tiny gaps in the shield wall. And yet, what he saw chilled him to the very core. 'Oh shit,' Jay whispered to himself, as he caught sight of the hundreds of blood-crazed orks charging towards them, 'this isn't going to be good.'

The orks came rushing forward, running in that lolloping staggered gait of theirs. They looked to Jay like a bubbling, boiling mass of pure hate intent on the destruction of anything and everything that got in their way, and that is exactly what they were.

Jay began to wonder what madness possessed him to place himself in the way of the oncoming loathing that was about to hit the shield wall. But then that shield wall was all that stood between the enemy and the rest of his family.

Sergeant Wiglaf was watching the approaching enemy also. He walked slowly along the line of men as he shouted out the orders. 'Shields!' he called out at the top of his voice, and the watchmen brought their shields up, covering themselves from nose to knee. The orks reached the barricade and began tearing at it. 'Spears!' The men of the watch thrust at the orks, fighting with them for possession of the last obstacle before the open road to the market square. Orks fell, speared by the watch as they tore the barricade apart. But, for every ork that fell two more took their place and soon the barricade was gone to pieces and scattered in every direction, and the orks rushed forward once more. 'Wall!' The men locked their shields together on his command. 'Brace!' And with that Jay, and every other man in the rear ranks pushed their shields forward to support the men in front.

The enemy was only yards away, yards away and closing the distance rapidly. Jay buried his head and shoulder into his shield, leaning forward as he pressed against the back of the man in front of him. No sooner had Jay braced his legs than he heard the deafening sound of shield smashing on shield and felt the enormous impact of the ork charge. His legs buckled, his feet slipped on the cobbles and he felt as if he had been pushed back two feet or more.

Somehow Jay regained his footing, his feet searching out the edge of a cobble to push against. All around him the other men were doing the same, bracing their legs and pushing back against the enemy with all the strength they could muster.

In the front rank men thrust their spears, stabbing at anything, face, head or chest of any ork they could see. The orks raised their scimitars, striking down at the men holding them back. Some men fell, unable to lift their shields to protect themselves from the ferocious blows dealt out by the orks.

Behind them Sergeant Wiglaf was moving along the line, shouting for the watch to hold the enemy back and throwing his own shoulder into any section that appeared to be buckling. 'Hold them men, hold them. Use your spears. Kill them.'

Above the men of the watch, in the towers and on the wall archers were shooting down into the seething mass of orks. But there were too few archers and far too many orks.

It felt to Jay like trying to stop a volcano from erupting with a cork. There were only 120 men of the watch to defend the road and a thousand orks pushing them back.

Worse still, though unseen by the men of the watch, the orks had gained a foothold on the wall. Those large beasts, the orks with the thick iron breastplates and broad rimmed helmets, were now up there.

They chased the archers back along the wall before setting about attacking the towers with their axes.

On the wall the men fell back, barring the doors of the towers against the orks. But the ork axes were large, and the orks wielding them were powerful. Too soon the doors of the towers were smashed and splintered and them, with the doors gone, a desperate battle followed for possession of the tower.

Try as they might the men of the watch could not hold back the mass of orks. Inch by inch, foot by foot they were being pushed back. It was like a rugby scrum, and the orks had by far more muscle on their side. For the men in the front rank were desperate; they were being squeezed, crushed almost, by the ork in front and their own men behind. They could barely use their spears: they were too tightly compressed. The orks were also stuck in the same hopeless crush and were also unable to use their weapons. So the two sides pushed against each other, face to face, eye to eye, their breaths hot against each other's face. And both knowing that it was the men of the watch that would give way first.

There was but one thought in the minds of the men of the watch: they had to keep their feet. If they slipped and fell, if they allowed their line to buckle and break, it would be over; they had to keep pushing. They all knew that they could not run, for if they turned to run, the orks would be on them in a heart beat. They knew also that if they fell the orks would burst through their line and trample them underfoot. So they pushed, their legs burning from the strain, but they pushed against the enemy with all the strength that was left to them.

Moorbe and Kate reached the road by the bridge gate to see that the men of the watch were only twenty yards from the bridge road gatehouse. Despite their best efforts they had been pushed back nearly a hundred yards. But there was worse, and Kate had seen it, seen the danger to the defences. Kate raced to the gatehouse door and hammered on it demanding that they be let inside. A tiny flap in the door was opened and the sergeant looked out.

'Let us in,' Kate demanded breathlessly.

She heard the door being unbarred and quickly grabbed Moorbe, pulling him inside. Once inside Kate looked for the sergeant in charge. 'The roofs,' she panted, 'there are orks on the roofs of the houses.'

The sergeant understood what Kate was telling him: the orks were using the roofs to outflank the men in the streets. Hurriedly the sergeant ran up to the gatehouse tower and directed his archers to shoot at the orks on the rooftops. Kate followed the sergeant up. She still had her bow, and a full quiver of arrows, and somewhere down in the streets were her father and little brother.

Once at the top of the tower Kate found herself a place among the archers. She could see the orks jumping from rooftop to rooftop, stopping only to look down on the men fighting below. The archers on the gatehouse roof began picking them off, shooting at them as fast as they could. Kate raised her bow, fitting an arrow to the string. She took aim but then hesitated as it suddenly occurred to her that she had only once ever fired a bow. Kate let her arm fall, wondering what she thought she was doing. She had allowed herself to get too caught up in Moorbe's foolhardy actions to think clearly. Now, still panting from the exertion of chasing Moorbe round the town, and looking out over the battle taking place below, Kate was suddenly paralysed by doubt.

She felt a paw touch her elbow and looked down to see Moorbe standing up on the battlements and looking up at her. 'Picture the shot in your head, Kate. See where the arrow strikes in you mind and it will strike there when you release. Trust me in this, Kate. If you see it, it will be so.'

Kate took a deep breath and raised her bow. She drew the arrow back, aiming at an ork that about to jump on to the last house before dropping behind the watchmen. Kate imagined the arrow striking the ork in the chest, and as she did, she slowly let out her breath and released the arrow. The ork raised its sword and made to leap down onto the street below but as it did the arrow struck the creature and pierced its black heart.

'Good shot, girl,' the sergeant shouted as the dead ork fell down to the street with a sickening thud. 'Do it again.'

Kate fitted another arrow, aimed, and again imagined the arrow striking the ork's heart. She released, watched the arrows flight, and saw it kill a second ork.

'Come on, lads,' the sergeant shouted, 'this girl is showing you up.'

The other archers looked at Kate for a moment then went back to their task, taking greater aim so as not to be embarrassed by some girl.

Moorbe glanced up at Kate and gave a smile, of sorts. 'I told you, Kate,' he said softly, 'you have a power; if you see it in your mind, it will be.'

Kate stared at Moorbe for a moment but then the sounds of battle below drew her attention. She fitted another arrow, aimed and brought down another ork.

Below the gatehouse of the bridge gate there was movement in the street. Beohrtric, who had followed Kate and the chancellor to the gatehouse, was forming up his men. He had seen how the men of watch had been pushed back, seen how they were outnumbered and close to breaking. Quickly he had called the rest of his riders forward, holding them back in the side street and out of sight of the orks.

Beside the wall the watch was being pressed harder and harder, pushed back further with every passing second. All too soon they would be pushed back to the market square: that is, unless they should slip and fall then it would be over for all of them.

The men on the wall could not help them much as they had their own battle against the orks trying to take the towers. The men at the top of the gatehouse could not help either: they were too busy shooting at the orks attempting to scramble across the rooftops.

Beohrtric knew that it was down to him and his riders. If the orks got into the market square then all was lost. All he could do was hope that the men of the watch could stay on their feet as the orks pushed them back past where he was waiting.

The men of the watch were pushed back again, and the orks saw the open side street. With a cry of victory the ork rushed into the side street, some of them to lap round the shield wall, others to flood through the streets and come on the other fighters from behind. But their joy at finding the open street was short-lived. No sooner had they racing into the street than they were confronted by a solid wall of riders with lowered spears.

'Now,' Beohrtric shouted, 'charge!'

A horn sounded in the side street, echoing off the walls as the riders charged into the shocked ranks of the orks.

It was hard to say who was the most surprised: the men of the watch as the horsemen raced past them or the orks as they were speared and trampled under hoof.

The orks fell back, running away from the charging horsemen as best they might. But so tightly packed had the orks been, so many of them had forced their way up the street, that it was near impossible for them to retreat. Boehrtric and his riders charged into the thick of the orks, spearing and hacking down as many as they could. They pushed the orks back nearly to the barricade but then they found themselves under attack from the orks that had taken the wall.

Beohrtric was forced to retreat as his men were being picked off around him. He had charged the orks with fifty men: only thirty-five returned.

Yet as Beohrtric was pushing the orks back a mutiny of sorts was taking place in the ranks of the watch.

'This is useless,' Maullen told Sergeant Wiglaf. 'We cannot move, cannot fight, and I for one am sick of stinking ork breath in my face.'

'Get back in line, you fools,' Wiglaf shouted back. 'Reform the shield wall.'

'Why, so we can get crushed again?' Maullen asked loudly.

'That's how we fight,' Wiglaf said. 'Now reform the wall.'

'There's another way,' Maullen told the angry sergeant. 'Little Boots, Little Boots, get up here.'

Jay walked forward, feeling even smaller than his oversized padded jacket made him look.

Maullen grabbed hold of the front of Jay's jacket, nearly lifting him off his feet. 'Quickly, lad. Are you sure the way you showed us will work?'

'Well, er,' Jay stuttered.

'Will it work or not, Jay?' Maullen demanded.

'Yes,' Jay said, looking Maullen directly in the eye.

'This is madness,' Wiglaf screamed at the men. 'Get back in line, reform the wall before the orks return.'

'What's it to be, men?' Maullen shouted. 'Do we form a shield wall and get crushed or do we follow Little Boot's orders and kill some orks.'

'Reform the shield wall,' Wiglaf shouted, but one of the men grabbed the sergeant and pushed him out of the way.

'We're going with Little Boots,' he said.

The horsemen had cleared the street. The orks were advancing again: slowly at first but quickly speeding up to a full charge again on seeing the disorder ahead of them.

Maullen patted Jay on the back. 'Your in charge now, lad,' he said.

'First,' Jay called out, his voice breaking in a high-pitched squeak. He cleared his throat and called out again, this time more clearly. 'First formation.'

The two companies of the watch broke from the shield wall and changed to a more open formation each of ten men wide and six deep. Jay stood between the two companies.

'Spears, ready,' he shouted, and men lifted their spears, holding them above their shoulders.

Ahead of them the orks were charging back up the street, scimitars held high as they shrieked and called out their war cry.

'This is madness,' Wiglaf shouted, but the men ignored him and waited for Jay's order.

Jay watched the orks running towards them, watched and waited till they were no more than twenty yards way. 'Spears, now,' Jay shouted and the men threw their spears with all the force they could muster.

The front ranks of the orks were stopped, many of them falling as they were hit by the avalanche of spears. Those that had seen the spears coming and held up their shields now found the spears stuck fast in them and dragging their shields down.

The front rank of the watch then drew their swords, holding them level at waist height as they advanced on the orks.

The orks cast their shields aside, raising their scimitars in both hands as they made to strike down on the approaching men. But, before they could strike, the men thrust out their shields, hitting the orks full in their faces while stabbing them in their bloated bellies.

Another rank of orks fell as the men covered themselves with their shields and advanced again. Orks rushed forward, trying to get at the men, but they rushed forward onto the points of the swords that stabbed out the moment they got close.

The men kept on advancing in this way, striking with their shields to knock the orks off guard, stabbing their swords into the soft, unprotected bellies of the enemy, then covering themselves with their shields as they stepped forward again. And after the front rank had fought and killed two or three ranks of orks, Jay shouted out, 'Change.' The front rank suddenly turned around, covering their back with their shields as they filtered back through the ranks.

The orks saw this and assumed the men of the watch were trying to retreat. They rushed forward, ready to cut them down. But it was only the front changing over and the second rank had their swords levelled and waiting for the orks.

So it went on. The men fought two or three orks then changed over for the next man to do the fighting. If a man fell then the next man stepped forward and fought in his place. All the while the watch was advancing and all they had to do was just as Jay had shown them on the training ground: thrust, stab, recover, step; thrust, stab, recover, step.

Orks had fought men many times, but not like this; this was something new to them. They fell back, confused and not knowing what to do. But each time they fell back the men came forward thrusting and stabbing and killing many of the orks.

From atop the gatehouse Moorbe could see the men of the watch advancing, could see them cutting down rank after rank of ork as they fought to retake the street they had been pushed from. But also from his vantage point he could see the next tower along the wall.

Orks had broken into the tower and taken the lower level. Even as Moorbe watched he could see the men in the top of the tower fighting frantically to hold onto the upper level and to their lives. If the men of the watch kept advancing they would soon be under attack from the orks above them.

'Kate,' Moorbe said sharply. 'Kate, get the sergeant, we must retake that tower.'

Kate grabbed the sergeant and pointed to the next tower. Quickly the sergeant organised his men. Leaving but three archers on the gatehouse the rest formed up with the sergeant and opened the door. They ran along the top of the wall, collecting other men at arms as they ran towards the tower. Archers, now standing directly over the orks shot down into them, killing as many as they could.

As the sergeant and his men reached the door of the next tower, it flew open and one of the massive axe carrying orks burst onto the wall. It swung the axe, smashing the sergeant's shield as he attempted to defend himself. The sergeant's arm was broken and the force of the blow sent him tumbling off the wall and to his death among the mass of orks and goblins below.

The second man in line thrust a spear at the great ork. But his spear hit the ork's thick iron breastplate and ricocheted off. The ork grabbed the spear, twisting and yanking it from the man's grasp. It swung its axe again, a backhanded swing aiming to part the man's head from his body. The man ducked the blow, pulling his sword and stabbing upward and into the ork's neck. The ork fell from the wall.

Another of the beasts charged onto the wall; it saw its fellow fall and raised its axe in both hands ready to strike the man that had killed it. Kate plucked an arrow, fitted it, aimed and released faster than seemed humanly possible. The arrow struck the ork in the eye and it fell back dead: its axe still raised above its head.

Yet killing those two orks did nothing to reclaim the tower; if anything it had been more like pulling the cork from a bottle of champagne. No sooner were the two great orks dead than dozens more came stampeding through the door and onto the wall.

Ahead of Kate there were three men at arms trying to hold back the flood of orks. But they were brushed aside, overwhelmed by the orks in a matter of seconds. The gates had been opened then and it was impossible to stem the tide.

Arrow after arrow was loosed off by Kate, as they were by every other archer able to hold a bow, but still the orks came forward. The men on the wall began to retreat; Kate began to retreat, all the time loosing off arrows in a futile attempt to hold the orks back.

Kate reached into her quiver only to find she had no more arrows. The orks were nearly upon her, their jagged, sharpened teeth snarling at her, their large reptilian-like eyes wide with some demented bloodlust as they charged forward. She swung her bow with all her strength, striking an ork across the side of its face; at the same time she drew her sword and stabbed at the next ork.

The ork Kate stabbed went down but the other, the one she had struck with her bow, was only stunned. Quickly it regained its senses and grabbed hold of Kate's arm and twisted it violently. Kate gave a cry as the pain shot up into her should. She fell to her knees and the ork holding her arm raised its scimitar.

Kate closed her eyes, expecting to die at any second. Instead she felt something hit her back: not the sharp blow of a scimitar but something like a kick. She heard a ferocious bark and growling behind her and the ork released her arm. When she looked up Kate saw the ork staggering backwards with Moorbe's fangs sunk deep into the creature's throat.

Moorbe tore the throat from the ork and then leapt at a second. As he did Kate felt herself being lifted. Somebody had grabbed the rear of her jacket and, in one effortless motion, hoisted Kate back on to her feet.

'Stay on your feet, lady,' the big man said to Kate. 'you fall, you die.' And with that he charged into the thick of the orks swinging an axe and driving them back.

Kate was astonished. She had not seen the man before and he was not dressed as the rest of the gate guard were. In fact he looked as if he was dressed in nothing more than his pants and a nightshirt, and the skin of both his face and arms were covered in burn scars. But one thing was for sure: he knew how to use his axe and he was using it to devastating effect on the ork.

With his first swing he took the head of one ork. Then he jabbed the axe into the face of the next, knocking it backwards, before whipping the axe round and striking the ork in the middle and nearly cutting it in two. He pulled the axe out, spinning it and himself round before burying the axe deep into the head of another ork and splitting it from crown to chest.

Moorbe was fighting alongside of the axe man, biting at and tearing the flesh from any ork he could get his fangs into. He leapt at another ork, sinking his teeth deep into the ork's arm. The ork cried out in pain but at the same moment brought up a dagger.

Kate heard the cry, not that of the ork but the blood-chilling yelp that came from Moorbe. She watched helplessly as the ork swung its arm with Moorbe still hanging on. The ork smashed Moorbe against the hard stone battlements and Kate heard him yelp again along with what sounded like the snapping of a thick twig.

'*Noooo*,' Kate screamed. All reason left her at that moment. She raised her sword and charged forward with but one intention: to kill every ork she could lay her blade to. Behind her the men had also seen

Moorbe fall and seen Kate charge into the thick of the orks. Without hesitation the men drew their swords and charged forward also.

The orks too had heard Kate and saw her running at them. But they had not heard the scream of a distressed girl. Nor did they see some young and rather thin girl. What they heard was the war cry of some inhuman creature, a cry that tore at their ears and clawed at their minds. And what they saw was something unnatural charging towards them. Her hair was like fire and her sword flickered with white hot flames. A light, a chilling bright blue light, brighter than any light they had even seen or could have imagined, shone around her and from her and, as she came forward, it was as if the girl was wreathed in pure flame: the orks fled before her.

'Get forward, you maggots,' Gol-nar shouted. 'There's but a handful of them, you cowards. Get forwards, kill them, kill them all.'

The orks and goblins by the bridge gate had fallen back after the charge by the riders. Now Gol-nar come forward and was driving them back into the attack. He had brought several more of his half-goblins with him and they were then pushing the orks and goblins forward, kicking them, cursing them and beating them with whips and the flats of their swords.

'Attack, you scum, kill all the men; show them how orks can fight.'

The orks and goblin had gone back into the attack but now they were stalled again and again beginning to fall back as the men of the watch advanced upon them.

Gol-nar and his half goblin men pushed their way through the densely packed ranks encouraging, shouting, cursing, or anything in fact to get their lads back into the fight, but as they went forward, the orks were falling back around them. Unexpectedly Gol-nar found himself and his goblin men at the front of the orks and facing the men of the watch. More accurately, Gol-nar found himself facing a short man in an ill-fitting padded jacket.

'Change,' Jay shouted, and again the front rank turned and filtered back as the next rank stabbed out at the orks and goblins before them. The front of the enemy fell before the stabbing blades of the watch and Jay came face to face with the six tall, black-cloaked figures.

They had their swords drawn and slashed out at the watch as they advanced. One missed completely, but the three swords that stabbed at him did not. Another struck the shield of the man approaching him only to see its sword bounce off. A split second later the goblin man was struck in the face by the shield and he staggered back dismayed as a sword flashed out and disembowelled him.

In the centre the man next to Jay thrust his shield at the tallest of the goblin men, knocking his sword arm away. He stabbed with his sword but the goblin sidestepped the thrust as he brought his other hand round in a left hook, but a left hook armed with a long curve dagger. The blade caught the watchman in the throat and he was dead before he hit the ground.

Jay slammed his shield into the goblin man's arm, knocking the dagger from his hand. He stabbed with his sword but missed as the goblin man grabbed his shield and yanked hard on it. Jay held on to the shield trying to pull it back as the goblin man heaved at it again. This time Jay was dragged forward, nearly lifted off his feet, and spun round. He was tossed aside as the goblin man let go of the shield and Jay staggered back, dropping to one knee as he tried to prevent himself from falling.

Jay found himself surrounded by three of the goblin men, surrounded and cut off from the men of the watch.

The first goblin took a swing at Jay, the blade flashing in the sun as it arced down at Jay. He lifted his shield, holding it above his head, and as the blow from the goblin struck his shield and knocked Jay down further he thrust his sword into the goblin's belly. The next goblin ran to attack Jay but before it could swing its sword Jay brought his shield down hard onto the creature's foot. The goblin man howled in pain, lifting its injured foot as it hopped around in agony. Jay stood up and thrust his sword out, catching the howling goblin under its ribs and driving the tip of his sword into its lung.

The third goblin man, the one that had dragged him out of the ranks, came at Jay then, its arm drawn back and its sword levelled as it delivered a ferocious backhanded blow designed to take Jay's head from his shoulders. Jay dropped to his knee again, lifting his shield to protect himself. But Jay had seen the blow coming too late and neither dropped quickly enough nor raised his shield fast enough. The last thing Jay saw was the curl notched edge of the goblin's scimitar as it passed before his eyes. Then there was the intense searing pain as the blade made contact with his skull and the world went black.

'Little Boots, they got Little Boots,' someone shouted.

'Little Boots is down,' shouted another.

The men of the watch surged forwards en masse, stabbing and hacking at anything that got in their way.

Jay's body lay limp on the ground as the battle raged over him. Orks grabbed at him, keen to carry off a trophy. But the men of the watch also grabbed for his body, every bit as determined, if not more so, that his body would not be taken.

A tug of war developed between the two sides: the men pulling on Jay's arms as the orks and goblins pulled on his legs. His body was lifted from the ground as the two sides pulled him back and forth. Jay's helmet had been knocked off by the blow and a deep wound had been opened in his head. His face and hair were nothing but a mass of blood and his eyes dim, hollow and staring.

'Get the body, get the body, maggots,' Gol-nar screamed, resolute that he should have his prize. Then Gol-nar saw Maullen approaching with sword raised and a look of utter loathing on his face, and Gol-nar was not so sure about Jay's body anymore.

Maullen brought his sword down, a blow that Gol-nar only just blocked. A second later Gol-nar was knocked back by a thrust of Maullen's shield. Gol-nar leapt forward swinging wildly at Maullen.

Maullen took the swing on his shield and stabbed at Gol-nar. The goblin sidestepped the thrust, raised his scimitar, and swung quickly. He missed Maullen who had ducked under the swing then, as he came up again, Maullen swung his sword, aiming at Gol-nar's head. The goblin blocked the sword swing but failed to see that Maullen had tilted his shield and was jabbing its edge at Gol-nar's middle. The blow from the shield knocked the air from Gol-nar's lungs. He doubled over in pain only for Maullen to turn his sword and stab down into the goblin's spin.

Gol-nar fell face down into the cobbles at the very moment when the men of the watch, hacking at the arms of the orks, finally pulled Jay's body from them. The small limp figure in that ill-fitting and blood-soaked jacket was passed back between the ranks. At the rear Sergeant Wiglaf took Jay's body and carried it away from the fight. He lay him on the ground slipping on the blood-covered cobbles as he did so and knocking Jay's head.

Jay groaned and Wiglaf stared at the boy. 'You're alive,' Wiglaf gasped. 'By all my fathers and my father's fathers, you're alive.'

Again Jay groaned as he began to come round. Then he felt the pain from his wound and he cried out. The goblin blade had caught Jay as he was going down but it had also caught the cheek guard and nose guard of his helmet. Rather than kill Jay the force of the blow had been taken by the helmet and knocked his head backwards but as his helmet came off, the blade had carved out a part of Jay's forehead and left a flap of skin two inches wide and as many long.

Wiglaf pressed a bandage to the wound in an attempt to close the flap of skin and stop the bleeding. 'Stay still, Little Boots, and we'll get you to the healing house,' the old sergeant said gently. 'Just you wait, lad, when the girls see a scare they think hero, and seeing this one will have them as wet as winter.'

'He's alive,' Maulen gasped as he looked over Wiglaf's shoulder. 'That goblin blow should have taken his head off.'

Wiglaf wrapped a bandage round Jay's head and looked up at the big man. 'I guess the lad's got a thick skull: lucky for him. He's a bit knocked about but he'll live. Now, let's get Little Boots here back to the healing house.'

'No,' Jay protested weakly, 'I can't go there.' He tried to get to his feet but the old sergeant held him down.

'The lads are doing all right, Little Boots,' Wiglaf said soothingly. 'You've done your share for today.'

Jay sat up and touched the bloody bandage round his brow. 'It's not that,' he tried to explain. 'When Mum sees this she gonna kill me.'

On the road by the ferry gate the men of the watch had been able to hold back the endless attacks by both goblin and orks. The enemy had never been able to break into the old tower, and during the whole battle, the men in the tower had kept up a continuous barrage on the heads of the orks.

The street was littered with hundreds of goblins and orks bodies. Mixed in with them were also the bodies of the watch that had fallen defending the road, but defend it they had. They had been told before the battle began that the ferry gate must be held. They had fought to defend it – they had died defending it – and it was still in their hands.

All day the men of the town watch had faced the enemy, fought them, and held them back. They were still facing the enemy, and for that reason they did not see the ferry gate being opened behind them.

The boss was sitting on a log and enjoying a leisurely lunch and sipping a rather good wine with some of his men. He had seen all he needed to see: the palisade burning down, his orks and goblins charging into the town. He had heard the sounds of battle. And he was content. What could a few hundred do against the thousands he had brought? Sure they might have had good defences, and yes he would lose more than he had planned over coming them, but it was all about the numbers and the numbers were on his side.

He saw a rider approaching as he took another sip of that delightfully tasty wine. 'Well, gentlemen,' he said with a grin, 'it would seem that news of our victory has come at last.' The boss laughed; those around him enjoying lunch laughed: it was only the rider that was not laughing.

The man dismounted, strode up to the boss, and bowed low. 'Boss, there are men on the ferry.'

'Rats jumping from the sinking ship err?' the boss laughed.

'No, boss,' the rider said standing upright. 'The men are entering the town: hundreds of them.'

'Impossible,' the boss shouted dismayed.

'It is true, boss, I have just seen them. Hundreds of men both on horse and on foot.'

'Under whose banner?' the boss demanded.

'Under the king's banner, boss,'

One of the boss's lunch party stepped close to him saying, 'My Lord, if the king has come out…'

'That imbecilic ditherer would not dare come out,' the boss hissed.

'But if he has, My Lord,' the other insisted quietly. 'If he has come out then it would be best not to be found here, My Lord. There may be others coming from the north, perhaps even the dwarves.'

For a long moment the boss was deep in thought. He looked north then back south at Two Rivers. He looked across the river to the east, the back at his men. 'We break camp,' he said at last, 'ride east till nightfall then we shall consider our options.'

'Boss?' the messenger asked, 'what about the army, boss? Should I give word for them to fall back?'

The boss looked towards Two Rivers again before saying, 'Leave them, if they cannot win with all the odds in their favour what use are they?' And with that the boss and all his men rode off eastward as fast as their horses could carry them.

Ed was standing in the middle road. He was at the rear of the shield wall that was locked in a bitter struggle with hundreds of orks and goblins. The battle had raged all day flowing first one way then the other, yet neither side could gain the upper hand. It was a stalemate but, like all stalemates, it was becoming a battle of attrition and in that case it was a battle that the orks would win. Many orks and goblins had fallen, dozens of them being cut down in every attack and counter attack. But the orks could take the losses, take them and hundreds more besides. But every man that fell was one too many and it was bringing the men of Two Rivers closer and closer to defeat.

Ed heard a sound behind him that he had dreaded hearing all day. It was the sound of feet running behind him and towards him. He spun round, expecting to see a host of orks charging down the street into the rear of the shield wall. Instead he saw Beohrtric leading a large party of men.

As soon as his men had arrived, Beohrtric had ordered the ferry gate open. His men began to ferry themselves across the river, overloading the little ferry with fifty or sixty men at a time. No sooner had they landed than Beohrtric ordered them into battle: first securing the ferry road then clearing the walls and securing the road at the other side of town. Now he was coming forward with more men to clear the middle road, and coming not a moment too soon.

With all his men in position, Beohrtric ordered that the horns be sounded. From every road and every tower the horns sounded. They echoed off the walls and buildings until they became a deafening tumult.

Once the horn had sounded, Beohrtric's men, drawn up in tight formation, began to advance. They walked forward, beating out the time of their paces with spear on shield.

The orks began to fall back as the streets were too tight and they were too exhausted to fight these densely packed and heavily armed men coming at them. Clearing the streets the orks fell back to the open ground before the new wall, and as they did, Beohrtric's men spread out from the streets and formed one solid unbroken line.

Another horn sounded and Beohrtric's men charged forward, pinning the orks and goblins against the wall.

The fight was brief and bloody as orks and goblins were being cut down in their hundreds while they desperately tried to scramble back over the wall. Even when they had, Beohrtric's men followed them, jumping over the wall and chasing them through the ashes of the palisade.

Once out in the open, Beohrtric unleashed his riders, letting them pursue till not one of their enemy was left alive within sight of Two Rivers.

Kate walked slowly back along the wall. She felt drained, exhausted, and ready to drop. She could not think how many orks and goblins she had killed; it was all just a blur, a bad dream that she was sure she must wake up from at any minute. Beside her, walking close by her like some bodyguard was the big man carrying his axe. Only now, with the battle over, did Kate remember who he was. She had seen him carried in by the other from Guidepost. Everyone thought he would die, so badly wounded and burnt he had been, but against all the odds, he had lived.

'Thank you, by the way,' Kate said, smiling up at the big man.

'For?'

'For saving me back there,' she pointed out.

The big man shrugged but said nothing.

Kate stopped and stared at the man, but he turned away, unable to hold her gaze. 'I see you're as talkative as you were in the healing house.'

Again the man shrugged. 'Don't feel like talking, begging your pardon, miss,' he said quietly and walked past Kate back towards the gatehouse.

'Wait a minute,' Kate shouted after him. 'What's your name?'

The man stopped, his head went down and his broad shoulders sank. Slowly he turned to face Kate. 'Dead men have no need of names,' he said as he turned and walked away.

Kate could only stare at the man, stunned by his words. She began to follow him slowly but then her eyes fell on an odd sight. Not far from the second tower of the wall she saw a naked man lying among a pile of dead orks. She walked towards the man then noticed he was still breathing.

'Some help here!' Kate shouted to the men on the wall. 'There's a wounded man here.'

Men rushed to Kate as she knelt beside the naked man offering him what comfort she could. 'You just lie still. We'll get you to the healing house soon.'

The man shook his head slowly. 'Do not trouble yourself, Kate. I'm all done.' He raised his hand and patted Kate's.

'Chancellor Moorbe,' Kate gasped, 'but you're, you're a man.'

Moorbe forced a weak smile. 'I always was, Kate.'

'No,' Kate said. 'You're not a dog. The spell is broken you're changing back.'

Moorbe laughed softly, but the pain was too great for him and blood was coming up with his breath. 'Kate, you must keep up your studies,' he smiled, 'the spell is broken because I am broken. I felt my back splinter when I hit the wall. The spell is broken because I am dying.'

'No,' Kate cried, 'I won't let you die. I won't. You said I just have to see it and it will be.'

Moorbe smiled again and held Kate's hand. 'In time you may have that power, Kate. Then you will be the most powerful sorcerer to have ever walked in Angron. But not yet I fear.' He closed his eyes and his hand slipped from Kate's.

Kate was crying when the men arrived at her side. They looked down at her and at the naked man laying beside her.

'Who is he?' one of them asked.

Kate sat back and looked up at the men. 'Do you not recognize your chancellor?' she asked the men. 'This is Chancellor Moorbe; he died defending me, defending this town and all your families. Use your cloaks to cover his body and carry him like the hero he was.'

The men did as Kate bid them, fashioning a litter from their spears and cloaks on which they carried the body of Moorbe back to his tower one last time.

Standing among the ashes of the palisade, Beohrtric, Cenfus, and Ed watched the riders chasing down the last of the enemy.

'Well,' Ed said slowly, 'I suppose we won.'

Cenfus smiled broadly. 'We're alive so yes.'

'At least it is over,' Ed sighed.

'Over?' Beohrtric shook his head slowly. 'This has been but the beginning.'

Printed in Great Britain
by Amazon